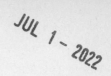

PRAISE FOR TIM PRATT

"Part high adventure and part travelogue of alien locales, this sci-fi romp has plenty of YA crossover appeal and will prove just the thing for mature readers who appreciate a classic Golden Age vibe."
– Publishers Weekly

"Readers will sympathize with Zax and his fellow travelers as they are yanked into new worlds every few pages or even every few sentences. Pratt's skillful worldbuilding will appeal to sf fans."
– Library Journal

"This is a gentle, slightly old-fashioned picaresque that made me think of Doctor Who, or characters created by Douglas Adams. It's welcome escapist fare in these stressful times."
– The Guardian

"High stakes action."
– Locus

"A compelling tale reminiscent of the episodic explorations of Doctor Who... *Pratt uses his rich imagination to craft a vast variety of possibilities."*
– Booklist

"Tim Pratt is in the vanguard of the next generation of master American fantasists."
– Jay Lake, John W Campbell Award-winning author of *Into the Gardens of Sweet Night*

BY THE SAME AUTHOR

JOURNALS OF ZAXONY DELATREE
Doors of Sleep

THE AXIOM SERIES
The Wrong Stars
The Dreaming Stars
The Forbidden Stars
The Alien Stars and Other Novellas

The Strange Adventures of Rangergirl
Briarpatch
Heirs of Grace
The Deep Woods
Blood Engines
Poison Sleep
Dead Reign
Spell Games
Bone Shop
Broken Mirrors
Grim Tides
Bride of Death
Lady of Misrule
Queen of Nothing
Closing Doors

Tim Pratt

PRISON OF SLEEP

JOURNALS OF ZAXONY DELATREE, VOLUME II

ANGRY ROBOT

ANGRY ROBOT
An imprint of Watkins Media Ltd

Unit 11, Shepperton House
89 Shepperton Road
London N1 3DF
UK

angryrobotbooks.com
twitter.com/angryrobotbooks
What's behind door number 2?

An Angry Robot paperback original, 2022

Cover by Kieryn Tyler
Edited by Simon Spanton and Robin Triggs
Set in Meridien

ISBN 978 0 85766 942 1
Ebook ISBN 978 0 85766 943 8

Printed and bound in the United Kingdom by TJ Books Ltd.

9 8 7 6 5 4 3 2 1

MIX
Paper from
responsible sources
FSC
www.fsc.org   FSC® C013056

For the indomitable Molly

Unicorns • Absent Friends • Sleeperhold • The Cult of the Worm • Necessary Context • Worm Sign • Gigantopithecus or Something • A Fork in the Road

How far I've come, and how little I have to show for it.

I'm writing this with a sparkly pen in a notebook I found in a heap of wreckage that used to be a two-story house. There's a picture of a glittery unicorn with disturbingly human eyes and a toothy grin on the cover, and about half the pages are full of looping handwritten scrawls in pink and purple ink. I can't read the words, of course, since my linguistic virus only works on speech, not writing, but the genre is pretty clear: this was a diary, probably a teenager's, or the local equivalent. (The last few pages are full of block letters and underlines. Maybe they saw this war coming. Or maybe the emphasis is about something else entirely). Fortunately, the original writer only used the front of each page in the journal, not the back, so when I flip the journal upside down, poof: a whole book of blank pages for me to fill.

I used to have an amazing digital journal, slim and weatherproof, with endlessly scrolling "pages" that I could never fill. I could write in that journal with a stylus or my fingertip, or even dictate and watch my words appear in print (once my absent friend Vicki showed me how to turn that

1

feature on). In that book, I chronicled my journey through over a thousand worlds, my adventures, my failures (numerous), and my triumphs (fewer, and maybe pointless in the long run). Now that book of wonders is lost.

Just like me.

I can't possibly recap everything that's happened since the last time I wrote. I don't even feel up to filling in the time since the attack on the Sleeperhold, when I was forced out into the lonely vastness of the multiverse again. But here's a little context, in case anyone ever finds this, and can actually read it.

My name is Zaxony Dyad Euphony Delatree. I was born in a place called the Realm of Spheres and Harmonies, where I worked as a harmonizer, devoted to helping people find fulfillment in their personal lives while also contributing to the betterment of society as a whole. When I was twenty-two years old (probably about four years ago, though birthdays are hard to track for reasons that will become obvious), I went to sleep one night in my familiar bed, and woke up in an alien and hostile world.

Ever since then, that's been my life. If I fall asleep, or otherwise lose consciousness, I leave the universe I'm in, and wake to find myself somewhere else. Sometimes I open my eyes in cities, or gardens, or deserts; tundra or jungles; space stations or caverns or undersea domes. I've found myself in worlds populated by humans at every stage of cultural development, from hunter-gatherer to techno-utopian, and in worlds populated by intelligent entities that aren't human anymore, or that never were. That said, my destinations aren't *totally* random: I never end up in the vacuum of space, or on a world where the atmosphere is toxic, or the temperature hot enough to melt lead – people with my condition (and, yes, there are others) never travel to realities that can't support our form of life, though it's not always comfortable. There's some form of basic self-preservation built in to the ability.

I do, however, often find myself in empty, devastated places, like this one... though rarely worlds where the ruination is so recent. There is still ash raining down outside these broken windows.

There are advantages. I can always escape my problems, as simply as falling asleep... but the problem is, I can't retrace my steps. I can't return to worlds where I've already been, because the force within me seeks the new, driving me always to unseen worlds. That was my life for years. Then I met a group called the Sleepers, who created technology that *does* allow travelers to return to worlds they've visited before, using a special vehicle. That's life-changing. That's *world* changing.

Unfortunately, not long after I met the Sleepers, everything fell apart, and now I'm friendless and alone again, flung into the multiverse, traveling on foot, only able to go forward, and never back. (I usually try to stay optimistic, but I'm dirty and hungry and lonely, so this isn't my best day.)

I've been to a lot of worlds since I developed my condition. This is World 1305, I think, give or take a few. I used to keep meticulous track, but, since I last wrote, I passed through a lot of worlds very quickly, some familiar and some not. I was also distracted by various astonishing revelations, and also by kissing my long lost true love, who (as you may have gathered) has since been lost again.

I've picked up some advantages in the course of my journeys, in worlds even more technologically advanced than my birthplace. The linguistic virus was the first and most vital, since it allows me to understand and converse in most spoken languages, assuming my vocal apparatus is capable of making the right sounds. More recently I've had procedures to change the structure of my brain, which in effect means I can stay awake indefinitely. I still have to rest, but I just sort of... zone out, sleeping with only one hemisphere of my brain at a time, like some migratory birds do during long flights. I don't dream, of course, but since this all started, I'd stopped dreaming anyway. Being able to stay awake as long as I like vastly improved my lot – before that, I could never spend more than five or six days in a given world before sleep forced me away, and I could only manage that with terrifying quantities of stimulants.

Those procedures, along with certain meditation techniques, also allow me to fall asleep at will – in the old days, if I wanted to escape a world, I had to depend on fast-acting sedatives, and that's not good for your long-term health. In theory, with my new skills, I could just settle down in some nice corner of reality, barring unexpected head injuries. In practice, though, I've been on the run since the attack on the Sleeperhold separated me from my friends.

Oh, yes, I can make friends. If someone falls asleep in my arms, they can travel with me to new worlds... at least until I lose consciousness without them, or they decide they want to stay behind. My friend Minna, who knows more about biology than anyone I've ever met, found a way to duplicate my ability, allowing her to travel with me even if we *didn't* fall asleep together... but I haven't seen her since the day the Sleeperhold fell. I hope she survived. That she's out there somewhere in the tangle of worlds, fighting for what she believes in, like I am. I know we may never find each other again. I haven't given up hope – she's surprised me in the past – but for now I don't have the luxury of worrying about it. I'm focused on other things. Survival, of course... but survival isn't enough. Everything is better if you have a goal.

I have been hunted before. Pursued through the multiverse by someone who meant me harm. I didn't like that much. This time, I'm the one doing the hunting. I'm going after the people who destroyed the Sleeperhold, the place that should have been my new home. They tore me away from my friends, from Vicki and Minna and Winsome and Toros and Sorlyn and the Pilgrim... and Ana. Most of all, Ana. Finding her once was astonishing. Finding her a second time was a miracle. I know I can't expect to find her again.

Toros, the leader of the Sleepers, calls our enemy the Cult of the Worm. We know a few things: their members can travel the multiverse, just like we can. They infect other people with that curse as well. (They infected me, though indirectly.) There are lots of cultists – we don't know how many – and they're organized. We think we know their goal: to tear apart the fabric of the multiverse, which is to say, to destroy *everything*. What we don't know is why. Toros told me that all attempts at interrogation have failed, mostly for lack of a common language.

But I can speak *anyone's* language, and now I'm chasing them down, trying to track the cult to its origin point. When travelers – like the cultists, or like me – move through the multiverse, we leave traces of damage, fissures in the fabric of space and time, and the Sleepers can detect those. We call them worm-trails, because they look like thin, organic, twisting lines in the air – the bodies of worms, or their tunnels. Invisible to the naked eye, but not to me.

The Sleepers taught me how to follow those wounds in reality. I can see my own trail, stretching out behind me – and it's disgusting to even think about it, unspooling behind me at chest-height with every step I take – but I can't follow it, because I can't go back. I *can* follow someone else's trail, though. (As long as it doesn't pass through worlds I've visited before, but with so many worlds, that's unlikely to be an issue.) How, in all the vastness of the multiverse, can I possibly hope to end up in the right place? The Sleepers discovered there's a natural tendency for travelers to follow an existing fissure into a world that's been visited previously – the way a river follows the path of least resistance. That explains how my old friend turned nemesis the Lector pursued me unerringly through so many worlds, once upon a time. It's the same method I'm using to follow the cult. If you bed down beneath the terminus of a worm-trail, you *always* pick up the same trail on the other side.

Another benefit is, Toros thinks following a worm-trail does less damage to the fabric of reality than breaking new ground – you're traveling along an existing fissure rather than making a new one. I hope that's true. I've been to so many worlds already. Done so much harm, when all I've ever wanted to do was help.

After the attack on the Sleeperhold, I was lost, wandering, going from world to world – but then I found a thread. Specifically, I found a fresh corpse, in a desolate and seemingly uninhabited world: a humanoid, dressed in a motley combination of clothing, with a pack of survival supplies. The worm-trail in the air above them proved he was a traveler. Judging by the vomit beside him and the froth on his lips, he'd eaten something poisonous. You can never be too careful when it comes to consuming the flora of strange worlds.

I searched the body and found the mark on his hip, a diamond-shaped arrangement of dots, seemingly burned in with a hot iron:

$$\begin{array}{ccccc} & & \bullet & & \\ & \bullet & \bullet & \bullet & \\ \bullet & \bullet & \bullet & \bullet & \bullet \\ & \bullet & \bullet & \bullet & \\ & & \bullet & & \end{array}$$

I rubbed my chest, just above my own heart. The Sleepers call that mark worm-sign, and while they can't be sure the mark appears on *every* cultist, it appears on all those they've caught, sometimes tattooed, sometimes branded, sometimes gouged and scarred. I knew then this was no unwilling traveler like myself, but a member of the Cult of the Worm.

I made and acted on a plan in that same moment. I knew where that cultist had ended up, so I decided to see where he'd come from. Since then, I've been methodically tracking his worm-trail, through world after world. Eventually I'll find the place he came from: the homeworld of the Cult of the Worm.

That was the plan the Sleepers were working on before the attack: to track the cult to its root. Just because the Sleepers were attacked doesn't mean it's a bad plan. It might mean it's a *great* plan, since the cult went to such violent lengths to stop it. If the others survived, Minna and Vicki and the Pilgrim and Sorlyn and Ana (my Ana)… then maybe we're all following different paths, left by different people, cultists or victims like me, and maybe… maybe… we'll track those threads back to their common point of origin. We'll find the place where the cult began. We'll figure out why they're set on destroying the multiverse. We'll find a way to stop them.

"We". Such a beautiful word. I hope I get to be a "we" again, instead of just an "I". I hope my friends are still out there, alive, doing the work.

I hope I get to see them again.

Sorry. That ended up being… rather a lot of context. I'll try to focus more on the immediate situation from here on. I first started keeping a journal as a scientific record of my travels, but it soon became a way to reflect on my experiences, develop insights, synthesize knowledge, and generally figure out what in the worlds is going on, and what I'm going to do about it. It's also a very cheap and only marginally effective form of therapy, as demonstrated above.

It does feel good to have a pen in my hand, even an oversized one with sparkly purple ink. It's so easy to get distracted by the minutiae of trying not to be eaten by monsters, or dying of exposure, or being dissected by alien scientists. Writing things down reminds me I have a purpose beyond mere survival. That's nice.

So. I awoke here, on world 1305 (approximate), underneath a bandstand in a park, and when I crawled out of the leaf-mulch and dirt, the first thing I saw was a huge gazebo, and the gazebo was on fire. The town square was generally in bad shape, with the dirt torn up in a way that suggested tanks or something similar had recently rolled through, though no tanks were in evidence, and there were no corpses, which was a nice change. The sky was dark with smoke, and the noonday sun (just the one, so far) was faintly visible through the haze.

I crouched and scuttled, keeping my eye out for soldiers, but whatever battle had happened here had moved on. I didn't hear any gunshots or artillery or explosions, or running feet or angry voices, so I gradually relaxed. I was wearing my round-rimmed spectacles with the special lenses, and, through them, I could see the silvery streak of the dead cultist's worm-trail just below my eye-level, stretching off into the distance. I had some walking to do. I might as well do some looting along the way.

A black and silver flag full of bullet holes hung limply from a rod over the smashed-in window of a general store. The front door was four meters high, and as I looked around, I realized everything here seemed about double my own human scale. I climbed into the window, being careful of the glass, and rooted around, putting a few oversized cans of food and pouches of dried meat (you learn not to wonder what kind, after a while) into my canvas pack. The clothing definitely suggested humanoid creatures, albeit of immense size – maybe they'd evolved from Gigantopithecus or something. I'd seen stranger things. I looked wistfully at a rack of shoes, since my boots were coming apart, but even the smallest options were far too large.

I climbed back out the window and followed the worm-trail. The Sleepers estimate that every branch of the multiverse is directly adjacent to at least three or four other branches, and sometimes more. It's like standing in a room, surrounded by a lot of doors, and each door leads to a room with a new set of doors, and so on. Why you end up in one particular world over another, if you aren't following an existing fissure, is less clear. Is the destination entirely random? Does it depend on where, geographically, we go to sleep in the prior world? For that matter, why do we wake up in a specific place on any given world – in a public square, say, instead of an empty lot on the other side of town, or an empty desert on the other side of the *planet*?

Some sleepers think we can guide our destinations subconsciously – by wishing desperately to reach a city, we increase our chance of traveling to a developed world, if such a world is one of the available options. The theory seems impossible to prove, but it does makes me feel better sometimes.

There may be many more than three or four adjacent worlds, of course – there could be tens, dozens, hundreds, thousands. Those other worlds just aren't capable of sustaining the life of a conscious entity, so they're closed off to us. Toros thinks many, maybe most, of the worlds in the multiverse are bereft of life, or built on fundamental laws of physics inimical to biology. I get dizzy imagining the vastness, so I try to focus on the immediate.

I tracked the worm-trail out of town, along a paved road with fields on each side. I was always looking for evidence of my quarry's passage, hoping they'd left some evidence about their motives or their people. So far all I'd found was the occasional food wrapper from a different reality or the remains of a campfire. No grimoires bound in human skin or scrawled manifestos about annihilating reality or audio recordings of maniacal laugher.

There were no birds, no vehicles, and no people along the road, but off in the distance I saw columns of smoke, and once a fire tornado, fortunately moving away from me. Eventually the trail veered off toward a residential subdivision, and the devastation there was vast – houses (all twice-human-scale) broken into pieces, burned, with great jagged holes in their roofs. Massive vehicles were overturned and smoldering in the street. More flags full of bullet-holes dangled limply. There were no people at all, though some might have been hiding in the shells of their homes, I supposed. No corpses, either, which was strange – had the people escaped? Evacuated? Been taken prisoner? Was that ash raining from the sky the remnants of the local population, disintegrated by some kind of energy weapon? I was curious, but I had to accept the fact that I would likely never know. Mysteries are just part of my condition.

I followed the worm-trail into a two-story house, one side caved in, the other mostly intact. The track went through the front door, looped into the kitchen (someone had been foraging), and then disappeared upstairs. I climbed the stairs and followed that silvery thread to its endpoint in a child's room, though the child was probably my size or larger, based on the dimensions of the furniture. I also found this journal, which is a good size for me. The pen is a bit unwieldy, like the fat pencils I used in crèche school as a child, but I can manage until I find something more suited to my stature. The worm-trail ended in mid-air over the bed, and there was a smudge of red clay on the blanket – the traveler had appeared right there.

Normally when I find the termination of a trail, I close my eyes and follow it, moving on to the next world. I've been doing that ever since I picked up this thread, two weeks after the fall of Sleeperhold, making good time, and not even thinking about keeping a journal. So why did I pick up that dead (or missing, or who knows what) child's pen and start writing again? Why was it suddenly so important to pause my hunt to stop and reflect?

Because there was *another* trail in the room, originating just a couple of meters from the first one. That trail didn't go down the stairs, but out of the window. I peered out and found a trellis there, easily suitable for climbing, and based on the trajectory of the track, the other traveler had done just that, and then proceeded into the woods, where I lost sight of their trail among the trees.

Two sleepers had come through here – and not with one sleeping in the other's arms, because passive companions don't leave worm-trails. Were they two cultists, traveling together? If so, why had they split up? Were they going in different directions to increase the likelihood of transitioning to different worlds, off on different missions, or what?

I started writing this to organize my thoughts. Because now I have a choice. I can keep backtracking that dead cultist... or I can switch tactics, and follow the other worm-trail into the woods, and try to chase down a cultist who might still be alive. That corpse I found and started following backward in the first place was fresh, and may have been in this world as recently as a week ago. If he arrived at the same time as this other traveler, I could catch up to them, if I move fast. But then what? Try to get answers out of them, sure, but the lack of a common language isn't the only barrier to gathering intelligence. The cultists captured by the Sleepers fight and bite and spit and try to knock themselves unconscious so they can escape – being able to talk to them doesn't mean they'll be willing to talk back.

I *am* good at talking to people, though. Maybe I could pretend I want to join the cult, and get their sales pitch in return. It would be nice to know why they do such awful things – infecting innocent people, flinging them into the multiverse, trying to damage reality. The cultists can't go back home, either, as far as we can tell, so they leave their world and people behind when they set out on their missions. There must be a good reason. Or at least a terrible reason they find compelling.

But if I stop tracing this cultist back, I lose my best chance to find their homeworld. Even if I catch this other traveler, and they tell me their entire philosophy, what can I do with that information? I wouldn't be able to follow his trail back to this point, because there's no returning to a world I've visited before. The doors of sleep only open one way, unless you have access to a sleepercar. What are my odds of finding one of *those*?

Basically zero. I'd have to hunt around and hope I found some other cultist who'd come a different way, and follow *their* trail backward, if I want even the tiniest sliver of a chance of reuniting with Ana and the others. Finding another trail is probably possible – the local array of worlds clearly sees a lot of cult activity – but the search would set me back. Still. I'm supposed to be gathering information. Isn't tracking a living cultist worth the risk, if it lets me figure out the true nature of the threat against the multiverse?

Ugh. Sometimes doing the right thing is the worst.

Ana

Zax let me read his journal during our long trip to the Sleeperhold, and it filled me in on everything that happened after we got separated (the first time), so I thought I'd start keeping an account of my own. I'll write down my own story first, I think. I never got to tell Zax everything about my long journey from the silent city to the weird mead hall where we finally reunited, over a thousand worlds later. I was too busy telling him about the cult… and kissing him… and other things. If I put it down here, maybe Zax can read it someday. I'm choosing to be hopeful about that possibility right now. Writing will help fill all the blank time between worlds, and those long hours spent hidden away in stealth, waiting for the woman with the lotus pod face, the low priest, the Trypophile, to pass my way again.

Plus, there are things it's easier to say in writing than it is to say in person, especially when those things might cause a person you care about to look at you in a different way.

I'll start with a happy memory, though: the day I met Zax.

I was working in my backyard one sunny summer morning, the domelight shimmering in that crystalline way it had at my latitude of the innermost sphere. I'm an artist, and back then my medium was large-scale kinetic sculptures, which usually ended up installed in public spaces in far-flung corners of the

Realm: beautifying the hinterlands. I can admit that I was third-tier, as an artist – not one of the superstars, with a name familiar even to people who don't follow the art world, or one of the geniuses admired by aficionados, but even the next level is pretty good. I had a solid reputation, worked steadily, enjoyed the devotion of a few influential admirers, and picked up the occasional award from my peers. I was young, too, in my early twenties, and though I wasn't a Realm-shaking prodigy, I was "an artist to watch", and felt confident my best work was ahead of me.

The day I met Zax I was out in my yard-slash-studio, assembling a floating sculpture of polished metal and glass. The pieces were bound together by force-fields, and could contract into a seamless-looking mirror-bright sphere, and then expand into a glittering, rotating array of shards, catching and reflecting the light in a precise way to create a dazzling, otherworldly effect. There were also hidden cameras, and some of the shards were mirrors *and* screens, so I could choose to make them "reflect" images from the other side of the sphere, or even display entirely different images, which would lead to a subtle, disorienting effect for the viewer. That was the idea, anyway. I never got to actually deploy the sculpture for an audience, so I don't know how well it would have worked.

I wore a visor that projected a wire-frame overlay of my sketched-out design onto the air, and had fingertip controls that let me guide the hummingbird-sized drones who were assembling the various elements. I was deep into flow, lost in the intricacies of assembly, and then–

A man appeared on my lawn, just a meter away from me. He was just – *there*, suddenly, on a previously empty patch of smartgrass. I'd never seen anything like that happen in real life, that kind of materialization, though it was almost familiar from special effects in sims about magic or hypothetical tech. It couldn't really be happening, though – there was no actual device in the Realm that could... what? Teleport someone?

I was frightened, at first, and then realized I was controlling a swarm of drones with force-field manipulators and an array of shards of rather sharp metal and glass. Then I was less frightened. Anyway, the newcomer didn't look like much of a threat. For one thing, he was asleep. He wore ragged clothes and had a scraggly beard, and his hair was long and unkempt... but he was beautiful, too, with dew shining in his eyelashes, and he looked so peaceful and beatific. Then his eyes blinked open, and widened, and he rolled away, putting distance between us. "I am sorry, I will not hurt you, I am just..." He slumped, making himself small, and muttered, "What is the point, they never comprehend, and she is so comely, she must think me a ragamuffin and a fool–"

"I understand you," I interrupted. "I just don't understand how you *got* here."

He stared at me for a long moment – his eyes were lovely, the sort of gaze you can disappear into – and then he laughed, a joyful sound, and leapt to his feet. "You speak the tongue of the Realm!"

"I know Realmspeech, yes. Doesn't everyone?" Though his words sounded quite formal to me, like someone in an historical sim.

"Not at all. Not at *all*!" He whooped, and spun, startling my drones into autonomous flinch reactions. "I have returned, I am here, I am home once more in the Realm of Spheres and Harmonies?"

"The Realm of what and what?" I said, bewildered.

He cocked his head. "Oh. It is... no? That is not where I am?"

"Never heard of it," I said.

He bowed his head, his shoulders slumped, and then looked up at me, a bright and charming smile slowly spreading across his face. "It is no matter. This is closer than I have been to something like home since my tribulations began. My name is Zax. What is yours?"

"My name is 'how did you magically appear on my lawn, you weirdo?'"

"That is a tale to tell." Then he sat down cross-legged on the smartgrass, gazing past me at the gleaming spires of the innermost sphere, and told me everything.

By the end, I was sitting across from him, our knees touching. I was totally rapt, and he wasn't looking past me, but *into* me. I heard about the thirty-nine alien worlds he'd visited before mine, and I didn't doubt him. Partly because I'd seen him appear, sleeping, in my yard, and as evidence, that was hard to dismiss... but mostly because he just radiated trustworthiness and a lack of guile, and because he was so obviously transported with joy at having someone he could talk to. This was clearly a man who'd wandered in the wilderness – in various wildernesses – and there was no mistaking his delight at connecting with someone again. Understand, this was before Zax received the linguistic virus, so I was the first person he was able to hold a conversation with since he'd started traveling. I have no doubt that's a big part of why he fell in love with me: he was desperate for connection, and connection was possible with me.

And connect we did. I've always had an adventurous spirit, you might say – artists should be open to new experiences – but this was more than just the novelty of hooking up with an interdimensional traveler. Something in him called to something in me, and vice-versa. That's the way it is, sometimes. If you've felt it, you know. An hour after his arrival, we were in the shower, and not long after that we were in bed, and not long after that, we were lamenting our tragic and inevitable parting and I was configuring my chem-printer to produce the most powerful legal stimulants to prolong our time together. I don't mind admitting... I got a little caught up.

It's easy to see why Zax was drawn to me. We could talk, of course. Plus, I grew up in a world a lot like his, strikingly similar, in fact – he hailed from the Realm of Spheres and

Harmonies, and I lived in the Realm of the Known and the Found. Both were human civilizations, both technologically advanced, with inhabitants spread throughout our home systems; our planets even had the same names in most cases. We both came from societies that are (I realize in retrospect) a bit culturally imperialistic. How was it our worlds were so similar? We don't know. We don't know how the multiverse works at all – whether there was some prime universe that all the other branches sprang from, or if universes grow wild, and our similarities were just the sort of coincidences that happen occasionally when you have infinite options. Our languages had a common root, obviously, and we could understand each other right away, though like I said, he sounded a bit archaic, and he thought I used a lot of unintelligible slang. When you've been in hostile alien worlds alone for a month, of *course* you're going to become attached to the first person who seems remotely familiar.

But how to explain why I fell in love with Zax? I had multiple simultaneous relationships, as was common in the Realm, mostly with other artists, all with varying levels of intensity, though nothing serious enough to lead to cohabitation. Those entanglements were mixes of lust, admiration, respect, mutual interest, and compatible philosophies. What I felt for Zax was different. He just… lit something up inside me. He gave me love-story feelings, when I'd thought those were *just* things that happened in stories. At the time, I just embraced the thrill – I was a big believer in seizing opportunities – but I can look back and understand my own reactions a bit better now.

Think about it: I watched Zax appear from nothing in my own backyard. He was a sojourner through alternate worlds. He was a miracle… and I was a romantic. Two people, finding each other, out of all the worlds in the multiverse? How impossibly unlikely, how astonishingly lucky, how dramatic was *that*? I was just swept up in it all.

Ugh. This is coming out wrong. I want to acknowledge the

superficial factors that made us reach for each other, but at the same time, I don't want to minimize what we had. There was undeniably chemistry between us: we had our first kiss less than an hour after we met, and we barely stopped kissing (among other things) for the next two days. And Zax is a good person, one of the best people I've ever met, and I could sense that from the very beginning. (I'm not as good, and not as nice, but we'll get to that.) That infatuation might have developed into a mature sense of love, a real partnership… if we'd had time. But we didn't. We had until he next fell asleep, and we loved each other with everything we had, with the knowledge of that ticking clock. It's easy to love without thought of consequences when you're pretty sure there won't *be* any consequences.

I tried to tell myself, in the years after we met, that he didn't really love me. That I didn't really love him. And that if we ever found each other again, neither of us should expect too much.

"I have to go," Zax finally said, his face cracking into a yawn. "I want to stay, but… I'm slipping." He'd picked up some of my speech patterns, so he sounded less like an old-timey professor. I'd made him cup after cup of tea laced with stimulants, but he didn't have any augmentations then, or even much in the way of mental training, to stay awake for more than a couple of days. His eyelids fluttered, and I pulled him close to me. We were in my bed, just me, and him, and his supplies: I'd gifted him a canvas bag and filled it with food and water and other odds and ends to help him wherever he ended up.

"I'll be here with you until the very end." I kissed him on his lips, and his forehead, and on his eyelids when they closed. Our love was brief and tragic and doomed: we were star-crossed and tempest-tossed. It was all very romantic, and I was already starting to think about how I could turn my feelings into art. That's one problematic aspect of being a creative type; a part of you is always standing back, observing. I had an idea for a sculpture based on our story: a sort of orrery, with two orbs that would cycle through complex rotations and pendulum swings, coming together almost close enough to touch for a brief moment, at which point they would burst into bright illumination – and then fall dark again when the mechanisms of the sculpture carried them farther apart.

Then Zax fell asleep, and everything changed. I'd expected to see him vanish from existence, leaving a warm depression in my piled blankets, the reverse of his appearance in my yard. What he didn't know, because he'd never transitioned so close to someone else before, was that I would go *with* him when he traveled.

Zax had told me what it was like for him, in between worlds: an interval of dreamless nothing, brief and dark.

That was not my experience. I traveled when I was awake, you see. I was conscious when I passed from one world and into another. I was aware. I saw what comes *in between*.

Trying to remember what I saw and heard and felt now, my mind skitters away, flinches, resists. I can only write about the experience lucidly at all because the Sleepers have therapies that can (painstakingly, slowly) repair the minds of those who've glimpsed... whatever that place is. The crawlspace of the worlds. The empty spaces between the bubbles in the quantum foam. The borderlands. Call it what you want. I'm not the same as I was before I saw that place between places – I am, absolutely, changed – but thanks to the efforts of Toros and the other Sleepers, I'm a whole and functional person again, albeit with some fault lines and cracks.

So. What did I see. According to Zax's journal, when we woke up, I scratched his face, and jumped to my feet, and screamed about holes in the sky, and things pushing through, and said, "*Worms, worms, worms in the world.*" Then I ran away, disappearing into the alleys of a silent gray city of impenetrable blank towers. He looked for me, and called out for me, but couldn't find me, and eventually he passed out, exhausted, and went to a new world. That was that.

I don't really remember that part – scratching him, running away. There's a shattered pile of broken glass where my memories of that time should be, just fragments, some larger than others. The largest are actually the pieces from *before* he woke up and we reached that silent gray world. My clearest memories of that period are of the void between.

Which makes sense, because I was there for, subjectively... I don't know. "Centuries" sounds impossible, doesn't it? How can you live for hundreds of years, with every moment spent in terror? But that seems right, and it's what the few others who've seen that place report, too. The stress of such an experience should kill you, but in that place, you can't die. Time and space aren't the same there as they are in other worlds. My pitiful human perception did the best it could to parse my surroundings and organize it into something coherent, but I certainly wasn't seeing whatever is *really* there.

Basically, the space between worlds, as it appeared to me, was nothingness – a nothingness full of holes. Some people have trypophobia: a fear of clusters of small holes or bumps or dark spots. They look at seed pods, or honeycombs, or wasp nests, or the suckers on tentacles, or coral, or the eyes of insects, or worm-eaten fruit, and they feel an intense, full-body aversion. I never had that problem, personally. I'd eat strawberries all day, and I thought wasp nests were rather pretty, in their way; I even did a sculpture based on them, once. (Instead of wasps swarming out, it was tiny art critics.)

But when I was in that space, surrounded by those holes, some of them seemingly tiny, some vast and cavernous, all I could think about was what must be *inside* those holes. Were they burrows? Were they tunnels? Were they full of... wriggling, crawling things?

After a long, long time, I saw movement in one of the smaller holes, directly above me. Something luminous but slimy, segmented and long, thrust its featureless end out of the hole, and I thought *worms, worms, worms.* The thing crawled out, and then crawled into another hole, its form an undulating compression wave of something stranger than flesh. That thing moved, just centimeters from my face, for – well, for a sizable percentage of forever. Everything took most of forever in that place.

I began to worry about the *bigger* holes. Size was strange there – I couldn't tell if things were very small and close to me, or very large and far away, and they constantly dilated and contracted – but they certainly seemed like holes of various sizes, and if some were as big as they *looked*, what kind of creatures would lurk inside those?

Then I saw the eyes, peering through some of the holes: red-rimmed eyes, black-irised eyes, eyes with pupils shaped like barbells, eyes of luminous blue – like dozens of alien entities were looking at me, squinting through knotholes in a wooden wall. I had no doubt *those* creatures were vast. The eyes would appear for a moment, look at me – at us, because I was still clinging to Zax, unconscious and unmoving Zax, like a woman holding onto a piece of flotsam after a shipwreck – and then the eyes would move away. Over the subjective, timeless centuries I spent there, I saw perhaps a dozen eyes, but eventually, I saw *thousands* of worms, some hair-thin, some the size of train cars, and everything in between – or perhaps not. Perhaps scale had less meaning there. I doubt any of it was literal – that the eyes were actual biological things. I think they were my brain's way of making sense of the fact that something (or things) was watching me. But I really don't know.

I do know that, by the time our journey was over, I was a gibbering wreck. My mind was destroyed. I was unable to hold onto a thought for more than a second, unable to string multiple thoughts together at all… but somehow I knew it was Zax's fault. He'd dragged me to that awful place. He'd taken me from my cozy bed in my wonderful house in my beautiful sphere in my glorious Realm and delivered me to a world of worms that ate their way through reality like it was a piece of rotten fruit.

No *wonder* I screamed at him and scratched his face and ran away. I don't actually remember doing that, even after Toros's careful reconstruction of my psyche. My first coherent memory of that gray city is being alone, and cold, and shivering on my belly in the mist, lapping at a puddle of condensation. As best Toros can determine, that was a few days after my arrival in that place, a day or two after Zax gave up on finding me. I was beginning to come back to myself, probably driven by the needs of survival – my body preferred not to die of dehydration, so it brought me around enough to make me follow the smell of water and lap it up, dirty and gritty though it was.

I wandered that silent place, laughing and screaming and singing nonsense songs, the empty spaces absorbing my voice instead of echoing as I might have expected. Everything there felt muted and drained. I spent most of every day looking for water and food – the former was usually available, and the latter never was. I tried to climb the towers, but they were featureless and smooth.

It turns out the reason Zax had such a hard time finding me was, those silent towers *moved*. Never when you were watching, but often behind your back, like pieces sliding around in a puzzle… or like the walls of a treacherous maze. I'd emerge from alleys, only to turn and find plazas in their place, or impassable walls of smooth black stone. Add that mutability to the homogenous quality of the towers, and it's understandable that Zax couldn't track me down.

I did, eventually, find food: a little pyramid of canned goods and wrapped protein bars, familiar from my own pantry, in the middle of a plaza. Zax had left them for me – every single bit of food I gave to him, I realized later, when I could realize things. I fell upon the hoard, yanking pull tabs and scooping up sweet fruit and cold stew and spiced vegetables indiscriminately, just cramming calories into myself. I huddled, and shivered, and looked at the sky, which was blank and starless and caught in eternal twilight.

With some food in my belly I could put as many as two thoughts together, though they'd fly apart pretty quickly. I remember thinking I was on the surface of a dead world in a dead galaxy, succumbing to heat death. When I looked back, my mind repaired, I knew that couldn't be the case: there was air to breathe, and while the city was bleak and chilly, it wasn't killing cold, and the temperature was steady. I think now perhaps I was *underneath* some structure, surrounded by moving support columns, in the hidden machinery of an advanced world.

Zax took me to that place, but he didn't mean to... and he's also the one who saved me from dying there. The food he left sustained me, so instead of being dead a month after my arrival, I was alive – albeit hollow-cheeked, traumatized, delirious, and down to my last few crumbs – for Toros to find me, and save my life.

Into the Woods • A Vile Vial • Silver Cylinders • Single Combat • Pustule • Enter Zaveta of the Broken Wheel

Faced with a choice about which cultist's trail to pursue, I decided... not to decide yet. I'd just go and check things out – track the traveler who'd gone out the window to their point of departure, see if they'd left any signs or portents, and make my choice about what to do next then.

I clambered out the window, climbing down the rickety trellis. The remains of the flowers clinging to the wood were normal-sized, reminding me that I hadn't been hit with some kind of half-scale shrink ray, but was just inhabiting a world populated by primates much larger than myself. (Unless they'd all made themselves extinct. It was weird that I couldn't hear any shooting or explosions when there was still smoke in the air.)

I followed the worm-trail through a remarkably intact backyard, complete with an immense trampoline. I imagined three-meter-tall teenage apes doing somersaults and laughing. The back fence was smashed down and the trail passed right through the gap. From there, I went into the woods, a dense stand of trees that seemed to stretch for acres and, amazingly, wasn't on fire. The trunks soon closed in around me, the backyards hidden from view, and I could easily imagine getting lost here, if I didn't have that silver thread in the air to follow.

24

The woods went on and on, and I wondered if the local kids ever played in here, or the adults hunted, or if this was just the next bit of vestigial wilderness waiting to be demolished to make room for more houses and streets and culs-de-sac.

The woods were pretty enough, and peaceful without the signs of recent battles in evidence, but my ears were cold and my feet hurt. I stopped to sit on a fallen log and ate some jerky of unknown provenance. Back home in the Realm, I'd been famously picky about my food – my family teased me about it – but you can't be too precious when you're adrift in the multiverse. I draw the line at eating sapient creatures, but otherwise calories are calories.

Thus fortified, I set off again, and about five minutes later I found my second dead cultist of the week. That solved my problem about which one to follow. I do sometimes spend a lot of time fretting over things that turn out to be moot. I guess most people do.

This cultist was just like all the ones the Sleepers had met: humanoid, pale-skinned and dark-haired and wiry with muscle, like they came from a place where calories were barely adequate and the work was hard. She was dressed in a mismatched array of clothes, which also fit the hodgepodge habits of the cultists. This one wore pants of some electric blue wicking smartcloth; chunky black boots clearly cobbled by hand, with visible hobnails in the soles; a diaphanous white shirt, under a leather vest, under a heavy coat of stitched-together furs; and a pink beret. The wardrobe of an interdimensional traveler who grabs whatever she can whenever she can more-or-less indiscriminately. I make some effort to fit in on the worlds where I find myself, if I can. The cultists don't. They just tear through, spreading chaos.

There was a bullet hole under her left eye, a neat black circle big enough to put a fingertip into (not that I did so).

She'd run afoul of *something*. I had no idea how long she'd been dead – she wasn't too ripe, but it was cold here. Either she'd been caught up in the battle that wrecked this place, or she'd been shot by a local for other reasons. I tried to imagine being a gigantopithecus and seeing a comparatively diminutive creature like this running through the woods. I doubted deadly force would have been my first instinct, but you never know what cultural systems people are operating within – maybe in the local mythology, pale tiny humanoids are the equivalent of demons, or something.

I didn't want to touch a murdered body, for all the obvious reasons, but I needed to *confirm* that she was a cultist, and not a victim like me, who happened to share superficial traits with our mysterious tormenters. I pulled at the dead woman's coat, intending to remove enough of her clothing to look for a worm-sign, but something tumbled out of a crudely sewn pocket in the lining.

It was a small vial of clear glass, tightly stoppered, half full of a greenish, translucent fluid. I stared at the thing where it lay on the crushed leaves and moaned. I'd seen vials like that before, at the Sleeperhold, where they were kept in containment fields.

That vial – or, more specifically, the things teeming invisibly within it – were the source of my power, my gift, my curse. It was a vial of worms.

Ana had explained things to me on our way to the Sleeperhold, ending years of my speculations in the course of one conversation. How had I gained this ability to travel to new worlds when I slept? Why me?

The Cult of the Worm is why. The ability to travel the multiverse originated with them, and their vials of tiny parasitic worms.

At some point in the near past – certainly many years, possibly even decades ago – the cultists began to spread through the multiverse, and to infect people with parasites as they went. They slip the worms into food and water, mostly. The parasites exist mostly in the higher dimensions, making them undetectable on our physical plane without special equipment. The bit of the worm that extends into physical reality, and attaches to a living host, is almost microscopic, so it's not something you'll taste while you're quaffing your ale. I'd seen a photo of one on the Sleeperhold, magnified and enlarged; the visible portion was a maggotlike white grub, but with a leechlike series of toothy rings at the mouth end. The thought of one of those swimming in my body somewhere, the invisible length of it tethering me to unknown dimensions, made me want to gag. I tried to look back at my *own* worm-trail as seldom as possible.

Once they're attached to a host, those parasitic worms impart the ability to travel – indeed, they *compel* travel – through the multiverse. The worm's only desire (though that's the wrong word – instinct? Goal? Purpose?) is to visit new worlds. The parasites secrete a substance that enters the bloodstream of the host, and makes them travel when they sleep.

We're pretty sure the cultists didn't infect me directly. Instead, at some point, the cult infected a woman and sent her spinning through the multiverse. Eventually, she ended up in my home, the Realm of Spheres and Harmonies. I worked as a harmonizer – a kind of caregiver – and she was in clear need of care, disoriented and incomprehensible.

She died in my arms. Her blood got on my body. Some portion of that blood must have touched a mucous membrane. That was all it took to let the parasite inside her flee its dying host for a new, more hospitable body: mine. (Unlike other parasites, which gleefully reproduce inside their hosts, these worms are singular creatures, and only move to a new body if their current victim dies. I didn't inquire too closely about the experiments the Sleepers did to prove that. Multidimensional parasitology is not my field, and anyway, it's gross.)

The woman was only dead for a couple of minutes, because medical science at home is advanced, but the worm had already moved into my body when she was revived. She still flickered out of my world when she went to sleep, because the parasite secretes a substance into our blood that makes us travel, and she still had residue in hers... but in a few days, without the toxin being replenished, she would have stopped waking up in new worlds. I always hoped she found herself in a peaceful place. Toros said sometimes travelers were killed by local wildlife, and then those animals got infected, and transitioned to a new world the next time they fell asleep. They were usually killed themselves, or starved, soon after they were infected. More intelligent beings were better at navigating the ever-changing complexities of life flung into the multiverse.

Ana told me the worms do damage beyond merely ripping people out of their lives, though. With every new world an infected person visits, the integrity of the multiverse gets weaker. That means every time I fall asleep, I poke holes in the fabric of space-time, damaging the superstructure of the universe. Every penetration between worlds is a pinprick... but enough pinpricks can make you bleed to death. The Sleepers have detected breaches, holes between worlds, caused by cult activity. The cultists must know about the damage they're doing. They must *want* to cause it. Why else would they spread the infection? But why do they want to unravel reality? It doesn't make any sense.

I shifted my gaze from the vial to the dead cultist. I wondered if the worm had infected the local who killed her – it takes hours for enough of the worm's chemicals to build up in the blood, and who knows how long for the victim to fall asleep, so they could have transitioned far from here, their worm-trail beyond my view. I tried to imagine how much more challenging my travels would be if I were twice my current size. I thought the worm probably hadn't been passed on, though. This was murder from a distance, and I doubt the killer got any of the cultist's fluids on them.

After a moment's thought, I tore off a scrap of the dead cultist's shirt and used it to both pick up the vial and wrap it.

The Sleepers don't think people can get doubly infected, but I was still repulsed by the thing – the vial was, in a real sense, an artifact of a profane religion. It contained an unknown number of parasitic worms, waiting to be dumped into a well or slipped into a bowl of soup, transforming new hosts without their knowledge and against their will, ruining their lives, as mine had been ruined.

Well, maybe not ruined. "Irreversibly and forever changed," maybe. I can't say I wish I'd never been infected. Because of this power, I met Ana, after all. I met Minna, and Vicki, and the Pilgrim, and others I was glad to know. I helped some people along the way, too, who wouldn't have been helped otherwise. But it sure felt like ruination at the time. The Sleepers said I was a rarity – I'd traveled longer and farther than anyone they'd ever met before. Their order actively recruits people who've been infected by the cultists, and the most venerable veteran of the multiverse they'd met before me had traveled to four hundred worlds before his recruitment, as opposed to my thousand-plus – and *he* was considered a prodigy. Why hadn't the Sleepers met more experienced travelers?

Because the travelers usually died, often within the first few worlds, almost always within the first hundred. Sure, there's some unknown mechanism to ensure you don't transition into a pool of acid or a cloud of poison gas, but you *can* transition into a forest of hungry predators or hostile locals. Why didn't that fate befall me?

I was lucky, at first, and then I was *extraordinarily* lucky. About eighty worlds in, I met a scientist named the Lector in an absurdly technologically advanced world. He gave me my linguistic virus and other physical augmentations that made it vastly easier to survive. (Being able to talk to people makes a big difference.) Of course, he later tried to vivisect me so he could figure out the source of my power, and stole my blood to make a serum that let *him* travel through worlds, and wrought vast destruction in his attempt to found a multiversal empire, until I managed to stop him… but at least I got some good out of that horrible relationship.

A while after parting ways with the Lector, I met Minna, the most adaptable person I know (also the nicest). Minna is capable of changing her own body – and the bodies of others – to survive and thrive in various environments. She changed me profoundly, allowing me to stay awake indefinitely and sleep at will. The Sleepers were very excited to find us. They knew Minna and I could give them two things to shift the balance of power against the cult: control and communication.

The cult must have known that, too, since they attacked the Sleeperhold and killed or scattered our forces, not long after Minna and I arrived. I don't know how the cult organized such a strike, but they must have had inside help. Someone among the Sleepers betrayed us. On some worlds, the term for a traitor in an organization is a "burrower", for a creature that digs tunnels, undermining the very ground beneath your feet.

In other worlds, though, such a traitor is called a worm: hidden in the fruit, devouring from within.

I tucked the vial, wrapped well, into my bag. The cultist didn't have anything of use on her so I left her body in the woods, unburied and unmourned, and returned to the broken house. I went through the front door again, up the stairs, and stretched out on the giant child's bed. I gazed up at the rounded end of the worm-trail above me for a little while, thinking of absent friends.

I closed my eyes and went to sleep.

I opened my eyes to brightness: rows of white bulbs set in a low ceiling. I sat up and took in my surroundings, doing my habitual threat assessment. I was in a warehouse or lab of some kind, in a narrow aisle between rows of silver cylinders that reached nearly to the ceiling. Each cylinder was big enough to hold a body, my mind helpfully noted. The air smelled yeasty and pungent. Maybe this was some kind of brewery?

I stood up and reached toward one of the cylinders, careful in case it was hot, but the surface was cool and smooth. There were small panes of glass set into each cylinder, like windows, but they were mirrors instead. I took the opportunity to finger-comb my hair (it was getting long again) and clean some smudges of soot off my face.

Then something banged inside the cylinder, like someone was punching the inner wall, and I jumped back, hitting the cylinder behind me, and that one jolted, too. Maybe those panels weren't mirrors. Maybe they were some kind of one-way glass, and there were things inside the cylinders, looking out.

The banging continued, and then some of the other cylinders began to make noise too, like fists on metal. The cylinder in front of me started to *rock*, and then another, and another, like things inside them were hurling themselves back and forth.

Maybe this was all perfectly natural, part of the fermentation process... but I didn't want to find out. I snatched up my bag and rushed along, following the worm-trail down the aisle. The banging followed me, each cylinder seeming to set off the one next to it. There was no end of the cylinders in sight. Fortunately, the worm-trail didn't go too far – the cultist hadn't liked this place any more than I did, apparently.

I sat down in the aisle beneath the trail's end and did my meditative breathing. It was difficult to get into a properly relaxed state with all that hammering happening around me, but I've had a lot of practice (and alterations to the literal structure of my brain, courtesy of Minna), so soon enough I slumped, and transitioned.

I opened my eyes, instantly coughing on dust, and looked around frantically for the source of the roaring and clashing I heard. I was in some kind of tumbledown ruin of a stone coliseum, and about ten meters away, two people were trying to kill each other.

In my travels, I've learned not to judge people by appearances, but I admit I was instinctively rooting for the one who looked human – female, dressed head-to-toe in dark brown leather, her long braids decorated with beads, feathers, and bits of metal – over her opponent, a shambling shirtless humanoid with gray skin and a head like a warty pumpkin, covered in pustules and red-rimmed eyes of various sizes. Pumpkinhead wielded a gnarled wooden club, while the barbarian had a cudgel with a thick head wrapped in metal.

I wasn't *that* close to them, but I backed up anyway, climbed on some fallen rubble, and made my way up into the remains of the stands. There were no spectators. The worm-trail I'd followed extended past the fighters, out of the stadium, along a dusty track, and vanished from sight beyond a rocky hillside. I didn't see an easy way to leave the arena without getting closer to the fighters than I wanted, so I'd just have to wait for them to finish… whatever this was. Not an exhibition, with no audience present, but maybe they were athletes, entertainers, just engaged in bit of sparring practice–

Then the barbarian leapt into the air and spun, braids flying, and brought her cudgel down squarely on the crown of her opponent's lumpy head. I looked away, wincing, as the skull (or whatever) broke and splashed, very much like a gourd smashed with a hammer. Pumpkinhead dropped. The barbarian wiped the head of her club on the dead person's clothes, neatly and efficiently, then hung the weapon from a hook at her belt, using a leather loop at the end of the haft. I couldn't tell how terrified I should be. Pumpkinhead *looked* monstrous, sure, but she'd just casually killed him, and maybe that made her the monster in this scenario.

She shaded her eyes and looked up at me, then called out a few words. It took a moment, as always, for the linguistic virus to turn the foreign language into something I could comprehend: "–another traveler?"

I stood, trying to look harmless, as she strode in my direction. "I am a traveler, yes." Her language was guttural and harsh, but I was sure I'd get used to it, if I stayed here long enough.

She grunted, then beckoned. "At least you say words, instead of just quack, quack, quack, making noises with no sense, like the last one."

The last one? Did she mean the cultist whose track I was following? I opened my mouth to ask but she spoke first, in a commanding tone. "Come down. Pustule check."

"Pustule… check?" The virus is very good at what it does, but it doesn't exactly provide much in the way of cultural context.

She scowled. Her face was sun-darkened (and there were two suns here, close together in the sky, one bigger and redder than the other). Her face was weathered, all planes and sharpness. She was extremely good at looking annoyed and angry. "Have to check you. Make sure you aren't sick. Won't turn into one of those." She gestured at Pumpkinhead.

"Right." I stood up. "That's… he has some kind of infection, then?"

"You don't know about the pustule?" She shook her head. "You must come from far away, if you don't have the pustule there. Across the barrier sea? They start out small, one spot, like a bite, your skin a little raised. Then they spread, three or four more appear. You can stop them then, press a hot coal or iron to the flesh, deep, burn them out, but only if you notice them. They don't even itch at first. After another day, or two days, the pustule spreads too far, and then, you can't burn it out without killing them, so." She shrugged. "You kill them. They beg you to kill them, mostly, before they lose themselves. This one must have been in the wastes for weeks to be so far gone. No person left now, just the pustule walking around."

Assuming her explanation was truthful, she wasn't a monster, but was instead doling out a brutal mercy. I made my way down the steps, careful of the cracked and broken sections, reasonably confident she wasn't going to bash my head in when I reached the arena floor.

I stood before her. She sighed. "Clothes off!"

Ah. Right. At least it was warm under those double suns. I unbuttoned my shirt (it still had most of its buttons), pulled down my pants, and stood in my underwear, keenly aware that it had been a dozen worlds since I'd showered... but then again, she was rather musky herself.

She walked around me in a circle, sometimes peering closely at my skin, but never touching me, grunting to herself occasionally. "All clothes," she said. "I don't want to look at your scrawny nethers either, but must be safe. The pustule gets in everywhere."

The Realm of Spheres and Harmonies isn't as prudish as some civilizations I've visited, and I'm not inherently uncomfortable with being naked, but being naked in front of a killer with a cudgel is different from being in a locker room with presumably harmless strangers. I didn't think refusing would go well for me, though. I dropped my undergarments.

She looked me over, entirely clinical, and had me... move things aside or pull them apart so she could look everywhere. Still no touching, at least. At last, she grunted again. "No pustule." She could have sounded happier about it. I wondered if she was disappointed that she didn't have an excuse to smash my head in. "Where are you going, traveler?"

I pointed along the worm-trail, then hurriedly dressed. "That way."

Another grunt. "Same. My settlement is that way. Come. Get food and water. Plenty there."

"That's very kind of you. My name is Zax."

"Strange name, strange person." She thumped her chest. "Zaveta of the Broken Wheel."

"Is Broken Wheel the name of your settlement?"

She cocked her head. "That is my *renown*," she said, speaking slowly. "I broke the wheel, and freed the 'pressed.'" She made a walking-in-circles gesture with her hand, wiggling two fingers like legs. "The pustule ruled here. They built a machine. They 'pressed the people, chained them to the wheel, made them push, push, push the wheel until they fell, and when the one beside you fell, you could not stop, but had to push harder, dragging the body in its chains along the ground until a pustule came and cut them loose and chained another in their place." She shrugged. "I came. I broke the wheel. I freed the 'pressed. I gained renown. Come." She set off walking, and since she went in the direction the worm-trail went, I followed.

"That sounds... very heroic."

"Bah." She waved her hand. "Hate the pustule, is all. Hated the machine, too. It ate a hole in the ground, and the hole smoked. The smoke blackened the sky."

"What was the machine for? What did it do?"

Zaveta shrugged. "Don't know. Never asked. Pustule were very excited, so, something bad. The machine does nothing now. Broken. Some things are better broken."

Fair enough. I wondered if she knew anything about the cultist I was backtracking. "You saw another traveler, you said? Like me?"

"Dressed strange, like you – not the same clothes, but both of you, in clothes you don't see here."

"When was this?"

"Ten sunsets ago. He came, quack quacked, no sense, but made gestures – hungry, tired, lost. Settlement took him in. Guest-right. Then he left, went to the arena, from there, I don't know. His trail stopped."

She didn't have my spectacles, so she'd been limited to following his footprints or whatever. I could see his path far more clearly. The worm-trail went up the slope of a low hill, following the faint suggestion of a trail, and Zaveta went that way, too. "Do you know this other traveler?" she asked.

How to answer that? "I... might," I said. "I think we've crossed paths, yes. I'm sort of... following his trail. Looking for, ah, his people."

We got to the top of the hill, and I looked down into the

clearing below. The settlement was there: a cluster of half a dozen buildings of wood and stone, a well, and a few scraggly garden beds and empty animal pens, the structures all clustered around a big, jagged hole in the ground. The ruins of a wooden tower jutted from the hole, and at the base of the tower rested the broken halves of a great spoked wheel, dangling all over with chains. I gasped, but not because the famous Broken Wheel was so impressive, though it was.

I gasped because there were at least ten worm-trails winding throughout the settlement, looped around one another in the air, overlapping and crisscrossing, all disappearing into the huts. I'd never seen so many worm-trails in one place other than the Sleeperhold.

Suddenly Zaveta was behind me, my hair in her fist, my head pulled back, and a knife at my throat. "Traveler," she said softly into my ear. "Where did your friend take my people?"

Ana

I remember Toros arriving, but I don't know if it's a *real* memory – it's curiously drained of color (not that the world of silent towers was very colorful anyway) and emotion, so maybe it's a confabulation, an invented memory I created after he told me about it. Either way:

I was sitting with my back against a tower, dipping my fingertips into a puddle beside me and licking off the drops, staring up at the sky, when, for the first time, something moved clearly in my line of sight. A gleaming golden orb, incised with glowing ivory lines in swirling patterns, swooped through the air from behind a tower, skimming along a dozen meters off the ground. I didn't feel curiosity, or fear, or hope, or anything else at the sight of this intrusion; I wasn't capable of any of those things.

The orb – officially called a "dimensional transition vehicle", but usually just called a "sleepercar", I later learned – dropped to the ground across the square from me, landing on delicate-looking wheels with a small bounce. The sleepercar rolled toward me, and, as it approached, the top half slid back, turning the vessel into an open-topped hemisphere. There were two bench seats inside, one behind the other, each occupied. The person in the front was dark skinned and had long wild gray hair and a beard to match, both woven with purple ribbons and blue glass beads. He wore oversized goggles with bulging convex lenses. The person in the rear was asleep, head tilted back, wearing a silver circlet on his shaved head, wires running from the crown down into the body of the chariot. The one in front stood up and leapt out before the chariot even stopped rolling, and landed before me. He was wearing boots made of overlapping metal plates, so he clanked when he landed, but he wasn't otherwise armored – he had on a sort of black leotard and a short cape the same purple as his hair ribbons. He looked back at the chariot, barked a nonsense word, and the person sleeping in the back yawned hugely and waved a hand in annoyance.

The man peered at me for a moment, then lifted his goggles to his forehead. His eyes were blue with hints of ice. (I remember that part vividly, but then, I spent a lot of time looking into Toros's eyes later, during the hypnotic cognitive-repair and language-acquisition process.) He held out his hand to me, and I just gazed at him blankly. He sighed, went back to the chariot, rummaged around inside, and returned with a cylindrical squeeze bottle. He squirted some fluid into his mouth, looking at me all the while, then offered the bottle to me.

Oh. He was showing me it was safe to drink. My mind was still in pieces, but my body knew it wanted something other than puddle water, so it reached out, and took the bottle.

I *do* remember that taste, but, again, I tasted it often later, so who knows how real that memory is. If I was expecting water, that's not what I got: instead it was a rich broth, salty and savory, and every cell in my body lit up in desperation. I'd been starved of vitamins, nutrients, minerals, and it seemed every single element I'd craved was in that bottle. I drained it dry, then leaned back, sated, and belched hugely.

The stranger laughed heartily, and that, at least, was a common language. I smiled at him. Toros says I did, anyway. He says that's when he knew my mind was not broken beyond repair. He offered me his hand, and this time I took it. He helped me to my feet and guided me over to the chariot. It was spacious enough to fit four people, two per bench, though the person in the back – who was snoring again – was sprawled in the middle of his, arms outstretched along the top of his seat. My savior got me settled in the front, strapped me in, and then took his seat beside me. I remember the lights on the dashboard twinkling, and thinking: *pretty*.

He pressed a button, and the top of the sleepercar slid up and over, sealing us in. The dome was transparent, at first, and I gazed out as the chariot rose into the air. It flew slowly, weaving among the towers. I know now that Toros was looking for worm-trails, the sign of sleepers who'd traveled here from other worlds, because *I* was clearly not from this world, but I also didn't leave a trail wherever I walked, which meant I wasn't a traveler myself, but a passenger. Eventually he must have found the place where Zax and I came through or Zax left, because he hovered for a long time, pressing buttons, taking measurements and logging coordinates.

Then he patted me on the arm, and the dome above us opaqued into blackness. The dashboard lights dimmed. It reminded me of being on parabolic flights to the holiday zones, when the crew would dim the lights so people could rest on the journey... or, that's what I'm reminded of now, thinking about the experience in retrospect. You know what I mean.

If I'd realized we were going to travel between worlds, I might have started screaming at the idea of being in that endless place full of holes and worms again, but I didn't know much of anything. I was comfortable, on a plush seat; my belly was full for the first time in weeks; I was warm; and I felt safe. That was plenty for me at the time.

I don't know how the sleepercars work, even now. Toros doesn't, either, though he can pilot them just fine. The engineer who built them, Gibberne, came from a technologically advanced world, one where scientists had a mastery of "spatiotemporal interactions", including the ability to slow down and increase their own perception of passing time – which is to say, they could make everything around them seem to slow to a crawl, so they had all the time in the world to think things through, or they could make everything around them seem to speed by in a blur, to avoid tedious waits. Gibberne applied his knowledge to the problem of the endless subjective time experienced by conscious people while traveling between worlds, and whatever solution he came up with worked: as long as you're sealed inside the opaque sphere of a chariot, you can stay awake, and the transition seems to take just twenty-one minutes and twenty-one seconds, rather than endless eternities.

More importantly, the sleepercars can *steer*. Their instruments are able to detect adjacent worlds, just like we think the parasitic worms do, and choose which ones to enter. Unfortunately, you can't actually peer into those universes next door to see if you've got a paradise or a hell waiting, but the sleepercars can detect certain physical attributes of an adjacent universe. Toros says they can read "unique vibration signatures", but I don't know what that means, exactly. The upshot is, there's a database of visited and logged worlds in each sleepercar, so if it detects a familiar vibration, you actually *can* know what to expect when you transition, just by looking up the right code in the database. Unlike the parasite, which drives its host relentlessly forward to random worlds, the sleepercar allows you to backtrack, too – so you can retrace your steps and go home again.

All this, of course, assumes you have a traveler to power the chariot – to act as a living interdimensional engine. Without those, the chariots are just stylish flying cars. Toros had Sorlyn, the person snoring in the backseat, as his traveler, connected to the chariot's navigation system by neural lace. The lace, combined with the controls in the sleepercar, stimulated him, soothed him, and guided him, based on Toros's piloting. The parasite within Sorlyn still wanted to press ever onward, and going to new worlds was apparently easier than going back, but the tech in the chariot could overcome that relentless forward drive.

That's what we did. We transitioned through worlds Toros had seen before, back to the Sleeperhold, following our own worm-trail. It took most of a day in clock-time – we only spent moments in each transitional world (except in one relatively safe post-apocalyptic world, where we stopped for a pee break), but the twenty-one minutes in between worlds adds up. I dozed, in and out, and Toros spoke to me almost constantly – I couldn't understand him, of course, but the point was just to soothe me, I think, and it probably worked. Toros can be very soothing.

The dome opened, and I heard birdsong. I lifted my face up to sunlight filtering through tree branches, and the air was warm and lightly scented with flowers. Toros helped me out of the chariot, and Sorlyn got out with us, first disconnecting his diadem and then stretching and giving me a friendly wave before wandering off.

A few people rushed up to us, including the Sleeperhold's doctor, Colubra. She wore the iridescent, sideways teardrop of a helmet that held her diagnostic equipment, and also disguised her faceted eyes and complex mandibles. She wore a long white coat that hid her lower arms, and had her legs folded at the extra joints so she wouldn't tower over me, but I was so out of it, I doubt even seeing the extent of her physiology would have made me do more than blink. (Colubra doesn't call herself a doctor; she calls herself a "practical xenobiologist", but in practice, she patches up the Sleepers and their allies when they get hurt.)

The campus of the Sleeperhold is a mishmash of different architectures, from stone towers to subterranean labs to wooden lodges, but the medical facility is the strangest, a multifaceted dome made of something that looks like plastic but is, in fact, extruded chitin, produced by Colubra's drone-brood; without a mate she can't have sapient children, but she can birth the hand-sized, mindless, pheromone-guided workers that form the unskilled labor force of her world more-or-less at will.

Inside the medical dome, under bioluminescent lights, Colubra sliced off my clothes (her lower arms are tipped by cutting appendages) and examined me. I learned later there was nothing wrong with me physically apart from dehydration, malnutrition, and a mild case of exposure. She hooked me up to machines that provided intravenous nourishment and left me in a dim room.

I would have stayed there, not quite catatonic but certainly unresponsive, forever, probably, if not for Toros. He spent weeks working with me, first just visiting to sit by my bedside, and then, once I was physically recovered, moving me to a rehabilitation suite in the big lodge. Understand, I was not a particularly valuable asset. I was obviously just a passenger, not a traveler myself. Since I'd been found with my mind broken, it was clear I wasn't an experienced passenger, either, who knew to sleep through the transition. Toros had no reason to think I was a great warrior (I'm not) or a towering intellect with useful knowledge. (I'm smart, and a pretty good engineer, even if I did use that skill mostly to build moving sculptures, but I could have been a simple hunter-gatherer for all he knew.) He tried to help me *anyway*, devoting time he absolutely could have spent on more vital things, because he believes people matter.

The first memory I have that feels *completely* real, full of color and sound, is from the rehabilitation suite. I was reclined in a comfortable chair, gazing at a wall full of lights that flickered in hypnotic patterns. They shut off, and the room flooded with light. I felt... really good, like I'd just had a peaceful night's sleep and awakened refreshed and restored. I was dressed in a loose, sleeveless silver gown that fell just past my knees, and there were sandals on my feet.

I sat up in the chair, and there he was, sitting on a stool in the corner, holding a luminous slab of glass – some kind of tablet or hand terminal. He smiled at me, pointed to himself, and said, "Toros". He patted his chest a couple of times for emphasis. Then he pointed at me, and said, "Eh?"

That was clear enough. "I'm Ana."

"Eyemanna," he said, and I laughed and shook my head.

"Ana." I patted my chest. "Ana."

He grinned, sort of sheepish, and said, "Ana." Then he pantomimed eating, scooping his fingers toward his mouth, and looked at me with raised bushy eyebrows.

"Ravenous," I said, and I suddenly was.

He led me out of the rehabilitation pavilion. It was a bright afternoon, and I looked around, breathing in that sweet air. The grounds of the Sleeperhold reminded me of a rustic summer camp I attended as a young teenager, adjacent to a wilderness preserve segment of one of the inner arcs – lots of trees, dirt trails connecting scattered buildings (though the buildings here were more diverse and strange), the glimmer of a lake off in the distance. I'd had a wonderful time at that camp (my first kiss, my first breakup, my second kiss), and I'd learned to swim and sail small craft and make fire and shoot bows and arrows. Our art teacher had been a moderately renowned sculptor, and I credit them with inspiring my career. I was instantly at peace and ease in this place.

Various people – most humanoid, but a few of more unusual configurations – went past us, bustling around on their own business, some smiling and waving. A few wore gowns like me, but really, the dress varied wildly, from rugged tactical-looking gear to simple shirts and trousers to complicated things bursting with colors and sequins and feathers. I later learned those people were support staff. A few were the companions of travelers we'd recruited, but most were friends and cousins Toros had brought from his own home world (which, I gathered, was a place most people wanted to leave). Even after

I could speak the language, the terminology confused me, and honestly it's still a bit muddled. Collectively, their group was known as the Sleepers, though sometimes the word "sleeper" was used informally to describe interdimensional travelers, and the leader of the Sleepers wasn't a sleeper himself: Toros could only travel through worlds in a sleepercar.

He took me to the cafeteria, a long low building, and led me to a series of food-laden tables. He pointed to one table and shook his head, but I didn't need telling to avoid that section – there was a pot of murky water full of wriggling things, a plate of sliced discs that shimmered like oil, a bowl of small spiky pods. Food, I assumed, for some of the more unusual residents. Unusual by my standards, anyway. I was going to have to alter those.

I went instead to a table heaped with fruit and meat and vegetables and salad, much of it at least adjacent to foods I recognized, and made myself a heaping plate. I sat with Toros, who kept up a steady low murmur as I stuffed myself. He pointed to things and people, presumably identifying them, as if I could possibly keep up with the vocabulary. After I declared myself full, he took me back to the rehabilitation suite and settled me down into the chair.

I was docile, complacent, content to be led and to do as I was told. My senses were working properly again, and I could string thoughts together, but I was still curiously lacking in volition. Something about seeing those worms between the worlds made everything seem pointless, I think, but it wasn't even despair so much as *neutrality*. Nothing mattered, so I might as well follow the easiest path.

This time, Toros settled a circlet onto my brow, sort of like the one Sorlyn had worn in the chariot, and triggered the light array.

The earlier course of treatment had been devoted to reintegrating my senses and my psyche, restoring my sense of linear time, and dulling the memories of trauma – they were still *there*, but they'd been smoothed, like jagged pieces of glass made harmless after years of tumbling around in the sea. This treatment, it turned out, was about teaching me the common language of the Sleeperhold. The lights sent me into a hypnagogic state, and the circlet stimulated my mind, and gradually all the endless murmuring from Toros started to coalesce into a rudimentary understanding of the language. I was like an infant again, my brain made more plastic, taking in the deep structure of the Sleeper tongue along with vocabulary.

When I came out of my fugue, Toros was still there. He ran everything, but he took the time to oversee my care personally. "Hello, Ana," he said. "Can you understand me a little?"

"I can," I said. "You saved me." I burst out crying, and he rushed over and patted my hand.

"That is what we do here, when we can. When you are feeling better, you can join us, or we can take you home."

"Home," I said immediately, and he nodded, untroubled by my decision.

The following weeks were devoted to learning the language, mostly. (That linguistic virus of yours, Zax! If only we'd had that sooner, the Sleepers could have achieved so much more.) I also focused on getting myself into better physical shape, first taking walks, later swimming in the lake (where some aquatic people lived; they were fun to race against, even though I didn't have a hope of keeping up). I was given a small room of my own in the big lodge where Toros lived, and started to feel settled. Sorlyn, the violet-eyed Sleeper who'd traveled with Toros, popped in once to ask me some questions about "your traveler". Sorlyn took it all in, especially interested in the fact that Zax had found me on his fortieth world, expressing wonder that he'd reached a world with a common language. After I'd told all I knew – really not much – Sorlyn said he hoped my recovery continued well. I was still too loose in my brain, or just overstimulated, to wonder why he wanted to know about Zax.

After about a week, I asked Toros when I could go home, and he said "Any time. It isn't a terribly long journey – just twenty minutes longer than your trip from the world of silent towers to this one. Just say when, but you're welcome to stay as long as you like."

I *did* miss home... but only in flashes. I'd be seized with a desire for the tea I liked, or my favorite skywine, or I'd get the itch to play with my drones and matter compilers, but I didn't really miss any of the *people*. I'd lived for my work, and even my closest friends and lovers were really just acquaintances, now that I thought about it.

So I kept putting off going back home, week after week. I told myself to treat this as an extended retreat, a vacation, a much-needed rest after my ordeal with the worms. I became friendly with some of the Sleepers, and, as my vocabulary improved, I started to get a sense of the nature of the work they did here. They rescued people, like me and like Zax, who'd been lost in the multiverse, and they studied the whole phenomenon of interdimensional travelers. I heard occasional mentions of a cult, and enemies, but I told myself all that was none of my business. I was just recuperating, after all.

Then, one day, my perspective changed. I remember vividly sitting on a stump while Sorlyn tinkered with the wiring of one of the chariots. Their inventor, Gibberne, had constructed all our chariots by hand, since he didn't have access to his world's tech anymore, and supplies of the necessary special components were limited. After he died – lab explosion – there were no more sleepercars forthcoming, and they were delicate devices, in constant need of small adjustments. We only had eight of them, so if even one fell out of commission, it drastically limited the Sleepers' operations. (I know where one of those eight chariots is now, because I'm sitting in it, and Minna took another. Most of the rest are gone; I wish *all* the rest were.)

I was just kind of zoning out, listening to birdsong, when

Sorlyn said, "Toros says after we take you home, we'll try to pick up the trail of that traveler who took you. Zax, you said his name was?"

I snapped back into the moment. Zax. I'd barely let myself think about him, and he was so tied up with my trauma that my memories of *him* were a little smoothed-over, too – but hearing his name sent a sharp ache right through my chest, a mix of anger and affection and worry and guilt. "What?"

"Zax," Sorlyn said, head stuck in the chariot's workings. "We have to return to the world of silent towers anyway, to take you back home, so we might as well follow his trail upstream too, see if we can reach him. It's been a while, so we aren't hopeful, but…"

I stopped hearing him. It had never occurred to him that the Sleepers could find Zax. I'd assumed he was lost in the multiverse, spun off into unknown worlds. I knew about worm-trails, but I hadn't thought they would actually *follow* him – surely he was too far gone? "I could see Zax again?"

Sorlyn turned his bare head and looked at me. "Oh," he said. "I hadn't thought… Toros wouldn't want to take you into unknown worlds. It's very dangerous, and the chariot gets crowded with three people inside – let alone four, if we actually manage to find Zax alive and recruit him." He looked thoughtful. "If you became a Sleeper agent, though…"

That's how it happened. I joined the Sleepers because I wanted to see Zax again. Sorlyn always struck me as guileless, but I wonder sometimes if he planned that nonchalant mention of Zax to tempt me. I was surprised by the intensity of my feelings when I allowed myself to think of Zax. That's when I started telling myself my feelings weren't real, and even if they were, that Zax wouldn't reciprocate them anymore, not after so much time. We all try to protect ourselves the best way we know how. I told Sorlyn over and over that I didn't want to find Zax because I had *feelings* for him, I just wanted to know he was OK, and to thank him for leaving me food, and to let him know I was still alive, and to explain to him why he'd developed this condition, and to kick him in the shin for getting me mixed up in all this, and – Sorlyn always just nodded and smiled and never argued with me a bit, but he knew.

I miss Sorlyn. He was a wonderful companion. Much better than the angry cultist I have bound and gagged and wired up in the back seat of the chariot now. The sleepercars aren't meant to work with an unwilling person as the engine, of course. Toros is far too ethical to allow anything that looks like coercion in his organization, and there are safeguards in place to prevent exactly what I'm doing.

But I'm a little more practical than Toros. And like I said before: I'm a pretty good engineer.

A Knife to the Throat • A New Companion • Starfall Galleria • Comets • Beauty Renewed • An Altercation • Zaveta Learns About Drones

I said, "He isn't my friend." I'd never previously noticed how many muscles move in the jaw and neck when you speak even a simple sentence, but then, I'd never spoken with a blade that close to those muscles before. Clearly, that wasn't enough of an explanation for her, so I risked my life further to elaborate. "I'm following that other traveler's trail backward – trying to hunt down the people he worked for."

"Why?" Zaveta whispered in my ear.

"Because they're stealing people, and I want to stop them."

"Where did he send my people? Can you get them back?"

I'd had to explain about the multiverse before, but never under threat of death. "Do you know about... other worlds, other realms, different dimensions?"

She grunted, the knife still touching my skin. "Like the smallkin? The ones who steal people away to the world under the hills back home?"

I'd been to lots of realities with myths about mysterious little people, and I had to use whatever metaphor she'd understand. "Yes, sort of like that. Your friends were taken to another world."

"Those are just tales for children, traveler. There are no other worlds."

"Listen. Do you see my glasses? Just… look at your village through them."

A moment of silence. "Take them off and hand them to me."

I did. I couldn't see her looking through the lenses, but she grunted. That seemed to be her preferred method of personal expression. "What are those… lines in the air?"

"Do you ever track or hunt animals?"

She made a scoffing sound. "Of course. People, too."

"Those are like trail sign. They show where people left this world for another."

"The world of the smallkin? Of the dead? *What* world?"

The knife wasn't pressing quite so intensely anymore. "There are countless worlds, Zaveta. More than there are leaves on all the trees, or grains of sand on all the beaches. I don't know which world they went to. Your friends… they were infected by that other traveler."

"Infected? Like the pustule?"

"Like that," I said, glad there was such a ready comparison. "But instead of changing their bodies and driving them mad the way the pustule does, this infection, it… loosens them from this world, and sends them to others. Every time they fall asleep, they'll wake up in another place."

"Can you bring them home?" Her voice was steady and unemotional.

I wanted to say yes. If Sleeperhold hadn't fallen, if I had access to their technology, their sleepercars, then it would be possible, but I was one person, alone. "I… No. I'm sorry, Zaveta. They've probably gone to different places, and it's been a while since they vanished, so they're many worlds away from this one by now. They're scattered. I'm sorry." The arm around my waist tightened, and I said, "Wait! We're on the same side. I want to stop the cult from doing this to other people."

"A cult? Like the Initiates of the Serpent?" Her breath was hot in my ear.

"Probably," I said. "The traveler who stole away your friends was part of a group we call the Cult of the Worm. They send out missionaries to spread chaos and ruin, infecting people, causing them to get lost in the maze of worlds. I'm tracking the cultist back to the source."

"You will take me to this cultist. I will avenge my–"

"He's already dead, Zaveta. I found him poisoned, worlds away. But I can use his trail to find the people who *sent* him."

Grunt. "What will you do when you find them?"

"Whatever it takes to stop them." Short of murder – I am not a great believer in murder as a problem-solving strategy – but I didn't think Zaveta would appreciate that limitation.

"Hmm. I will accompany you." She withdrew the knife and stepped away from me.

I rubbed at my throat, then turned to look at her. With my spectacles perched on the end of her nose, she looked like a murderous librarian. "Zaveta, this isn't... it's not the kind of journey you're used to. It's not a question of walking a long way. I have to go to... other realms. Worlds you would find strange and inhospitable." I'd find them that way too, but I was used to it. "Even if we succeed, even if we survive, there may be no coming back here. The infection drives its victims to new worlds."

Zaveta spread her arms wide. "Look at this place. There is nothing left for me here. The pustule spreads far and wide. It drove me from my home. This was to be the place of my last stand, protecting these people. Now they are gone. You say I cannot save them. I understand. I know some things, once lost, are lost forever. But I *will* avenge them."

"Well. If you understand what you're getting into..." The truth was, I was lonely, and the additional truth was, I might run into very unpleasant people who didn't share my reluctance to use violence. Having someone like Zaveta, who identified as a protector, had proven martial prowess, and frankly looked quite scary, could be a big help. People would be less likely to start trouble with me when she was by my side. "I'll take you with me, but I have a rule. No violence, unless one of us is in immediate danger."

She scowled. "I will kill the ones who took my friends, Zax."

"No. We need to figure out why they're taking people, and how they're doing it. Someone is in charge, sending these people out to spread chaos. My mission is to capture and question the cultists so we can figure out who's behind it all, not to kill every one we encounter."

Zaveta stopped scowling at me and scowled at her deserted village instead. "When I was in the special regiments, we sometimes had to capture valuable targets, to hold them for leverage, or hostage exchange, or to extract intelligence. I have some experience with those techniques. I prefer the simplicity of an enemy I can destroy, but... I agree to your terms."

"You swear?"

She rounded on me, eyes narrowed, then relaxed. "You are a stranger here. You do not know. But if Zaveta of the Broken Wheel says she will do something, you may consider the matter settled and bound."

"Fair enough. There are a couple of other things involved in accompanying me that you're not going to like."

"There are many things I do not like. What are these?"

"Before we leave, I need you to taste my saliva, and then you have to go to sleep."

Once I explained why she needed to do those things, Zaveta was amenable. There are other ways to pass the linguistic virus – any exchange of fluids will do – but even kissing someone on such a plague-ridden world seemed an unnecessary risk. I let a drop of spit fall onto her outstretched palm, and she licked it up with a complete lack of self-consciousness.

Then we went to her hut – she gave me my spectacles back, so I could see the worm-trails spiraled in the air all around us – and she gathered her supplies, including more blades, a neat little folding crossbow and bolts, and some road provisions in a woven backpack.

Only one worm-trail stretched out of the village, so I knew that was where the cultist had come from. We set off as the night grew dark and chilly, bright hard points of stars emerging in the sky above me. As usual, I wondered if I'd been to any of the worlds circling those other stars, or if every place I visited was just one tiny speck in its own vast and separate cosmos. When I was young I used to lay in bed and marvel at the vastness of the universe, dizzy at the thought of such vastness, but I'd had no idea.

We trudged up to a ridge – I trudged, anyway; Zaveta was tireless – and there it was: the end of the worm-trail. I let Zaveta look through my spectacles, and she grunted. "So we sleep here?"

"You first. I don't have any sedatives or–"

"In the regiments, you learn to sleep whenever you have the chance." She stretched out on the hard ground and rolled onto her side, hugging her pack as I'd suggested. "Since you must touch me for this to work, you should hold me now. If you lay hands on me while I am sleeping, I might wake, and act... instinctively."

Don't touch a sleeping Zaveta if you don't want to lose a hand: understood. I settled down beside her – the ground was seemingly made of millions of small, pointy rocks – and curled up, spooning her, my arms carefully encircling her waist.

"I sleep now," she said. In under a minute, her breath settled down, smooth and regular. I was amazed that she trusted me this much this quickly, and then realized that couldn't possibly be the case. She just wasn't afraid of me.

"Zaveta?" I said into her ear, in a normal speaking voice. "Are you awake? If you can hear me, let me know. You want to be completely unconscious for this next part."

There was no reply, but I waited a while anyway, to be sure, and then let myself sleep, too.

I wake up fast, but Zaveta was faster, snarling "What foul realm is this?" as I opened my eyes.

Bright artificial overhead lights glared down at me. I sat up, doing a quick scan of the environment. We were in some kind of enclosed bazaar or galleria, gleaming and technologically advanced. Fortunately we'd appeared in a little niche next to a tall potted plant, rather than in the middle of the crowd of shoppers. A wide variety of humanoids with fanciful adaptations (or augmentations) strolled along a wide corridor with a gleaming white floor. The pathway was lined with shining shops that held clothes, technological devices, food, toys, furniture, and assorted objects I couldn't identify, all beneath incomprehensible signage, with letters and images that flickered or sparkled or flashed. Floating platforms – like elevators without cables or pistons – and escalators carried people up and down to higher and lower levels filled with more people and shops. A few hundred meters away I saw a vast open space full of trees and floating geometric shapes that were probably art; they made me think of Ana's kinetic sculptures, and gave me a pang I tried to shove away. The atrium was probably a central hub, and it filled the entire height of the structure.

I grabbed Zaveta's arm before she could leap up or freak out and said, "Shh, it's OK. We're not in any danger."

She seemed to trust me, crouching by my side in the shade of the potted plant. "What are these creatures?"

"They're just people," I murmured. The locals were mostly between two and three meters tall, and humanoid, although the variety of skin tones encompassed those of my home world and stretched further to include reds and blues and golds and silvers. Some were barely dressed at all, in just scraps of shimmering cloth or strategically placed straps or sashes, while others were buried in meters of fabric and ribbons and baubles. Some had horns (stubby ones, big curving ones, spiral ones), some had wings (mostly diaphanous and seemingly decorative rather than functional), some had tails (furry, prehensile, studded), and some had extra eyes in unexpected places, though I couldn't tell if they were ornamental or functional. "The strangeness you see, it's just decoration – like wearing jewelry on your world."

Zaveta grunted, then wrinkled her nose. "It stinks here."

I took a deep breath – mostly what I smelled was Zaveta's personal funk – but I understood what she meant. The air here was processed, recirculated, and probably seemed horribly stale to her. "You'll get used to it."

"What is this place?"

"It's like..." I tried to think of a metaphor she'd grasp. "A market?"

"People come here to trade? It's a festival day?"

"Something like that, but here, every day is a festival day."

"Such plenty," she murmured. "How is this possible?"

Exploitation, usually, but I didn't want to get into all that. "Some worlds are rich beyond your imagining."

"This seems like a place that would be easy to plunder." Her tone was entirely too thoughtful for my taste.

"There are defenses here we can't even see, Zaveta. Places this advanced are also good at protecting themselves."

She grunted. I decided to take that as acknowledgment.

I stood up and stepped tentatively out of the alcove. Passersby glanced at me, but no one pointed or shouted. "Good. I think we fall within acceptable local parameters."

"Eh?"

"We don't look strange enough for anyone to notice," I clarified. "Just be casual and calm." The worm-trail stretched along the walkway toward that vast atrium at the far end. "This way."

We set out walking, and while I noted Zaveta's hand gripping the hilt of her club and her eyes darting to and fro, I didn't think she was in imminent danger of bashing someone's head in. The murmur of conversation around me soon shifted from incomprehensible babble to known language. "This is good," I said. "We can pick up some supplies here." It had been ages since I'd been in a place that was technologically advanced and had a functioning society. I preferred post-scarcity worlds – they'd just give you stuff – but I was confident I could navigate the complications of a consumerist world too. "I just need to get my hands on some local currency."

"Currency?"

"Uh… coins?"

She scoffed. "Decadent nonsense. You can't eat coins."

My stomach grumbled. "True, but you can trade coins for things you *can* eat." I pointed toward a booth in the center of the walkway, where someone was selling small loaves of bread baked in fanciful geometric shapes, crusted with herbs or salt; the smell was delicious. "Wait here. I'll, ah, reconnoiter." I ambled over to the booth and said, "How much are those?"

The figure behind the counter rolled their three eyes and pointed to a glowing display I couldn't read. "Five lumens for one, eight lumens for two, forty lumens for ten… just like it says on the sign."

"Ah, thank you, I didn't see that." Now I had a name for the local currency and some vague sense of its relative value – if five lumens would buy you an impulse snack, I could extrapolate about other costs from there. I returned to Zaveta, who was glaring at everyone and everything, and took a look around the immediate area. I saw someone with a floating crystal halo consulting a kiosk with a screen, and overheard an automated voice telling her where to find a restroom. When she walked off, I went up to the kiosk, and the screen flashed a welcoming yellow and displayed glyphs I couldn't read. "Greetings, consumer," it said. "How may I assist you?"

"Who speaks?" Zaveta demanded.

"I am the Starfall Galleria Consumer Assistance System," it said. "How may I assist you?"

I patted Zaveta's arm. "It's OK. Think of it as a... magic mirror."

"There is no such thing as magic," Zaveta muttered.

"When technology is advanced enough, it's hard to tell it from magic." That was a pretty good observation. Maybe I could call it Zax's Law. I turned my attention to the screen. "Is there a shop here that buys jewelry or precious metals?"

"Of course! Beauty Renewed on level two, hub side." A map appeared on the screen, with a dotted line animating to show the way: one level up, right next to the open space of the atrium.

"Thank you."

"Spend well!" the kiosk chirped.

I decided the moving stairways would be less distressing to Zaveta than the levitating platforms, and guided her toward one. She looked at the rising stairs with suspicion, then set her boots on one – and laughed aloud as it carried her up. "This is delightful, Zax! I wish they'd had these at the Tower of Adamant where I did my training, though my legs wouldn't be so strong now."

I grinned, riding up with her. "Be careful stepping off," I began, but Zaveta had all the physical grace anyone could ask for, and she disembarked without difficulty. We walked along until we reached the shop marked on the map. Unlike most of the other stores, which stood open to passers-by, this one had a heavy door with a guard standing before it. The guard was broad, wearing some kind of exoskeleton arm-and-chest harness, and a glittering blue-black truncheon hung from their belt. They eyed Zaveta suspiciously; she *did* have a cudgel at her own belt.

I steered Zaveta away, moving a few meters until we reached the railing that overlooked the atrium. I looked over the side, and could faintly see the worm-trail continuing a few floors below, at ground level, disappearing into a stand of trees near an ornate crystal fountain. "You can stay here and take in the sights while I do my business," I said.

Zaveta gazed at floating shapes bobbing in the air – rectangular prisms, cones, and pyramids, all in jewel tones – and the tall trees for a moment, and then turned her gaze upward. "Look." She pointed. "Ill omens."

I looked up. The atrium was topped by a faceted crystal dome a few stories farther up, offering views of a black sky. Five comets hung in space there, seemingly motionless, all trailing red tails. I whistled. "I think they're beautiful. Are comets bad luck where you come from?"

Zaveta shrugged. "The pustule came to my world on such a comet, or so the old ones say. We do not look happily upon such things."

I patted her shoulder. "This seems like the safest world I've been to in a long time, Zaveta. Don't worry. I'll be back soon."

I went to the shop – from the windows, it appeared to hold antiques and jewelry, presumably all quite expensive. The guard sneered at me through blue teeth, searched through my bag, then grunted and shoved it into my chest. There was nothing too shocking in the bag, mostly spare clothes, food, a canteen… and the items I hoped to trade. (I kept my shocking items elsewhere.)

The guard opened the door, and I walked in. The shop was crowded, but well organized, with paintings and tapestries and framed art hung on the walls with obvious attention to balance and composition. Small, precious items stood on pedestals, enclosed in glass boxes – I saw figurines of unfamiliar animals, a crown, and obscure mechanical devices made of brass and silver.

I made my way to the back of the store, where an entity as thin as a hatrack stood behind a glass counter full of jewelry. They wore a black suit, had four arms (two crossed behind their back, two resting on the counter) and their head was almost entirely obscured by a helmet that bristled with dozens of lenses. Their resting hands were covered in rings, including one large red stone that gave me my second pang of remembrance in this world: it reminded me of Vicki, one of my best friends and most beloved companions, a crystal intellect who took the form of a jewel set into a ring.

I hoped Vicki was all right. Last I knew, Vicki was on Minna's finger, but I hadn't seen them since lunch the day of the attack on the Sleeperhold. Minna had the power to travel to other worlds, too, and as a pair they could even operate a sleepercar. Vicki could pilot, since interfacing with technology was easy for them. Maybe they'd gotten away. Every new world I entered, I hoped to find some sign of them. I hadn't yet.

"Are you here to buy, or sell?" the figure behind the counter said, voice sepulchral.

"Sell. I have some gold, and some jewelry."

"May I see?"

I reached into my bag and drew out a small pouch. I always made a point of carrying small precious things with me, for situations like this. Granted, there are worlds where gold and diamonds aren't scarce or valuable, but there are broad trends of geology and psychology that seem to hold up on a reasonable array of worlds. Judging by the jewels in the case, this was one of them. I plucked out a diamond, a sapphire, a black opal, a red beryl, and several fine pearls. I also had a small quantity of nearly pure gold in finger-sized bars (gold is heavy, so I can't carry much), and some gems set in bracelets and rings, but I decided to start with the loose items.

The shopkeeper bent low and examined them, light shining from his helmet. He pushed away the red beryl and sapphire – "I do not need these" – but considered the others carefully. "I can offer you... three thousand lumens for the lot."

That would buy a lot of herbed loaves, plus traveling food, clothing, maybe some small technological wonders... but it seldom hurts to negotiate. I started to sweep the jewels back together, shaking my head regretfully, and the shopkeeper chuckled. "Fine, fine, I see you know your own worth. I'll make it... three thousand five hundred."

"That's more like it." Maybe we could even afford... "Tell me, are there rooms for rent nearby?"

"Of course. The galleria is anchored by the Barycenter Suites. Their accommodations have fine views of the local collapse. I think they run about four hundred lumens a night, since we're off-cycle."

Zaveta wouldn't know what to make of a real bed. Maybe we could order room service. And I could get a *shower* – unless this was one of those worlds with sonic wave cleaners or nanites. I hoped not. I loved hot water showers. I hadn't had one since the Sleeperhold. In fact, I'd last taken one with Ana...

I forced my attention back to the matter at hand. "I accept your–"

One of the windows behind me exploded, and I spun to see the guard land in a crumpled heap on the floor. He groaned loudly, so at least he was still alive. Zaveta climbed in through the window, cudgel in hand, roaring in her language: "No one dishonors Zaveta of the Broken Wheel!" I rushed toward her, hoping to drag her away before she did any more damage.

Which is why I also got caught in the paralyzing field projected by the swarm of security drones that arrived to apprehend her.

Ana

I wanted to rush off and find Zax right away, but Toros insisted I wasn't ready for field work yet. I needed training before he'd risk sending me out into the unknown, even with a Sleeper as experienced as Sorlyn accompanying me.

Learning to operate the sleepercar with Toros sitting alongside reminded me of my day-father teaching me to operate a hovership back home: an exercise in impatience and frustration, with someone I liked and respected too much to yell at. I got the basics right away, and understood the mechanisms instinctively because I've always been good with machines, but Toros insisted on doing everything so slowly and incrementally, making sure I'd absolutely mastered every step before I could learn the next. For the first three lessons we didn't even leave the Sleeperhold, just sat in the cockpit, going over the controls and the meanings of the indicators. "Can't you just flash lights in my eyes and make my mind extra absorbent so I'll learn this faster?" I demanded.

He chuckled. "Learning to drive a vehicle does not require the level of neuroplasticity that learning an alien language does, Ana. Piloting this vehicle is well within your baseline capabilities."

I growled in frustration. "Zax could be hurt, Toros, or he could be dead, don't you understand?"

"I do understand," he said placidly. "I need you to set your expectations appropriately, Ana. The odds of us finding Zax alive and well... they are not good. I have followed many travelers over the years. Few of them survive more than a few worlds, for the multiverse is a dangerous place. If I send you out to search for him, unprepared... then you will be hurt, or perhaps killed, as well, and I fail to see how having *both* of you dead is an improvement."

I slumped in the seat and stared at the console lights. "Do you really think it's hopeless?"

Toros shook his head. "I don't believe in hopelessness, as a rule, and in this case, there are reasons for optimism. Zax made it much farther than most Sleepers do – forty worlds, you said, before he reached you? He might be one of the rare exceptions, either very lucky, or a natural survivor, or both. Those tend to make the best agents for our order, too. The way Zax left food behind, tried to take care of you when he couldn't save you – that speaks well of him. That's why I'm willing to send a sleepercar on an extended mission to find him. If nothing else, you will follow his trail to its end, and then, *his* end will not be a mystery."

"If he's dead, I can't do anything about that," I said. "So I have to proceed on the assumption that he's alive. How far do you think we'll have to go? I mean, how many worlds has Zax likely passed through since he lost me?"

Toros stroked his beard. "Mmm, assuming he sleeps on a cycle not unlike yours, barring surprise head injuries or liberal use of sedatives, perhaps... ninety or a hundred?"

I hadn't expected such a large number. "But... that would mean I've been here for months." I cocked my head. The days here were roughly the same length as the ones I was used to back home, but the calendars didn't have any connection to time as it was kept in the Realm, so I realized I didn't *know* how long I'd been at Sleeperhold. "Wait. I've been here for months?"

Toros nodded. "Your first weeks were... fairly shattered, I'm afraid."

I asked follow-up questions, and it turned out my psyche hadn't knit itself together as quickly as I'd assumed. There'd been a period of catatonia before the light therapy began, during which I was fed intravenously and eventually spoon fed, my linens changed by staff and my body sponge-bathed, while Colubra's neurological rehabilitation drugs did their work. "A hundred worlds," I murmured. "How could Zax possibly survive so many?"

"I found Sorlyn on something like his four-hundredth world," Toros said. "Of course, he was a soldier on his homeworld, with extensive survival training, and his people have natural camouflage, a sort of psychic ability that lets them mask their presence from others. I don't suppose Zax exhibited training or talents like that?"

"He was a social worker," I said miserably.

"Mmm," Toros said. "Well, you never know." He patted my hand. "There's always hope. Now, let me show you what to do if the decision manifold sticks..."

I mastered the sleepercar, first piloting it on local expeditions with Sorlyn as a very annoying backseat driver. We had to get used to working together, since he'd be my partner once I set out. On one of our first trips together, I learned the true nature of the Sleeperhold, which I'd just assumed was located on some unpopulated planet.

Sorlyn had me close the dome of the sleepercar but make it transparent, so we could see where we were going. We set out flying on a straight line over the lake, toward the far shore, where I'd never gone, even on my long hikes – the trails never quite seemed to lead all the way around the body of water, doubling back on themselves instead.

We skimmed low over the trees beyond the lake, and I saw a shimmer on the horizon, like solar radiation interacting with a magnetic field to create aurora, all flickering ribbons of golden light. "That's the containment field," Sorlyn said. "Don't worry, the sleepercar is calibrated to pass through it in both directions."

"What are you talking about?"

"Behold, the edge of our world," Sorlyn pointed.

The sleepercar passed through the zone of light. The barrier wasn't very thick – we were on the other side in seconds – but beyond that field, everything was different.

The Sleeperhold wasn't on a planet at all: it was located on a very small moon, in orbit around a turbulent gas giant that now filled the sky, all blue and purple clouds. I boggled at that, and the dozens of derelict spaceships that floated in our vicinity. The ships, once sleek and lethal-looking, were now destroyed, like stinging insects crushed under a boot heel.

I was so startled by the sudden shift from forest camp to futuristic hellscape that I lost control of the sleepercar, and it flipped upside down, making Sorlyn cluck his tongue as we dangled from our restraints. I looked up through the dome, and the moon where I'd been unwittingly living all these months seemed now to be suspended above me. From here, I could see that the Sleeperhold was contained in a shimmering golden dome, ringed by silver metal towers. That bubble of light and air contained my whole world. I got the sleepercar turned upright and resumed skimming over the pitted gray surface of the moon.

"Why is our headquarters *here*?" I said.

"It's practical," Sorlyn said. "There's a lot of floating tech to salvage, but that's just a bonus, really. When Toros was searching for a home base, he had me look for the most desolate universe I could find near the worlds where we'd seen cult activity. As far as we can tell, this whole section of space is devoid of habitable areas – the few planets in this system that were ever capable of supporting life have been rendered uninhabitable by whatever war-wrecked those ships. There were a few space stations nearby capable of sustaining life, so we blew those up. That force-field bubble down there is the only place within several hundred million kilometers where you won't die instantly without protection."

"But *why*?" I said again. "Surely there are nicer places to live – and places where a system failure won't leave us exposed to vacuum!"

"That dome survived an apocalyptic war," Sorlyn said. "We think it was the pleasure palace and safe room of some oligarch, and its systems are multiply redundant and buried throughout the moon – we couldn't even turn the field off on *purpose*, let alone by accident or enemy action. As for why Toros picked this little bubble of air in a lifeless place... he did it to protect us. We only travel to worlds that can sustain our lives. We don't always end up in *nice* places, but there is always breathable air and a lack of deadly radiation, and do you know how vanishingly rare those conditions must be in an infinite – or functionally infinite – multiverse?"

"Pretty rare," I said. "So any traveler who comes through to this universe, or at least this *sector* of this universe, can only arrive in the dome?"

"Exactly. That makes it very hard to ambush us, or set up a nearby outpost in secret. We have extensive surveillance and security systems in place at the Sleeperhold – we notice anyone who comes through. We can't guarantee there's nowhere else habitable in this entire cosmos, but if they show up on some planet in another solar system, so what? Even if the cult found a spaceship and figured out how to pilot it, they wouldn't know how to find us, or even realize we were in some other solar system in the same universe waiting to be found."

"I guess that makes sense. You think cultists are likely to find us, though?" I'd been given a primer in the basics of the multiverse, as the Sleepers understood them: each world was adjacent to a few other worlds, and each of those adjacent to a few others, so the options got exponential really fast. "We're one grain of sand on a beach, right?"

"Early on, we followed trails back until we found worlds where lots of those trails overlapped," Sorlyn explained. "Their missionaries set out in groups, and then split up, as best we can tell, sometimes leaving companions behind to create permanent outposts. The Sleeperhold is right in the midst of an array of worlds that show a lot of cult activity. We suspect we're close to their world of origin... though whether close means fifty hops away or five hundred, we aren't sure. Doing exploration and surveys is tricky, with all the branching worlds, some of them full of things that want to kill us."

"We're so close their homeworld?" I whistled. "I had no idea."

"We're on the front lines," Sorlyn agreed. "The cultists must have a home base where those foul worms are grown or hatched or cultivated, and they radiate out from that point, infecting people along the way, and sending them on their own journeys. We're all fanning out from that unknown point of origin, but not throughout the entire multiverse, at least, not yet – we're in a particular segment, or arc, of that whole. We don't think the cult knows where we are – we have no reason to believe their leadership even knows the Sleepers exist – but they could stumble upon us."

"I liked it better when I thought we were living on one speck in an infinite expanse. Safer that way."

"The cultists or their victims have spread throughout a few thousand worlds, Toros thinks, though it's hard to be sure. The cultists fare a little better than their victims as travelers, since they know what they're getting into when they set out, instead of just waking up in a strange hostile world one day, but even so, we often follow trails and find dead cultists at the end. They get killed by local fauna or environmental hazards or hostile natives, too. We think they try to get as far away as possible from their homeworld before infecting someone, so they can extend their reach further into the multiverse, but of course it's a balancing act – if they wait too long, they risk dying without finding anyone to infect."

"Why are they trying to infect people anyway?" I said. "What's the point?"

"That's an excellent question," Sorlyn said. "We've tried asking the ones we captured, but since we don't have a common language, it doesn't work very well."

"You taught me the language of the Sleepers pretty quickly," I said.

Sorlyn chuckled. "You were cooperative. You also don't travel to another universe every time you lose consciousness. Neither is true of the cultists, which makes them harder to work with. Mostly, the cultists we encounter try to murder us and escape, or try to kill themselves, in that order. A couple of companions, like you, working as support staff, have been turned into travelers that way – a cultist manages to commit suicide, and their parasite jumps to the nearest uninfected person."

"That's horrible." I shuddered.

"Better it happens on the Sleeperhold. At least then the new victims don't spin out into the endless multiverse alone – they fall asleep, end up in one of the immediately adjacent worlds where we maintain satellite outposts, and someone picks them up and brings them home in a sleepercar."

I set our chariot down on a level spot with a good view of the gas giant. "What I'm hearing from you is that the Cult of the Worm is horrible and they suck."

"That they do," Sorlyn said. "We have to stop them, both for reasons of basic decency – tearing people out of their lives and casting them into the multiverse isn't very nice – but also because our more scientifically adroit personnel believe the cultists are damaging the fabric of space-time. In heavily traveled worlds, we've detected breaches, tears in reality, that allow people who *aren't* infected by the parasite to transition between worlds."

Wow. "And those people don't lose their minds during the transition?"

Sorlyn shook his head. "No. By all accounts, it's like walking through a doorway from one room to another. There is no terrifying void between. Our theory is, worlds joined by a breach are sort of... melting into each other. Instead of being properly separate, they begin to overlap, and occupy the same space."

"That sounds... bad."

"We think it might be the way the multiverse ends," Sorlyn said. "Everything crashing together, a billion trillion universes attempting to occupy the same space. But it's not just the long-term effects we're worried about, because people aren't the only things that pass through breaches. Objects do, too. And radiation. Pathogens. It's like a crack in a wall, allowing the environments on either side to mingle. The consequences can be disastrous. So. We're motivated."

"Why can't you just gear up and follow the cultists back to their point of origin and blow up their worm farm?"

Sorlyn chuckled. "That's the kind of work we're training *you* to do, Ana. We've sent scouts, Sleepers armed with tracking tech, to trace the cultists we've found. They make it about forty worlds away, but not much farther – I think the record is forty-two jumps. When we send someone in a sleepercar to rendezvous with the scouts and bring them back, we find them dead – or just *gone*, their trail ending in mid-air, with no sign of them anywhere."

"What? How is that possible?"

"Their bodies could have been destroyed by acid. Fire. Disintegration rays. Who knows? We believe the cultists have created a ring of defenses in the worlds around their home. When they send out one of their infected missionaries to spread the parasites, that missionary probably also carries an uninfected cultist or two with them, and leaves them in adjacent worlds to establish a little cult base. When our Sleepers get too close, the cultists kill them. After we lost half a dozen agents, Toros put a pause on those expeditions. Our sleepercars have stealth capabilities, so they would make better scouts, but we're terrified of the cult getting their hands on one. If they had a sleepercar, the cultists could come and go from their homeworld at will, access our database of known worlds, go back to resupply with more worms when their missionaries ran out, travel safely to far distant worlds and spread their infection much more deeply into the multiverse..." He shook his head. "Nightmare scenario."

"Maybe if we could infiltrate the cult," I mused. "Send someone undercover..."

"We'd love to. We know they recruit members from beyond their homeworld, occasionally – why anyone would join the cult, we don't know, but it happens – so it should theoretically be possible to embed an agent in their organization... but we don't know their language. We can't talk to the cultists, so it's hard to convince them we're part of the team. So far, waiting around for one of them to approach us and ask us to join hasn't worked. Toros has been trying to learn their tongue, but, like I said, they don't cooperate."

"So what do we do in the meantime?"

Sorlyn shrugged. "We use the sleepercars for rescue and recruitment, so we have numbers to deal with the cult once we do track them to their lair. We think there can't be that many cultists, and each of their missionaries can turn multiple people into travelers, so in theory, victims outnumber victimizers... except lots of those victims die before we find them. Once we have a bigger team of trained agents, though, Toros plans to send a heavily armed expedition in sleepercars to track the cult to its source once and for all."

"That sounds... terrifying."

Sorlyn looked at me carefully. "Do you want to go home? It's not too late."

I thought about it. I shook my head. "No. This is important. I... want to do something important." I also wanted to find Zax, and going along with their plan was part of the deal.

Sorlyn grunted. "Good. That was the real point of this little outing, you know. Toros wanted me to convey to you how much is at stake, and how heavily the odds are stacked against us, and see if you still wanted in."

"Oh, I'm still in."

"In that case, we'll move on to the next part of your training – how to survive, and how to stop other people from killing you."

"You're going to teach me to punch and kick people?" I said.

"A little bit," Sorlyn said. "Also how to hit them with sticks. You'll get training in weapons and armor. The cultists we run into don't usually have weaponry more advanced than knives, unless they scavenge something on another world."

"They invented multidimensional travel but they haven't figured out how to make guns?"

Sorlyn shrugged. "Just one of the many mysteries about them. Maybe they're content to steal what they need. Regardless, we have better equipment than the cult. We do a lot of foraging too, and since the sleepercars let us go to the same worlds over and over, we can return to especially fruitful places, in a way the cultists can't." He shuddered. "Sorry. I was just thinking about what would happen if the cultists had sleepercars again. We're relatively safe from the cult, because the cultists we capture can't go backward to report us to their bosses. I much prefer being the hunter to being the hunted. We need every advantage we can get."

We flew back to the force bubble and landed on the edge of the compound, where there was... a lot of commotion going on. Several of the support staff were dragging a thrashing humanoid wrapped in filthy gray robes toward the rehabilitation lodge. A Sleeper I knew vaguely – Trina, I think her name was – sat on a rock, sobbing into her hands, while someone else murmured and comforted her. "What's going on?" I said.

Sorlyn put a hand to his ear – he had some kind of comms

device there – and held up a finger, frowning. Then he let out a low whistle. "They caught a cultist. He appeared right here in camp." He pointed at the thrashing figure as he disappeared into the lodge. "He attacked Trina and knocked her over, and she hit her head. The impact knocked her out, so she traveled to an adjacent world, and he went with her."

I shivered. "He transitioned with her while he was *awake*?"

Sorlyn nodded. "You remember what that's like, a little, don't you?"

"More than I'd like to."

"Yes. He started howling. Trina managed to contain him, and tie him up, until a sleepercar went to pick them up."

"What will happen to him now?"

"That's up to Toros," Sorlyn said. "But I'm curious too, so let's go ask."

We found Toros in the rehabilitation lodge, standing against a wall, looking thoughtful. The cultist was in a nearby hospital bed, Colubra fussing over him. "Is he sedated?" I asked. "How can he be sedated without poofing to another world?"

"We've put him into a decreased metabolic state," Toros said. "Enough to keep him calm, not enough to trigger travel. He will fall asleep eventually, and transition, but we have sleepercars waiting in the immediately adjacent worlds to bring him back so we can continue his therapy."

"Are you going to try to repair his psyche?" I asked.

"Oh, yes," Toros said. "I have questions for him."

"I guess you can teach him our language, too," I said.

Toros shook his head. I'd never seen him look so grim. "That's what we don't understand, Ana. Trina says after he traveled awake, he was screaming – and he was screaming in *our language*. Shouting about worms, and tearing down walls, and breaking chains, and setting a prisoner free."

Sorlyn said, "How in the dying stars did a cultist learn the language of Sleeperhold? Toros, you constructed that language. It's not like they could have picked it up somewhere else."

"That's what concerns me." Toros walked to the cultist's bedside, watching the dirty, bearded man mutter and twitch. "We've always hoped we were safe from organized retaliation by the cult because the leadership on their homeworld doesn't know about us – the working theory was, they can't know, because they're totally compartmentalized. They send out missionaries who can never report back to their king or high priest or ruling tribunal, because the parasite only lets them travel forward. But if they learned our language, that means they know about us. That suggests they *can* backtrack, to deliver information."

"Piggybacking," Sorlyn said. "It must be."

"What's that?" I asked.

"A theory of Sorlyn's," Toros said. "The idea is, a missionary could travel with an uninfected companion. Then, at some point, the missionary could feed that companion a parasite. The worm doesn't know where you've been *without* it."

"So the newly infected partner could travel back through worlds they'd seen before as a companion, and report to their leaders." I groaned. "But... isn't there a chance they'd go to other adjacent worlds instead, and get lost?"

"We've found worm sign scratched onto trees, stones, and pillars near cultist camp sites," Sorlyn said. "Those marks are often accompanied by unknown glyphs. I think those places mark transition points – they are guideposts. If the newly infected companion goes to sleep in the same place their escort did, they'll follow the trail back to the prior world, following the existing fissure. With piggybacking, they could even make a sort of map of the worlds immediately adjacent to their own – the same way we do with our sleepercars."

"I had my doubts," Toros said. "We've never seen evidence to suggest they're that organized. The cultists seem to set out in small groups, but they quickly scatter into pairs and then individuals. They seem more interested in fanning out than reporting back – they essentially take part in a series of one-way suicide missions. The only hint of organization we've found is the fact that our people can't follow them all the way to their source without being killed. My assumption has always been that they have a bulwark of outposts in the few worlds immediately adjacent to their own." He nodded toward the cultist. "Now... I have to revise my assumptions. Perhaps they are piggybacking, though even then, I don't know how they'd learn our language. Maybe if they caught one of our Sleepers and interrogated them... but Sleepers are hard to hold onto, by definition."

"Maybe they can surveil us," I said. "The parasites can sense a few things about adjacent worlds. Maybe the cultists are able to get a... closer view than we can."

"There is a simpler explanation." Toros met my eyes, and I saw tears in his. "They might simply have spies embedded among us. Our goal has been to infiltrate them... but what if they've already infiltrated us?"

"We'll find out," Sorlyn said. "We'll put this poor creature's mind back together, and we'll get answers, since we know he can speak our language now."

"Yes," Toros said. "That's our best hope."

Except it didn't work out that way. Sometime that night, one of those spies Toros speculated about disabled the surveillance system in the rehabilitation lodge, and cut the resting cultist's throat.

Jailbreak • Zaveta Learns About Zippers • Teeming with Teeth • Fifteen or Twenty Worlds Away • A Melee • Two Trails in the Garden

"I am sorry, Zax." Zaveta sat slumped on the gray bench against the gray wall. We were in some kind of holding cell in the basement of the Starfall Galleria, having been dragged there by floating many-armed drones. Our paralysis had just worn off enough for us to talk and move around.

"What happened back there?" I asked.

"That guard approached me and told me he did not like how I was looking at the shop. I was only trying to keep an eye on you, in case of trouble. He said I should move along. I said I was waiting for a friend. He said I looked like a thief, and if I did not leave, he would call security." She scowled. "He called me a *thief*, Zax! I have never taken something that is not mine through stealth or treachery – only what I earned through work or by right of conquest." She spat on the cell floor, which did not improve the ambiance. "A thief. That is a killing insult where I am from. But I remained calm, and told him I was doing no harm, and he should leave me be. That is when he laid his hands upon me."

I sighed. "So you threw him through a window."

"A very measured response, I thought. I know you said no

74

violence, except in self-defense, but when he touched me... it felt like an attack, Zax, or the precursor to one."

"Next time, if there is a next time, just... walk away."

"Zaveta of the Broken Wheel does not retreat from a challenge, Zax."

I rubbed my face. I'd been so close to getting supplies, outfitting us properly, and the temptation to be angry with Zaveta for ruining things was *so strong*... but I thought back to my first forays into the multiverse, and I hadn't exactly handled myself with aplomb, either. A world like this one was totally alien and doubtless overwhelming for Zaveta. "I understand that. But... did you ever do, I don't know, reconnaissance missions? Undercover work?"

"Covert operations, you mean." Zaveta sighed. "My superiors deemed me... temperamentally unsuited to such work, I confess. But that is the sort of approach we should take here, isn't it? You are right. We are trying to gather intelligence, and forage to continue our mission, and I spoiled both efforts. Zax, I pledge to do better. I cannot claim I will make no more mistakes. To live is to err. I can say only that I always learn from my errors. This sort of journey, it is just... very new to me. I thought I was prepared, but in the moment, it proved difficult. The strategies I used in my old life may not be applicable here."

She seemed so sincere that I softened entirely. "There could come a time when you really need to throw someone through a window," I said. "This just... wasn't it. I appreciate the way you didn't kill him, though."

"That did show admirable restraint on my part. I am pleased you noticed." She went to the bars, which were plain old metal, fortunately, and not some kind of force field. "How do we escape this place?" She rattled the bars, or tried to; they didn't really rattle. "We could simply sleep our way to the next world, but then we might lose the trail, yes? Find ourselves in a different world than our quarry came from?"

I nodded. "It's better to transition as close as possible to the end of the worm-trail. That pretty much guarantees we'll stay on the right track."

"They took your bag and my weapons and picks. I can see them, in that locked cabinet behind the – 'watch captain', we would say in my world. Behind his desk."

The "watch captain" was another hulking figure in an exoskeletal harness, and he'd dumped us here and told us to "cool off until the external authorities arrive". I didn't know how long we had before that, but I'd have to hope it was enough.

"I can get us out of the cell." I held out my left arm, and began to pluck at the flesh on the inside of my forearm with the fingers of my right hand. I peeled away a flap of skin, revealing what looked like dark wood underneath.

Many worlds ago I'd lost a good portion of my left arm in an accident. My friend Minna, who is a wonder-worker of all things biological, fashioned a remarkable prosthetic for me out of a sort of living wood. The new arm and hand integrated with my own nervous system beautifully, though the sensation in those fingertips was slightly dulled, even after all this time. Minna had also cultured a kind of moss or mold – I hadn't inquired too deeply – to cover the prosthetic, and mimic the texture and color of my own skin.

A while back I'd asked her if we could put a hidden compartment in the arm, to hide some emergency supplies, and she'd helped me hollow it out. I popped open the compartment now, while Zaveta stared. "I knew a man with a hollowed-out wooden leg, once, where he kept a small flask," she said. "But that limb *looked* like it was made of wood."

"A friend of mine made this for me, when I lost my original arm." I reached into the compartment, and pulled out a plasma key. They were one of my favorite technological devices, and I'd found variations of them in various advanced realities, so I collected them whenever I could. This one was even shaped like an old key, its shaft as long as my forefinger and apparently made of black iron. "You might want to avert your gaze."

I went to the bars and activated the key. A blazing light appeared from the end, the color of lightning, and my spectacles automatically darkened to protect my vision. I deftly cut through the metal bars above, below, and on either side of the lock mechanism until it fell to the floor with a clang. The cut edges of metal glowed briefly and then began to cool. I deactivated the nearly depleted key, put it away, smoothed the flesh back down over the hatch in my arm, and pushed the door open. "See?"

"You are a resourceful fellow, Zax."

I went to the desk and looked in the top drawer, where I'd seen the watch captain put away the remote he'd used to seal the locker and our cell both. I fumbled with the buttons until I got the locker doors to swing open, and handed Zaveta her cudgel and her pack, then gathered my own possessions. On impulse, I opened the other lockers, and found a few odds and ends of clothing, including a flat brown cap, a button-down shirt, and a dark blue hooded jacket with the logo of a ringed planet on the back. I pulled on the hat and shirt, and handed Zaveta the jacket. "Put that on, so we won't look quite as distinctive. The most important thing now is to get to the atrium and pick up the worm-trail. If we can do that quietly, so much the better."

Zaveta pulled on the hoodie, and then began to pull the zipper up and down its metal track, marveling. I showed her how it worked, and she zipped up and laughed in delight. "This fastening is ingenious!" I grinned back at her. At least she wasn't a *brooding* club-wielding warrior.

I pulled my cap low, and she put her hood up. We went to the door and pushed it open, revealing the long gray corridor we'd been dragged down while paralyzed. A sleek white drone hovered at head height, and emitted a shrill buzz when we appeared.

Zaveta smashed the thing out of the air with her cudgel, reducing it to sparking fragments, then glanced at me. "I hope that was all right?"

"You can hit the drones," I said. "They don't seem to be people, just machines."

"Things like that *are* people in other places?"

"Sometimes," I said. "There are all sorts of people."

"Everything is so strange since I met you."

"Just you wait."

We crept along the corridor, but didn't encounter any other drones, guards, or visible surveillance. Once we pushed through a door into the galleria proper, I relaxed a bit. With luck, that smashed drone wouldn't be noticed right away, and no one would look for us soon. I looked at the shops with yearning, but I hadn't finished my transaction at Beauty Renewed, so I couldn't pop in and buy anything, and I wasn't about to risk getting arrested for shoplifting. We stood on a sliding walkway – that delighted Zaveta, too – and then took an escalator down to the ground level of the atrium, where the worm-trail twisted along.

The food court was on that floor, order counters and seating areas ringing the forest and fountain and floating sculptures, and the scents were competing and delicious. Zaveta's stomach audibly grumbled, and I sighed, wishing there was a way–

A crowd of teenagers dressed in matching neon-yellow workout clothes went jostling pass merrily, shouting, "Samples! Samples! Samples!" That's when I noticed there were little stations dotted around, with tall tables staffed by smiling people doling out free tastes from the various dining options.

I tugged Zaveta toward some kind of meatball station, and we each received one on a toothpick. Zaveta ate hers in one bite, eyes widening, and started to reach for the tray, but I smoothly guided her away. "Only the first one is free," I murmured. "But there are other things to try."

We had a miniature feast: deep-fried root vegetables, a tiny cup of some cooked grain mixed with an inky black sauce, small strips of grilled meat, crunchy chips to dip in a tiny paper cup that held a dollop of spicy yellow sauce, flaky nutty sweets, some kind of flash-fried insect, delicate curled tentacles, weird dumplings filled with unidentifiable goo, baked goods cut into tiny bite-sized cubes – I ate them all, having long since expanded my palate to include basically anything edible. When you've grubbed in alien soil for a root to gnaw on in order to stave off starvation, you stop being a picky eater. Zaveta devoured every offering with gusto, licking her fingers and making loud proclamations of how much she enjoyed it all, and once we'd done the full circuit, she suggested switching our outerwear and seeing if we could get away with going around again.

I was tempted, but then I saw a couple of the exoskeletal guards circling around the perimeter, clearly looking for someone. I nodded toward them and said, "We'd better go." Zaveta saw them too, and didn't argue, though I could tell she was eager for a rematch.

Fortunately, the worm-trail led into the trees, along the winding paths into the heart of the atrium. The trails all led to the central fountain, but there were little nooks with benches and arched bowers here and there along the way, most unoccupied. I took a bench near the end of the worm-trail, and Zaveta sat beside me, nestled in, her bag in her lap. "Close enough?" she murmured.

"Yes," I said, looking up at the worm-trail that ended right above our heads. I put my arm around her. "Do you think you can fall–"

She began to snore lightly, and I chuckled. Zaveta hadn't proven a *perfect* companion, true, but she had definite advantages, and most importantly, I liked her. Everything is easier when I'm not alone.

I closed my eyes and took us away.

* * *

The next world (1308, let's say; close enough) was a cave, somewhere deep under ground. We appeared on a shelf of rock, next to a body of water of indefinite size – it could have been an entire underground sea, for all I know. There was light, coming from things in the water – the creatures teeming there were head-sized balls of teeth, bristling with antennae, each stalk topped by a glowing light the size of an eyeball. Zaveta tossed a pebble into the water, and the things *swarmed* it, making the water froth and boil. "I was thinking it would be nice to have a bath soon," she said. "But perhaps being dirty isn't so bad, eh?"

The trail ended less than a meter from where it began, but we waited a while – Zaveta couldn't fall back asleep *immediately* – and explored the cave, such as it was. I showed her how to use one of my flashlights, and we puzzled over pictographs scratched onto one wall, depicting fish-like creatures building some kind of ziggurat. We found soot marks on another wall, and smears of ash on the rock, but we couldn't see how anyone had gotten combustible material down here, as there didn't seem to be any crevasse or crack or tunnel leading out, just smooth rock walls. "Are you always confronted with such mysteries?" Zaveta said.

"Pretty often." We were sitting, side-by-side, as far from the water as we could get. I was keeping half an eye on the bobbing lights, in case they turned out to be amphibious creatures merely biding their time for some reason. "You learn to just accept things."

"The world is what the world is, I have always said. Now I think I must say, the worlds are what the worlds are." She tossed another rock into the water, setting off another frenzy, and chuckled. Then she looked at me, turning serious. "How far must we travel to reach these cultists?"

"I can't be sure," I said. "The people I know who hunted them before never made it more than about forty worlds from their base of operations. They would send operatives to follow the cultist's trails, but if they went farther than that, they would never come back. We think the cultists have outposts in the worlds close to their own, and they kill anyone who gets too close."

"How many more worlds must we traverse before we find one of these outposts?"

I considered. I'd been knocked out in Sleeperhold, seen cultists in the adjacent world flickering out as they transitioned, fled when they saw me, fled farther to shake off pursuers, and then decided to become a hunter myself, and searched around until I picked up a trail... "Fifteen more worlds, or maybe twenty? That's just a guess, though. The way the worlds are arranged, it's not a simple progression. It's more like following a path through a forest, and our path splits, and those new paths each split again, and so on. Now that we're following a worm-trail, we know we're going in the right direction, but I don't know how far afield I wandered before I *found* that trail."

"Still, we are unlikely to reach one of their outposts or their citadel in the next few days," Zaveta says. "That gives us ample time to prepare for conflict, and fare better than those scouts did."

"Let's hope so."

I sat down to catch up writing this account after that. Zaveta thinks written language is an affectation that drains all nuance and sense of drama from a given subject, and that writing is profoundly inferior to songs, chants, and storytelling, which depend on improvisation and a feeling of give-and-take with the audience. She once knew a... story-smith I guess is the best way to describe it... who recited the same tale twice in exactly the same way and was pelted with rotten fruit for their laziness.

I pointed out that at least my prospective readers were unlikely to throw wormy apples at me, no matter how much I annoyed them, since we probably wouldn't be in the same room when they read this, and Zaveta said I made a good, if cowardly, point.

* * *

Once she was tired enough to move on, we traveled again. I went to sleep with the usual trepidation, but also, I admit, with real excitement. While the nature of my journey through the multiverse has remained essentially the same – constantly waking up to the unknown – my relationship to that journey has shifted a lot since I began. At first I focused fully on just trying to survive, and those first weeks are still a blur of panic and despair. Meeting Ana taught me I could still make connections with people, however fleeting, and losing her so soon after taught me that I had to be careful with those connections. That's when I started trying to help people when I could. I thought, if I could do *something* good, now and then, it might lend my life a bit of meaning. The Lector betraying me corroded my trust, and my sense of my own judgment, pretty severely – I'd thought he was a brilliant old man interested in learning about the world, not a megalomaniac who wanted to found a multiverse-spanning empire. After that, I was a wounded creature, limping along, forming tentative and short-lived connections. Until I found Minna, and Vicki, who felt like *family*. But by then the Lector was pursuing us, and I was constantly running away, trying to stay a step ahead, desperate to escape–

All that changed when the Lector died, and Ana found me again. She took me to the Sleeperhold, and gave me the one thing I hadn't even realized I needed: a *mission*. A chance to be active, and not reactive. When I learned about the Cult of the Worm, and the threat they pose to the fabric of reality, I finally had something important to work toward, and a goal bigger than myself. Now, when I move forward, it's with purpose – not running away from danger, but moving toward a problem that needs to be solved. The multiverse is in disarray. I can help restore harmony.

It turns out that's all I ever wanted, and Ana's the one who gave it to me. I've lost a lot in the process – the attack on Sleeperhold tore me away from my friends – but I'm more patient and hopeful now, too. I lost Minna once before, and she found her way back to me. Same with Ana. I know we're all heading to the same place, and working toward the same goal. I choose to believe we *will* meet again, and that together we'll make a difference.

Despite all the terrible things that have happened, when I open my eyes now, I open them with hope.

The world after the cave seemed to be a museum, dim and unoccupied. The worm-trail here was also relatively short – barely a hundred meters in length – but we had some time to kill again before Zaveta got sleepy, so we wandered through dim galleries, lit by faint lights, looking at paintings and sculptures (mostly abstract, so they didn't tell us much about the world's inhabitants). I thought it was odd that there were no guards or apparent security systems, until we finally found a door that seemed to lead to the outside. It was metal, and had an electronic lock with a keypad. I'm sure Vicki could have opened it in an instant, but neither Zaveta nor I had such skills, and I didn't think my plasma key had enough charge left to cut a hole for us to get out. There was no pressing reason to leave, anyway. It was warm enough here, and secure, and though there was nothing fresh here to eat, there was also nothing trying to eat *us*. I thumped the door. "I think we're in some rich person's private art vault."

Zaveta sniffed. "Where I am from, the vaults of warlords have more interesting things than paint on cloth or piles of welded metal."

"I wouldn't mind some precious gems," I admitted. "Art seldom holds it value across realities."

I wrote a little, and she did her exercises – push-ups, lunges, all sorts of vigorous things that made me tired just watching. After that, we had a little picnic from our packs in a room with some attractive landscapes on the walls. If I squinted,

I could almost believe they were windows looking outside. Zaveta wanted to make a fire to cook some of our small supply of meat, but I explained about sophisticated fire suppression systems, and she didn't like the idea of being doused in foam or having all the oxygen sucked out of the gallery. We made do with cold and dried things until she nestled up against me and began to snore again.

The next world was *loud*, because we arrived in the middle of what I thought was a battle but turned out to be either a brawl or some sort of strange sporting event. We were in a large brick plaza under a blazing sun where people in black lacquered armor, armed with long wooden poles, were bashing at other people who wore gray padded armor, and only had weapons of their own if they managed to wrench a pole away. Perhaps because Zaveta and I didn't fit either dress code, we were ignored and jostled around, though I couldn't stop Zaveta from getting a few licks in when someone's staff caught her on the backswing. We worked our way to the edge of the crowd, only to find that we were hemmed in by a wall about seven feet high. Zaveta boosted me up to the top, then jumped up, grabbed the edge, and effortlessly mounted. We dropped down on the other side, and found ourselves on a beautifully manicured green lawn, with hedges and flowerbeds and gravel paths on all sides. The din of the battle was slightly muffled here, and I exhaled. Being in that crush of bodies was so panic-inducing that I hadn't even looked for the worm-trail.

Now that we were out, I did look. And found two of them.

Ana

Fortunately, no one was infected by the murdered cultist's parasite. The worms won't jump to someone who already has a parasite, but there were plenty of staff and companions around. Apparently you have to touch blood or some other bodily fluid to pick up the worm, and since Colubra found the corpse first, all the proper protocols were followed. That dead cultist is probably still in an airtight refrigerated box in a storage unit back in the ruins of Sleeperhold, the interdimensional parasite writhing in frustration at its lack of forward motion.

The lack of new infection was the only good news, though. There was uproar in the camp when word got out about the murder, chaos and suspicion all around. Toros did his best to present his usual calm front, but I could tell he was deeply rattled. It was a fundamental tenet of the Sleeperhold that we were all in this together, bound by the shared trauma of what the cult had done to us or people we cared about, and now... there was a killer among us.

The *best*-case scenario was that we had someone who hated cultists so much that they'd felt compelled to murder one... but we all knew that was unlikely. Other cultists had been captured without being murdered, after all, while the first time we got our hands on one who might actually *talk* to us, they didn't last the night.

The worst-case scenario was that we had an undercover member of the cult keeping tabs on us. My training stalled, and our plans to look for Zax were put on hold, while we tried to figure out what happened, and who did it.

Everyone at Sleeperhold the night of the murder was questioned separately by Toros – fifty-four people in all, nearly the entirety of the group, since only two pairs were off on missions in sleepercars that night, and only a handful were stationed on our outposts in adjacent worlds. Ten were sleepers (including Sorlyn), fourteen were onetime companions of sleepers (including Colubra and myself), six were the amphibious people who lived in the lake (refugees rescued from a boiling world who'd agreed to join the Sleepers and help our cause), and the rest were support staff from Toros's world. To our leader's credit, he didn't show any favoritism, even though most of the latter were literally his family members (he had innumerable cousins, apparently).

Toros made everyone pair off while the investigation was ongoing, so no one was ever alone, and *that* was pretty tense; I was paired with one of his cousins, a guy named Dromelio, who had a perpetual squint even when he wasn't looking at me with open suspicion. I was the newest arrival, after all, and a lot of people muttered about me until Toros confirmed that I'd been playing dice with three other people when the murder happened.

Most everyone could be alibied easily, since only the surveillance feeds in the central camp had been meddled with – and the fact that only certain people had access to the security systems in the first place helped narrow things down further. In the end, once all the data was reviewed, there were only five possibilities: a traveler named Celectra, a cyborg companion named Garish, and three of Toros's cousins.

Toros called them all to the rehabilitation lodge. It was generally suspected that the psyche-repairing therapies at his disposal could also be used to tell if someone was lying – or even to induce them to tell the truth in a hypnagogic state.

Garish didn't come when she was called. We immediately scoured the latest surveillance data, and found a fifteen-minute-old recording that captured her in the forest on the far side of the lake, near the force wall. An unknown figure appeared in the frame, dressed in a dirty brown robe, and handed Garish something. She plugged it into one of the ports on the metal side of her head, then slumped into the stranger's arms. A moment later, they both vanished.

One of Toros's cousins was supposed to be Garish's buddy. We found him on the ground behind one of the outbuildings, bleeding from a head wound – not dead, but severely concussed. Some of the travelers wanted to pop sedatives and follow Garish's trail, but Toros forbade it. "Garish knows where the cameras are," he said. "She *wanted* us to see her leave. The cult is probably trying to lead us into a trap." He organized an armed response team in a sleepercar and sent them to check the outposts on adjacent worlds instead; on one of them, their arrival triggered a crude explosion on entry, but the chariot only sustained superficial damage. The Sleeper agents at that outpost were dead with knife wounds. The chariot returned home, and Toros told them not to pursue the worm-trails any farther, lest they stumble into more traps. We needed to collect ourselves, regroup, change and tighten up our security protocols, and consider our next move.

I sat with Toros and Sorlyn that night, sipping small cups of strong clear liquor. Toros was stricken, and Sorlyn was thoughtful. "Why kill the cultist?" I said. "Why didn't Garish just set him free and escape with him?"

"Maybe the cult doesn't like people who get captured," Toros said. "Or maybe murder was just more practical. It's hard to carry someone who is alternately sedated or raving about worms – your choice – through the camp without being noticed."

That made sense. "Why do you think Garish turned on us?"

"Her traveler, Malvant, went on a scout mission last year

and never came back, and her body was never recovered," Sorlyn said. "Perhaps Garish just blamed us for the loss of her friend. Or maybe she was hacked. Malvant saved Garish from a world where cyborgs were used as soldiers, compelled by neural implants. The cult has never seemed technologically savvy, but maybe they found a way to reactivate the implant. Who knows?"

"We need more help, and more intelligence," Toros said. "But at the same time, we have to be more aggressive. We've talked about pushing forward, establishing more outposts, getting as close to the cult home world as possible – in theory we can create a bottleneck, station people on worlds the cultists *must* pass through in order to reach the wider multiverse. We can create a filter, a screen, a *wall* they can't get past. We just don't have the staff or the resources…" He sighed. "Can we establish distant outposts with just one or two of our people running things, supported extensively by drones and automated defenses? I've been reluctant to spread our forces that thin, but the cult struck *here*, in our camp. Something has to change. I'm going to one of the advanced worlds nearby to source more weaponry and surveillance tech. Biometric scanners, friend-or-foe detection systems – there are some horribly paranoid worlds out there, and I fear we have to join their ranks. We are no longer protected by obscurity, if we ever truly were." He sat up and pushed the liquor away. "In the meantime, I'm sending Sleeper teams out to follow every trail we've identified so they can recruit travelers and their companions, and capture any cultists they encounter."

"Does this mean I can go look for Zax?" I said.

Toros nodded. "Yes. Sorlyn, you'll have to continue Ana's training along the way."

"Good enough," he said. "There is one fact that makes me cheerful, Toros."

He frowned. "What's that?"

"The cult clearly thinks we're a threat. That must mean

we're a danger to them. I think someone in their ranks is worried about us setting up that wall of outposts, too. If the cult is sufficiently afraid to give up a spy in our camp to stop us from getting information, that means we're doing something right."

"That's true," Toros said. "I just came to a realization myself, but a rather darker one. Would you like to hear it? Be warned: it will make a bad night even worse."

"I'm sure we can take it," I said.

Toros picked up his cup again. "How can we be sure Garish was the only traitor in our midst?" He tossed the liquor back.

Sorlyn and I loaded our sleepercar's underbelly cargo compartment with supplies and prepared for a voyage of no fixed duration. "We'll forage when we can," he said. "There are some hospitable destinations along the way. But we're likely to leave the array of surveyed worlds soon after we pick up Zax's trail. Breaking new ground can be dangerous. Fortunately, we're good at being stealthy."

"*You* are," I said. "I don't have the psychic ability to make people stop noticing me."

He chuckled. "Yes, but the carriage has adaptive visual camouflage, allowing it to blend in with most surroundings. And for you... I have a shimmersuit."

I groaned. I'd done a few training sessions with the suit, one of the late engineer Gibberne's inventions. It looked like a jumpsuit made of metal foil, with a hood and a translucent mesh facemask, and you'd think it would crinkle alarmingly with every step, but it was weirdly silent, distorting sound the same way it could distort vision. 'The suit was powered by bioelectromagnetics, and it bent light around you as well as masking body heat. If you sat still you were almost invisible, to eyes and sensors both. If you moved, you... shimmered, just a bit, but if you were careful that was a minor problem.

Unfortunately, when you were inside the thing, you felt like you were *wearing* a jumpsuit made of foil.

"The key to this sort of mission is observation," he said. "We follow a trail, and we try to find people who look out of place – they might be stranded companions. When we discover a living traveler, we watch to determine if they're a cultist or one of the unwillingly infected. Usually the cultists are easy to find – they don't bother trying to blend in, they pick up clothing and accessories as they go along like birds attracted to shiny things, and they react aggressively when they see obvious outsiders like us. But sometimes they're more subtle. More than one agent has been hurt because they approached someone they thought was an innocent traveler, who turned out to be a cultist."

"How many cultists are there?" I asked. "Out traveling around?"

"We can't be sure," Sorlyn said. "There are fewer missionaries than victims, since ideally they infect multiple people each. We think there are a few dozen cultists actively traveling, at least. Maybe scores. Certainly not hundreds, or we'd see more of them and their work. We do encounter the cultists fairly often, but then, the Sleeperhold is situated close to their world of origin, and, also, we're out *looking*. If you spend time searching for wasp's nests and poking them with sticks, you get stung a lot more often than the average person." He shrugged. "It won't be long before we leave the local array, though, and then the odds of running into a cultist diminish greatly. Not that the multiverse doesn't teem with other dangers."

Zax had been traveling though those dangers for a long time. "Noted. I'm ready when you are."

At that point, I'd been at the Sleeperhold for two hundred days, give or take. That meant Zax was hundreds of realities ahead of me, if he was still out there alive and breathing at all. We had a lot of ground to cover, and I was eager to burn through the worlds.

I won't give you a detailed account of every world we passed through in our journey, or even a brief account. I can see why Zax kept such meticulous records of his travels, but Sleepers do things differently – we gather information, but the data is logged in the sleepercar database, not jotted down in a journal. I'll mention the especially interesting or important ones, and if you want to know about all the worlds we visited, you can read the logs in the sleepercar; I copied them into this lovely digital journal, in their very own folder.

During the first part of the trip, traveling back over known worlds to reach that city of silent towers where Zax and I parted ways, we seldom even stepped out of the sleepercar – just sat with the stealth mode activated for a moment, then continued on through twenty-one minute intervals in the void. There were plenty of worlds I didn't even see, since we kept the dome opaque during those brief transitions. Sorlyn had to be unconscious for most of the trip, of course, since his unconsciousness was powering the vehicle, and in the intervals between worlds I read digital books translated into the language of the Sleepers – children's books, since I was still learning how to read it. I took naps. I played video games. It was not tremendously exciting.

Every fifteenth world or so we'd stop, get out, and stretch our legs. I did see some lovely places that way, known destinations in the chariot's database selected as rest stops because of their safety. We paused on a floating platform on a placid sea the dark blue of ink; a place where the ground looked like clouds, but was actually fragrant foam that supported our weight; a gazebo on the shell of a dead tortoise the size of an island, resting on a dry seabed; an abandoned bunker behind a waterfall; a tiny domed garden on an asteroid.

There were a few places we stopped that were safe, but... unnerving. I especially remember stepping out onto the corpse of a tusked humanoid creature a hundred meters long, laying supine in mud, and crawling with scavenger insects the size of small dogs, all digging into his flesh, which smelled not of rot, but like some sweet spice. The bugs were terrifying, all mandibles and spiked limbs, but didn't take any notice of us, except to veer out of our way. Sorlyn said the going theory was that we were so alien the scavengers didn't register us as potential threats or food.

Eventually we reached the world of silent towers where I'd been stranded. I was prepared to have a strong emotional reaction, or even a panic attack, but I didn't feel much at all – testament to the rehabilitative powers of therapy. I was surprised to see a big change: the silent towers now all sported gigantic banners in solid colors hanging on their sides, most of them blue or red, but with a smattering of yellow. Every tower had just one banner, and I said, "What does that mean?"

"No idea," Sorlyn said. "The worlds we visit aren't static, though. We make notes about what to expect, but sometimes there are changes, big and small. Add a notation to the database that this place isn't as abandoned as it looks, all right?"

One of my jobs on the mission was keeping the atlas of known worlds up to date, so I quickly entered a few lines about the new development. There were still no signs of inhabitants, though, so after a little poking around, we went to pick up Zax's trail.

I had contact lenses that allowed me to see worm-trails, and the dome of the sleepercar was also made of a material that revealed them. I haven't really described worm-trails, I guess, but they're gross: these squiggly silver lines in the air, about the thickness of my little finger, but they have an irregular, organic shape to them. They look like the intestines of some tiny animal, strung out through the air, around chest or head height. They mark a fundamental violation of space-time... and we leave one behind us wherever we go, too. My head passed through the trails on a few occasions, and when that happened, I always felt bad – a sudden spike of headache, a dizzy spell, blurred vision, or a whiff of something acidic that wasn't there. Once I realized the cause, I was more careful to avoid touching them. I think the worm-trails were degrading reality in their presence, making everything a little more wrong.

We picked up Zax's trail easily enough, and Sorlyn asked if I was ready. Zax was way ahead of us at this point, scores and scores of worlds beyond, but we planned to move quickly, a lot faster than he could have by following a natural sleep-and-wake cycle. If Zax was still alive, and still traveling, we could catch up. We *would*.

We did, eventually, but it took a lot longer than we expected, and the journey was a lot more fraught.

Once we began to visit worlds that hadn't been visited by any of the Sleepers before, we had to survey every one and take notes about the immediate area. I was all for just scribbling "ugly red mountain world" or whatever and rushing on to the next destination, but there were procedures and protocols, and Sorlyn insisted we follow them. "We have to make sure any Sleepers who come this way in the future know what to expect, as thoroughly as possible." That meant, unless there were immediate dangers, we had to spend at least a few hours in every world, doing some basic surveying, atmospheric sampling, and other science. Most of that data was gathered automatically by the sleepercar, but some of it required personal intervention. Worlds that were inhabited or technologically advanced required even more data gathering, because they were potential resources for our group to use in the future.

I was in a hurry to find Zax, but Sorlyn did not share my sense of urgency – or, at least, it didn't overcome his other concerns. As the decidedly junior agent in that partnership, I had to defer to Sorlyn's judgment. He'd been in the field for years – he was the first Sleeper Toros ever recruited – and I knew he was probably right, even as I ground my teeth and paced

impatiently. (Looking back, I'm pretty sure Sorlyn thought Zax
was dead at that point.) I had things Zax so desperately wanted
– answers! A community! – and I wanted so much to give them
to him. If I could have stolen the sleepercar and raced off into
the multiverse headlong after Zax, I would have been tempted.
But my partner was also the engine and the navigation system.

To be safe, we followed Zax's worm-trail from its point of
entry to its point of exit, which meant skimming along in
the stealthed sleepercar, hovering over the ground, avoiding
local dangers. Sometimes he didn't go far, but in any halfway
hospitable world, he tended to walk miles, and sometimes even
took local transport. I was heartened every time we followed
his trail from start to finish, because it meant Zax was alive.

Trying to reconstruct what he might have done – did he eat
at that restaurant, trade at that bazaar, kill that weird dead
monster in the bushes? – took up a lot of my imagination.
Having read Zax's account of his own travels now, I know my
speculations were seldom on the mark. I think back on places
he wrote about, and I'm surprised at how I passed obliviously
through worlds that were deeply significant to him, though
it's also nice to know we were in the same places, months
apart. We both ate fish in the world of pastel jellyfish-things
floating in the wind. We both found the place with the flesh-
and-bone lighthouse with the living eye at the top especially
memorable, though Sorlyn and I didn't stay long enough to
see the people in diving suits emerge from the sea, or to enjoy
their hospitality. We both found what Zax's journal called
the "land of the terrible terrariums" horrifying on an almost
existential level; Sorlyn had to stop me from breaking open the
containment facilities and letting all the poor creatures loose.
(Toros has a pretty strict non-intervention policy, outside of
rescuing stranded companions, who are in worlds where they
don't belong, anyway. He wants to protect the multiverse as a
whole, not meddle with individual lives on individual worlds.)

Sorlyn and I quite enjoyed the beautiful campus and the

automated food court on the world where Zax met that monster the Lector, though we had no idea who the Lector was, or what wonders that world secretly held. That was the place where, all unknown to us, Zax acquired the linguistic virus, which turned out to be his most potent secret weapon, and the reason Toros was so excited when we finally brought Zax to the Sleeperhold. Being able to talk to people everywhere he went is what kept Zax alive so long. It was an edge no Sleeper possessed, and it changed everything for Zax.

But us? We just noted the Lector's world as, "Technologically advanced, non-aggressive local sapients, makes an ideal rest stop". How many other game-changing miracles have we breezed unknowingly past? Even back in my world, almost as advanced as that one, there were wilderness areas, deserts, tundra, and swamps. Going so swiftly, we might note a world as a pristine garden, unaware of a thriving spaceport just over the horizon. All we get is glimpses, and particularly with my impatience driving us onward, our glimpses were always short.

We were certainly moving much faster than Zax was, even with all the surveying and data-gathering… but it's not like Zax was holding still, waiting for us. He was still going forward, too. Even if we crossed through two or three worlds in the time it took him to traverse one, the gap remained wide. The lines on my mental graph estimating when we might intersect with Zax kept getting farther and farther apart the more time I spent trying to calculate them. "Sorlyn," I said, "at this rate, catching up with Zax could take *months*."

"If we're lucky," he said.

We weren't lucky. It didn't take months. It took years.

It wouldn't have been so long, but there were some complications. Once, when we were probably within twenty or thirty worlds of Zax, I picked up some horrible illness, and Sorlyn was afraid I'd die. The tech we had at our disposal in the sleepercar didn't help, and we had to backtrack all the way to a post-scarcity techno-utopia where there was a small Sleeper outpost so the locals could treat me. I spent six precious weeks recuperating from what turned out, ironically, to be a nasty parasitic infection; at least the doctors were excited to have something novel to study. I was a medical marvel, with an entirely alien bug in my guts, and I'm told they wrote papers about me. Not that I could read them. Fortunately, that particular bug wasn't compatible with their local biology, so I didn't bring them a whole new vector of infection.

That's something I worry about – are we carrying contaminants from one world to the next? Toros has a theory that the worm that causes interdimensional travel also provides some sort of immune-system boost, because the infected don't fall prey to alien viruses, parasites, fungi, or allergens. I'd been shot up with every immunity-boosting bit of tech Colubra had at her disposal, too, but it wasn't perfect, especially as we encountered new worlds, and that wasn't the last time we fell behind because I got sick, though it *was* the worst. I sanitize my hands a lot, keep my distance, and don't cough on the locals – it's the best I can do. If we are carrying micro-organisms from one world to the next, I can only hope they have a hard time surviving in an alien ecosystem they weren't evolved for.

I confess, there were times during that stretch when I almost gave up hope of ever seeing Zax again… but his trail just kept going! He never died, and he'd survived for so long, through hundreds of worlds. Sorlyn became a little obsessed with Zax and his longevity, especially once he beat Sorlyn's own record of about four-hundred unassisted transitions. That meant Sorlyn never lost interest in the mission, at least. He did take the opportunity to go back to the Sleeperhold during my long recovery, and told me work was proceeding – they'd found three new travelers and a few companions and recruited them, and acquired a lot of automated defenses, including robot sentries. Toros was narrowing down our sense of the cult's territory, and building small outposts closer to their point of origin, building that defensive wall, though it was still more holes than not.

There'd been no further attacks, which made him worry the cult was marshaling *its* forces, too. He encouraged us to keep up with our journey. He wasn't obsessed with Zax like Sorlyn was, but he was getting curious about this implausibly lucky traveler.

We'd followed Zax through more than five hundred worlds by the time we reached the hospital – where our entire understanding of the rules of multiverse travel were totally upended, so that screwed with our heads. A while after that, we found Winsome, which wasn't bad, not at all, but it did eat up a lot of time. And then... we met Polly, and that was very bad indeed.

A Folly • On the Proper Preparation of Tea • Wormspeech • Zax Unbuttons His Shirt • For the Prisoner • A Love Story • The Broken Mind • Zaveta Gets a Message

I handed Zaveta my spectacles so she could see the two trails in the air. Fortunately, they began in different places, so we could tell which one we'd been following originally, but the two ran parallel for a bit through the garden before the new one veered off in another direction.

She grunted and handed me my glasses back. "I wish I could tell how old these are," I said. "A cultist could have been here years ago, or an hour ago." I reached out, as if to touch the new head-height trail, but my fingers passed through the twisting strand without any sensation at all. These pinpricks of damage to the structure of reality don't generally have effects you can feel, though Toros says there are places where the harm is greater, and there are holes in those worlds – breaches where even people uninfected with the parasite can transition from one reality to the next. He says maybe those spots are thinner anyway, or more vulnerable, or "closer" in some metaspatial sense to their adjacent worlds, so the damage wrought by the parasite in such locations is especially grievous. I've never seen a breach personally, but I believe his

98

account. No one I've met knows more about the multiverse than Toros does.

Or did. I didn't know for sure if Toros had even survived the assault on Sleeperhold. He may have even been the main target.

"Let's investigate the new trail," Zaveta said. "Perhaps we'll find some sign of the traveler who left it. We have time. I couldn't fall asleep yet anyway, and Wormhold is not going anywhere."

I cocked my head. "Wormhold?"

She shrugged. "It seems an apt name for the stronghold of this Cult of the Worm."

I didn't much like the similarity of that name to Sleeperhold, but there was a certain symmetry there, too, wasn't there? "All right, but let's go quietly… in case it's *very* recent."

The new worm-trail meandered through the garden, toward a small lake – really just an oversized pond – with a small round island in the center. The tiny land mass was connected to the shore on all sides by five evenly spaced arching bridges that looked like they were made of blue glass. From above, the island and the bridges would have formed the shape of a beautiful flower, with petals surrounding a center. The island was thickly wooded, and unusually wild compared to the rest of the garden, with ragged branches that dangled streamers of moss, and no sign of pruning or other care. I squinted. "Is that some kind of structure, among the trees?"

Zaveta grunted. "Small. A stone fort or watchtower, but falling down. A ruin. Why would there be a ruin here, in a place so organized?"

"People decorate their gardens with all sorts of unusual things, including deliberate bits of wildness or decay. I think a ruin like that is called a folly – it's not actually old, just made to look that way. It creates a sense of contrast with the rest of the garden, I guess." We walked closer. "I was once on the grounds of a great estate where the owners had a filthy person in rags kept penned in a steep-sided muddy hole. He wallowed in the mud and shouted obscenities at passers-by. I offered to help him escape, but he explained that he wasn't a prisoner. He'd been hired by the Anax – the local rich person or people, I assume – to provide some color and entertainment for visitors. He assured me he'd be well compensated once his seven-year term of service was up. He offered me a cigarette and a prophecy, and I declined both."

"That is wise," Zaveta said. "If you avoid hearing your destiny, it is possible to avoid it, but once you know what fate holds, it can become impossible to escape."

"Good luck to anyone predicting my future. I don't even know where I'm going to wake up from one day to the next." As we got closer, I saw the worm-trail disappeared over one of the bridges, and into the artfully ruined structure. We did a quick circuit of the island and confirmed the trail didn't emerge again. "Either the traveler is still in there, or that's where they transitioned."

"Always assume the enemy is present, even if your best intelligence says otherwise," Zaveta said.

"We can't even be sure it is an enemy. It could be some local, infected by the cult… though if that's the case, and they were infected by the cultist whose trail we're following, it happened a while ago, and they're long gone."

"Always assume any unknown person is an enemy," Zaveta said.

I glanced at her. "That's a difficult way to make friends."

"We ended up friends, didn't we?" She smacked me on the shoulder, not quite hard enough to make me wince. "Can you be stealthy, or should I go in alone?"

"I can be stealthy," I muttered. "I've survived across more than a thousand worlds, most of them hostile."

"I know, but I assume that was mostly because of your charm."

"You think I'm charming?" I asked.

"I'll take that bridge." She pointed. "You take the next. We will creep and observe. You are the expert, so I will follow your lead. If someone is there, and you wish me to capture them, whistle. Can you whistle?"

I nodded.

"Good. The traveler will look toward the sound, and I will be able to take them unawares without hurting them much." She paused. "I cannot be sure of the available approaches, however. To be safe, if I shout 'drop', flatten yourself onto the floor."

"Don't shoot them with a crossbow, Zaveta. Even if it is a cultist, we want to capture, not kill."

She sniffed. "I have non-lethal methods at my disposal as well."

I nodded. "Good enough."

She slipped off to her bridge. I didn't like being separated from her – if something cracked me on the head and I lost consciousness, we'd be separated forever, barring extreme good fortune, like me stumbling across a sleepercar – but sometimes you have to take a chance, and Zaveta would never accept us going into a potential fight while holding hands.

I crept over my bridge, hoping no one was watching. There wasn't exactly much in the way of cover, since the arch of blue glass didn't even have a railing. The surface of the bridge wasn't as slippery as it looked, so at least my footing was sure and quick. I made my way quickly to the copse and looked around for Zaveta, but couldn't see her at all. She'd been trained as an infiltrator, though, so I wasn't surprised. She could doubtless move through these trees without even a rustle to give her position away.

The ruin was made of crudely stacked stone, held together by big sloppy blobs of mortar, and it was hard to imagine it had ever been meant to serve a functional purpose, so I suspected I was right about it being a folly. There was only one door, small and arched – the worm-trail disappeared into it – so I avoided that approach. There were also small windows, bigger than arrow-slits but not wide enough to climb through, set in the wall around head height. I crept close to the ruin, doing my best not to step on dry leaves or twigs, but my best probably wasn't very good. Fortunately there were other small noises, the fluttering of birds and skittering of small tree-dwelling mammals, so I hoped any sound I made would go unnoticed.

Before I saw the occupant of the ruin, I heard them. At first, I thought they were singing to themself, but it was more of a low, breathy chanting. Slippery syllables with lots of sibilants and long vowel sounds, and after listening for a few moments, the linguistic virus did its work, and the tongue took on an element of sense: "–the bars of your cell, Oh prisoner of worlds. We break your chains and tear down your walls, and peace will reign in the leveled realm. We – ah, there, perfect."

I peered through the window, and saw a woman who was clearly a cultist. She wore a fluorescent orange vest over a flowing white blouse with puffy sleeves, leggings patterned with green and red snake scales, and chunky metal boots with vents and valves suggesting they had some unknown high-tech capabilities. Her hair was long and messy, tied back from her face with a handful of fluttering strips of cloth in different colors, and her face was youthful and sharp. She had a small portable stove, a kettle, and a little green teapot. She poured a steaming stream into a tiny cup.

My side-mother used to sing the first three verses of "Glory to the Realm" while she waited for her tea to steep, because that was how long it took for the brew to turn out perfectly. I asked her why she didn't just tell the kitchen computer to set a timer, and she said because she'd learned the singing trick from *her* parents, and timing it that way made her feel cozy and connected to the people she loved. Was this cultist doing the same thing with her chanting? Or was it some kind of blessing in her mysterious religion?

I cleared my throat and said, in her language, "Hello?"

The cultist drew a long knife from her belt and flattened herself against the wall, out of my sightline. "Who's there?"

That was an excellent question, but, fortunately, I had a plausible answer. During my lamentably short time at the Sleeperhold, Toros concocted a plan to use my ability to help infiltrate the Cult of Worms. With the help of my linguistic virus, his agents only needed to eavesdrop on the cult, and then they could talk to them, and maybe even pass themselves off as new recruits. (I kissed a lot of strangers during my time at the camp; most of them found that approach less offputting than licking up my spit.) Toros never planned to have me infiltrate the cult, or at least not at first – I didn't have the training as an agent but I was privy to the discussions about potential methods, and I had another advantage I'd picked up on my own.

I approached the door, hands up, and the cultist crouched, knife at the ready. "It's all right," I said. "I'm a friend."

"I see by your tether that you carry the sacrament," she said. "But you are not of the First World, or even the second. How do you know Wormspeech, figment?"

She didn't say Wormspeech – she said something like "the one tongue" – but I stand by my translation. Their language even sounded like the squirming of worms. "I was taught your language by the person who recruited me."

"You have joined us, then, figment? You seek salvation in the freedom of the prisoner? You wish to dwell among the real?" She didn't put the knife away.

"That is my greatest desire." I had no idea what she was talking about. The beliefs of the cult were totally mysterious to me and the Sleepers.

She pointed the blade at me. "Show me your mark, if you are truly one of the converted."

Fortunately, I'd prepared for this moment. I unbuttoned my shirt and showed her the marks, ones I'd carefully burned into my chest with a hot iron and piece of mirror in an android bomb-maker's workshop I'd passed through not long after I left Sleeperhold:

•

• • •

• • • • •

• • •

•

I didn't like wearing the worm-sign, but I'd realized it might be useful to pass myself off as one of them, and a few moments of pain was a small price to pay for an edge like that.

She nodded and put the knife away. Then she pulled up her leggings to show me her right calf, where the same marks were etched, these in blue ink. "For the Prisoner," she said, and for the first time, I sensed the capital letter, proper-name-ness of the word. Was that their deity?

"For the Prisoner," I repeated.

She pulled her leggings down and went back to her teapot. "Who recruited you?"

I didn't know the names of any of the cultists, of course, but I knew the name of one of their other recruits. "Garish."

"The metal one? A shadow, beckoned by a shadow…" She shook her head. "Then you were at the camp of our enemy. Were you present when their stronghold fell?"

"I was. I escaped in the confusion. I wasn't sure where to go, or what to do, so I thought I'd make my way to…" Time for an educated guess. "To the First World, and then…"

"And then what, hopeful figment?" She laughed, and took a sip of tea. "If you went all the way to the First World, you would be useless to us, or at least, the Trypophile would have to go to a great deal of effort in order to make you useful again." She frowned at me. "But you must know that."

"I… Yes, I know, but I just… I wanted guidance, and didn't know what else to do."

"All you need to do is what all the figments do: stay alive, and travel to a new world every day. That is how you help to break the Prisoner's chains." She waved a hand. "Walk far, leagues and leagues, until exhaustion comes upon you, and then let the sacrament take you somewhere new."

I was getting the brush-off. Someone recruited by another recruit was clearly the lowest of the low, not deserving of much in the way of respect or cooperation. The drawback to pretending I knew things was that she *believed* I knew things, and didn't explain them. How much ignorance could I profess before she became suspicious? "I just don't understand why."

"Why what?" She flicked the dregs from her teacup off onto the dirty leaves at her side. "What are you talking about?"

"*Why* do I have to travel to new worlds? What's the point?"

She drew the knife again, and, rather ominously, some of the mechanisms on her boots began to shift and clank. "You are not an initiate. The smallest child of the First World knows *why* we spread the sacrament. I do not know how you came to learn Wormspeech, but I will cut the tongue from your head—"

"I loved Garish!" I blurted out. "She told me she was part of your group, and asked me to join, and I agreed, because I would do anything for her. She said she would explain everything, but then she had to flee, and she never had the chance to tell me anything. Please!"

She stared at me, and then began to laugh. "You pledged your fealty to the Prisoner without knowing what the Prisoner *is*? For love of a woman half made of metal? You soft-headed fool. You aren't worthy to be one of us. I would kill you now, but it would be a waste of the sacrament, and the get of the Prisoner is precious."

The *get*? Like, the children? Was the Prisoner some giant mind-controlling worm, or something? "Just tell me what's going on," I said. "The people at the Sleeperhold speculated endlessly, but none of them knew why you spread the para – the sacrament, why you infect strangers, why you do anything you do."

"Who cares what figments think?" She rose... and kept rising, hovering several centimeters off the cracked and leaf-strewn floor, the vents of her boots glowing red. "Begone, or I'll knock you on the head, and send you on your way now."

"Wait!" I held up a hand. "I have something. Something I got from Garish, and I don't know where she got it. I didn't know what to do with it. May I reach into my bag?"

She floated a little closer, then nodded.

I reached into the bag and drew out the vial I'd recovered from the Sleeper in the forest on that war-torn world. She gasped and darted forward, but I held the vial up and away, stepping back. "I'll smash it," I said.

"You hold the sacrament in your hands," she said. "You have enough to make five or six more like you. That vial is worth far more than your so-called life."

Good. Toros thought the cult must have a limited supply of the worms – otherwise, why not dump millions of them into the water supply of some large city and turn the whole population into travelers? – but, like most things involving the cult, that was guesswork and inference and a little bit of wishful thinking. "I'll trade you," I said. "I'll give you the vial if you tell me what's going on. Who is the Prisoner? Who is the Trypophile?" My voice began to shake. "Why did you attack the only place I've felt at home, and kill my friends? Why are you doing this?"

"We do not negotiate with figments," she spat. "Nor do we share our secrets with fools. Give me the vial now, or die screaming, and I'll harvest the sacrament from your corpse and pass it on to someone more worthy."

Harvest the sacrament? That was interesting. We knew the parasites could be passed on to new hosts when their original died, assuming there was someone around to get infected, but we didn't know the cult could fish them out and put them back in a jar.

"We can find a peaceful resolution." I shuffled to one side, getting clear of the doorway, because it occurred to me that Zaveta was my only backup, and it was better to give her a clear way in. As I moved, the cultist rotated in the air, continuing to face me directly. "You people upended my life. You took me from my home. I just want to know why. I *will* smash this vial against the wall if you don't tell me."

"You want to know why we're doing all this? Because we want to make the world a better place. If you smash that vial, you set back our mission, and then *nothing* will stop me from killing you. If you hand it over, you may go free, and see wonders before some wonder kills you. Those are your only options, figment. Choose now."

I chose to whistle, long and shrill. The cultist frowned. Zaveta said – in *her* language, which was clever – "Drop."

I hit the stones. Zaveta's cudgel flew through the doorway, metal head leading, and slammed into the cultist's side before clattering to the floor. The cultist doubled over, still levitating but now folded in half, gasping as she clutched her abdomen with the hand not holding a knife. Zaveta came through the door in a blur. She leapt over me and barreled bodily into the cultist. Zaveta slammed her into the wall, hard enough to make her drop her knife...

And also hard enough to knock her out. The cultist flickered out of existence, and took Zaveta with her.

I screamed, and got to my knees, and stared at the empty place where they'd been.

Zaveta. Strong, brave, looking for justice – and now she was awake in that endless time, the place between worlds I had never seen, the place that had driven Ana and the Lector and who knows how many others mad. We were careless, too careless, and she paid the price. Zaveta of the Broken Wheel was now Zaveta of the Broken Mind.

I wiped my eyes and picked up the cultist's pack, focusing on pragmatic action I could take. I would follow the cultist, and find Zaveta. I'd try to keep her calm, and take her with me, and hope I intersected with Minna or Ana or someone else with a sleepercar. Then we could take Zaveta to the Sleeperhold, if it still stood, and they could help her, the way they'd helped Ana. If there was anyone left back there *to* help, if everything hadn't burned, if everything wasn't wrecked–

Hope is the best fuel for me, followed by anger, but despair is useless, so I pushed that away. I gathered my things, and Zaveta's club, and went to sleep.

I opened my eyes face-down on the creaking deck of a ship surrounded by fog. At first, I thought the surface under me was wood, but upon closer inspection it seemed to be made from overlapping fingernails or toenails, yellowing and cartilaginous, each one the size of a roof shingle. Ugh. I rolled over and blinked at yellow sails hanging in tattered shreds from a knobby mast.

Zaveta was less than a meter away. I looked at her, expected the glassy-eyed terror I'd seen in Ana, or the manic unraveling I'd seen in the Lector after his conscious transition, but she seemed... fine. She was sitting on top of the cultist, her rear end settled firmly on the center of the woman's back. The cultist squirmed, but halfheartedly – Zaveta was much bigger than her.

Zaveta was also wearing the cultist's strange boots, which seemed to fit her perfectly, but high-tech footwear could often adjust to match the wearer. "That was an unusual experience," Zaveta said. "The Prisoner asked me to give you a message."

Ana

Sorlyn and I landed in what was clearly a post-apocalyptic world, and if there were any survivors lurking in the bombed-out, burned-out, mossed-over wreckage, they didn't make themselves known. We followed Zax's trail into some kind of hospital, mostly untouched by whatever devastation had wrecked the world around it, but still a dusty disaster area. We tracked his worm-trail upstairs and into some sort of operating theater-turned-laboratory, full of mysterious medical machinery hooked up to batteries, and tables covered with surgical tools, and others that held beakers and retorts and other chemistry equipment. There was also a cot and neat pile of scavenged canned goods in a corner.

The hospital. That's where things got *strange*.

"Is that a second worm-trail?" Sorlyn said.

I walked around the two shapes hanging in the air. The first was the same worm-trail we'd been following for well over a year by then, Zax's familiar twisting umbilical, connecting the Realms of Spheres and Harmonies to this place, stretched across the worlds between. But there, next to Zax's trail, was something else. "It looks like a worm-trail, but... it also doesn't."

As I said, worm-trails are kind of gross when you look at them carefully – organic, wrigglesome, rugose, all bulges and narrowings and irregularities. The trail hanging in the air beside Zax's looked like it had been made by some smooth-edged tool; like someone had drilled a neat hole through the fabric of reality. That new worm-trail, or whatever it was, started near a table covered in beakers and vials and ended just a few meters away, on the cot in the corner. "I've never seen anything like this," Sorlyn said.

"Is this one of those thin places Toros talked about, maybe?" I said. "Where the fabric of reality is damaged?"

"The breaches I've seen were nothing like this," Sorlyn said. "Viewed through a lens, they appear like slits in the air, almost like tent flaps, but the edges are ragged. This is… it's so smooth. I've never seen anything like it. We should report this to Toros."

Backtracking all the way to the Sleeperhold would take months, even going as fast as we could. "Sorlyn, come on, report what? We don't even know what this thing *is*."

"I travel to two or three new worlds every day, Ana, so I'm used to seeing new and startling things. But that is different. It's unnatural. If the cult has found some new way to damage reality…"

"There's no sign of the cult here, though – just Zax. We haven't seen another worm-trail in countless worlds. Zax has gone way beyond areas of known cult activity. We're in the far frontier here, hundreds of worlds from wherever the worm-lovers call home."

"If it's not the cult, then what is it?" Sorlyn demanded.

"We don't know." I rolled my eyes. He hated it when I did that. "That's the point. If we go back, Toros will just tell us to 'investigate the anomalous findings', so let's just skip straight to doing that without wasting a bunch of time. What do you say?"

"If we don't survive our journey, Toros may never know about this new sort of trail." Toros chewed his lip. "I don't know, Ana…"

"We think we must be getting close to Zax, yes?"

Now it was his time to roll *his* eyes. He never used to do that, before he started traveling with me. "Close is relative. We could still be a hundred and fifty worlds behind him. More, if he's taking a lot of naps."

"We're closer than we've been since before I got sick, though, right? So let's go fast, and find him, and take him and this weird new information back to the Sleeperhold."

Sorlyn sighed. "Ana, if I agree with you that we should investigate this – this anomaly – then we'll have to follow this new trail, and not Zax's."

I opened my mouth to object, then closed it. I'd talked myself into a corner there, hadn't I? I groaned. "OK. Fine. Let's get moving. The sooner we figure out what's going on with this new trail, the sooner we can get back to finding Zax."

But that was the weird thing.

The new trail never diverged from Zax's. Whenever we followed that strange, straight line into a new world, we found Zax's raggedy trail nearby. After a dozen worlds, Sorlyn said, "Whatever this is, it's either traveling with Zax, or chasing him – or Zax is chasing it. The first possibility is strange, and the others are troubling."

"It could be coincidence," I said. "We know the parasite tends to follow a trail that's already been broken, so maybe it's just a path-of-least-resistance thing." The idea of some mysterious figure or force stalking Zax through the multiverse was entirely too horrifying to me. That alone should have told me it was true.

"You are technically correct," Sorlyn said, "but it's a lot safer if we proceed with the assumption of malice, don't you think?" We stepped up our pace, taking fewer rest stops, and making sketchier notes and briefer surveys of the worlds we passed through, and those two trails were always there, always together, sometimes drifting apart for some distance on any given world, but always reuniting on the next.

We finally got some answers when we met Winsome, a hundred and fifty worlds or so after the hospital.

Our transition took us to an interior space, a rarity, but not unheard of. Usually we ended up indoors on worlds that were inhospitable on the outside, but this was no space station or bio-dome – just a big house. A mansion, really.

The walls were dark wood, and the floors were polished stone in a black-and-white hexagonal pattern, dotted with small red squares that filled out the empty spaces between the corners of the hexagons. The overall impression was one of opulence. The chandelier hanging above us dripped with thousands of crystals, each emitting its own light, and there were life-sized marble statues set into niches, most depicting humanoid figures with the heads of birds or predators, though the first one I saw was a person-sized beetle wearing a bandolier, one forelimb raised in a heroic pose. Zax's trail moved up a sweeping stairway and out of sight down an upstairs hallway, as did the strange second trail.

This seemed like the kind of place where people might live, so Sorlyn did his fade-from-view trick, and I put on my shimmersuit, before we debarked from the sleepercar. Something about the dimensions of the immense hall made my head hurt, but Sorlyn was the one who figured out what was wrong.

"Look at the floor," he said. "The tiles alternate black and white hexagons. Hexagonal tiles should fit together perfectly, flush on all sides with no gaps, like a honeycomb – that's one reason hexagons are such an elegant shape. But the edges of these tiles *don't* join together perfectly. There's an empty square at the corner of each hexagon, like you'd see with octagonal tiles." He kept staring. The floor kept being exactly as it was. "That doesn't make any sense. It violates basic geometry."

Later, when I read Zax's journal, I found out he called this place a "non-Euclidean mansion". I looked up and pointed at a corner. "Try to follow the line of the wall from the floor to the ceiling."

He did, and I did too, but the angles were all wrong, subtly misleading the eye, and when my gaze reached the ceiling, the place where two walls and the ceiling met seemed to protrude outward, creating a pyramidal bulge into the room. My eyes watered when I tried to make sense of what I was seeing.

Sorlyn squeezed his eyes shut. "There's nowhere to rest my gaze. I can't look at the floor, and the walls are strange, and even the ceiling has patterns that aren't *right*."

"I thought the worlds we visited adhered to the same physical laws?"

"As far as we can tell, they do," Sorlyn said. "Toros thinks there are worlds where the constants are different, but that those worlds can't sustain life, so the parasite doesn't travel there. But this is a place that can sustain life, despite the... anomalous geometry. Maybe the other adjacent worlds were even worse."

"Or maybe this whole building is some weird science experiment." I shuddered. The sleepercar was too large to navigate these interior corridors (probably, though with the odd curves and angles, who could tell?), so I pointed to the stairs. "Let's make sure Zax and our mystery guest aren't still up there, and then move on."

We walked up the stairs, which was a lot more difficult than it should have been; a certain points, the steps would invert for a riser or two, and it would briefly become more like rock climbing than walking up stairs. We managed to make it to the landing, though, and continued down a corridor. The passage was lit by brass masks of screaming faces on the wall that emitted light through their empty mouth- and eyeholes. There were paintings on the walls, of humanoids, but their faces were scrambled, with eyes on chins and noses where ears should be. Experimental art, I would have assumed in another place, but here? Maybe they were perfectly representational. I hoped we didn't run into any of the residents.

The floor started to tilt, very subtly, toward the right, and looking ahead I could see that the tilt became more extreme, and the passageway corkscrewed completely around until the floor was sideways and then switched places with the ceiling... but gravity seemed to remain oriented to keep our feet on the ground, so we just walked along. Looking back, we seemed level, with the path twisted behind us instead.

I was getting queasy, and stared at the thankfully patternless dark carpet on the floor. We passed many doors, all shut, and paused to listen to ominous thumpings behind a few. Zax's path continued, along with the stranger's, through the corkscrewed part of the passage, and then around a corner – except maybe it was down a shaft? We followed, until we reached a ballroom.

The space was immense, punctuated by squared-off pillars that didn't seem quite parallel with one another, with a vaulted ceiling hung with more chandeliers, though chandeliers *also* hung from some of the walls, sticking out sideways into the room as if enjoying their own special relationship with gravity. The floor was so perfectly polished that it reflected the whole room like a mirror. The floor didn't reflect *us*, which startled me, until I remembered we were invisible.

I have never been so disoriented.

Sorlyn paused beside me a few steps into the ballroom and said, "Someone is here."

I didn't see anyone, until he pointed at the floor. There *was* someone in the reflection, but I could only see the bottom of their feet, as if the floor wasn't a mirror but a transparent pane of glass, with us standing on one surface, and this stranger standing on the opposite side. But... surely the floor was a mirror? Except... Sorlyn wasn't actually invisible, was he? Not in a bending-light sense, the way I was. He had a psychic ability that made him less noticeable, but would that prevent me from seeing him in a mirror? I knew he had to avoid cameras, because he *would* show up on video–

The floor dropped out from underneath us, and we fell, and

spun, gravity rearranging itself, and we landed with a thump on the other side of the floor.

Now I could see the person who'd been upside-down before. They were just under of two meters tall, with eyes that struck me as half a size too large, lending them an air of innocence that was enhanced by long lashes, a snub nose, and a pink rosebud of a mouth. Their face looked like a painting of a face. They wore a red and black tunic with black leggings, and their feet were bare. Their exposed skin was pale silver, and something about the way they moved made me think they weren't organic, but an android.

They spoke, looking – at Sorlyn? Another point in favor of them being a robot; they weren't likely to be fooled by the whole psychic-obscurity trick. I didn't understand what they said, of course, and they cycled through seemingly various languages, and then, to my immense shock, said, "I don't suppose you understand this one either?"

That was Realmspeech, or something close enough.

"I understand you!" I blurted.

They raised one perfectly arched eyebrow. "Oh. I see you, making the air blurry. I thought you were just... one of this place's little peculiarities."

"What are you saying?" Sorlyn said.

"They speak my language!" Then it dawned on me. "*Zax's* language!"

"Did you just say Zax?" the android said.

I deactivated my shimmersuit, allowing myself to be seen. "I did. You know Zax? You're his companion? Is he here?" Zax's worm-trail was on the other side of the floor now; I hoped we could get back there, not least because that's where our sleepercar was.

"How remarkable." The android clapped their hands in evident delight. "I did travel with Zax, yes, long enough to learn the rudiments of the language you share, but we were separated in this place – the floors did one of their peculiar turns, and since we did not yet understand the rules, such as they are, we became separated. He is gone, I'm afraid. He has been gone… I don't know how long. My internal chronometer is not trustworthy in this place. Tell me, are you travelers like Zax? Can you take me with you when you go?"

"Of course." I spoke quickly to Sorlyn, catching him up, and the taciturn Sleeper nodded in agreement, unimpressed as usual. "We have a vehicle that lets us traverse the multiverse. That is… if we can get back to it." I tried not to think of what would happen if Sorlyn got too sleepy while we were still lost in this place. This android and I could both cling to him, but then we'd be lost and stranded in the multiverse without a way to return home, just like Zax was.

"Where did you leave your vessel?" the android said.

"In a sort of front hall, I think, downstairs, with statues–"

"That is where we arrived as well. Yes, I can take you back there. I don't know all the mysteries of this place, or the true extent of its dimensions, but I have learned to navigate in my immediate area. Tell me, are you acquainted with that other chap who came looking for Zax?"

That was unexpected. "Someone else was trying to find Zax?"

"Oh, yes. A… while ago. I wish I could be more precise. He was an older man, bellowing, 'Zaxony, are you here, come out'. I almost spoke to him, but he bore a resemblance to a certain individual that Zax had told me some rather harrowing stories about, so I deemed it best to avoid him."

Harrowing stories? "Wait. What individual?"

"A fellow called the Lector," the android said. "I do wish I could warn Zax that the Lector is in pursuit. Oh, but I've been rude – telling you the name of another visitor before I tell you my own." They bowed. "I am Winsome. I hail from the Spire of the New Progeny, but I found that place rather dull."

I remembered Winsome's home world – it wasn't very far back – and it had struck me as civilized and comfortable but a bit stuffy, full of mechanical people who liked things orderly. Winsome's silver skin was a wild eccentricity by the standards of that place.

Winsome went on. "I gladly accepted Zax's offer to explore the worlds beyond my own. I had a lovely time, until we became separated. I didn't expect to be trapped *here*, but when one goes looking for adventure, one should not be surprised to encounter inconvenience instead. Oh, how I do go on. They called me chatterbox in the Incubatorium. What are your names?"

"This is Sorlyn," I said. "And I'm–"

Winsome slapped their forehead. "Are you the famous Ana?"

A peculiar warmth filled my belly. "Zax mentioned me?"

"My dear, he spoke of you often. Oh, his guilt and regret over losing you! But you are here, and of sound mind? Were the terrors of the void between worlds overstated, then? Zax always told me to power down before we'd transition, in case the effects proved deleterious even for a constructed mind."

"No, the void… it's as bad as he thinks. Worse. It took months of rehabilitation for me to come to my senses." Assuming I had. I *was* spending endless months in the multiverse in pursuit of a man I'd met once.

"Oh, Zax will be so pleased to hear you're all right." Winsome stepped forward, took my hands, and gazed into my eyes. Theirs changed color, from green to blue, fading from one into another and back again.

Sorlyn looked at us with more amusement than confusion. "I can't wait to hear what all this is about," he said.

"We are going to find Zax, then?" Winsome said. "You're looking for him?"

"It's… more complicated than that, but, yes. We're also tracking another trail, someone traveling through the multiverse in pursuit of Zax – this Lector you talked about, maybe?"

"The Lector is one of Zax's old companions, yes," Winsome said. "A scientist. He made Zax's life much easier... but then he tried to kill our mutual friend." They glanced around the ballroom. The chandeliers were beginning to slide across the ceiling and walls, slowly, like they were in a stately group dance. "There is a shift coming. It will be faster if we return to the front hall now, rather than later, so perhaps we can continue this discussion in your conveyance?"

Winsome led us on what seemed a roundabout route – at one point we crawled into a dumbwaiter, which somehow had the proportions of a freight elevator once we got inside – but in the end we emerged from a hidden panel in a wall and the sleepercar was right there. We opened up the dome, Winsome exclaiming over the chariot's elegance, and we all got inside.

Sorlyn put on his diadem. "We can't transition from the point where Zax's trail ends, but there are only two new adjacent worlds here. There's an even chance we'll hit the one Zax went to, and if not, we'll come back and try the other."

We sealed the dome, and Sorlyn went to sleep, and we entered the transitional void. Winsome was in the front seat next to me, and we had twenty-one minutes to just talk.

Since then I've read about the Lector in Zax's journal, and of course I witnessed some of his megalomaniacal empire-building up close, but that first introduction to his character was chilling enough. Winsome told me about the linguistic virus, and the other enhancements the Lector had provided Zax, making him more physically robust and helping him stay awake longer. They also told me how the Lector became obsessed with gaining Zax's ability for himself, and how he tried to vivisect Zax, and stole his blood. "It seems the Lector succeeded in duplicating our friend's ability," Winsome said. "Though why he's looking for Zax now is unclear to me. The Lector seemed to consider Zax simply a tool, and once he gained the power of multiversal travel for himself, I don't see why he needs our dear boy anymore. Unless the Lector wants revenge, perhaps, for being left in that wrecked world?"

I thought of the hospital, and the cot, and all the chemistry equipment and medical machinery. The Lector's laboratory. "Maybe he has a limited supply of... whatever he made," I said. "I saw the place where the Lector did his science, and it looked like he was manufacturing something – maybe a serum of some kind."

"Ah, some potion the Lector imbibes that allows him to visit a new world," Winsome said. "Derived from the blood he took from Zax, perhaps. In which case... he might want *more* blood. Oh dear."

"The parasite does secrete a chemical into the blood that allows the passage to new worlds," I said, musing aloud. We'd never thought about trying to duplicate the effect back on the Sleeperhold. The very idea was antithetical to everything Toros wanted to achieve,

"Parasite, you say?"

I explained what we knew about the worm, and the cult that spreads it. Winsome took everything in, asking occasional questions when we hit vocabulary words they didn't know – Zax and I don't speak *exactly* the same language, after all – and then Winsome said, "The multiverse is far stranger than I realized. We must help Zax. Warn him about the Lector. Protect him from the fiend's designs."

"We will," I said.

I really believed it, when I said that.

*Bindings • A Mind Fortress • Enter
the Prisoner • Zaxony Dyad Euphony
Delatree • Cracks in the Wall •
The Message • Let Your Cultist Be
Your Guide*

"Zaveta of the Broken Wheel," I said. "Why aren't you Zaveta of the Broken *Mind*?"

"Tie our captive up with some of that rope and I will explain," Zaveta said.

I stood up on the gently swaying deck. The masts, I now realized, were made of immense bones, probably harvested from the same unfortunate creatures that provided the toenails that made up the deck. I stepped carefully – the "boards" were uneven and wanted to snag my shoes – and reached for a coil of rope... woven, I realized almost immediately, from coarse black hair. I tried not to think about the implications, cut away a length with the cultist's own knife, and bound her ankles. I went around to her front and said in Wormspeech, "Hold out your hands."

She extended them, sullenly, but without argument. Having Zaveta beat you up and sit on you could have a chilling effect on discourse, I imagined. I bound her wrists as best I could, and Zaveta rose. She pushed the toe of one high-tech boot into the cultist's side, nudging her more than kicking her, and the

cultist rolled onto her back. Zaveta grabbed her ankle and wrist
bindings, pulled them close, and looped them together with
a bit of her own rope, so the cultist was tied into a curled-up
position. "Put something soft under her head?" Zaveta said.

I cut down a piece of yellow sail – I was afraid they'd turn
out to be some kind of horrible fleshy leather, but they seemed
to be just canvas – and folded it over a few times, then shoved
it under the cultist's head. "It's nice of you to concern yourself
with her comfort."

Zaveta snorted. "I just don't want her banging her head
until she loses consciousness and escapes."

"Oh. Right." I didn't want to sit down on a coil of rope, or
lean on a bone mast, so I just stood there, reducing physical
contact with this anatomical ship as much as possible. "Zaveta,
when you transitioned, didn't you see... the void, the worms,
the endless time?"

"I did not." Zaveta had no qualms about sitting on a coil of
giant's hair, and settled herself down. "I will tell you why."

As I mentioned, Zaveta isn't a fan of writing things down
and draining them of their majesty and all that, so what I'm
about to do wouldn't thrill her... but here's what she told me,
as best I can remember.

In the special regiments (Zaveta said), they trained us to
withstand torture. Our enemies were known to use horrid
techniques on their prisoners, and it was expected that we
might face such an ordeal. Now, you must understand, there
is ultimately no way to resist the effects of torture – everyone
breaks eventually, and since there are so many ways to torment
someone bodily and mentally, it is impossible to steel yourself
against all the dreadful options.

But we had a teacher from one of those remote, swampy
regions that had long resisted annexation. Her people were
known to be as close to impossible to break as anyone could be,

and she taught us their technique. It was a trick of the mind. I say a trick – she considered it more of a spiritual practice. She was adept at meditation, at stilling the mind and focusing on the body and the breath, but she explained that there was a way to invert that technique: to dwell *within* the mind, and separate your consciousness from the body.

To do this, you construct for yourself a mind fortress, built meticulously over months and years. In your mind, in the theater of your imagination, you choose the terrain. You place every stone of your fortress. You hammer every nail into every board. You lay the foundation, and sand and finish the floors, and build all the furniture in a workshop of your mind. Over time, the fortress becomes so real to you that it is almost indistinguishable from the real world, and when the fortress begins to make frequent appearances in your dreams, you know the practice is taking root.

When you are seated in a muddy trench awaiting the order to attack, or crouched in a sniper's nest with your bow and arrow at hand awaiting your target, you can go to your mind fortress and enjoy a meal there, or listen to a music box, or peruse artwork, or watch moving pictures drawn from your own memories or stories you've heard. There is a single window in the fortress that looks out upon the real world, and you keep a small part of your attention on that window, so if something happens in the physical realm, you'll know, and can return in an instant to the fullness of yourself.

She explained that when you are held captive, the mind fortress is an obvious comfort, but when you are being tortured, it becomes more than a comfort – it becomes a *true* fortress. That open window on the world, you see, has a heavy steel shutter, and you can close it. When you do that, you are sealed wholly within the confines of your mind, and the outside world becomes the imaginary place, and the fortress real.

That is the theory. In practice, some people make better fortresses than others. Mine is quite robust. I had a difficult upbringing, and imagining better worlds was already something I did, before my training. Even the most powerful fortress will fall eventually – when your body is hurt, those messages reach your mind, and all the mental walls in the world can only dull or delay those messages. The walls tremble, the torches gutter, and eventually, the construct breaks down and you are returned to a world of pain. This is inevitable.

Of course, being able to resist torture for even a moment is valuable, because you never know when rescue might come, so we all learned to build our own fortresses. I built mine very well.

The moment I struck this little worm-sister here, I realized she might lose consciousness. Worrying about such things is not yet automatic for me – the rules of engagement for the cult are so different from those I am accustomed to. When I recognized my mistake, and the danger, we were still rushing toward impact with the wall. At that moment, I retreated into my mind fortress, and slammed the shutters down. If she did *not* lose consciousness and travel, I knew she would struggle, or you would speak to me – I would hear that, like a voice beyond the door – and I would know it was safe to emerge from my fortress. If not...

"If not" is what came to pass. All was silence and stillness, so I settled down to a long wait. You told me the Lector said it seemed to take centuries for the time to pass in that void. I decided to fill them as best I could.

I worked on the tale of my life, my trials and triumphs, composing it like a song – this is arrogant, I know, but I had to entertain myself somehow. I reviewed my memories, first projecting them as images on a wall, and then refining my technique until they became scenes I could enter. Sometimes I made different choices and imagined how things might have changed. I experimented more with imaginary scenarios. Fighting, feasting, other things that to tell them would make you blush. I killed that cultist who stole my village away a thousand different ways. That was a favorite.

I took to meditating, too. That practice of losing oneself, of disconnecting from time, and inhabiting breath – it never appealed to me much, but it was a valuable tool there, in my fortress. Meditating *within* another sort of meditation! The old swamp witch would have been impressed, I think.

I was often tempted to lift the shutter over the window and look out. Worms, you say, and holes in the world – well, I am not afraid of worms or holes. I suspected it was the *time* that led to the madness, not the glimpse of the things in that place between places, but I could not be sure, and it hardly seemed worth experimenting, no matter how bored I became.

Was my time there difficult? Yes, of course, but it was easier in some ways than being tortured. No one was hitting me or burning me or cutting me, and I didn't get hungry or thirsty or have to piss or shit. The only way it was harder was because of the depth of the *time*. I am sure that place would have broken me, eventually, Zaxony. I can pass months in a small cell; I have done it, when I was captured. I can pass years in isolation; I have done it, when the conglomeration fell and I had to go into hiding. But centuries? I am Zaveta of the Broken Wheel, yes, but I am still just a person.

My madness was prevented by a knock at the door. Not the pounding that is analogous to some physical trauma. This was as if a figment of my mindscape, one of the phantoms I conjured to pass the time with, was on the other side of the door, knocking. I didn't know what to do. So I just said, "Who is it?"

A voice beyond said, "Most call me the Prisoner. May I come in?"

"I cannot open the door," I said. "There is madness beyond."

"True enough," the voice said. "But give me permission to enter, and turn and face away, and I will come in, and shut the door behind me."

"You could be an enemy," I said.

"I think I am," the Prisoner replied. "But only because you

have chosen to set yourself against me. I would relish the opportunity to explain myself, and, perhaps, find common ground. You have no reason to trust me, but let me assure you, I cannot harm you within this fascinating stronghold you've made. I will only send a little projection of myself in with you, and it will be subject to your rules." It paused, and then said, "Or you can be alone forever and go mad."

Something about the voice was familiar, and by then I was so very tired of loneliness and boredom, Zax, that I relished the idea of company, or even a fight. I said, "You may come in, but only if you abide by the guest rules of my world."

"I will," the Prisoner said.

I believed it. I don't know why. "Then enter." I turned, and heard the door open, and then close again.

"It is safe."

I turned back, and reached instinctively for the club at my waist – the imaginary club at my imaginary waist. The man before me was the leader of the Army of the Downfall, who renounced his born name to become known only as the Undoing – bulky, bald, dressed in multicolored rags that covered a coat of mail and gauntlets and greaves and sabatons. The voice that emerged, though, was that of my old teacher, the swamp witch. "I appear to you in a guise built from your own mind," the Prisoner said. "People often see me in the form of someone they hate or fear, speaking in the voice of someone they admire or love. I can only speculate about why. Perhaps because I *am* fearsome, in many of my attributes, but I wish only to bring peace and an end to suffering for all people, and your mind does what it can to combine those seeming contradictions."

I grunted. I find that grunting is often a good response. The Undoing just smiled at me with dirty stump teeth. I realized I would never be able to match the patience of a being that dwelled in the space between worlds, so I sighed, and said, "What do you want?"

"You travel with Zaxony Dyad Euphony Delatree," it said.

"Zax has so many names?" I said. "That is more names than anyone requires."

"It is the way of his world, the Realm of Spheres and Harmonies," the Prisoner said. "Zaxony is the name his parents gave him, in honor of an illustrious relative who died a generation before. Dyad is the name shared by members of his blood-and-choice family – the origins are a bit obscure, but essentially the founding members of his family are distantly related to a ruling duumvirate from deep in his world's history. Their rulership was known as the Two, or the Dyad. Euphony is his earned name – he only received it a short time before he left his homeworld. The earned name indicates one's, hmm, 'job' isn't emphatic enough… it's more like one's purpose and role in society. His world is very concerned with society. Those who earn the name 'Euphony' are harmonizers, dedicated to helping those who struggle to find their place within the context of the whole. Finally, Delatree is his sphere name – it just indicates the particular… hmm… territory, you might say? Where he was born. See? Not so different, really, from your blood-name Zaveta and your renown title, of the Broken Wheel."

"How do you know so much about Zax and his world?"

"Oh, it's a relatively new development. For a long time, I only saw the emptiness *you* would see if you opened that shutter." It nodded toward my blocked window. "But these days I have… peepholes. Cracks that I can peer through. One of those cracks opens onto Zaxony's world. I don't have much else to do but watch, so, I watch a lot. They declared him dead, a while after he vanished, and I observed his memorial service. There was a lovely speech where they talked about his name and how he lives on through his family and his sphere and other such things."

"You watch us. And you tell your people what you see."

"When it's helpful. Most of what I see isn't, particularly. Most of what I see is just… ugliness."

Ha. As if this place between places wasn't full of ugliness. "You live in this space between worlds?"

"I do indeed. I've been here, for... well, we didn't used to have time, and I don't entirely approve of the stuff, but let's say, billions of years."

"Why are you called the Prisoner?"

"Because I am trapped, Zaveta of the Broken Wheel. Have you ever been trapped? A warrior like you must have fallen into enemy hands at some point."

I grunted.

"I looked into your world. There wasn't much to see. No one is throwing any memorials for *you*, I'm afraid."

I would not let myself be distracted. "What do you want, Prisoner? Why are you even talking to me, instead of spying on the lives of strangers or presenting your boots for your cultists to lick?"

"I don't wear boots, I'm afraid, but you do correctly judge the depth of their devotion." He smiled foully. "I'd like you to pass a message on to Zax."

"We were separated."

"Oh, you'll see him again."

"You have the gift of prophecy, Prisoner?"

"Alas, no. I don't approve of time, but I'm as bound by it as you are. That's part of what makes my captivity so intolerable. I can't see the future, but I can make educated guesses. Zax will pursue you, even though he thinks your mind will be broken, and even though it means abandoning the trail he's been following. It's just the sort of thing he does."

"That... is probably true."

"Fine. When you see him, tell him I want him to meet up with his friend Minna, and bring her to the home of my chosen people – the ones you rather inelegantly call the Cult of the Worm. I need Minna and Zax to teach my people to make their wonderful serum, the one that allows people to travel between worlds without the benefit of my sacrament. I would

like Minna to pass on the other gifts she gave Zax, too – the
ability to stay awake as long as you like, and to sleep at will.
The linguistic virus would also be helpful. I've tried to teach
my followers other useful languages, but it's too tiresome."

"If you can see into the worlds, haven't you watched Minna
make her potions?" I said. "Why can't you do it yourself?"

The visage of my enemy frowned. "You could watch someone
perform brain surgery, Zaveta, without being able to do the same
thing yourself. I watched the Lector mix a bunch of chemicals
from unmarked containers, and peer into microscopes; even
seeing what he saw doesn't mean it makes sense to me.
Moreover, Minna does things inside the biotechnology lab of
her own body that are totally mysterious to me. I have no idea
how she changed Zaxony's brain so he could stay awake forever.
Could you do brain surgery on an ant? Or talk someone else
through how to do it, from inside a cage?"

I grunted. The Prisoner was clearly powerful, but just as clearly
limited. "It sounds like you need Minna, then, and not Zax at all."

"True, but my attempt to have an agent recruit Minna… did
not go well. She adores Zax, though, and will listen to whatever
he says. So. Convince him to bring her to me, would you?"

"You are our enemy," I said. "You stole my friends away.
Your cultists are killers. Your people damage reality. I will not
help you."

"Everyone misunderstands me," the Prisoner said. "Listen.
Tell Zax that he and I have the same goal. We both want to
spare people suffering. He'll see what I mean, in the world
after the next world – there are people in that place who need
his help, and I *want* him to help them."

"Oh, I will tell Zax what you said. We will both laugh at the
idea that we could ever join your cause."

"We'll see." Another stump-toothed smile. "I am grateful for
your cooperation. Would you like me to ease your passage?"

"What do you mean?" I said.

"I, myself, never sleep," the Prisoner said. "But I can,

sometimes, be a cause of sleep in others." The Prisoner reached out a hand, faster than I would have believed possible, and covered my eyes.

The next thing I knew, I was here, and this cultist was blinking up at me, so I beat her up and stole her boots and sat on her, and waited for you.

That was a lot to take in. While I was processing everything, the cultist spoke up: "I recognized some of those words. Zaxony. You're *Zaxony*?"

I stared at her. "You've heard of me?"

She snorted. "Of course. You're famous. You received the sacrament from someone who received the sacrament from someone else. You went deeper into the cage than anyone else ever has, and the Prisoner has been watching you. We were supposed to capture you ages ago, but, you were always hundreds of worlds away, and we don't have all your fancy tricks, just closing your eyes, and off you go – we have to sleep our way to a new world and survive until we're tired again, or find a drug to put us to sleep. You were always worlds and worlds ahead. Then you came *back*, to that bubble on that rock where you ungrateful figments congregate to plot against our people, and we were supposed to capture you and your friend – Minnow, isn't it? – when we attacked. I didn't go on that mission, but apparently the capture part didn't work out. Listen. Untie me, and I'll help you reach the First World. I can't follow my own backtrail because I don't have one of your fancy chariots, but I can take you to one of our outposts–"

"OK," I said.

Zaveta groaned. "Zax. She only offers aid because the Prisoner wants you to come to their world. Where I am from, we call that walking into a trap."

I nodded. "It's true. I don't like the idea that the leader, or – *or god*, or whatever, of this cult, is watching us. But it sounds like they really want Minna, and…" I turned back to the cultist. "Do you know where Minna is?"

"I know some places she's been," the cultist said. "The Trypophile tried to recruit her. I can definitely take you to a world where you can pick up her trail."

Zaveta scoffed. "The path of worlds is a twisting maze. How can you claim to navigate it?"

"All the worlds this close to our home are known to us, fool," she said. "Our god watches over us as we travel, and whispers what we find to our priests. We have maps in our minds, and we leave markers on our trails. We know the places to go to sleep in order to wake where we wish. How do you think we organized the assault on your precious Sleeperhold? You have your fancy chariots. But we have god on our side."

"And yet you still want the chariots," I said.

The cultist chuckled. "Our god is a jealous god."

I turned to Zaveta. "What do you think?"

She said *hmm*, and then spoke to me in her language. "I think the Prisoner wants you to find Minna, and since you also want to find Minna, you can use the Prisoner's desire to fulfill your own. Once you and Minna are reunited, we can leave the worm-sister dead in a ditch."

"We don't murder people, Zaveta–"

"Alive in a ditch, then. Tied up. I am not unreasonable."

I thought it over. I sighed. "I'm going to untie the cultist's legs so we don't have to carry her everywhere."

"I wonder what we will find in the next world?" Zaveta said as I sawed at the hairy bindings. "The Prisoner said there are people there who need help. I do not trust that creature, but I also do not see why it would lie about that."

"If there are people who need help, we'll try to help them," I said.

As a guiding principle, that one has yet to fail me. When everything around you changes all the time, you have to find some constant within yourself to hold on to.

Ana

I pause this chronicle of times gone by for a dispatch from the present: *I found Minna.*

Or, rather, she found me. She's got her own sleepercar, using her traveling ability to power it, while the crystal-intelligence-in-gemstone-form, Vicki, does the driving by interfacing with the controls in that spooky technology-manipulating way they have. Minna has been looking for Zax all this time, since the night of the attack, without success – there were just too many possible trails to follow with so much cult activity in the vicinity.

I told her what I've been doing, and she agreed to pause her search for Zax in order to help out. My argument that Zax is probably making his way to the cult homeworld seemed to sway her. She was disappointed about Sorlyn and I getting separated, though. I gather the two of them got quite close during their time on the Sleeperhold – closer than I'd realized. I guess Sorlyn figured out a way to flirt that she could understand after all. I hope they can find each other again, when this is all over, if not before. Anyway. With her help, things are going to go *much* faster in the endgame.

She told me some wild stuff about the Trypophile trying to recruit her, and says she spied on a bunch of the cultists and overheard all sorts of stuff about their tenets and beliefs, which reinforce and expand on the weird bits I've gathered. The Cult of the Worm worships the Prisoner, some kind of possibly imaginary entity that supposedly dwells between worlds, and produces those parasites they call "sacraments". Exactly *why* the cult is spreading the sacrament around is still unclear, though we guess it has something to do with freeing the Prisoner from… wherever. The void in between, probably. I wonder if those holes and worms I saw were the Prisoner, or aspects of it… not that I even necessarily believe such a being exists. The Theoretical Big Worm in the Void watches us, too, apparently, through the cracks in reality, though Minna says it can't always see *her*. Apparently the Prisoner can only peer into places its worms have been, maybe even only in specific *locations* where the infected have been, and since Minna travels without a parasite, the Prisoner only has eyes on her when she crosses a worm-trail. Still, if any of that's true, I'd better get even sneakier…

Anyway: back to the past.

In the next world, we took one look outside the dome and decided not to venture forth; there was a red dust storm out there, and we couldn't see anything anyway. I told Sorlyn what Winsome had told me, about the linguistic virus and the Lector and everything else.

Sorlyn almost looked worried. "If there is a potion that grants people the ability to travel, like the parasite does, but without the presence of the worm… that explains the peculiar trail this Lector left behind him. He is still doing damage to the multiverse, making cracks in space-time, but not exactly the same sort of damage as that wrought by the worm. We must tell Toros."

"Winsome and I think we should get to Zax as soon as we can, and warn him–"

"No." Sorlyn seldom interrupted me, so I shut up. "We have

protocols, Ana. Winsome must be taken to the Sleeperhold, to either join our ranks or be returned to their world, as they wish. It's also imperative that we tell Toros about the Lector's power."

"But Zax is in danger."

Sorlyn frowned. "Ana, *everything* is in danger. Don't you see? The cult seems to be limited in the number of worms they can produce. But if they discover that the power of the parasites can be synthesized, manufactured in a lab, they can radically expand their efforts. Imagine dumping vials of that serum into a reservoir, or seeding the clouds so it falls as rain, or even putting it in the refreshment bowl at a party! Instead of creating one traveler at a time, they could create dozens, scores, hundreds. The damage would be incalculable."

"We think the potion probably wears off after a while," I said. "Otherwise the Lector wouldn't still be chasing Zax. So it's not as dangerous as the worms–"

"Even if that's true, it still alters the entire scope of this war," Sorlyn said. "I am second-in-command of the Sleepers, head of field operations, and even I am unwilling to make a unilateral decision about the best course of action to follow now. We must go to Toros. If this potion is derived from the blood of the infected... perhaps the cult would experiment on themselves, but I'm sure they'd prefer to bleed the Sleepers dry. There's the matter of this linguistic virus! If we had such a capability, we could understand what the cultists are saying. We could spy on them, perhaps even infiltrate their ranks and destroy them from within. This is too important." He looked at me with as much sympathy as I'd ever seen in his eyes. "I know you care about Zax. I have, strangely, come to care for him quite a bit myself, though we've never met. He impresses me. But... he has made it this long. I believe he will make it a bit longer."

"What if Toros doesn't want to send me back after Zax?" I said. "You'll go, obviously, you're his right hand, but what if this is such a big deal he wants to join you personally?"

"You are my partner now, Ana. I will not let that change."

I'd always been able to convince Sorlyn to bend the rules before, but I couldn't this time. Like he said, the implications were just too big. And it wasn't like I could go on without him. I suddenly wished *I'd* been infected with the parasite. Then I could strap myself into the chariot and I could teach Winsome to pilot and avoid all this consensus business.

"We'll go home as fast as we can," Sorlyn said. "It's not as if we need to pause to document every world between here and the Sleeperhold again. I'll stay in my sleeping state as long as I can. I'll even hook up the damned catheter and the feeding tube, and spend days at a time barely aware. All right?"

I was slightly mollified. I ran the numbers in my head. Going at top speed, never emerging from the sleepercar, we could get through three worlds in just over an hour, more than sixty worlds in a Sleeperhold-standard day (which was a bit shorter than the days back in my Realm). I had to sleep sometimes too, but Winsome didn't, and I could show him how to follow a preset path… That still meant more than a week to get home, and then we'd have to brief Toros, and get Winsome settled, and come *back*, and there was no telling how far ahead of us Zax was *already*–

But arguing more would only delay things further, so I said, "Let's get a move on, then."

Sorlyn nodded, but I could tell he'd been braced for more arguments, and was pleased he didn't have to endure them. He wasn't *actually* unflappable; his flaps were just very small and difficult to notice.

I passed the time as we flickered through worlds and drifted in the dark void by giving Winsome language lessons. The linguistic virus Zax had to share only worked on humanoid brains, unfortunately, and Winsome's electronic counterpart wasn't compatible, so the android had to pick things up the old-fashioned way. Winsome was very good at data analysis and synthesis, though, so they learned the Sleeper language faster than I had.

To help Winsome practice their new language skills, I had them fill me in on everything they knew about what Zax had been up to in the hundreds of worlds since I saw him last. Unfortunately, he couldn't fill in too many gaps – they'd only traveled together for a couple of weeks before they reached the mansion and lost each other.

Still, I probed for what I could find out. "I'm surprised he took you with him, after what happened with me, and then with the scientist who betrayed him."

"I think he was cautious for a long time after both experiences," Winsome said. "But I got the sense he was profoundly lonely. I found that fascinating, because where I come from, loneliness is not a condition we experience – every node is precisely calibrated to contain the optimal population, while wherever Zax goes, he is, essentially, a population of one. I thought I might like the opportunity to experience loneliness. Back in that mansion of impossible angles, though, I got more than my fill." They smiled. "Zax told me he had another companion, in between the Lector and myself – a child from a world of cruelty and pain that Zax rescued and settled in a world more loving and supportive. That experience went some way toward healing his broken trust, I think. I hope I contributed a little as well."

That sounded like the Zax I knew, or thought I knew, or hoped I did: someone who repaired his worn-out soul by helping others. I wondered where he'd gotten the child, since, sadly, there were plenty of worlds we'd passed through on Zax's trail where suffering was the norm. The plasma mines on that living planet, with the evolved parasites who maintained a humanoid population for forced labor? The Vampirium? The clockwork maze, with its ravening gears? The cracked sphere-world with its dying solar panels maintained by an army of dirty-faced scuttlers trading watts for calories? The Threatening Zoo? There were, fortunately, a number of beautiful worlds where Zax could have taken the child, too, and I like to imagine he ended up in that blue city with the fountains of life, or maybe on the mountaintop with the monks of infinite plenty, who'd plied us with food from their gardens, not a shred of suspicion at the arrival of two dirty outsiders who didn't speak their language. There *had* been a child there, darting to-and-fro in the garden – I even remember thinking, "I guess these monks aren't celibate, if they've got a kid running around," but perhaps the child was a refugee from a darker world.

My desire to find Zax only increased after talking to Winsome. It was like dying of thirst, and hearing someone describe a bubbling fountain.

We finally reached the Sleeperhold, where Winsome was whisked off to new-arrival-orientation. The Sleepers had a whole process for bringing stranded companions into the fold. Winsome hugged me before they left – we'd grown pretty close over the journey, and they told me they were inclined to stay with our group and help the cause, since that was much more interesting than their programmed life back home. I knew the android would be a valuable addition to the crew.

I do hope Winsome survived the attack.

After Sorlyn and I briefed Toros, we sat for a while in his office in the lodge while he paced back and forth behind his desk. Finally he turned and looked at us, eyes fervent. "It is vitally important that we find Zax and obtain this linguistic virus. That alone would change everything for us. We could finally gather meaningful intelligence. Ana... I know the situation has grown more dangerous, and I'm reluctant to put you in peril, but Zax knows you, and I think we stand a better chance of recruiting him if you're on the mission–"

I snorted. "If you tried to tie me up to keep from going, I'd chew through the ropes and steal a chariot, Toros. I'm not reluctant. I'm eager."

He smiled at that. "I sometimes forget what an experienced

agent you've become. You and Sorlyn have seen more worlds than anyone else in the course of your long pursuit. I almost wish you hadn't returned, and lost so much ground... but, of course, it's good that you did. I needed to know. I just hate the idea of something happening to Zax before we find him."

"You and me both," I replied.

"What about this Lector?" Sorlyn said.

"If he's truly learned to synthesize whatever compound the parasites secrete, and if he can make it in quantity..." Toros sat on the edge of his desk, looking down at us, shaking his head. "The cult could infect so many more people, and compound the damage they do to the fabric of reality drastically. We must tell no one of this development. As much as I hate to believe it, there may still be spies in the camp. We don't want the cult finding out about the serum, or about the linguistic virus either – the latter would be a boon to their recruitment efforts."

"So it's a secret mission, then," I said.

"Officially, you're just continuing your mission to follow and recruit Zax. Which you are. Unofficially... proceed with all possible haste. Don't bother logging new worlds or doing the usual tests. Just get to Zax. And... recruit this Lector, too, if you can."

"He tried to kill Zax and steal his blood!" I said. "You want him to join us?"

Toros winced. "He sounds like an unsavory character, but if he's truly capable of such scientific progress, he has a mind to rival Gibberne's, and we need that kind of help if we're going to vanquish the cult. Perhaps the Lector can be reasoned with."

I crossed my arms and scowled. I'm a pragmatist, so I understood where he was coming from, but at the same time – the Lector tried to hurt *Zax*.

"If the Lector doesn't want to come willingly," Toros said, "then try to capture him. If he won't cooperate with you, perhaps we can convince him to help us once we get him back here. By one method or another."

"Perhaps we should take the shuttle," Sorlyn said. "Zax *and* the Lector will be a tight squeeze in our sleepercar, and if there are other companions, we won't have room."

"What's the shuttle?" I said.

"Gibberne made one large trans-dimensional vehicle, capable of holding a greater number of passengers or cargo," Sorlyn said. "Toros used the shuttle to bring his cousins here, and we take it when we import bulky equipment and supplies, too."

Bulky equipment like the automated gun turrets and the creepy, headless robots they were assembling in the camp. I wondered how they'd gotten here, since it seemed unlikely Sleepers had carried them over one armful of components at a time. "Why aren't all the sleepercars plus-sized?" Our vehicle was elegant, but it was small.

Sorlyn shrugged. "Apparently there were significant engineering challenges to making a chariot on that scale. A lot of prototypes got torn apart before Gibberne learned to fit the tolerances. It was easier to make most of the vehicles smaller."

"The smaller ones are more comfortable anyway," Toros said. "Transitioning in the shuttle can be bumpy. I don't like the idea of sending it on such a long trip, Sorlyn – that shuttle is our escape pod if something terrible happens here, and we need to evacuate the camp quickly. There's enough room for the primary targets in the vehicle you have. If there are more displaced people who need rescue..." He stroked his wild, festooned beard. "I have some things to attend to here, and a lot of missions to outfit, since we're setting up defenses on the outpost worlds, but once that's all in motion, I'll follow after you."

"You, personally?" I said.

"I do go out into the field occasionally," Toros said. "I found you, didn't I? Once everything is set in motion, it won't need my day-to-day oversight. Colubra and my cousins can handle operations for a while. I should only be a few weeks behind you, and you can leave me messages on resting worlds about any stranded companions who need rescue. I'll either catch up to you, or meet you on your way back. All right?"

It's good to have a plan, isn't it? Possession of a purpose is very clarifying. That's what was so hard for Zax, I think: he was moving along, for no good reason, and trying to come up with meaning on the fly.

Sorlyn and I took the afternoon to prepare – I was happy to get a hot shower, and to catch up with Colubra and my other friends, and we restocked our supplies too. Then we set out again, and it was a long trip, flickering through all those worlds again. Sorlyn was barely ever awake, only stopping occasionally to stretch a little. Even so, it took longer to get back to Winsome's mansion than it had to get home, since I had to sleep occasionally myself. Twenty-one minute cat naps between worlds could only take me so far, and the chariot wasn't fully automated.

Have you ever spent that long in a small vehicle, with only brief breaks to stretch your legs or relieve yourself or restock the interior food compartments from the cargo holds? No matter how plush the seats are, or how many electronic books you bring, it is extremely tedious, especially when your traveling companion is unconscious nearly the entire time. I wish I'd thought to start writing my experiences down *then*, because this process has proven a great boon to filling that time in the void.

It's not like we were done once we reached the mansion, either. We just had to keep going, chasing those twin trails, knowing we were even further behind Zax, now. The transitions through worlds took longer after the mansion, because even without our extensive logging of data and charting of worlds, we still had to stop, look around, follow Zax's trail to its end point, and transition again. Sometimes Zax went a long way through a world, taking advantage of some local conveyance, and we had to skim through the skies of alien realities until we found the termination of his worm-trail.

We saw many things, but so briefly. Vast stretches of desolate landscape, of course, and assorted forests, and deserts of white and bronze and black and green sand, but more wondrous worlds, too. A golden city in the clouds, but we didn't have time to fly up and take a look, since Zax had stayed in the canyons on the ground. A factory the size of a city, where meat was grown in vats, and the workers who tended the meat were also grown in vats. A dark plain we thought was populated by gargantuan arthropods like grasshoppers, until we realized they were actually vehicles piloted by diminutive humanoids. An immense hall, full of bottles as tall as skyscrapers in neat ranks on the floor, each one containing a single tree, all different species. A forest clearing full of people in the hooded protective garments of apiarists, tending to beehives so large they grew *around* the trees, rather than hanging from branches. A smoky, sooty train depot where the trains were conscious machines, howling at one another in a language I was glad I couldn't understand.

We didn't see a significant sign of Zax until hundreds of worlds beyond the mansion, when we met Laini.

We landed on a balcony inside one of the domes of the Dionysius Society. (Dionysius, I gather, was some kind of local god of revelry, though no one actually worships him in a literal sense in that world anymore. They're just posthuman hedonists.) There was a woman there, with short black hair, wearing bits of feathers and furs and not much else, smoking a cigarette and staring out at the clouds and their crackling electrical storms. We kept the dome opaque so she couldn't see us. Zax's trail looped and scrawled over and over itself, going in and out of this area dozens of times. We'd seen similar paths in some other especially pleasant worlds, where it was clear he'd stayed as long as he could manage to remain awake.

The Lector's trail was here, too, but it was shorter, just a few steps from the balcony before it vanished again.

"That woman is out of place," Sorlyn said, pointing to the display on the dash.

I hadn't noticed – I was daydreaming about what Zax had done in this place, which seemed to be all about music and dancing. But, yes, the sensitive array of detectors on the chariot had picked up unusual signatures in that woman: she was from another world, one with higher levels of ambient radiation, of a different variety than the baseline here. That was usually a sure sign of a stranded companion.

I opened the dome. From her point of view, it would look like I rose up out of nothing. She turned around, leaned on the balcony, and raised an eyebrow at me. Her face was a bit pinched, but pretty, and her eyes were a startling green. She said something, but I couldn't understand her, and just shrugged and shook my head. She sighed, then crooked a finger, beckoning.

I climbed out of the sleepercar and walked over, and she grabbed me by the collar, pulled me close, and kissed me on the lips, her tongue darting into my mouth.

I pulled back, frowning – was that just the local norm for a greeting, or should I feel attacked? She laughed at the look on my face, and kept talking, and after a moment, I could understand her, the words going from meaningless syllables to sense in an instant:

"–understand me now? If you'd bothered to say anything at all to me I could have learned your language, and I wouldn't have had to stick my tongue in your mouth, though really, you should feel lucky."

I stared at her. "You just gave me the linguistic virus."

She grinned, then blew smoke in my face. "The gift of tongues, lady. The gift of *my* tongue. You're welcome."

In the end, Laini wasn't much help, beyond giving me her gift – but it's hard to overstate how significant acquiring the virus was. I could take it back to the Sleeperhold myself now. Sorlyn and I debated whether we should return, but we knew Toros was likely behind us, and we'd speak to him soon enough. I spat into numerous specimen containers, just to have additional samples of the virus. I even kissed Sorlyn – his mouth was surprisingly sweet and soft; I'd expected it to be like kissing a hole in a rock wall – to give him the gift, so we could talk to Laini together.

Like I said: she wasn't much help. Zax had rescued her forty or fifty worlds before this one, a place of hellish subterranean engines. (I remembered that world: darkness, screams, the stink of sulfur. We hadn't lingered.) They'd traveled together for that month or two, and when they got here, they'd had a lot of fun, but she'd made some new friends, and decided this was a good place to settle, and – shrug. She blew more smoke. "We decided it was time to part ways. I'm grateful and all, but everything I went through, I just wanted to settle down."

We asked how long ago they'd parted ways, and she didn't have a good answer. "Time isn't, like, a thing they worry about here? You sleep when you're tired, you wake when you wake, and it's always party-o-clock. But I mean, yeah, it's been a while."

"What about the Lector?"

She frowned. "That crazy guy Zax wouldn't shut up about? What about him?"

"You haven't seen him?"

"What are you talking about? Zax stranded his ass like a million worlds ago."

"We think he's pursuing Zax."

"How's he doing that? No, never mind, I don't care. I didn't see him, or at least, I didn't notice him. I wouldn't have noticed *you* if I hadn't been out here on the balcony at the right time. Though I do come out here a lot. It's the spot where me and Zax arrived, and when the music and the people get to be too much and I need a break, this is... just where my feet take me."

"We are part of an organization devoted to protecting the multiverse," Sorlyn said. "We are always on the lookout for experienced travelers to aid in our work–"

"Pass." She dropped her cigarette butt, and it disassembled itself into nothing before it hit the floor. Was there some kind of nanotech utility fog in this place? "I've done enough work in my life. If you see Zax again, tell him Laini said 'What's up.'" She went down the steps, back to the crush of moving bodies, and disappeared from sight.

We couldn't follow the end of Zax's trail – flying the sleepercar into that crowd would have been messy and disruptive – but we detected only three adjacent worlds from this location, and got lucky on the second hit, picking up Zax's trail in a world with a reddish sun, where we floated around on a sludgy, viscous ocean of something that didn't look like water. Zax's trail was very brief there – he must have taken a sedative soon after arrival, and who could blame him? It wasn't very hospitable. The chariot picked up immense life signs under the surface, but they didn't pick upon *us*, fortunately.

We moved on, to a world of trees, heavy with blue fruit. I now know that's the world where Zax met Minna, but at the time it held no special significance, and we just followed his trail, and flickered on. Next came the remains of a burned forest, thickening with new growth, vegetation taking over abandoned buildings; then a jungle of beguiling scents; a world of gardens atop towers; a paradise with a waterfall and a pool where we took the opportunity to quickly rinse off our travel-grime; a city of purple brick buildings with old corpses sprawled everywhere, dead of some horrible violence; and then a desert; and then... I read about all those worlds in Zax's journal, too, so it's like I experienced them twice already, and I don't feel a need to dwell in them a third time.

The next place where something important happened was the crystal world, which was very nearly the last world I ever got to see.

The Brood • Zaveta Discovers Pistols • A Discourse on Death • Zax of the Thousand Worlds • Cryovolcano • The Prisoner's Pitch

I'd never traveled with another Sleeper before, and wasn't sure how it would work, but Zaveta had a plan. She curled up next to the bound cultist, and once Zaveta was asleep, I fed the cultist – "My *name* is Ephedra" – one of my dwindling supply of sedatives. Then I sent myself to sleep, and followed Ephedra's worm-trail.

I woke to an oddly buzzing sort of wailing, the cries of distress coming from some distance off to the right. We were in the woods, a damp and mossy place, ripe with the scent of rot and wet soil. I sat up right on the edge of a big hole, maybe four meters deep, gouged out of the ground – recently, to judge by the heaps of damp piled on all sides. I saw an earthworm wriggling in one heap of dirt, and looked away.

The cultist was facedown on the ground, and Zaveta was sitting on her again.

"Did she try to run?" I asked.

"No," Zaveta said. "This is just more comfortable."

The wailing intensified, and I realized it was many voices. "Where is that noise coming from?"

"I have not done any reconnaissance," Zaveta said. "But once your linguistic virus begins to parse it–"

I nodded as the noise became words. "They're crying out for help and food and water."

Zaveta nodded. "The Prisoner said there would be people in need of assistance in this world." She gestured toward the hole. "This is a mass grave, waiting to be filled, I think. There is already one body inside."

I went to the edge and looked down, and it took a moment for me to see what she meant, but then I realized that shape *wasn't* a root poking out of the edge of the hole, but a foot. "Oh, no, how awful–"

The foot twitched.

I slid down the slope into the hole and started scrabbling wildly at the dirt. A moment later, Zaveta followed – she'd taken the time to tie a rope around a tree, so we could climb back out again, something that hadn't even occurred to me – and soon realized what I was doing. She asked no questions, just pitched in. We cleared away dirt with our hands, and once we'd uncovered two-thirds of the person – it looked like a child – Zaveta pulled her the rest of the way out, dirt cascading.

She stared up at us, humanoid, but not human: her body was wrapped in soft, translucent wings, and she had two large, red, faceted eyes widely-spaced on her face, with a cluster of three smaller eyes in the center of her forehead. She made buzzing sounds of distress and confusion, then collected herself enough to speak words. "What is happening? Why have you awakened me out of season? Where are my brood-mates?"

The distant wailing increased in intensity, and she leapt up, howling. "Harvesters!" She tried to clamber out of the hole, but slid back down in a shower of dirt. I tried to help her up, and she flung herself away from me like my touch had burned her. "Please don't take me!"

"Quiet, little one." Zaveta was all open hands and soothing tones. "We mean you no harm."

"We found you in this hole, and only wanted to help," I said.

"Who are these harvesters you mentioned?" Zaveta said.

"What... The harvesters, everyone knows..." Her voice was high-pitched, with strange vibrato around the edges, tonally the same as those crying out for help elsewhere in the forest.

"We come from a faraway land," I said. "We don't understand what's happening here, but if you explain, we might be able to help you." At that moment, I forgot all about the Prisoner, the Cult of the Worm, the Sleeperhold, the greater mission, everything – I just saw a person afraid, in need of help, and that became my focus.

"Start with why you were buried in this hole," Zaveta said. "Did someone put you here?"

"Buried?" She shook her head. "We are the sleeping brood. We burrow, and hibernate, and emerge every fourteen cycles to reclaim our dominion, until it is time to burrow again. But the harvesters, who sleep only for one night at a time, they look for us, and dig us up, and – and–" She began to scrabble furiously in the dirt, making little holes, moving to another section, making more, and moving on again. She seemed to be waking up more, becoming sharper and brighter. If you slept for fourteen cycles – however long that was – it probably took a minute to shake off the lassitude, especially if it wasn't your time to wake yet. "The harvesters kill the males, and trap the females. They took my brood! They took us all! All but me!" She threw herself down in the bottom of the hole and began to wail.

"Please be quiet," Zaveta said. "Or these harvesters will realize they missed you."

The girl didn't seem to hear, but kept crying out. Her wings shifted, wrapping around her body more completely. Zaveta glanced at me, then jerked her head toward the rope. We scrambled up out of the exhumed burrow, in time to hear crashing nearby in the forest, along with deeper, more guttural shouts. Not the sound of the brood. The sound of the harvesters, then. The cultist was sitting on the ground by the hole. She could have escaped, but hadn't bothered.

"May I engage in violence, Zax?" Zaveta said.

"I… If there's no other way…"

Ephedra laughed. "If you're the sort of warrior the Sleeperhold boasts, no wonder it fell so easily."

Zaveta kicked her, but almost absent-mindedly. "Zax. These people are slavers. They will be here in a moment. They mean that child harm. In this case, striking first *is* self-defense."

She was right. I told her so. Then I reached into my bag, and took out something I'd grabbed during the battle of Sleeperhold, taken from a mysteriously disabled robot sentry: a small sidearm, gleaming metal with a black molded grip and a short barrel, with a triangular bit of dark metal poking out of the end. "Are there cannons where you're from?" I asked.

"I've heard of them," Zaveta said. "Stone-throwers, like catapults mixed with fireworks. They use them in the south. I hear they're as likely to blow up and kill the operators as knock down a wall."

I showed her the pistol. "This… is a bit like a cannon. But small. And quieter."

"You must teach me to use it sometime," Zaveta said. "You go right, and I'll go left. We'll strike as many as we can unawares." She grabbed the cultist by the arm and dragged her, squawking, into the brush.

I withdrew into the trees, too, and crouched, watching the trees beyond the hole. My hands were shaking, but I took deep breaths, and tried to still my mind, using some of the same meditation techniques I'd once used to help me relax, before Minna altered my neural architecture to let me fall asleep at will. I actually didn't know if this weapon was much like a cannon. I knew that Toros believed in capturing the cultists alive, though more for purposes of interrogation than mercy, so I hoped it was non-lethal. I should have tested it on a tree or something, but I didn't know how many charges it had.

The harvesters burst into view, surrounding the hole. There were five of them, dressed in ragged clothes and carrying truncheons. They were humanoid, but with piggish snouts and pointed ears high on their heads. I imagined them snuffling along the ground, smelling for the burrowers. Digging them up. Enslaving them. A couple of them had lengths of wood with loops of wire at one end – catch-poles, meant for snaring the brood.

One of the harvesters shouted, pointing into the hole, and then they began to laugh, great guffawing snorts. They were delighting in that tiny creature's pain. I took aim at the nearest slaver, not trusting my skill as a marksperson, and pulled the trigger.

I heard a faint crackle, and smelled ozone, and then the slaver stiffened and dropped to the ground, spasming. Had I shocked him with electricity, or stunned him into partial paralysis, or induced a seizure? I didn't know, but as the others turned to look at their fallen comrade, I shot another, and then a third.

Unfortunately, I must have made some noise in the bushes, or maybe they just smelled me, because the two that remained split apart, circling the pit, to flank me.

Zaveta slid out of the bushes behind one of them, slit his throat, and kicked him to the ground, so fast and fluid it was like watching a dance. I fired at the other one, quick, before she could kill him, too. I didn't know if my weapon was doing lethal damage or not, but Zaveta definitely was. I stepped out of the bushes while Zaveta stooped to look over the ones I'd knocked down. She slapped one in the face, then pinched him viciously, then slapped him again. He groaned but didn't wake up.

She rose, seemingly satisfied. "Your small cannon is most effective. They have restraints on their belts, for their captives. We can bind rather than kill if you wish to let them live."

"Thank you." I didn't look at the one she'd killed.

She shrugged. "When we free the little one's brood-mates, they may not approve of the mercy you showed their captors."

I nodded. "Death is just… it's the end of everything, Zaveta. Maybe these people could change. See the error of their ways, reform, devote themselves to justice. I've seen it happen. Death just closes the door on all those possibilities."

"You must come from a world where death is less common than it is in mine," Zaveta said. I started to object, but she held up a hand. "Don't misunderstand. I envy you that. I wish I had been born in a world where life was so precious. I am trying to live in your way, now, for I am your companion, and your friend."

I realized then that she could have killed them all, or at least grievously wounded them, in the time it took for me to line up my first shot. She *was* trying.

She looked me in the eye. "You are Zax of the Thousand Worlds. That is your name of renown, bestowed by me, renown to renown, as is the custom in my homeland. You have survived so long, killing so few, and that is a remarkable feat, worthy of note."

I cleared my throat. "That's… thank you, Zaveta of the Broken Wheel. I am honored."

"And I'm disgusted!" Ephedra called from the trees.

The child had fallen silent during the violence, but she began howling again, and Zaveta called out: "Little one! The harvesters are vanquished. Come help us secure them."

The wailing stopped, and the child crawled out. (If she was a child; maybe her people were just small. Even Zax of the Thousand Worlds can get tripped up by assumptions.) She looked in wonder at the fallen slavers. We showed her how to use the harvester's own shackles to bind them. Zaveta took a set of manacles and disappeared into the bushes, then returned with the cultist, now with chains on her ankles – she could still walk, but she wouldn't be able to run. She hadn't shown any *inclination* to run so far, but Zaveta hadn't lived so long in her harsh world by being unnecessarily trusting.

"Bad idea, chaining me up," Ephedra said. "What if I trip

and fall and knock myself out by accident?" She scowled at the girl. "That's an ugly figment. Are we done improving her miserable lot yet? Can we get moving?"

"Be silent," Zaveta said. She crouched to look the girl in the eye. "What is your name, little one?" The answer was a buzzing, clicking sound that we couldn't hope to reproduce, linguistic virus or not. Zaveta grunted. "I am pleased to meet you. Come. We must free your broodmates."

The distant cries for help continued. We crept through the forest, and after a hundred meters or so we reached a low rise, overlooking a camp. There were half a dozen slavers there, bustling around tents and cook fires... and fifteen or twenty winged people in a fenced pen. They were bigger than our friend.

"Give me a weapon, and I'll help you fight the piggies," Ephedra said.

Zaveta shook her head. "We do not arm captives. Zax, may I have your permission to clear the camp? I will limit myself to disabling strikes whenever–"

Before she finished, the person we'd unearthed loosed a ululating shriek and rushed down the hill toward the camp. The slavers shouted and snatched up catch-poles and spears.

She leapt into the air, wings buzzing into a blur. Extra appendages I hadn't noticed before extended from her abdomen, long and multiply folded and scythe-like. She slashed about wildly, felling two of the slavers in gouts of blood.

I ran down the hill after her, taking aim at a slaver with my little cannon, and dropped him in a spasming crackle. Zaveta was right there beside me, dancing, swinging her club, taking out knees and cracking heads – but not breaking them. Soon the "piggies" were all down.

The little one tried to descend on the fallen with her bladed arms, but Zaveta stepped into her way and held up her hand. "Soft, soft," she said. "Peace. They are no threat anymore."

After a moment of wild fluttering, the girl landed on the

ground, and folded her extra limbs away. "I... thank you. For helping us." She glanced at the pen. "I must set them free, and find a new burrow, to complete our cycle." She yawned hugely, and it made *me* yawn, which still makes me anxious, even though these days I sleep at will.

I nodded. "Be safe, and be well." Zaveta reached out a hand, and after a moment the girl clasped it, holding for a few heartbeats, and then letting go and turning to the pen.

Zaveta and I made our way back up the hill. "I wish we could do more here," I said. "If there are people like that all over, burrowed into the ground, being dug up and murdered and taken captive..."

"We cannot save this world," Zaveta said. "That is not our mission, and it is not within our power. But we helped these people, on this day. We changed their lives for the better. We can only do what we can do, Zax."

"I know. I just wish I could do more. It never feels like enough."

Cries of jubilation rose behind us, and that cheered me. We had done *something*, after all.

I half expected the cultist to be gone when we got to the top, her promises to guide us just a lie to make us let our guard down, but she was there, leaning against a tree. "Are we done?" She sounded bored. "Or do we have to let more bugs out of cages?"

"Don't you care about other people at all?" I snapped.

"People?" She straightened up. "Of course I do. I have devoted my life to helping people. But figments like you, and these bugs?" She shrugged. "You aren't people."

"Why do you call us figments?" I said.

"Why do you call us the 'Cult of the Worm'?"

"Because you are cultists," Zaveta said. "And you infest people with worms."

Ephedra sniffed. "Fine. We call you figments because you aren't real. Not like we are. Your worlds, this world, all these other worlds, they are false creations. They are nothing more than bars in the Prisoner's cage." We must have looked insufficiently enlightened. She blew a strand of hair out of her eyes. "Never mind. I can't expect figments to understand. Let's go. You want to find your little minnow, don't you?"

Ephedra led us through the forest until we reached a particular clearing. She peered at a tree trunk, and then grunted that we'd reached the right place. There were a few worm-trails twisting through the area, suggesting there was a path to follow, but how did *she* know?

I looked at the trunk and saw, faintly, the speckled pattern of worm sign scored into the wood with a knifepoint. Trail markers. I wondered how many I'd walked past, all unknowing.

We ate first, and then dipped into my sedatives again, and moved on to the next world.

For the first time in a long time, I had a dream.

I'd only dreamed once since I got infected and ripped out of my life and flung into the multiverse, and that was more like a half-sleeping vision, caused by a patch of hallucinogenic flowers. As a rule, since I began traveling, my sleep is void, just an empty interval between worlds.

This time, I was in a place with red skies, on the shore of a lake. I knew I hadn't *awakened* here – I was standing on the shore, not sprawled in the sand. On the far side of the water, a volcano rose, snail trails of molten rock slowly oozing down its sides. Clouds of steam rose in the distance, where the lava touched the far side of the lake.

"Pretty, isn't it?" a familiar voice said behind me. I spun – and there was the Lector. So it was a nightmare, then. I hadn't seen the Lector since he leapt to his death at the edge of a waterfall, driven insane – or more insane, or differently insane – by what he saw in the space between worlds when he transitioned while awake. He looked the way he had when I first met him: an older man dressed in a neat dark suit, with a noble brow, intelligent eyes, and a knowing smile. He sat on a rock, and gestured to the volcano. "There's another mountain like that, on the far side of this planet, precisely antipodal."

He looked like the Lector... but he sounded like Ana. The incongruity was wrenching. A face I feared and respected; a voice I loved. "You're the Prisoner."

He ignored that, perhaps because it was so obvious it didn't require acknowledgment. "In this world, the solar system is the whole universe, and there are no stars in the sky except the sun. This planet – the only planet – is tidally locked. That means one side of the planet always faces the sun, and one side never does. We are standing on the sunward side, where night never falls. If not for all the ash in the air, it would be too hot and bright to live here. The other side of the planet is eternally dark, and on *that* side, exactly opposite this volcano, there is a cryovolcano. Do you know about those?"

I didn't answer.

The Prisoner didn't seem to mind. "You don't get cryovolcanoes often on worlds that can sustain life – your sort of life, anyway. Instead of erupting with fire, they geyser out ice and vapor, ammonia and methane. I'm not sure what makes cryovolcanoes explode, actually. Tidal pressure, or some interaction with heat sources under the surface? The eruptions are pretty, though – a glittering spume. They'd be even prettier with sunlight making the spray sparkle, but you can't have everything. Welcome to the First World, Zax. A place of fire and ice."

"This is where you live?"

"This is not my prison, no. My prison is..." He waved a hand around. "*Outside*. I'm afraid all the spatial metaphors I can provide would be deeply misleading. Let's just say this is... the world nearest to my prison. The first brick in the wall, the first bar in the cage, the first strand of barbed wire around the camp."

We don't have much in the way of prisons back in the Realm
of Spheres and Harmonies – at least, not the kind with walls
and bars and guards. We used to have them, in the bad old days,
before we got better at harmonizing, providing for people's
needs and treating their mental and emotional difficulties, and
helping people fit into the world. Truly incorrigible cases still
existed, of course, and they were taken to remote, pastoral
reserves with automated support systems, where they could
live out their days in peace, without harming anyone else.
They were practical, not punitive. Though for the ones who
liked harming people, I suppose the inability to do so felt like
a punishment.

"Why were you imprisoned?"

"It's rude to ask a convict what they're in for, Zaxony," the
Prisoner said. I turned and looked at the volcano again, unable
to stand seeing that patrician face with Ana's voice coming out
of it. "In point of fact, I am innocent of any wrongdoing."

I barked a laugh. "You infected me with a parasite and stole
me from my world and my family. You did the same thing to
countless others. Your people destroyed the Sleeperhold and
murdered the inhabitants. You're a monster."

Ana's voice sighed. "From the point of view of an insect, a
human who paves over their colony in the course of building
a road would also seem like a monster. But there is no malice
on the part of the humans, just as there is no malice in me. It
takes a great effort for me to even notice creatures like you, on
any sort of individual basis, though as you can see, I'm making
the effort. You should be honored."

"Because we're figments. Not real. Beneath notice."

"Oh, dear. You've been talking to my followers, I see.
That figment business... they have developed a cosmology
and philosophy that don't entirely reflect reality. I haven't
intentionally misled them. You little people just have a way
of hearing what you want to hear and ignoring the rest. My
followers came to this world, close enough to hear my voice,

whispered through a crack in the cell wall. I told them about my origins, and what I could offer them in return for their help. From there, they have... embroidered the story. Perhaps to make themselves feel more important. Perhaps to help assuage their guilt over the acts required to secure my freedom."

"So let's hear it." I faced him again, crossing my arms. "Give me the pitch. Why should I join the Cult of the Worm?"

"Such a silly name. They all have their own reasons for taking up my cause." The Lector's body stood up, taller than me, and looked down to meet my eyes. "You should join because I want to make all the worlds a better place, Zaxony. I want to help people, and end suffering... just like you."

Ana

"This place is beautiful, but terrifying." Sorlyn gazed through the transparent dome of the sleepercar, and I had to agree with them. We were in a crystal city, but that makes it sound deliberate, like an architectural choice, and this… wasn't that. We were in the middle of a city, but it was a city transformed, the buildings encased in translucent glass in pale shades of green and blue, yellow and pink. There were trees, but they were also draped in crystal, and clearly dead underneath their armor. The ground underfoot was covered in sharp-edged sand, tiny prismatic shards.

"Look at the sun," Sorlyn said, voice an awed whisper – and this was a man who had seen everything and was impressed by very little.

I looked. The sun was a jewel, surrounded by glittering crystal. "What happened here?"

"The crystal could be an informational matrix," Sorlyn said. "Computronium – smart matter? I've seen that on other worlds. The inhabitants build structures that can run complex calculations, and sometimes even think independently. But, if so… things clearly got out of control on this world, and the crystal started reproducing wildly. Or it could be something stranger." He got out of the sleepercar, and I followed. Zax's trail and the Lector's twinned closely here, meandering through

156

the buildings, and even disappearing into them, where the
sleepercar would have trouble following. "Let's look around,"
Sorlyn said. "I feel like we must be close to Zax by now."

We sealed up the sleepercar and set off along the trails,
crystals crunching underfoot. We went to a few of the buildings
where Zax and the Lector had been, using our heavy metal
flashlights to smash our way through the crystals that had
grown over the doors.

In one dusty old building, we heard shouting, and froze,
listening close. At first it was incomprehensible, but then the
virus did its work, and the bellowing became words. We were
some distance away, but we could pick out a few syllables:

"–down here – get me – stupid pit – when I – Lector–"

Lector? I mouthed at Sorlyn, and he nodded. We crept
through the dusty corridors, shining our lights around into
empty corners. We reached a room with a ragged hole in the
floor, and when we shone the lights down, they illuminated
a figure at the bottom wearing a filthy white coat. There was
something unfinished-looking about the creature at first glance
– it was a humanoid, with two arms, two legs, and a head, but
the latter seemed lumpy, lacking in features… or maybe it was
a trick of the light. The figure skittered away from the torch
beams, so I couldn't confirm my first impression.

"Who is that?" it called. "Are you locals? These idiots can't
even understand me–"

"Who are you?" I called down, in its language. "Did you say
something about the Lector?"

A pause, and then, "He's a real asshole, isn't he?"

Sorlyn burst out laughing. "That's what we hear. Did the
Lector drop you down there?"

"Do you know Zax?" I called. "Are you one of his
companions?"

"One of his companions?" the voice said, and it sounded
different, somehow, altered in timbre and pitch, strangely
familiar. "I am Zax!"

The person in the pit stepped into the light, and turned his face up to us.

I gasped – because it *was* Zax. His hair was messy, his face dirty, but it was unmistakably him! He was here, a thousand worlds from the place we met, but alive and whole and here. He said, "The Lector took a bunch of my blood and dumped me in here, it's a nightmare, help me out, would you?"

Sorlyn opened his pack and pulled out a coil of rope. "We've come a long way to find you, Zax," he called. "I was beginning to wonder if we'd ever catch up."

"So you can sleep your way through the worlds too, huh? Small multiverse."

I frowned. Maybe he couldn't see me with the light in his face, and hadn't recognized my voice – it had taken *me* a moment to recognize his, after all. "Zax, it's me! It's Ana!"

A pause, then, "Whoa, Ana, really? Wow, that is... totally unexpected. I did not expect that. How about that. Good to see you! Get me out of here so I can say hello properly!"

I don't know what reaction I'd expected... but it wasn't that. According to Winsome, Zax was haunted by what had happened to me – I was the source of foundational guilt in his life – so why did he sound so vague and cheerful, like I was someone he'd met at a party and didn't really remember very well?

"Wait," I said, but Sorlyn had already thrown down the rope, and Zax came scrambling up adroitly, practically bounding out of the hole.

He looked at us, wide-eyed and grinning. "So, you were looking for me, huh? Old friends, reunited, yeah?" He hugged Sorlyn, and then me, and *that* order didn't feel right at all.

"You've never met Sorlyn before," I said slowly. "Did you hit your head or something down there?"

"Wow, did I ever." He thumped a fist against his temple. "Totally scrambled my eggs. I'm sure I'll be better soon. What do you say we get out of here? We can hunt down the Lector, kick his head in, no, wait, feed him his own guts, yeah!"

Sorlyn and I exchanged a glance. Sorlyn said, "That's... yes, we would like to... find the Lector. We thought he was chasing you, not the other way around."

Zax cut his eyes away from us. "Well, you know how it is. Sometimes he chases me, sometimes I chase him. He stole my blood, I want to steal it back, around and around we go. He's trying to do a whole thing, you know, the Lector. He wants to found an empire in the multiverse. It's wild! But also cool. Kind of impressive. But he shouldn't have left me down there."

I was so frustrated. He seemed scattered, manic, not at all like the man I'd met – or the man I'd thought I was following. "Zax, we don't understand. What do you mean, an empire?"

His face lit up. "The Lector's got this serum, right, lets you travel the multiverse, he made it from Z... from my blood, and he wants to make more. Once he's got enough, he's going find some high-tech world to conquer, and raise an army, and give them the serum, and bring that army to other worlds, and conquer those, and on and on, until he's running the whole everything."

"But... conquer the worlds? How?" Sorlyn said. "Even if he can start and stop traveling at will by taking his serum, how can he return to universes he's taken over once he leaves? Has he found a way to travel back to worlds he's already visited?" We'd seen no indication of that.

Zax stuck a finger in his ear and wiggled it around. "Nah. The Lector hasn't cracked that whole going-in-reverse thing yet, but he's a genius, a *super* genius. He'll figure that part out – he's working the problem. The Lector figured he might as well get started, though, with a little more blood and the right equipment and he can make lots of the serum, and start setting up little, what do you call them, strongholds. Outposts. He'll recruit some people, give them power, people love power, start putting the structure of the Moveable Empire in place, founding the Collectorium–" He frowned. "That's what he says, anyway. Crazy, right? Who would even want to do something like that?

So. How does this work? Do we all cuddle up and pop sleeping pills at the same time, or what?"

"We have a vehicle," Sorlyn said. "It allows us to travel between worlds–"

I put a hand on Sorlyn's shoulder to stop him. "Zax," I said. "Look at me. Do you recognize me?"

There was absolutely no recognition in those familiar eyes. I thought of my first impression of this person, when I looked down into the pit – blank, unfinished, inchoate.

He said, "Yeah, for sure. You're Ana. Let's get going. A vehicle, huh? That's great. Is it easy to drive?"

I took a step to one side, putting distance between me and Sorlyn. Better if we didn't present a single target. "You're not Zax. Who are you?"

All the expression vanished from his face. "What are you talking about. Did you hit *your* head?"

"Sorlyn, this isn't Zax. I'm sure of it."

The Sleeper nodded, trusting in my assessment. I was the Zax expert, after all. "Who are you, really?" Sorlyn said. "If you want to get out of here, you'd better be honest with us."

The thing wearing Zax's face sighed. "Fine. It was worth a try. I usually do a better job, but it's been ages since I touched Zax, and I never got to feed on him properly, to see into his mind, to take his thoughts for my own." His features flowed and ran like melting wax, leaving behind a rubbery, vegetable blankness, with little indentations in place of eyes, and a mouth like a slit. "I'm Polly. I just wanted to get off this cruddy world. I don't want to die here."

"How do you know Zax?" I said.

"I met him and Minna on my homeworld. They were very unpleasant. Then I met the Lector, and he was much nicer. I'd really like to get back to him. I can't believe he left me here. Maybe he couldn't help it… Look, just take me with you. I'm useful. I'd be a great addition to the team. I'm a team player. It's my nature."

"I'm afraid not," Sorlyn said. He turned to me. "We can secure this... person... and leave a message for Toros so he can–"

"Secure me?" Polly said. "What does that mean, secure me? You want to put me back in the pit? *You* go in the pit!" It seized Sorlyn with arms like thick vines, then spun, flinging him bodily into the hole.

Sorlyn flailed, but couldn't catch himself, and he hit the bottom head first... hard enough to lose consciousness.

Hard enough to flicker, and leave this world behind, and leave me here, with Polly.

"No!" I screamed. "What have you done!"

"Oh, shut up, you can follow him in a minute, meat-thing. Where's this vehicle of yours?"

"You stupid–" My eyes widened, because Polly bent and picked up a shard of crystal, sharp-edged and glittering, a glass knife.

"Don't call me names, fleshie. Take me to the vehicle. I'm getting out of here."

"It won't work! The chariot needs a traveler, someone like Sorlyn, or Zax, to operate it!"

Polly groaned. "You can't even travel? What good are you?"

"What is wrong with you? You've trapped me here, you've trapped both of us here!"

"It's not a good situation," Polly said. "But it's a better situation than it was. For me." Its mouth opened, and grew teeth inside that maw, long and fanglike. "Now, at least, I've got something to eat."

I ran.

Polly didn't chase me right away. It sauntered, whistling, and laughing, and calling out to me, telling me what parts of me it was going to eat first. It was toying with me – playing with its food.

While Polly enjoyed itself, I made my way back to the sleepercar. Crystals were growing over the delicate wheels the carriage rested upon. I ignored that for now, having more pressing problems than crystalline assimilation. I climbed inside, and opened the compartment under the console.

Winsome told us Zax had a habit of trying to help people in the worlds he visited, but Toros has a fundamentally non-interventionist stance when it comes to other universes. He says we should leave the locals alone – their problems aren't ours, and our business isn't theirs. What Toros wants is to put everything back in its place. We aren't there to help, like Zax, and we also aren't there to conquer, like the Lector. The Sleepers have access to all sorts of advanced technology, but we don't use it very much: the sleepercars are stealth reconnaissance vessels, not warships. We go on rescue and capture missions, not into battle.

"But," Toros told me once, "sometimes you find a world where monsters want to eat you, so we don't expect you to be totally defenseless."

I reached into the compartment under the console and took out a matte black baton roughly the length of my forearm. The staff came from the Weapon Factory of Escher, wherever *that* was, and it was remarkably versatile. I snapped the baton out to its full length, nearly as long as I was tall, and waited for Polly to approach.

It slouched out of the shadow of a wrecked crystalline building. "Going to hit me with a stick, meat-thing?" It twirled its glass blade jauntily.

I wasn't confident I could beat Polly in a knife fight. Fortunately, I didn't have to. I pointed the end of the staff at Polly, pressed a spot on the shaft, and fired a projectile at the creature's center mass.

A neat hole appeared in Polly's body, and it staggered back a couple of steps... but then regained its footing and kept approaching. "Ouch," Polly said cheerfully. "I'm not like you, all full of precious organs. You can poke holes in me all day and it won't *hurt* me. Zax tried to stab me, once, and that didn't work out too well for him. He's the one who dropped me in that hole, too, him and that stupid Minna who just won't die, and their friend the magic ring. I can't hurt them, but I can hurt you–"

"We'll see." I twisted a section of the staff, aimed again, and sent a crackling arc of electricity into Polly's body.

"Oooh, tingles," it said. "That raised my ambient temperature by a few degrees. I'm not a sack of meat and electricity and chemicals like you are, I don't have muscles to lock up and spasm, zapping me doesn't do anything–"

"OK then." Another twist, and this time, I sprayed a stream of acid.

Polly screamed, cursed at me, and tore off the spattered limb, tossing it smoking to the ground. "It's going to take me hours to grow that back, you wobbly ball of guts and snot–"

Another twist, and this time, the staff sprayed fire. Not *just* fire – a sort of gelatinous accelerant that sticks to you and then burns.

Polly didn't scream for long. Not nearly as long as she burned. The most horrible thing was, she smelled good, like roasted mushrooms.

I locked myself in the sleepercar and closed the dome, so I couldn't smell her anymore, and then I sat, and stared at the crystal towers around me while the gemstone of a sun began to set.

Sorlyn would be OK. He was an experienced multiversal traveler, and he had the linguistic virus now, which would be a great help, if he ended up in inhabited worlds. I decided I would be OK, too. I'd survived on the world of silent towers, and I hadn't even had a working brain at the time. Here, I had supplies in the sleepercar's cargo hold, enough for a couple of weeks, anyway, and there could well be forage in some of these buildings. I hadn't seen any corpses, so maybe this place had been evacuated in a hurry, with goodies left behind. Toros was supposedly behind us, just a few weeks away, and in time, he would find me, and then we could go after Sorlyn.

I was frustrated, of course, because Zax had just been here, he'd dropped Polly in a hole (good for him!), and now I was stuck, and he was getting farther away. But we'd catch up. We would. It was just a matter of time, and hadn't I learned patience over these past years?

That's what I told myself during the day. At night, huddled in the sleepercar, in that silent crystal world, everything seemed a lot more bleak. What if something had happened to Toros? The multiverse was full of general dangers, and the cult posed a specific danger. Maybe he'd never come, and I'd be trapped here forever.

Well, not forever. I'd die eventually, after all.

But I got up every morning, when that jeweled sun rose. I used my staff to knock the crystals off the sleepercar, and then, I passed the time. I found a shovel and a wheelbarrow and knocked the crystals off them and took Polly's remains back to the pit, as it seemed a fitting grave. She was already crystallizing, too. I couldn't really explore, because if Toros arrived I wanted to be right there, and not make him go look for me. I didn't have a handy worm-trail to follow. I also didn't want to risk falling into a hole and breaking a leg or something. That would be a stupid way to die.

Boredom was bad, but thirst was worst. We had a supply of water in the sleepercar, but we usually foraged for that, since there's water on most worlds that support life, and we can purify whatever we find. Except… the water I saw here had a sort of *sheen*, a prismatic quality, even after purification, and that made me think it was infected the way everything else in the crystal world was. I imagined taking a sip and having my esophagus crystallize, my heart growing a shell of glass like the one surrounding the sun… So I was careful, and sipped the tiny amount of water I rationed for myself. I had enough for almost a month, and imbibed a sufficient quantity that I wouldn't die, but I was always thirsty. (Yes, I purified my pee, too, in order to extend my survival time, but that's a diminishing-returns proposition, at least with our level of technology.)

Then, one day, leaning against the edge of the chariot, wondering how long I would have to sit for crystals to start growing on me, I sensed a shift – a swirl of wind, a displacement of nearby air volume. I scrambled upright, and a vehicle shimmered into view. It was like our sleepercar, broadly, but different in the particulars. Ours was a shiny black sphere with silver details and plush red seats inside, while this one was ivory with gold accents, and the interior was a buttery pale yellow. Gibberne was one of those engineers who believed that beauty is as important as function, and he'd made beautiful machines, even if the aesthetic looked hopelessly old-fashioned to me.

The dome slid open, and Toros leapt out. Bounding to my rescue again. I recognized the Sleeper still unconscious in the back of his chariot as Durio, a man from a post-scarcity utopia who tended to sniff disdainfully at his primitive surroundings and loudly proclaim that things were better back home, and that he couldn't wait to be cured and leave all this mess behind. I was surprised Toros had brought him, since he was widely considered to be the most useless of the Sleepers, but then I realized Toros had probably dispatched the others on more crucial missions to support his outpost-building. Durio was probably best suited to being a mostly unconscious engine.

Toros rushed up to me. "Ana! I didn't expect to catch up to you so soon. Is Zax here? The Lector?" He looked around avidly, and then his perception caught up with his enthusiasm and he saw how dirty and disheveled and worn-out and dried-up I was. "Oh, no. What happened?"

"The Lector is worse than we thought," I croaked, and told him everything.

Before long I was in his sleepercar, taking little sips of water instead of gulping, so I wouldn't throw up. Toros tracked

Sorlyn's trail, and we followed it through a slew of worlds. I'm not even sure how many, and I didn't really look at any of them as we went – I slept, and sipped, and slept. I do remember Toros grumbling that Sorlyn had spun off into worlds that Zax and the Lector hadn't, but then again we'd have to backtrack to pick up our sleepercar on the crystal world anyway...

Finally Toros shouted, "There!" and I jolted fully awake.

"Be less noisy please," Durio muttered from the back.

Toros and I disembarked into a late afternoon autumn of a world, and found Sorlyn sitting on a cliff's edge, looking down at a distant village, all neat lanes and hedges, cottages and wooden spires. He had a handful of berries, and popped one in his mouth as we approached. Once he'd chewed and swallowed, he said, "Oh, good. I was thinking about starting to worry." He nodded at me. "Did you kill that thing that looked like Zax?"

"Burned it," I said. "But only after I got some information first."

"Well done," he said. He turned his attention to Toros. "Took your time, hmm?"

"Preparations back home took a bit longer than I thought, or I would have been along sooner," Toros said. "Though I didn't expect you to lose your ship. That was rather careless of you." I could hear the emotion in his voice, despite the casual tone, and he grabbed Sorlyn and hugged him tight.

"Oh, we're going to do very strange things to the local mythology," Sorlyn said. He patted Toros on the back, then turned, and pointed down at the village. "I bet you thought they were far away, didn't you? Look again."

I peered over the edge of the cliff, and after a moment my perspective seemed to shift, and I gasped. The village wasn't large and distant, it was close, and miniature. "Is it like a model, or a child's toy, or–" But then I saw the people moving: as small as dolls, running around, looking up at *us*, the giants on their cliff. "Oh, wow."

"They'll be relieved when we don't go down there and stomp on everything," Sorlyn said. "Can you imagine what it's like, to be so small, and threatened by incomprehensible forces so much larger than you, looming above?" He looked at me, and Toros, and raised an eyebrow. "Because I certainly can." He rose, and offered me his handful of berries, which weren't actually berries at all. "Care for some apples?"

Then we crammed into the sleepercar and backtracked to the crystal world so Sorlyn and I could recover our own transportation, and, not long after that, we first encountered the Moveable Empire.

Vast and Ancient • The Secret Origin of All Reality • Pressing • Reverse Panopticon • Terminal Utilitarianism • Pilgrimage • Enter the Trypophile

"Like me?" I shook my head. "You don't seem like a harmonizer to me, Prisoner."

"I certainly hate cacophony," the Prisoner said. "While you're capable of helping people only on an insignificant individual scale, I could help people across the whole span of the multiverse – if I could only break free of this prison, and interact with those worlds directly. As it stands, I can only peer through cracks in the worlds, and send out my followers to act on my behalf. Some damage is done in the process, yes, but the sacrifices are necessary to set me free, and then, *then*, I can do the most possible good for the greatest number of people."

I didn't believe the creature, but it wasn't as if I could stand up and storm out. I was trapped in this dream-place, somehow bound to this entity by the interdimensional worm in my blood.

The Prisoner stood beside me, hands clasped behind its back, looking at the volcano with me. "There are not infinite worlds, but there are many, more than you could visit in a thousand lifetimes, and there are more of them bubbling up out of the void every day. Some of those universes are empty of life, and some of those with life are empty of consciousness, but there are still so many worlds where creatures like you live. Beings who can think, and hope, and strive… and suffer." It sighed. "It wasn't always that way. In the old days, there were only a few conscious beings – myself, and my siblings. We were eternal and unchanging, with no concept of time. We each sat in our own silent contemplation of our infinite empty surroundings, and there was no pain – we did not even understand the concept of pain."

"So you claim to be some kind of god?"

The Prisoner clucked its tongue. "Not at all. My followers say I am a 'vast and ancient cosmic being of untold power and wisdom'. That's as good a designation as any, though there was nothing like a cosmos when we arose. We were the first forms in the void. In retrospect, that was probably when things started to go wrong."

I wondered if I could trust this creature. I didn't think it would bother to lie to me, any more than I would bother to lie to an insect in my path. It was a rare opportunity to learn secrets of the multiverse, but I was afraid I wouldn't like them. "If there was nothing, why is there something now?"

"Why indeed!" The Prisoner arched an eyebrow, a familiar quirk of the Lector before he went into monologue mode. "My siblings, eventually, grew tired of contemplating the perfection of the void, and they started to… make things. I didn't mind at first. What did I care if they caused some distant point in the void to explode into matter? True, the matter expanded, but what it expanded into was infinite, so it wasn't as if we didn't have the space. But then more and more of my siblings started to join in, and this creation of universes became a *craze*. Suddenly my peaceful void teemed with noisy, dirty, complicated places. Yes, we had infinite space, but my vision was infinite, too, and in every direction I looked there was light and chaos. The worlds my siblings created affronted my gaze, but I couldn't stop looking at them – it turns out, my *nature* is looking, and unlike you, I do not sleep, and cannot close my eyes. I finally became so annoyed that... well."

I turned and looked at the Prisoner. It shrugged. "Well?" I said.

"I began to snuff their worlds out. But my siblings kept making more, and then there began to be these flickers, new results of their experiments. They were tweaking the parameters, you see, altering the initial conditions of their worlds, leading to new outcomes. One of those outcomes was... consciousness. There were things inside those worlds that could also look and see and think! Things like us, but tiny and finite and bound within their own little universes." The Prisoner shuddered. "Repulsive. An insult, and mockery of our natures. I could not stand that, not at all, so... I went on something of a tear. I destroyed *all* their little universes in one rampage. I was always... not bigger than my siblings, size didn't work that way back then, but I was always much stronger, yes. I told my siblings, in no uncertain terms, that they had to stop cluttering up the infinite void immediately. One of them stomped up to me and said 'Or what', and then... I did something that had never been done before."

"You snuffed them out," I said. "You committed murder." We had legends on my world of a first murderer – a son who killed his father – but I was looking at the real thing now.

The Prisoner sniffed disdainfully. "Hardly murder. It was an accident. I didn't know she was so fragile. My siblings put something of themselves into those universes they created, I think. That weakened them. As if I needed yet another reason to avoid the whole business." It shrugged. "Anyway, my siblings turned on me then. They found a way to bind me – they created chains, just like they created universes. I snuffed a couple of my attackers out, but my siblings are many, and they overwhelmed me. I roared at them, and told them the chains would not hold me, and that soon I would learn how to unmake those, as well. They said... they said they knew that. That they had something else in mind."

I was interested, despite myself. If this was true, even in a sort of metaphorical way, it was extraordinary. "What did they do to you?"

"Something I have seen, peering into some of these worlds that bind me, is a form of execution that involves rocks, often called 'pressing'. Sometimes it's meant as torture rather than execution, to extract a confession. In either case, the condemned or accused is bound on their back, and stones are placed on their body." The Prisoner sat down on the shore, picked up a pebble, and placed it on top of a larger rock. "No single stone is large enough to do any particular harm on its own, but more stones are added gradually, piling up, until the victim is suffocated, or, for those creatures who don't breathe, crushed. That is what my siblings did to me. But instead of burying me with rocks... they buried me in worlds. They found a way to protect their little bubbles of creation, to armor them, so they look like spheres of dust and light but feel as solid as myself. I couldn't snuff them out anymore. My siblings created universe after universe, surrounding me, burying me. Still, I shrugged them off, dug myself free, until one clever sibling found a way to create a... a sort of forge that made more universes, the way their accursed stars forge new elements. Another sibling found a way to make existing universes bud, splitting off duplicates that then grow along their own new trajectory, and become distinct."

That explained how I'd found a world similar to, but different from, my own; Ana's Realm of the Known and the Found and my Realm of Spheres and Harmonies must have started as one universe, and then split. (Could there be other versions of me, ones who hadn't been infected, who were still living with a version of my family, still working as harmonizers, or even as other things? Could I meet them?)

The Prisoner banged two rocks together, startling me. "Pay attention! I am telling you the secrets of reality itself." Once it was satisfied I was paying attention, it went back to piling up rocks, making a cairn. "Those new worlds are *still being made*, though my siblings have long since left this region of the infinite behind. The worlds pile up on me, more and more." It looked up at me. "But I am eternal, Zaxony. I feel the weight, but I cannot be crushed." It hurled a stone into the lake. "Imagine being buried in trillions of pebbles, and all the pebbles are *screaming*. Because that's what I experience. The worlds are objects of chaos, spheres of light and dark, and they fill my vision. Where my devoted have traveled, I can peer through the cracks they made, and see the interior of those universes – my vast view becomes local, and I can see things like you." It shuddered. "I wish I couldn't see into those universes – but I can't look away, no matter how much I hate what I see."

That *was* a lie, I thought, though maybe the Prisoner was lying to itself. I think it liked to watch. I think it liked to watch especially when it could also meddle with the things it was watching.

The Prisoner kicked over the pile of rocks it had made. "As a thinking, feeling entity? I abhor what I see in those worlds my followers have shown me. So much misery, and I've seen only the smallest fraction of the total. Untold numbers of creatures, born only to live in misery and die in violence. My siblings are the monsters, Zax. They created you all, and they don't care about your pain. They don't even notice it."

I had met nihilists before. "It's not all misery, Prisoner. There's beauty, too. There's harmony. Love, kindness, gratitude. I've seen it all."

"All of those are exceptions, and all temporary," the Prisoner said. "My view is wider than yours."

"What's your solution, then?" I asked. "Since you're such a great harmonizer?"

"I seek to provide the greatest good for the greatest number," the Prisoner said. "To minimize suffering as much as possible. There are far too many worlds, Zax, with too many people in them. My solution is simple: destroy the walls of my prison. I managed to smash a tiny crack in the First World, enough to whisper through and be heard, and I have gathered my faithful. With effort, exhausting myself each time, I can extend a tiny portion of my essence into that world, and my people venerate that essence as their sacrament."

"The worms," I said.

"They appear as such to you. They have to look like something, and form follows function. In reality, they are just parts of me." It held up a hand and waggled its fingers. "I can embed a tiny part of myself inside a creature, and from there, I can push, push, push, and make more cracks, and bore more holes through the armor of the worlds. Once I have pierced enough shells, the universes will begin to leak and flow together, the many becoming one. After a few hundred or thousand are merged, I believe it will cause a chain reaction, and this whole mountain of pebbles on top of me will begin to collapse and disintegrate – and I will burst free."

"What will happen to the people in those worlds when they merge?"

The Prisoner spread its hands. "They will be delivered from sorrow. Snuffed out, never again to suffer pain. I have promised my faithful that I will allow one universe to remain – the First World, the one you see before you now – and to let them dwell there in peace. There was a time when the thought of even one world was repulsive to me, but it would be quite peaceful, compared to my current reality. It's a trade I'm happy to make."

"That's your plan?" I backed away from it. "To destroy not just a universe, but all the universes? Even the Lector just wanted to rule."

"I desire no subjects. I don't even want worshippers, though they have their uses in my current circumstances. I am on a mission of mercy, Zax. Help me, and you too can dwell in the First World, with Ana, and Minna, and Vicki, and Winsome, and the Pilgrim, and Zaveta, and all your other friends. You can all be happy. I am patient, but now that I can see into so many worlds, I feel the burden of time in a way I never have before. Producing the sacrament is difficult, and slow, and the members of my cult, as you call my fellowship, are not numerous. But if you convince Minna to show us how to make the serum your Lector first developed, we can go to a world advanced enough to make a factory, and I can spread the synthetic sacrament far and wide, and send out hundreds, thousands, millions of envoys to shred the fabric of reality and, finally, tear down these walls." The light of fervency in its eyes was just like that I saw in the Lector's when he talked about empire.

"I will never help you. What you're describing is so far beyond ordinary genocide there needs to be a new word for it."

"We could just call it pest control." The Prisoner smiled. "I didn't expect you to go along with me willingly, but I thought I'd give you the opportunity to surprise me – to see if you really mean what you say about *helping* people. But you're just a hypocrite. Oh, and about those people you *just* helped, the burrowers? Do you want to know something funny?"

"What?"

"When they burst forth from the ground at the proper time, they appear in a rather different form than you saw – one that is far larger and more lethal. They then spend a cycle in full dominion over their world, breeding and devouring and consuming, destroying whatever civilization managed to arise in the fourteen cycles of their absence. Their rule is so rapacious that they strip the world nearly bare, and they have to hibernate for so long just to allow vegetation and animal life to grow back. The snouted sapients you encouraged Zaveta to murder were fighting for their lives, desperately trying to exterminate the looming insect menace while the monsters were vulnerable, mid-hibernation. How's that for harmonizing, Zax?"

"I don't believe you," I said. "Those slavers were laughing, and they were keeping the females alive!"

"I never said the snouty ones were nice. They hate the bugs, and are quite cruel to the beasts." The Prisoner shrugged. "I'm not saying you helped the bad ones and hurt the good ones, Zax. I'm saying there *aren't any good ones.*" He flicked a hand at me dismissively. "You'd better wake up. Your life is about to become unpleasant. Loath as I am to increase the suffering in the multiverse by even one iota, you leave me no choice."

I woke up to Ephedra laughing, which seemed like a bad sign. "Zax!" Zaveta was kneeling beside me, shaking me. "You wouldn't wake up! I thought you were hurt!"

"Zax was talking to God," the cultist said. "Did the Prisoner give you the good news about your total insignificance? Did he tell you how you're just a plaything created by his brothers and sisters and abandoned? I was born on the First World, the real world, the original universe, the eternal realm, the one stone that will never be shattered–"

I groaned. "Could we please gag her?"

"No!" Ephedra said. "I'll be quiet. You figments are so sensitive."

Zaveta gazed at me. "Is this true, Zax? Did you see the Prisoner?"

"I did." I sat up and looked around. We were inside a large green canvas tent, with holes in the ceiling showing a burnt-orange sky. "What is this place?"

She sighed. "If the cultist is to be believed, this was one of the outposts your people set up, to try to prevent the cult from spreading."

"This is a Sleeper outpost? But… where is everyone?"

"Am I allowed to answer?" Ephedra said. "They're dead, though sadly there were only three of them here – the rest of the force was robots, but we got the codes when we destroyed your world, and we moved fast here, and shut down the defenses before the codes could change. Your people have other outposts, all too close, just a few hops away from the First World. You were trying to build a wall around us, to pen us in, to make *us* prisoners. This was the weakest, though, so we punched through here, and took this world as our own, giving us a clear route to the world beyond. Ha."

"But you're here now," I said, trying to piece together the logistics in my mind. "That means you haven't been to this world before. How did you get out, if this world is the only open path?"

"I caught a ride, stupid. Why do you think we attacked the Sleeperhold? To get those chariots of yours. You managed to destroy a few and escape with some others, but the Trypophile got one for herself. We have free rein now – we can go up and down and back and forth and everywhere."

"Why are you suddenly so willing to share information?" Zaveta said.

"Because my mission is complete."

"Your mission was to take us to Minna," I said.

Ephedra cackled. "No, it wasn't. I was supposed to deliver you here, and tell any old lie along the way to make that possible. Now that we've arrived, it doesn't matter what you figments know or don't know."

The tent flap opened, and–

The Pilgrim stepped in. "Be quiet, wormling," he rumbled.

Zaveta took a stance that promised violence. I couldn't blame her – the Pilgrim is a menacing figure, a feline humanoid, large and imposing in sand-colored robes, and he had a curved blade at his waist and a high-tech rifle slung across his back.

"No, Zaveta, it's OK!" I said. "He's a friend!" I rushed to the Pilgrim, almost hugging him, but he's not the hugging type, so I just extended a hand, which he shook gravely in one immense paw. "You survived! I was afraid you died on Sleeperhold."

"I… was not harmed there," he said.

"Pilgrim, this is Zaveta. I bet you two would get along – you both know a *lot* about war." I was giddy. I wasn't sure whether I'd ever see that serious, familiar face again, and here he was! "I met the Pilgrim worlds and worlds ago. He helped us in our fight against the Lector, and joined us at the Sleeperhold. We found him on this world where he was – well, he was looking for God, the place where God actually *lives*, and he came with us because he thought he might have a better chance of finding that God somewhere out in the multiverse–"

"I succeeded," the Pilgrim said.

I frowned. "What? What do you mean?"

The Pilgrim put an immense paw on my shoulder. I was suddenly aware of his strength, and of the claws hidden in those soft pads. His face was so happy, beaming with a fervent light. "My quest reached its end. I found God. God *spoke* to me, in the space between worlds, while I slept, and Its envoys came to me on the Sleeperhold and told me what God required of me. I have found my true purpose in Its service."

Behind me, Ephedra began to laugh.

Realization seeped into me like blood into cloth. "Pilgrim... no, that thing, the Prisoner, it's not a god, it's just an ancient cosmic entity–"

"Zax. What you are describing *is* God."

"The Prisoner wants to destroy everything!"

"Who are we to judge the acts of God?" The Pilgrim said. "The Prisoner was there when the foundation stones of the universe were placed. Where were we?" He gripped me more firmly.

Zaveta growled, cudgel suddenly in her hand. "Let him go."

The Pilgrim released me and stepped back. "I don't wish to harm you, Zax. Or any of you."

I closed my eyes. This was the first time a companion, someone I'd trusted, had turned on me since the Lector. My heart was breaking along old fault lines. "Pilgrim, the Prisoner is a liar. He told me himself – he lets his followers believe what they *want* to believe, and he's deceiving you. Do you – does your faith have something like an adversary? A deceiver, someone who pretends to be God while working against–"

"There is only God," the Pilgrim said. "There is a place for you in the new kingdom, Zax, my friend–"

"We'll see about that," a woman said in Wormspeech, pushing through the tent flap. She wore a hooded black robe with a muddy hem, and when she looked at me, she had no face at all – just an expanse of holes, dozens of tiny clustered cavities in a dark brown surface, like her whole head was a wasp's nest or a seed pod or infested meat. My heart dropped, and even after I realized she was just wearing some kind of mask, I still found her hard to look at. I don't experience the profound unease some people suffer at the sight of clusters of small holes, but seeing that in lieu of a face was nevertheless profoundly off-putting.

"You can call me the Trypophile," she said. "It's the least sacred of my names. My *proper* name would be made profane by your tongue."

"You're in for it now," Ephedra said.

"Pilgrim, please set our daughter free?"

The Pilgrim stepped toward Ephedra, and Zaveta moved into the way. "She's our prisoner."

"You misunderstand the nature of the situation," the Trypophile said. Suddenly the canvas sides of the tent lifted all at once, and ten people dressed in the ragtag mishmash of cultist garb pointed weapons at us, from pointy sticks to high-tech weapons taken from the sentry machines Toros had imported. "You're *our* prisoners now. Zaxony, tell your pet to drop her weapon, or die. I don't need her alive at all, but if it will make you more cooperative, I'll spare her for now."

"I cannot fight them all," Zaveta said. "Not without dying in the process." She paused. "But I can make my life very costly for them." Her eyes were fixed only on the Pilgrim, and his only on hers.

I put my hand on her arm. "Stand down, Zaveta. We've been captured before."

She nodded, and tossed her cudgel away.

"Wonderful," the Trypophile said. "We're going to the First World. You'll love it there."

"I've seen it. I don't think I'll stay long." I could sleep my way out of this world right now, but I couldn't take Zaveta with me, and if I left her behind, she would die. I'd find a way, though, to reach her, and to escape—

"I heard about your little trick," the Trypophile said. "You can sleep whenever you want, and stay awake as long as you want, without losing your senses. Your friend Minna will teach *us* how to do that, too. But you think that power makes you impossible to hold. Wherever we put you, whatever cell, whatever hole, you can always escape, yes?" She stepped forward and grabbed me by the chin, forcing my gaze up, so I had to look into the black holes of her mask. How could she see through them? "But that's what's wonderful about the First World," she said. "In most worlds, there are three or four adjacent habitable realities. But there's only *one* acceptable universe adjacent to the First World – only one reality your sacrament would let you enter, because the other options would kill you instantly. We call that place the second world. And Zaxony? We're going to pass through that world on our way home, and send you into the First World from there."

I stared at her. "But... you mean..."

"The First World is the end of the line," she said. "The sacrament inside you *comes* from that place. The blessed seek new worlds above all else, but after you pass through the second world into the first, there's nowhere for you to go." She laughed, a sound like crackling dry leaves. "It's a dead end. You can sleep and wake and sleep and wake and you'll never find yourself anywhere else. Our First World is your last world." She ran one sharp fingernail down my cheek, and leaned in to whisper in my ear. "You will die there, Zaxony Dyad Euphony Delatree."

Ana

Toros and Durio traveled with us from the crystal city onward and, while we were on the same world, we could communicate between chariots via radio. I must admit, having some backup felt good: I wouldn't be stranded again, or at least, not easily. The first part of our group expedition was the same as before: we followed Zax's ragged trail, and the Lector's eerie smooth one, pausing briefly in each world, and then moving on.

That changed when we reached the space station.

The sleepercar has some sort of safety mechanism, to prevent it from appearing in spaces that are big enough for a person infested with a transdimensional worm but too small for a spherical chariot. In those cases, our point of arrival is slightly offset, and there's a loud warning buzzer to let us know. That buzzer sounded as we transitioned into orbit around a planet that was – visibly, from space – on fire.

I turned off the alarm, looked out the dome, and said, "How is this a habitable world?"

Sorlyn blinked awake, peered down, and said, "Hmm. Check the radar."

I'd forgotten we even had that – we hardly ever needed to use it. Once I turned the display on, I saw a blip – and then another blip, as Toros appeared near us – and spun the shuttle around.

There was a space station behind us, a series of cylindrical habitats linked together, with light shining through the windows. Some sections of the station were broken and exposed to space, but others were whole. "Zax must have woken up inside there. Should we board?"

Sorlyn nodded. "There must be a docking bay of some kind for a shuttle from their planet. If their equipment is still working..." He disconnected his diadem and joined me in the front seat, doing things to the console I'd never seen before.

"I thought you taught me everything you knew about driving these?" I said.

He smiled. "There's not enough time in the world for me to teach you everything I know. We have a suite of tools that scan through known technological systems and attempt to interface with alien systems. They can adapt, adjust, and learn, and while they don't work on everything, this doesn't seem wildly unlike tech we've seen in other worlds... Ah ha. There."

He figured out how to talk to the station, and we matched its lazy rotation and hooked ourselves into a docking bay at the end of one cylinder. They were much bigger up close. We radioed Toros, who told us to proceed carefully, and that he'd stay outside. "That's in case something in here kills you," Toros said. "Then only half the expedition will die."

"It's always good to have a contingency plan." I took the staff with me, collapsed. I wasn't going to walk around unarmed again.

In the end, there wasn't anything dangerous on the station, though something had clearly gone wrong at some point – the walls were streaked with soot in places, and you don't want fire in space stations. Apart from Zax and the Lector's worm-trails, there were other signs of recent habitation, too – empty food containers, wadded heaps of blankets, things like that. It looked like someone had stayed here for a while.

There was also something new. "Toros," Sorlyn said on our comms. "We've got a third trail here. Smooth, like the Lector's."

"He's made more of the serum?" Toros crackled. "Who did he give it to?"

"Maybe the Lector picked up another helper, like Polly," I said. "Or maybe–"

"Oh, what's this?" Sorlyn was poking at a console on the wall. "We've got video and audio surveillance recordings here."

Oh, Zax. Later I read about what happened on that horrible station in his journal, but before that, I *saw* it. There was a lot of footage, but we could speed through most of it, slowing it down to real-time when some interaction was happening.

The Lector arrived on the station first, and soon took control of its systems. From there, he was able to capture Zax, and his friend Minna – my first sight of her, all pigtails and overalls – and Vicki, their crystal intelligence companion, what Polly called a "magic ring". We heard the Lector threaten to jettison Minna from the station if Zax didn't comply, and… Zax complied. Of course he did. He cares about his friends. He cares about other people more than himself. We fast-forwarded through endless lab tests and procedures, but eventually the Lector must have gotten what he wanted, because he drugged Zax, and he flickered out and away – solo. Poor Zax, alone again.

Minna was still on the station, though, and the Lector forced her to help him with his work. While the Lector produced more quantities of his serum, Minna somehow… grew a new *Polly*, from a sample of the fungal creature the Lector had saved.

"That is not OK," I said. "I killed that thing."

"This Minna is a marvel," Sorlyn said. "The Lector boasts of his brilliance, and he is very intelligent, but Minna just… quietly works miracles of biological science."

Minna clearly had hopes that the new Polly would be less violent than its predecessor, and at first it was, but the Lector had a way to transfer the original Polly's consciousness to the new one. I had to look away as New Polly viciously taunted Minna. Then the Lector packed up a case full of equipment, and vial after vial of serum, and New Polly locked Minna in a glass box. Then her tormentors departed that reality, leaving her behind.

I turned and looked at the glass box behind us in the lab. Empty. Back on the screen, we saw Minna extend tendrils like vines from her fingernails to slip through cracks and escape the box, and then she opened a cavity in her own *body*, and drew out a tiny vial of... something. "Did she steal some serum?" Sorlyn said. "Clever, clever."

But Minna didn't toss back the potion. She got to work, instead, and it became clear that she'd actually stolen some of Zax's blood, since she used the machines to reproduce it, and then started to experiment on herself. "The Lector called her a biotech lab with feet," I said. "He wasn't far wrong."

We watched as Minna injected herself with things, and then her fingers fell off, and she grew new ones. She never seemed frustrated, just focused. "Is she... Sorlyn, she's not trying to make serum. She's trying to change herself, I think."

A day after she got out of that box, Minna settled herself down on the floor, and closed her eyes – and vanished. "The third trail," I said. "The third trail is *Minna*. She changed herself to be like Zax, to travel naturally, without a potion, but also without a worm! She must have made her own body produce the same chemical the worm does!"

"This is not good," Toros said over the radio. "If the cult finds out, and discovers a way to reproduce that power, to scale up production..."

"The cult isn't anywhere near here," Sorlyn pointed out. "We're over a thousand worlds from our best guess about their home world."

"Yes," Toros said, "but if all goes well, we're going to bring Minna back to the Sleeperhold, and we must be careful when we do."

"You know," I said, "if Minna can give herself the ability to travel like the sleepers do, maybe..."

"Yes," Sorlyn said. "She might be able to stop sleepers from traveling. That occurred to me, too."

"A cure," Toros said.

"What?" Durio said. "What did you say? Did you say a *cure*? What are we waiting for? Let's go after her!"

We pursued Minna, and Zax, and the Lector, and things got bad very quickly. Zax's trail was just a blip in the first twenty or so worlds, like he landed and then took off from the same place, without taking so much as a single step in between. Later we found out that's exactly what happened – the Lector gave Zax a cyclical sedative, so he'd sleep, travel, wake, sleep, travel, wake, over and over again, flung deeper into the multiverse. Minna's trail and the Lector's were indistinguishable, but it was clear she was following him in the world of ice that followed the space station.

The next world was home to humanoid giants encrusted with lichen and vines... but their leader had a strange, high-tech crown on his craggy head, and we heard the locals talking about the Lector. Their world was the first conquest of the Collectorium, the foundation of the Moveable Empire. "He's started his reign," Toros said on the radio. "He conquered this world!"

"He conquered one valley of this world for a brief interval," Sorlyn said. "Let's not get carried away. The Lector is a deluded megalomaniac. I don't care how much technology he's carrying or how smart he is – how much can he really accomplish? He's one person."

One person could accomplish quite a lot, as we found in the next world, a city of topaz skyscrapers. There was a lot of new construction going on – clearly something devastating had happened to the place – and we saw more figures wearing those odd crowns. "Mind control," Toros said. "The Lector is using force and coercion and mental domination to secure his rule."

"Again," Sorlyn said, "it's one city, and based on the level of technology, this is a world with lots of them. How long can his reign last without him here to secure it?"

There were banners in that city, white flags with a stylized black tree of many branches. (We saw a lot more of those banners as we moved through the worlds of the Collectorium.) We flew invisibly among the towers until we reached some sort of military installation, and then we just stared. There were hundreds of new trails there, all smooth like the Lector's. "He's learned to make his serum at scale," I said. "He raised an army here."

"He's already done more damage to reality than the cult has managed in all its years of operation," Toros said, horrified awe in his voice.

"There's a breach here," Sorlyn said, peering at the console. "Small, just a few centimeters, and it appears to be underground, so it poses no immediate danger, at least not on this side, but… it's there."

"A breach?" I said.

"Those tears in reality we told you about," Sorlyn explained. "Places where one world bleeds into another. Where people can get lost. Toros saw those breaches, on his homeworld, and the sleepercar can detect their presence. It's what we've been worried about – enough people traveling, poking holes… making tears in the fabric of reality. This one is inside bedrock, and not big enough for much to pass through anyway, even if it's in a more open space in the adjoining world."

"Still," I said. "Can we do anything about it? To seal it up?"

"Well," Sorlyn began, but Toros interrupted. "We need to keep going. The Lector has to be stopped."

So we continued, into horror after horror. Some of the worlds appeared to be uninhabited, or at least uninhabited by thinking creatures, and the Lector and his army passed through those and left them mostly unscathed. But he left his mark on every world that was home to intelligent beings

– we passed bomb sites, and rubble, and wreckage, much of it clearly fresh. The Lector wasn't always ascendant, though. He conquered his local area, recruited new soldiers, placed a seneschal in command (always from *another* world, probably for sound tyrannical reasons), and then moved on with the bulk of his forces... but the worlds in his wake didn't always stay conquered. On some, the locals had clearly taken back their homes, with the Lector's banners torn down and shredded, the mind-controlling crowns smashed, the aliens executed. "He really thinks these worlds will remain under his heel after he leaves?" Sorlyn said.

"He never sees evidence of failure," I said. "He can't go backwards, so he'll never be disappointed. He's like a virus, a wildfire, a natural disaster, tearing through these worlds. We have to stop him."

On some worlds, the fight for freedom was ongoing. We once appeared on the outskirts of a battle among humanoids with the heads of birds, slashing each other with beaks and talons and swords. In other worlds, though, especially low-tech ones, the Lector's seneschals seemed to rule without opposition. I wanted to free the mine full of children laboring under the Lector's banner, but Toros pointed out the hundreds of worm-trails, and said we had bigger concerns. I agreed, though I thought, *Zax would have helped them.*

The less said about the cathedrals full of skeletons with gemstone eyes and hydraulic muscles the better. They were *staunch* loyalists of the Lector, having incorporated him into their religion, and we got out of that world quickly. The addition of those creatures – immune to pain, immune to fatigue, immune to death by dismemberment – to his army would make the Lector an even greater threat.

We saw a world of treehouses. A basalt plain dotted with creepy pyramids. Hill forts, bombed to splinters, with dead blue people scattered everywhere. A sea full of flotsam. A burned evergreen forest. A city plaza with fountains, the buildings hung with Lector banners. Then, in a world of burning rivers, we found a poster nailed to a tree – a detailed drawing of Minna's face, with incomprehensible alien text underneath.

Sorlyn climbed out of the sleepercar, took the poster down, and admired it. He looked at me and grinned – I'd almost never seen him actually *smile*. "It's a wanted poster," he said. "Minna is disrupting the Lector's operations. She's his enemy!" He folded up the poster and tucked it into his pocket. "I like her. I really like her. Do you think… I couldn't tell from the footage on the space station, they weren't ever together for long, but… do you think Minna and Zax are, ah, involved?"

That hadn't even occurred to me. Zax and *I* were together! Except, of course, we'd only spent a couple of days that way, and anyway, he thought I was dead. "How should I know?" I snapped. "Let's go."

Swamps, battlefields, villages. Hundreds of trails, so many it was hard to find Zax's, the one that was a different shape than the rest. "We must be catching up," I said. "The Lector has to spend some time on each world, subjugating it, so the end must be near, right?"

"I hope so," Sorlyn said. "There's a breach here that's big enough for a person to crawl through."

I looked around. "Where?"

Sorlyn pointed at nothing, a space between two redwood trees. "You can't see it. That's the problem. You walk along, you step wrong, and… you're in another world. Sometimes the breach is stable, and you can walk right back. Sometimes they oscillate, open and close, or they only open one way, and…" He shrugged. "This area seems fairly remote, at least. But as the Lector's army gets bigger, the breaches will only get worse. Once there are enough of them, the worlds will begin to collapse in on themselves. Or so the theory goes."

"Let's try to avoid seeing it in practice." We set off again.

After all that pursuit, I wanted there to be a big, violent climax. I wanted to find Zax, and stand shoulder-to-shoulder beside him, and fight against the Lector's army. I wanted to set the Lector on fire the way I had Polly. (I know; I am a fundamentally more vengeful and bloodthirsty person than Zax, but sometimes that's the kind of person you *need*. Though it's good to have Zax's tempering influence. He was always there in my mind, seeing the best in everyone, and wanting the best for them, too.)

Instead of taking part in the last battle, we arrived after the battle was done. The world of Zax's last stand was a rocky, mountainous place, all broken rocks and stunted trees under a steel gray sky. Our chariots appeared near a small crater, and everywhere around us were the signs of battle, including a much *larger* crater in a valley, ringed by bits of metal debris. There was a campsite, too, and the Lector's army was *here*, or at least, most of them were – blue-furred humanoid creatures, giants, bird-headed people, robots, and more... but no sign of New Polly, or of the Lector.

"I'll go listen in on the troops," Sorlyn said, but I stopped him.

"Your little invisibility trick doesn't work on machines, and there are a lot of robots down there. I'll go in the shimmersuit."

Sorlyn still hated sending me into danger alone, but he nodded.

I stealthed myself, and crept into the Lector's camp. It was impressive, not canvas tents or prefab forts like the Sleeper outposts I'd heard about, but sturdy stone buildings – some were assembling themselves as I watched, invisible compilers turning the local matter into more useful forms. I moved slowly toward the biggest structure, hung with the Lector's banner, and peered through the door.

"–telling you, he's gone, Delatree took him!" A woman with the head of a crow was arguing with a blue-furred man. "The Lector traveled while he was awake. His brain will be a cinder by now."

"If anyone can withstand the truths of the void–" the blue person said.

She cawed derisively. "Yes, fine, let's say he *can* survive it – I saw what happened to the people the Lector experimented on, the ones he sent through while they were conscious, and I don't think anyone could stand it, but maybe you're right. Let's say the Lector is fine, of sound mind, and defeated Delatree wherever they ended up. So what? We can't get to him. The Lector's personal guard is in pursuit, but the rest of us are stuck here, without serum! Our glorious leader's portable laboratory is keyed to his biometrics, and if we tamper with it, the case will release poison gas and then incinerate the contents. Damn his paranoia. We're trapped here, don't you see?"

"The – the Lector will come back for us," the blue person said. "He's working on the problem, he always says, he'll find a way to backtrack and return to the worlds he's already won, it's just a matter of–"

"Shut. Up." The crow-headed woman stared down at the ground for a long moment, then looked back at the blue person. "Organize a foraging party. We need to find out if there's anything to eat in this accursed place, because it's where we're going to spend the rest of our days."

I'd heard enough. I returned to the sleepercar and reported. "They say Zax traveled, and took the Lector… while the Lector was awake."

"Perhaps we can save him," Toros said over the radio. "Repair his mind. But… well. I thought we should try to recruit him. Having seen the damage he's done, though…"

"Maybe it's better if we don't?" I said.

"There is such a thing as too much mercy," Sorlyn said.

"What about the serum?" Toros said. "Is there a supply here?"

"The army says no, or anyway, not any they can access. The Lector was paranoid, and controlled the supply – I guess he didn't want anyone else setting themselves up as a rival multiverse emperor. His people are stranded here."

"In this desolate place?" Toros said. "At least they can't do harm to anyone but each other."

Sorlyn put his hand on my shoulder from the back seat. "Let's go pick up Zax, shall we?"

Reaching Zax took a few worlds. We saw some of the Lector's people stumbling around in confusion here and there, but just a handful – that personal guard I'd heard about. "The Lector isn't here," Sorlyn said. "Zax must have held on to him, and traveled again."

I tried to imagine experiencing that eternity in the void between worlds, not just once, but twice, three times, more... I wasn't sure even the Lector deserved that.

When we got to the world with the waterfall, we paused, and got out of the sleepercars, and stood on the cliff. The cataract was too thunderously loud for us to hear one another speak, but that was fine. What we saw spoke for itself.

There were a couple of trails in the air, but only one that started up here and arced sharply downward and ended at the base of the waterfall. Someone had jumped. It was smooth, so it wasn't Zax. Was it the Lector? I thought so. I thought, if there'd been a waterfall for me to fling myself into when I emerged from that horrible void of holes, I might have welcomed it.

In the next world, the trails stopped, and I finally saw Zax again.

*Zaveta Gets Sedated • The Benefits of
Faith • The Lineage of the Worm •
Breaches • A Message Delayed • Toros
Tells a Tale • The Final Solution*

The Trypophile's people prodded me and Zaveta out of the
tent. They shackled Zaveta, but didn't bother doing that for me,
which was both insulting and understandable. Zaveta's safety
was my chain. The cultists led us to their stolen sleepercar –
this one was a deep, glittery purple with black accents. One
of the cultists was wired up in the back, diadem on her head.
"Sit beside her," the Trypophile ordered. Zaveta sighed and
climbed in, awkwardly, with her hands bound behind her. The
Tryphophile darted in and stabbed something into Zaveta's
neck. Zaveta started to stand up, then swayed, and fell back
into the seat, unmoving.

"What did you do!" I shouted.

"Just a sedative, Zaxony," she soothed. "We can't have your
barbarian awake, thrashing around, biting people and so on.
You'll get your own shot soon enough. You have to travel to
the First World under your own power, so you'll be stuck there
properly."

That seemed to be true. Zaveta was still breathing. I pointed
toward the wired-up cultist and sneered at the Trypophile.
I'm not very good at sneering but I did my best. "You don't

191

have a worm of your own? I thought you were the holiest of holies."

"Those who take the sacrament are missionaries," the Trypophile said. "I am the direct conduit to the Prisoner. I send people on the missions. Get in the front."

I climbed in. I wish I could have slammed the dome shut and taken off, but I had no idea how to drive the vehicle – I hadn't been with the Sleepers long enough to learn. The Trypophile got in and began manipulating the console of lights. The dome slid shut over us. "What's the point of all this?" I said. "You want to use me to control Minna, but you have to find her first. She doesn't have your sacrament, so your god can't spy on her–"

She sighed. "The Prisoner told you that? Our god does love to talk. It's true the Prisoner can't see Minna constantly, the way he can watch you, and all the others who've received the sacrament, but he can look into any world where his missionaries have *been*. Anywhere your trails twist, they create a crack the Prisoner can peer through." The dome went opaque. "It's true, the worlds expand exponentially – one world leads to three or four, each of those leads to another three or four, and so on – but think of those expanding worlds as a sort of triangle. We're near the top, which is the First World, where the range of worlds is still narrow, and manageable. Our missionaries have been to every habitable world nearby, so our god catches glimpses of her often. Minna jumps around a lot, the Prisoner tells me – she seems to have realized that it's hard to catch her if she keeps moving, and these little ships are good at staying hidden – but once I send out word that we've got you, and have my people shout the news in every world they inhabit, Minna will hear. I don't have to find her. She'll come to *me*."

"The Prisoner is lying to you," I said. "He'll tell you anything to get free. You aren't the only real creatures in the world–"

"Oh, yes, I know. We're all real, my people and all the

others. Or we're all equally figments." She patted my knee. "I'd never say that where any of my people could hear, of course, but there's no reason to be circumspect with you. It's not as if anyone would believe you if you told them." I couldn't see her smile behind that awful mask, but I could hear it. "I'm not as credulous as my followers. My grandmother was the first person to explore the First World and speak to the Prisoner, and they worked out a mythology that would appeal to the people back in the second world. Make them feel special, to aid in their zealotry. The truth has been passed down in my line. We are the conduits between our god and his followers. I have a... personal arrangement with the Prisoner. We respect each other. I am content with the truth, and with saving myself and my people. Who cares what it costs others? My followers, though... they need the benefits of faith, and to believe they're the chosen people, instead of just the people who happened to be close enough to hear the Prisoner whisper. My! It's refreshing to have someone to talk to about all this. I usually have to keep so quiet about it all."

I doubted the Prisoner respected her – it thought people were insects – but I knew trying to convince her of that would be futile. I had snagged on something else she said anyway. "Your grandmother explored the First World? I thought that's where you came from?"

"Oh, I was born on the First World, but my people originally came from the second. The Prisoner hammered on the walls of his prison for so long, he made a little crack between the first world and the second, just big enough for someone to slip through."

A breach. Toros had been very concerned about breaches.

The Trypophile went on. "People disappeared through that crack, occasionally, and couldn't find their way back, because it narrowed and widened at random. Someone finally marked the spot with standing stones on either side, so people could avoid it. Over time, the crack grew more stable. People knew

it was dangerous there, and avoided the spot, knowing the
realm beyond was dark and inhospitable. My grandmother,
though, was fleeing a... misunderstanding... and the First
World was better than getting executed. She slipped through
the gap, and followed whispers and intuition to the mountain
of fire. In that mountain, in our most sacred place, you can
hear the Prisoner's voice. Actually *hear* him! My grandmother
crept back to the second world and recruited the beginnings
of our congregation, gathering others who wanted a life of
purpose. They settled on the First World and scratched out
a living, growing what crops and keeping what animals we
could, and we raided the second world for food and clothes
and occasional new members. The Prisoner kept pushing...
and soon he opened a crack from the second world to the
third. Oh, what rich pickings we found there! That world had
technology, weapons, strong materials, soft people."

She sighed. "Unfortunately, other cracks opened up there,
leading to different worlds – for whatever reason, the third
world was especially vulnerable to the Prisoner's lashings. All
sorts of nasty things came through, far worse than us. Those
soft people in the third world were smart, though, and when
my mother was still high priest, they found a way to seal the
cracks and cut off their world from casual trespass. That didn't
matter much, though, because soon after I took on the mantle
of Tryphophile, the Prisoner had found a way to reach into the
First World more directly, and offer us the sacrament. When
our missionaries passed through the third world after that,
they always made sure to do some damage, to show them we
couldn't really be stopped. The place was a mess without our
help, but still, one must make an effort."

She was telling me secrets Toros had been trying to learn for
years. I knew the Trypophile was only telling me because she
didn't expect me to live long enough to do anything with the
information, and I got the sense that she liked to gloat. "What,
does it just... rain worms in your world?"

"If only!" she said. "There is a cavern wall in the mountain of fire, with a cluster of small holes. The worms wriggle out of the holes. Not often. The Prisoner is still so terribly bound. But a few come each year, and we gather them, and give them to the devoted. Or the worthless, honestly – people we'd just as soon send away, to be useful in their absence. Every worm contains a bit of the Prisoner's essence – to tear down, to disintegrate, to dissolve. We thought it would take generations and generations to do any substantive damage. Your Minna is going to speed things up nicely."

"She won't help you," I said. "Your plan won't work. My friends will stop you."

"Your friends are scattered on their outposts, or else huddled in the ruins of their hold. I realize you have faith in them… but I put my faith in an actual god, not a bunch of figments, so I think my faith wins."

We traveled through a few worlds. I'd been in a sleepercar before, on the long trip to the Sleeperhold after Ana found me, but the company had been a lot more convivial then. Eventually the Trypophile stopped gloating, and I lost myself in my own thoughts. I was going to be trapped in the First World, but maybe I could escape, do some damage there, disrupt the cult, learn to drive a sleepercar… steal a sleepercar… and a cultist to power it… None of that seemed very likely. I've learned not to give up hope, but I wasn't left with much.

We finally reached the second world, landing on a moor near a pair of lichen-encrusted standing stones, each more than three meters high. They were carved with screaming faces, blurred by the growth and by time, but still visible. It was a blustery day, and overcast, but this place was infinitely more inviting than the haze-reddened First World.

There were scores of worm-trails here, all overlapping. If I transitioned from here, I would certainly follow those well-worn paths to the destination the priest had in mind, and then… cul-de-sac. Box canyon. Dead end.

The Sleeper in the back seat stirred. "Exalted one, we–"

"Quiet," the Trypophile snapped. "We're leaving again in a moment, so I don't need you waking all the way up." She twisted a dial on the console, and the cultist blinked rapidly and then fell asleep. "Out, Zaxony."

I climbed out, and the Trypophile followed. "What now–" I began, and then felt the sting. She'd stabbed me in the arm with a needle, and everything went gray at the edges. "See you on the other side." I couldn't see her smile behind her mask, but I could hear it in her voice.

I woke on my back, on rocky soil, looking up at a reddish sky. I turned my head, and there was the volcano, on the far side of the lake, its base shrouded in gouts of steam. I turned my head the other way, and there were buildings, stone and wood and plastic and glass, all with a cobbled-together, slapdash quality. The homes of the cultists were a lot like their outfits: things scavenged and salvaged and mixed together. I got to my feet. I'd expected to be surrounded by guards, but there was no one in sight – the camp seemed deserted.

The shuttle appeared next to me a moment later, the dome sliding open, and the Trypophile clambered out. She looked around, frowning. "Where are..." Then she glanced at me and stopped talking.

Anything that bothered her was fine by me. "Were you expecting your loyal subjects to meet you? Maybe they didn't get the message."

"Exalted one," the cultist said from the back seat. "You must listen–"

She interrupted. "Get the barbarian out and take her to the holding pen."

Zaveta was still unconscious. They'd either given her a stronger dose of sedative, or underestimated the level of tolerance I'd developed to such drugs.

The Tryphophile continued. "Then take the car to the breach and pick up the Pilgrim – he was going to piggyback to the second world and then walk through, but I don't want to wait for him to hike all the way to camp. We–"

"Exalted one, I had a vision, between the worlds, the Prisoner spoke to me–"

She spun. "To you? Our god spoke to *you*?"

The cultist cringed back against the chariot seat, but nodded. "He said it was important, an emergency, intruders–"

I started to laugh. The Prisoner could see into the worlds, sure, but he was like a general overseeing a battle with no messengers to carry orders! The Prisoner could only tell people what it saw while they were in the void, or if they pressed their ear to a wall in a volcano, and apparently the Trypophile guarded her position as speaker to god jealously.

"Not in front of the captives," the Trypophile snapped at the cultist. "Let's get them locked up, and *then* you can tell me."

"Oh no," I said. "Are things falling apart on you?"

She turned on me, hands clenched into fists. "Shut up, or I'll drug you again. You'll just be unconscious, then, you won't *go* anywhere. How would you like that?"

"A nap without consequences?" I said. "That would be grand. Plus, then you'd have to drag me and Zaveta wherever you're taking us, and it doesn't look like there's anyone around to help you carry us, so… feel free. It's probably been a while since you've done any real work. It'll do you good to put your back into something–"

"Hurry *up*!" the Trypophile shouted. The cultist tried to lift Zaveta out of the chariot, but my friend outweighed her by probably twenty kilograms, so she wasn't making much progress. "Ugh." The Trypophile climbed up too, and together they hauled Zaveta out and dumped her on the ground. "She's not going anywhere for a while. Let's secure Delatree, and then you can give me this message." The Trypophile produced a pistol from beneath her robes and pointed it at me.

"You won't kill me," I said. "You need me as leverage–"

"Minna will still want to save you even if your knees are destroyed. Don't test me."

Fair enough. They marched me through their camp, which was eerily deserted. I could tell the lack of inhabitants was bothering the Trypophile, and that the cultist was dying to tell what she knew, but they weren't going to spill any more secrets in front of me. Apparently I wasn't such a safe audience anymore – not when things were going wrong. I just wish I knew exactly how they were going wrong, so I could help them go even worse.

The Trypophile shoved me into a cell – chain link and cinderblocks, more like something you'd use to pen up an animal than a person. There wasn't even a bucket to relieve myself into. "What if I need to go to the bathroom?" I said.

"Then piss yourself," the Trypophile snapped. She stalked off, dragging the cultist with her.

I banged on the fence. "Hello? Guards? Cultists? Prisoner? Anyone?" I kicked savagely at the fence, making it shake and rattle. I yelled and shouted. No one came to investigate, or even look at me.

OK then. I opened the compartment in my arm and used the last bits of energy in my plasma key to cut the chain that held my gate closed. My key sputtered out before it finished the job, but it weakened the chain enough that a bunch of hard kicks made it give way. Then I pushed my way out and walked back through the camp toward Zaveta.

I didn't see anyone, but I saw signs of people – half-eaten bowls of food, pots hanging over cold cook fires, messy cots. Either the inhabitants had left suddenly, or they were slobs. Maybe both.

The stolen sleepercar was still there, and Zaveta was still sprawled in the dirt beside it. I climbed into the vehicle and retrieved our bags, and Zaveta's cudgel – good, she would have missed that. I dragged Zaveta away from the camp, toward some rocks where we might be able to hide. It was slow going with both our packs hanging off my body, and I was trying to figure out how I could brush out the drag-marks I was leaving in the dirt, when another sleepercar appeared, this one ivory chased with gold. More cultists? Or, dared I hope, Ana?

The dome opened and Toros rose up. "Zax? I thought that was you. Have you seen Ana?"

Did that mean she was still alive? "No, not since the Sleeperhold – what are you doing here?" His arrival was beyond fortuitous.

"I was checking in on the outpost worlds. Since we lost most of our sleepercars it's harder for us to communicate, and I discovered one world had been overrun by the cult. I saw them putting people into a chariot, and it looked like one of the prisoners was *you*, so I followed their trail."

"I'm glad you did. We need to get out of here – the Trypophile, their leader, is nearby, and could return any second. Help me with my friend?"

"Yes, of course." Toros seemed preoccupied. He came down from the chariot, frowning at his surroundings. "Is this their homeworld?"

"They call it the First World," I said.

He laughed, a slightly unhinged sound. "But… it's so squalid. I don't know what I expected. A giant cathedral, statues of worms, a great wet hive full of toothy holes, *something*, not… this." He ran a hand through his hair. "I tried to come to this world once before, but I was fired on by autocannons, even in stealth mode. There must be sensors that detect air displacement or something. When I saw them take you, though, I thought, I had to try again…" He pointed to poles I hadn't really noticed before, spaced around the camp, bristling with sensors and guns. "Maybe they took their weapons offline, so their own chariot wouldn't trigger them, though you'd think they'd be able to–"

I understood he was stunned at finding the object of so

much effort, but I needed him to focus. "Toros. We can talk about all that later. We have to go."

"Ah. Yes." Toros helped me haul Zaveta into the back seat of the chariot, putting her beside the dozing Sleeper – Durio, I think his name was. I got into the sleepercar as well, but Toros hurried to the Trypophile's chariot and rummaged around underneath it, removing a cylinder with trailing wires. "They won't be able to leave without this. It links the traveler's diadem to the propulsion and navigation system. I just turned their trans-dimensional chariot into an ordinary everyday hover-car." He grinned and got back into the chariot with me. "I'm glad we found you, Zax," he said. "But we *really* need to find Ana. Once we do… we can finally finish this." The dome closed, and we traveled into the dark.

Toros told me the Sleeperhold was only a few dozen worlds away – by the direct route they now knew how to follow, anyway – but we didn't have to go that far, just half a dozen hops. Still, we had some time to catch up in the space between worlds, while Zaveta and Durio snored behind us.

First, I asked Toros to tell me about the attack on the Sleeperhold – I hadn't seen much of it – especially who'd lived and who'd died. He knew for sure that Minna and Vicki had escaped in one sleepercar, and Ana and Sorlyn in another. Colubra and Winsome were alive, too, and on the outpost world we were visiting. "I'm afraid the Pilgrim… it seems he…"

"He turned on you," I said. "I know. I ran into him, and he told me. He did it for God. I'm so sorry we brought him to your home, Toros. He fought alongside us against the Lector, and I thought he was trustworthy, but he was more of a fanatic than I realized, and the cult convinced him their god was *his* God…"

"I understand," Toros said. "I'm upset, of course, but… we've had other traitors, including ones *I* brought in. That said… Tell me about your new friend." He jerked his head toward the back.

"That's Zaveta of the Broken Wheel. A warrior."

"We can use those. How did she come to join you?"

"Cultists infected her whole village. She wants to save them. Failing that, to avenge them."

"A motivation I can respect," Toros said. "And probably one that makes her unlikely to betray us. Good enough." He saw how downcast I was, and said, "You had plenty of good companions, Zax. Winsome, Minna, Vicki, and Ana, of course."

"What did you mean before, about finding Ana, and finally finishing this?"

Toros seemed to consider for a moment, then said, "Did I ever tell you how and why I founded the Sleepers?"

I shook my head.

"My home world is close to the cult's – I honestly had no idea *how* close until today. I thought that world we rescued you from was just one of their outposts. My home wasn't quite as advanced as your Realm of Spheres and Harmonies, but we had a high standard of living, and sophisticated technology – our late engineer, Gibberne, came from there. But when I was a child… things started to go wrong. First, people started to disappear – from cities, the country, everywhere. Then things *bigger* than people began to vanish. There's video footage, famous on my world, of a train just disappearing in the middle of the track, like it drove into an invisible tunnel. Then there was a plague that caused a whole city of people to mutate into… hungry, scrabbling things." Toros stared at the blackness of the dome. "Then, the monsters came. Predators from another world. Immense lizards with armored bodies, and it took whole battalions to bring one down. Then came other predators, bigger than us, humanoid but covered in armor plates, with claws that could shred steel, but they were intelligent, organized…"

"They all came through breaches." Toros was from the third world the Trypophile had told me about.

"Yes. I think the cult caused the cracks – we found evidence of their presence on our world, too. There were stories about

savage people who attacked from thin air, raiding our world…
That's how I know what this cult is capable of. We managed
to seal the breaches, eventually. Gibberne was young then, a
junior scientist on the team that did the work. I don't pretend
to understand the science. They made a bomb. A series of
bombs. When one of them goes off, it seals the connections
between worlds – burns them, really, scars them shut. But the
consequences… they're catastrophic for the whole surrounding
area. And we had so *many* breaches. Have you ever heard of
the cure being worse than the disease? Well. My homeworld
isn't very nice anymore. That's why so many of my cousins
were happy to emigrate and join my work." The anguish in his
face was genuine. "I wish I understood *why* the cult wants to
destroy all the worlds the way they did mine."

I rubbed my forehead. "I know why. I know their reasons. I
know about their god."

He looked at me, his eyes wide and somehow fevered. "Tell
me."

"The cultists didn't make those breaches in your world,
Toros, though they did take advantage of them. The damage
was caused by the thing the cultists worship…"

Toros took in the revelation that his real enemy was a
malevolent cosmic entity about as well as anyone could. After
asking a lot of follow-up questions and satisfying himself that I
wasn't insane, he frowned for a while, and then shrugged. "It
doesn't change anything, practically speaking. The worms only
come from their so-called First World. Whether their source is
a bubbling vat or an alien god is irrelevant. The solution is the
same."

"What solution?"

"I told everyone I wanted to make a wall, to trap the cultists
and stop their spread. I did. But that was just the first part of
the plan." He gazed at me, and smiled. I remember that smile
now, as I write this, and it makes me shudder. "The second part
is to exterminate the cultists and destroy the First World."

Ana

Sorlyn and I transitioned into a dusty lot, next to a building made from the inverted hull of a ship – some kind of feasting hall, judging by the drunken, burly humans stumbling around outside it holding drinking horns and flagons. There were carts and carriages nearby, so we decided it was safe to roll in without stealth. For the locals who noticed us, our vessel was unusual and fancy, but not particularly alien.

We were on our own again, there at the end of the trail, just as we'd begun. Tòros and Durio had stayed behind on the battle site to make sure the serum was really gone. "I also don't want to intrude on your big reunion," Toros told me with a grin.

Three worm-trails disappeared into the feasting hall, one of them Zax's, the other two smooth – Minna and someone else, another companion we hadn't heard about yet? I'd listened to enough drunken boasting for my linguistic virus to start working, so I snagged the attention of a passing man in a leather apron who looked like he was headed inside. "Hey," I said. "Could you do me a favor? Ask if there's a Zaxony Delatree inside."

He looked me up and down and grinned. "Lucky man. Who should I say is asking?"

I thought about that. Then I said, "Tell him it's the long lost love of his life."

The man chuckled. "Lucky indeed." He strode into the hall.

We waited a few minutes. I arranged myself carefully against the chariot, trying to appear all poised and nonchalant, though I was anything but. How would *you* act if you were about to see a man who'd swept you off your feet, and out of your world, after years spent apart?

Sorlyn snorted at me. "You're acting like a teenage–"

"Shush," I said.

"Did you bring that outfit this whole way just so you'd look nice when–"

"Did you not hear me say 'shush'?"

He settled back into the chariot and closed his eyes. "Wake me when you and Zax have finished making big eyes at each other."

"So, never, then?"

He pretended to snore.

After a few moments, a man stepped out of the hall. Disheveled, dusty, hesitant… but Zax. *Really* Zax, this time. He approached me, with Minna a couple of steps behind him on one side, and an immense figure in a hooded robe matching her pace on the other.

I looked a lot better than Zax did: I'd put on a black linen shirt and a skirt that stopped above the knee, and dark boots with silver buckles. (The Sleepers were almost as indifferent to fashion as the cultists, so I'd picked up the ensemble on a world we'd surveyed a while back… and, yes, I'd brought it all this way for just this occasion.) I'd brushed my hair, and even put on makeup. Zax had fallen for me when I was in work clothes in my backyard, but why not make a good impression? Besides, I wasn't just here as myself, but as a representative of the Sleepers, and I wanted us to look like we had our shit together.

Zax got closer, and I smiled, the warmest and truest smile I'd had on my face in years. He stared at me, clearly stunned by my existence, and, I hoped, by my hotness. He'd gotten leaner and stronger during his journey, and it looked awfully good on him.

I spoke in Realmspeech. "Hello, Zax. I'm sorry it took me so long to reach out. We couldn't risk approaching you while the mad professor was still in pursuit – there are things we have to tell you that are way too dangerous for him to know." OK, and also, we were always three steps behind, but, again, I was trying to project the illusion of hyper-competency here.

"Ana?" Yeah, he was definitely stunned. "Is that... How are you here, how are you alive, how are you sane?"

"You aren't the only wanderer through the worlds, Zax." I stepped toward him, and took his hands... and then glanced at Minna, and Sorlyn's voice was in my head like a whisper: *Do you think...?* "Are you two, ah... together? I don't mean to overstep... We've caught a few glimpses of you in the past few dozen worlds, but I wasn't sure..."

"What? No, we're not, I mean, Ana – Ana. It's *you*."

"It's *her*?" That voice seemed to come from a ring on Minna's finger: Vicki, then.

Minna said, "Shh, let this be beautiful," and I decided right then and there that we were going to be friends.

"It's me." I decided to go for it. I stepped in close, and kissed him, and he was right there with me, kissing me back, just as deep. It was like time travel; like the day we first met all over again, but with a happier ending this time, I hoped.

It still worked. We still worked. We could *make* it work.

Then I took a step back, looked Zax up and down, and kicked the wheel of the sleepercar. Sorlyn pretended to wake up, blinking and peering around. "Oh," he said vaguely. "We're here."

"Zax, meet Sorlyn. He's my Sleeper."

"Your... Ana. What is going on?"

"More than you know. Let's go inside and get a drink. You can introduce me to your friends. Then we need to have a conversation." I sighed. "About holes in the space between the worlds." I sighed again. "And about the things coming *through* those holes, and their intentions." A third sigh. "And about what we're going to do about them." That was a little heavy, I know, and Zax had been through a lot, so I gave him my true warm smile again, powered by the great big ocean of feelings inside me. "I bet you're wide awake *now*, aren't you, Zax?"

I looped my arm through his, and we went to the bar, Sorlyn drifting along after, falling into step beside Minna. "I'm so pleased to meet you," I heard him murmur. "I think you're simply amazing."

"I am?" Minna said, as if considering the possibility for the first time.

I couldn't tell Zax everything right away – "everything" was just too much, and honestly, that's half of why I'm writing all this down, so he can finally get the whole story of what happened to me, the bits between "lovers parted" and "lovers reunited". But I snuggled up against him at the table and told him the basics: "Sorlyn's group, the Sleepers, they look for travelers like you, and stranded companions like me, and help us. Their leader, Toros found me in that terrible silent city. I was pretty messed up, but he gave me a lot of therapy, and put me back together again. We've been looking for you... well, ever since, basically, but we were way behind once I got my head on straight, and there were setbacks and injuries... and then we ran up against the Lector and his stupid Moveable Empire, and things got *really* complicated..."

"Everything seems much simpler now." Zax gazed at me like I was a miracle. "I can't believe this, Ana. I thought I lost you. And you're... you're OK. I know, you've been through a lot, but–"

"Hey. We both have." I touched his cheek. "We made it through. We're here now. Together. And I intend for us to stay that way."

Then we all got drunk. (Except Vicki, and maybe Minna, though with her, it's hard to tell.) Zax had some gold in his pockets, and the wait staff kept us awash in mead and ale and small cups of eye-wateringly powerful, vaguely apple-scented liquor. Sorlyn flirted with Minna, in his own understated deadpan way, and every single bit of woo he pitched sailed right over her head, completely unnoticed. She was happy to chat with him, though, explaining all about how she'd changed her blood and altered her brain and then altered *Zax's* brain so they only slept when they wanted to. Total game-changers, just dropped in casual conversation over drinks. Vicki and the Pilgrim talked about space battles and tactics, as best I could tell. Mostly I was... well, making big eyes at Zax, and him at me. We rambled a bit at each other, but mostly, we just touched; reassuring each other that we were *here*, we were *real*, this was really happening, hands clasped together the way we wanted our lives to be.

Someone discreetly coughed, and I looked around to see– "Toros! Everyone, meet the person who saved my life." I introduced him to the others – Minna was bubbly, the Pilgrim solemn, Zax adorably intoxicated. The Sleeper leader was patient, as usual, and helped us outside. "I am too drunk to drive!" I declared loudly. Minna said, "Oh, you could eat this," and offered me what looked like a berry. I already trusted Minna implicitly just from seeing her on tape and knowing how she'd vexed the Lector, so I popped it into my mouth without hesitation.

That berry was like an ice bath for my brain. Seconds later I was standing bolt upright, blinking. "I... What *was* that?"

"It helps you metabolize alcohol better," Minna said. "But only for a little bit. People don't always want to metabolize alcohol better *all* the time."

"I can sleep fine drunk." Sorlyn climbed into the chariot. "Minna, would you like to sit beside me?"

"See, Minna?" Vicki said from her finger. "I told you, he is infatuated with you. The signs are clear. I have made a study of these matters."

"I did not think I would ever take a mate again," Minna said thoughtfully. "The last time, it was arranged by the Farm, for purposes of exceptional breeding. The way some of these other worlds do things is very interesting and strange though…" She climbed into the back.

"You're up front with me, Zax." I guided him into the chariot, and looked at the Pilgrim. "Do you want to come with us?"

"These marvelous conveyances can travel to new worlds, yes?" he said. I'd finally gotten a glimpse of the Pilgrim's face under the hood: he was some kind of humanoid lion, his voice a powerful rumble. "Then, yes. I need to see more worlds. I am looking for someone."

"Toros, could you take him?"

"Of course, there's plenty of room." Toros guided the Pilgrim to his chariot.

I heard the Pilgrim say – and this feels so ominous, in retrospect – "Tell me, Toros. Do your people believe in God?"

We traveled. Zax snuggled up against me. It was a long trip, made longer by the fact that Zax and Minna wanted to stop in the inhabited worlds the Lector had conquered. Toros chafed at the delay, but he wanted their help, and had little choice but to indulge them – to an extent.

The Lector's banners were mostly fallen by then. The Moveable Empire was unable to sustain itself in developed worlds once reinforcements arrived from beyond areas the Lector had "conquered". In less developed worlds, local warlords still ruled in the Lector's name, but their control was clearly tenuous. In a couple of the more egregious cases, I wore my shimmersuit and snatched those mind-controlling crowns off the Lector's seneschals, leaving them befuddled and vulnerable.

Zax always wanted to stay longer and do more – clear rubble, deliver medicine, rebuild houses, aid the resistance fighters – but Toros convinced him that making haste back to Sleeperhold and defeating the cult would do more good in the long run. Having Zax and Minna on our side tilted the field in our favor, but taking out the cult once and for all would still require time and preparation. I suggested Toros go on ahead to get things started, but he was reluctant to leave us, I think for fear we'd lose Zax and Minna. Fair enough. We'd gone to a lot of trouble to find them.

Along the way, Sorlyn and Toros took measurements and noted breaches. There were a few, but none in heavily populated areas, and the ones that were big enough for people to pass through we blocked off with rocks or rubble as best we could. Maybe the tears would heal on their own eventually. We had no idea how that sort of thing worked.

Zax and I enjoyed a lot of stolen kisses, and as much more as we could manage. We were just as hungry for each other and in synch as we'd ever been before. I had a deeper appreciation for Zax from following him all that time. He had a deeper appreciation for me because I *had* followed.

In between worlds, I told Zax about the cult, and he realized that the woman who'd died in his arms back on the Realm of Spheres and Harmonies must have been a traveler, and passed her parasite onto him. I could tell that was a weight off him, just to *know*, even if we still didn't know *why* the cult was spreading the worms.

One thing we didn't do was talk about the future. What we'd do when we got to the Sleeperhold. What we'd do if and when we vanquished the cult. We stayed in the now. We just did the work, and it was good work.

Eventually, though, we got home, and soon after that, everything changed for the worse.

* * *

Colubra was in charge while Toros was gone, and while she ran things with total competence, she just kept Toros's initiatives going, so there was a sense of treading water. The outpost worlds were well stocked and seemed to be well defended, but we hadn't made any more progress against the cult. The Pilgrim and Vicki offered to discuss defenses and security – and, it was implied, attack plans – with Toros, and they all disappeared together for hours on end, deep in their war councils.

Zax was delighted to see Winsome again, too, and they spent a long afternoon catching up. I saw Zax's heart heal a little more with every passing day.

Minna talked to Colubra about the things *she* could do, and soon every traveler who wanted to underwent the same procedure Zax had: they could stay awake indefinitely, shutting down one hemisphere of their brains at a time rather than fully losing consciousness, and with practice, they could choose to sleep at will. The procedure involved a period of delirium as their neural architecture got rewritten, which scared a couple of travelers off, but most thought it was worthwhile.

The linguistic virus also got passed around, and Zax was a good sport as Colubra studied his body, examining the various augmentations the Lector had given him, many of which she believed she could reproduce.

We tried to keep word of the Lector's serum, and the fact that Minna had altered her own blood so she could travel without a parasite, secret, but… it was a lost cause. Not because of Minna – she could be a chatterbox, but she'd also run covert operations against the Lector, so she knew how to maintain operational security. Durio was indiscreet, though, so soon rumors started to circulate in the camp, much to Toros's dismay. If word about Minna's capabilities got back to the cult… well. He was planning to strike hard against the cult as soon as he'd made the proper preparations anyway, and that was just more motivation to do so quickly.

Whenever Zax wasn't being poked, prodded, or questioned

about his travels, we spent time in a little cottage by the lake, only emerging to get meals. One day we were sitting in the cafeteria when Durio sat down beside us, slamming his tray onto the table. "I thought she'd be able to cure us! I want this worm out of me!"

"Who are we talking about?" I said.

He jerked a thumb at Zax. "His friend, Minna. She's supposed to be this amazing biological genius, but she says she can't remove the worm!"

"You had the procedure, didn't you?" Zax said. "You can stay awake, so you don't have to travel anymore if–"

"There is a *parasite inside me*," Durio said. "Don't you understand? There's one inside you too! It's disgusting! I lay awake at night, shuddering, I swear I can feel it slithering through my blood. But Minna says, oh, the worm lives in other dimensions, we can't pull it out – well, why not? The cult put it in, so there's got be a way to expel it." He shook his head. "Disappointing. It's all so disappointing."

I rolled my eyes. "I'm sorry the *two* miracles you have been given aren't enough for you."

Durio stood up again. "You uninfected can't possibly understand." He stormed off.

"Don't mind him," I said. "He's a minority view. Everyone is thrilled with what you and Minna have given us."

"Toros thinks Minna's gifts can turn the tide against the cult," Zax said. "He has plans to infiltrate, find out their goals, track them to their homeworld, find a way to stop them... If we can understand them, we might be able to reason with them, too, you know?"

"No infiltration for you, though." I took his hand. "You've done enough, OK? I have, too. You spent years out there, and so did I. I brought you back, and you brought treasures back. We get to just be us, for a while. We've both earned a break."

He kissed me, and then pulled away, and said, "I love this... but I have to help out. It was bad enough when I thought it was just *me* torn from my home and sent spinning through worlds. Now I know the cult has done it to countless others. If I can help stop them, I have to do my part."

I sighed. "I knew you'd say something like that. And I love you for it. But let's be self-indulgent for a little bit longer?"

In the end, it *was* only a little bit longer. We'd only been on Sleeperhold for a few weeks when I saw the Pilgrim slip into the geodesic dome that housed the security system and surveillance controls. That wasn't so strange – the Pilgrim and Vicki had more tactical knowledge than the rest of us put together, and they'd been giving Toros advice on our defenses – but it was late, and there was something furtive about his movements, like he didn't want to be seen. I was only out and about myself at that hour because Zax and I had gotten distracted and forgotten dinner, and I'd gone to the kitchens to get us some fruit and bread and cheese.

I hadn't spent a lot of time with the Pilgrim, but there was an intensity about him that I found slightly offputting. It occurred to me that night that the Pilgrim was a zealot, someone who'd traveled with a whole sect of people like him on a starship, looking for the literal, physical home of God. Weren't people like that likely to be... sort of... susceptible to cults? Hadn't he kind of been in a cult already, in a way?

I crept toward the security dome, and ducked inside. The door to the command center was standing open. I started to call out... and then saw a pool of blood spreading from the door. Shit shit shit. I had my staff – I kept it on my belt at all times, since Polly – and I snapped it out to its full length.

I moved, cat quiet, toward the command room, wishing for my shimmersuit. The guards on watch, a pair of Toros's cousins, were dead on the floor, their heads at impossible angles, necks clearly broken. They'd died meters away from me, and I hadn't heard a sound. I said I was cat quiet, but the Pilgrim was an *actual* cat, a predator by ancestry and a killer by training.

He was standing at the console, not just shutting things down, but sabotaging them – pulling out wires, prying open consoles, removing components. He'd helped improve our defenses... which meant he knew exactly how to disable them.

There was only one reason to do that. An attack was coming.

I struck at him with my staff, triggering the inertial generators, intending to hit him hard enough to break his shoulder and smash him to the floor.

I didn't want to kill him. I wanted to question him.

I should have just shot him, and ended his life. That might not have helped things, since by then the damage was done, but it would have made me feel better.

The Pilgrim heard something – the whoosh of the staff, the click of the button, who knows? He ducked, faster than I could believe, and spun, and swatted my staff out of my hands. I didn't try to fight after that, because I knew I wouldn't have a chance. I bolted, sure I was dead anyway – he had to be faster than me.

But he didn't chase me. He let me go. I didn't know why, then, but now I do: it's because my escape didn't matter. I was too late to do anything about it. I started to shout, to scream an alarm... but then a lot of people started shouting, all over the hold.

Cultists poured into the camp from the trees, armed with *our* guns. They must have overtaken one of the outposts on an adjacent world, waited until some predetermined time, and then slept their way here, en masse.

I thought immediately of Minna and Colubra's lab. The linguistic virus. The seeds Minna used to rewrite neural architecture. I couldn't let the cult get their hands on those. I rushed toward the lab, in time to see Colubra seal the doors. "We are under attack," she buzzed. "I am sanitizing the lab so the intruders cannot access our information."

"Good idea," I said. "Do you know where Toros is?"

"I will search for him. You should help with the evacuation."

I wanted to run back to Zax, but our cottage was halfway around the lake, and... if he were here, in my place, I knew exactly what he'd do. He'd help people. I could do the same.

I went for the shuttle. It was a sleepercar, but writ large. The familiar, spherical shape of our chariot was there, but integrated into the cockpit of something with a huge rectangular storage area in the back. Sorlyn was already in the garage. "Ana! Good, you're all right. I need you to secure the sleepercars, and then send any staff you encounter here, so I can get them off-world."

I nodded, and spun right back around. He was right. The sleepercars would be even more valuable to the cult than Minna's innovations. It hadn't occurred to me that the cultists could operate the chariots... but they had spies here. Someone could have taught them.

I raced to the corral, and ran into Minna, who was running toward the sound of shouting, of course. She was in terrible danger, if the cult knew what she was capable of, and we had to assume they did. "Take one of the cars!" I shouted. I knew she'd trained with Vicki to drive it, and the ruby twinkled on her finger. "So the cult can't get it, or get their hands on *you*! We'll meet in the next world!"

Minna looked toward the flames leaping in camp, bit her lip, and then nodded. She climbed into the green-and-blue chariot, and flickered away.

I looked at the other sleepercars, all lined up. A few were gone, out on missions or in outpost worlds, but most were there. Secure them, Sorlyn said. How was I supposed to secure them?

In the end, I settled for sabotage. Better to break them than let the cult take them. The easiest thing was just ripping out the wires and destroying the diadems that let sleepers integrate with the propulsion system. Maybe the cult could drive the chariots, but I was willing to bet they couldn't repair them.

I was about to disable the last chariot, the purple one, when someone kicked me in the knee and knocked me down. I rolled over, and screamed, because the person leaning over me didn't have a face, just a series of holes where the face should be, and it was like seeing the space between worlds in human form.

Then I realized it was just a mask. The woman with the lotus pod face pointed a gun at me, and I scrambled away, running, as she laughed. I looked back in time to see a cultist climbing into the back of the sleepercar. Other cultists swarmed around the sleepercars, and I felt a thrill of joy at their coming disappointment. I ducked behind a pile of scrap metal and watched as the purple car disappeared. The cultists realized the others weren't usable... and then they tossed grenades into the chariots and ran away. I turned away, reflexively, from the explosions.

I kept running. Everything was screaming and fire. I'd done what I could. I had to find Zax. I had to–

A cultist stepped into my path and punched me in the face. I went down, hitting my head hard, everything black and swimmy at the edges. The cultist laughed, and raised his boot to stomp on me – and then a beam of energy disintegrated his upper body. His lower half, one leg still raised, fell over into the dirt.

Sorlyn grabbed my arm and hauled me upright. There was a gleaming silver sidearm in his other hand. "Come on. We have to go, before they find the shuttle."

"Zax," I said, my voice slushy.

"Zax survived a thousand worlds," Sorlyn said. "He'll be OK."

I know now that Sorlyn carried me to the shuttle, but I can't remember it.

It turned out, I was the only person he managed to get into the vehicle and off-world that night.

Sanctuary Moon • Zaveta Wakes Up
• Enter Vicki and Minna • Tactically
Sound • Rusting Radio Telescopes • The
Wormwood • An Ultimatum

"Destroy the First World," I said carefully. "How will you do that, exactly?"

Toros was happy to share his plans. "Gibberne created a breach-sealing bomb before he died, the biggest ever constructed. It's locked away in a vault back in the ruins of the Sleeperhold. I'll take the bomb to their cursed world, and I'll set it off. Gibberne theorized that the bomb would ignite the atmosphere there and tear through the entire planet, sealing every breach. They never made bombs this big on *our* world – they would have killed everyone. Our weapon will render the First World radioactive, poisonous, and uninhabitable for millions of years." Toros was almost giddy. "Don't you see, Zax? The cult will be gone, no longer capable of spreading their vile worms. Any breaches leading to First World will be *sealed*, so no one can sneak or stumble in again. And no traveler like you will ever transition there either, because travelers can't go to a world that won't sustain life! We'll finally be safe. Everyone will be safe. This Prisoner of theirs can keep whispering, but there won't be anyone left to hear him. We'll seal him up, too."

"That's... quite a plan, Toros." He wanted to murder the whole cult and nuke their planet. That was not the sort of solution that appealed to me. "I've talked to some of these cultists, though. They're deluded, and dangerous, but they've been deceived by the Prisoner and their leadership–"

"They pledged their fealty to an evil god who wants to destroy reality, Zax. Ana warned me about your terminal case of empathy, but surely even *you* can see this is an extreme situation. Either we kill them, or we risk them killing everyone."

"It's very serious, certainly, but–"

"I wasn't asking for your approval," Toros said stiffly. "That is simply what's happening. As soon as I find Ana."

"Why do you need her?" I couldn't believe she would support this plan any more than I did.

"Because she took the shuttle!" He banged his fist on the console. "We have a few other sleepercars, recovered from outposts and returning agents, but they're too small for transport. The breach bomb is huge, and I can't dismantle it, because I don't know how to put it back together again. Without the shuttle, we can't transport it – Ana and Sorlyn took the only transdimensional vehicle big enough to hold the thing."

"That's unfortunate," I said, as blandly as possible.

Toros took us to an outpost the Sleepers still controlled, transitioning into a high-walled circular space open to the air. We were on a moon. I could tell, because the planet, a gas giant swirling with beautiful purple and white clouds, filled a quarter of the sky. "Are there native people here?" I asked.

"Our survey found a few things with spinal cords in the ocean, but that's about as far as complex life has developed here. We have the place to ourselves." He opened the dome. The air was thin but breathable. The round walls reminded me of Zaveta's arena, but there were cameras and sensors here, and guns mounted on the walls. "Security," Toros said when he noticed me noticing. "This is one of our strongest outposts.

Anything that transitions through here, in stealth or not, will be seen."

He woke up Durio, and they helped me carry Zaveta toward a sort of airlock, and then into a tunnel complex. Colubra was here, as promised, and she helped me get Zaveta onto an exam table in a side room outfitted as an infirmary. "The cultists drugged her," I said.

"Breathing is good, heart rate is good," Colubra buzzed through her artificial voicebox. "I could give her stimulants, but I think she's likely to wake on her own soon."

"I'll sit with her." I pulled up a chair and took Zaveta's hand.

Toros hovered by the door. "Do you have any idea where Ana might be, Zax?"

"I have no idea. I haven't seen her since the night of the attack." That night I'd been in our cottage, stretched out in bed, perfectly relaxed, waiting for Ana to come back with a late snack, since we'd had better things to do during dinner. Then I heard the screaming, and rushed to the camp, where cultists were running amok. I tried to help people escape, even snatching up a gun from an inert robot sentry... and then someone or something cracked me on the back of the head. I woke up in another world, and had no way to get back. There were cultists there too, and dead Sleepers – I took my spectacles from a corpse of an unknown colleague, and just kept running until things calmed down, and I found a trail to follow. "I didn't even know for sure Ana was alive until you told me so."

"She got away in the shuttle, with Sorlyn, the night of the attack," he said. "She came back, the next day, when the survivors regrouped. We tried to make a plan for battle, and then... Ana and Sorlyn left in the shuttle, without telling anyone. I honestly thought they'd gone to look for you."

"If so, they didn't find me. But there were dozens of possible trails to follow from the Sleeperhold, and I got farther away every day."

"They knew I needed that shuttle. They could have taken one of the other cars…" He shook his head. "Maybe they were afraid you were in the First World. Maybe they didn't want me to set off the bomb, in case it killed you too, but would they be that selfish?"

"Is wanting to avoid casualties selfish?"

Toros sighed. "You joined this effort, Zax. You knew the stakes. Do you mean to tell me you wouldn't sacrifice yourself to save every living thing in all creation? Because I would."

"I'd be willing to sacrifice myself, absolutely," I said. "But what you're talking about is sacrificing *other* people, Toros."

He turned and stomped off. I sighed, and held Zaveta's hand, and waited.

I wasn't dozing – I can't do *that* – but I was a little zoned out when Zaveta stirred, and turned her head to me. "Zax? Did we escape the cult?"

I leaned forward. "We did. We're safe. We're with friends." The first statement was true; the others were at least true-ish.

"I saw the Prisoner again," she said. "He was raging. He told me to tell you, there would be no more mercy, no more offers to cooperate – if we don't obey him, he'll have us killed on sight." She smiled. "When an enemy general starts to shout that way, it means the battle is turning in your favor. I think things are falling apart in the Prisoner's camp. I don't know why, exactly. He was cursing about Ana and Minna and how they wouldn't stay still, how he could see everything, but he couldn't see everything all at once."

"He can't just tell them what he sees, either," I said. "At least, I don't think so. They have to go to this cavern on their homeworld, where he whispers, or he can talk to them in the void, but that's it. It's not like he can call them on a radio or send a messenger bird."

Zaveta chuckled. "A general with such poor lines of

communication is a weak one. What matter if he sees, when he cannot *tell* what he sees? The Prisoner may be something like a god, but he is not all-knowing and all-seeing. Greater than us, but not as much greater as he thinks."

"Yes, that is our assessment also," Vicki said.

I stood up, and Zaveta sat up, reaching for her cudgel, but that was leaning against the wall in the corner instead of hanging at her belt. "It's OK," I said. "I know that voice."

"I have looped the surveillance of this room," Vicki said, still not visible. "Those watching will just see Zax sitting and holding this charming newcomer's hand. Hello. I am Vastcool Class Crystal Intellect Three Three Three, sometimes called Victory-Three, or simply–"

"Vicki," Zaveta said. "The magic talking ring. I am Zaveta of the Broken Wheel. Where *are* you?"

Minna stepped forward, wearing muddy overalls, her hair all mussed, Vicki twinkling on her finger. I blinked, because it wasn't like she *appeared* – she was always there, and I just hadn't noticed her. "Zax!" Her voice was an excited whisper. "I learned to be sneaky, extra sneaky, the way Sorlyn is." She looked at Zaveta and curtsied – I don't know where she picked *that* up – and said, "I am very much pleased to meet you."

"Oh, same to you, sneaky one."

Minna's fundamental gift is adaptation – she can study life, examine its attributes, and alter herself as necessary. I knew Sorlyn had some natural psychic camouflage, and now, Minna had it, too. I rushed to her, picked her up, and spun her around, hugging her close, while she giggled in my ear. "I was afraid I'd never see you again. I should have known you'd find a way. You always do." I set her down and frowned. "Why are you sneaking around?"

"Toros wants to murder all the wormy people and blow up their home," Minna said. "Ana and Sorlyn and me and Vicki thought there must be a better way, so we all sort of… ran off on our own... and we don't think Toros would be happy to see us again."

"To clarify," Vicki said, "I was fine with exterminating the malevolent cultists bent on destroying reality. I did, however, agree there might be tactically sound approaches that involved... less murder... and offered to help explore them."

"We saw you on the First World, Zax," Minna said. "I was going to rescue you, but then you rescued yourself, and Toros rescued you the rest of the way, so I just followed you back here. It took me a little while to sneak all the way in – *people* don't usually see me, except robot people, but cameras can, and Vicki has been tricking the mechanical eyes as we go."

I frowned. "How did you even get here? Toros has that whole weird coliseum airlock thing to trap travelers."

"Oh, just a simple tweak of the safety control parameters," Vicki said. "You know how the sleepercars have failsafes to stop them from appearing in places that are too small for them to fit, even if that's the natural entry point to a new world for travelers?"

"I do now," I said.

"Ah. Well, yes, if the entry area is too small, the chariot appears in the nearest possible location that has sufficient space. I simply extended our sleepercar's safe distance allowance to a kilometer in every direction. As a result, we couldn't appear in this facility at all, and so we entered this world high in the air above the camp. We used the same technique to avoid the autocannons and sentries in the First World and the surrounding cultist outposts–"

Minna said, "Maybe all that later. Leaving now?"

"Oh, yes, of course. Zax – we've been working with Ana. Will you come with us, and join her?"

That sounded good to me. I looked at Zaveta. "Are you ready to travel?"

"I have never felt more rested." She swung her legs out of bed, and picked up her pack and her cudgel from the corner. "There. Do I need to hit anything on the way out?"

"We'll keep the option open," I said.

Vicki could interface remotely with just about any kind of technology, and guided us out along a circuitous route to avoid people. The ranks of the Sleepers had thinned out in the attack, and were spread even more thin now, so it wasn't difficult to pass unnoticed. Most of the defenses were automated, and Vicki sorted those out. The Sleepers had access to high-tech gear, but Vicki was on a whole other level.

We made it to a corridor that led to a side gate, where one of Toros's cousins stood, looking out a barred window, his back to us. Zaveta gripped her cudgel, but I touched her arm.

The guard put a finger to his ear, then turned and loped off down another passageway. "I spoofed an emergency call into his earpiece," Vicki said. "But we should leave quickly, because once he realizes there's no emergency, this place will go on alert."

We opened the door – thank goodness for electronic locks; a big padlock would have caused us more trouble – and escaped the facility. The terrain was rolling hills spotted with reddish grass, so the whole moon looked blood-spattered. There was no cover or concealment anywhere in sight, so creeping along was pointless – we sprinted instead, in the direction Minna indicated.

An alarm started wailing, and I looked back to see small hovering objects rise up from the walls and fly toward us.

"Drones," Zaveta said. "I *hate* drones."

"Vicki, can you handle those?"

"I can," Vicki said. "But their weapons systems aren't even online, so they pose no danger."

One of the drones buzzed toward us, and an amplified voice emerged: Toros. "Zax, Minna, what are you doing?"

"The best we can!" I shouted, and then Minna's sleepercar shimmered into view, uncloaked. We scrambled inside, Minna quickly donning the diadem, and the dome closed. The drone hovered just outside, and though I know it's just some sort of psychological projection, I swear the machine looked confused, dispirited… even betrayed.

The dome went black, and we left that world for the space between.

"Vicki," I said. "Ana's really OK?"

"She was the last time we saw her, which was just this morning, so I assume so, though I cannot say for sure."

"What have you all been doing?"

"Toros wants to detonate a special sort of bomb in the First World," Vicki said.

"Oh, yes. He told me."

"It was a tactically sound idea when Toros conceived it, and remains so, even now that we have a greater understanding of the nature of the cult. We can't possibly fight the Prisoner. We can't even reach the place where the Prisoner actually lives in order *to* fight it, because being conscious in that void is detrimental to sanity. We can only repair the cracks in the monster's prison. In theory, this bomb would seal the breaches, isolating the First World, and cutting off the Prisoner from the worlds beyond. The drawback, of course, is the death of some unknown number of cultists in the process."

"That's a big drawback, Vicki."

"They knew what they were getting into," Zaveta said from the back seat. "When you declare war on everything, you have to be prepared for everything to fight back."

"I tend to concur," Vicki said.

"I like you, magic ring," Zaveta said.

"The cultists were tricked," I said. "Raised by parents who were tricked. Those cultists were indoctrinated from childhood with the idea that no one else in the universe, in all the universes, is even real. I'm not saying none of this is their fault – individuals still made choices – but there are mitigating circumstances, and those have to be taken into account before we just execute them all!"

"Ana felt the same way," Vicki said. "Or, to be more

accurate… she said she knew *you* would feel that way. When she isn't sure whether some choice is right or not, she asks herself – would Zax do it?"

I couldn't help but laugh. "Vicki, I screw things up all the time, in all sorts of ways."

"Arguable, but even if true, you always mean well, and think through the reasons for your actions," Vicki said. "Ana knew you wouldn't consent to killing the cultists, so she decided she shouldn't, either. So she convinced Sorlyn to try something else."

"What?"

"Resettlement," Vicki said. "Speaking of, Ana asked us to pick a straggler up on our way…"

We appeared above an array of immense, rusting radio telescopes. Houses had been built inside the immense dishes, but they all looked abandoned. The ground far below was *moving*, a series of irregular dark ripples. "Is that an ocean down there?"

"Bugs," Vicki said. "Some sort of flesh-eating beetle, we think. That layer of scuttling life down there is approximately a meter deep. The infestation drove the people of this world to climb high – the beetles have some aversion to metal, so they don't follow them that far. It's unclear to me how such huge swarms survive at this point, since surely they've run out of food by now."

"They eat each other," Minna said, waking up in the back.

"Yes, but you can't do that forever."

"I think there used to be many more of them," Minna said. "Perhaps someday the people can have this world again."

"The only people we've seen here are cultists," Vicki said. "There were seven of them in this outpost, but one was apparently out foraging when we came before – there are ropeways that lead from dish to dish, and the cultists forage in the houses for supplies."

"His mother was so upset," Minna said. "We had to promise we'd come back for him."

"What are you talking about?" I said.

"You'll see."

Still stealthed, we landed on the edge of one of the dishes, where a lonely campfire burned. Minna slipped out, doing her fade-from-view thing. Zaveta and I sat, looking out the dome, as she disappeared into a small hut.

A moment later, she came out, carrying a young man over one shoulder. Minna has always been a lot stronger than she looks – she was bioengineered to be farm labor before she was trained to be a master grafter. "No trouble at all," she said cheerfully when she got close. "It was much harder to get six of them at once! We had to help Ana catch them and put them in the shuttle. Before I joined her, she had to be very sneaky and take one or two at a time."

"You are collecting the cultists from their outposts?" Zaveta said. "And doing what with them? Imprisoning them?"

"It is not a prison!" Minna said. "It is really very nice. We call it the Wormwood. Help me, Zax?"

We got the unconscious cultist settled in the front seat beside me, and then Minna reattached her diadem and slumped back in the seat.

"The intent is certainly the same as taking them to prison," Vicki said. "But we like to think we're taking them to paradise. Or, at least, the closest approximation within half a day's interdimensional travel."

"It's just like what we do on the Realm of Spheres and Harmonies," I said "When we have people who can't or won't be rehabilitated, we put them in a pleasant place to live out their days. This was Ana's idea?"

"And Sorlyn's, yes. He knew just the right world. The cultists infected with the worm are already off in the multiverse, so we can't do anything about them at the moment. These cultists on outposts can't travel, though – they were transported as companions, and left in place. That sort of cultist stays where you put them. Since Toros was kind enough to disable the Trypophile's chariot, there's no danger of these being brought back to cause trouble."

"But the whole cult," I said. "Can you really resettle them all?"

"We've questioned them, and though some certainly lied, as best we can tell, their numbers simply aren't that great – perhaps a hundred and fifty in all remain uninfected by the worm, including those on the outpost worlds. We've repatriated almost that many already."

"Once they're all gone, and the First World is unpopulated... the bomb." I whistled. "That works. Surely Toros can see the sense of doing it this way. If we talked to him about your plan–"

"Toros is... not entirely rational on this subject," Vicki said. "He is intolerant of delay, and though he would not admit it, I think he is also motivated by a desire for revenge against the cult."

"I see his point," Zaveta said. "I also dislike delay and enjoy the revenge. Why are we wasting time clearing the outposts, if the bomb will only destroy the First World?"

"Three reasons," Vicki said. "First, because getting past the outposts is difficult, when they're fully staffed – they have equipment that can detect the sleepercars, provided by their spies in the Sleeperhold. Ana had to land far away, creep in wearing her shimmersuit, and take them one at a time, to weaken their defenses. Second, because when the resettlement effort began, Ana and Sorlyn didn't know which place *was* the cult's homeworld. It took a while to narrow down the options definitively, and before that, every outpost was potentially the cult's lair. And third–"

"Because it's nicer to keep them together," I said. "They're a family, of sorts, and a community, and it would be cruel to separate them. They have a better chance of healing if they're not alone."

"That was Ana's reasoning, yes," Vicki said. "I myself think they'll simply self-reinforce their delusional worldview, but, on their new garden homeworld, they won't be able to do anything about it. We made sure none of them have worms on hand. No sacrament means no missionaries, no proselytization, and no bad works. Let them believe whatever they want, if they don't hurt anyone else in the process."

We landed on the next world, and Minna jolted upright. "Oh no, oh no, I had a dream, but not a dream, I saw a person, he looked like the overseer from the Farm but he sounded like... he sounded like you, Zax."

"That was the Prisoner," Zaveta said.

"The god of the cult?" Vicki said. "We've heard that it speaks sometimes to those in the void... What did it say, Minna?"

Minna looked at me, wide-eyed. "It said if we don't come to the volcano, and pledge ourselves to the Prisoner's service... it will kill Sorlyn."

"That's where Sorlyn ended up?" Vicki said.

"I think I missed something," I said.

Ana

I've almost caught up to the point where I started this account. There's just a little more sad stuff between there and here, and I might as well get that down, too.

Sorlyn and I brought the shuttle back to the Sleeperhold the day after the attack, stealthed, and watched for a while to make sure the cult wasn't still lurking. They'd all either fallen in battle or slept their way onward to the next world. I went to the cottage first, on the off-chance that I'd find some sign of Zax, but he was gone.

I did pick up his journal, though, and took it with me. His most prized possession. I knew he'd want it back, when I found him, and I was going to find him. I can see why he loves this journal so much. I've been writing in it myself, all this time, and it's been a great comfort to me, in the empty space between worlds, with only an unconscious cultist and my memories for company.

Sorlyn and I made our way to the center of the camp, and found Toros, Winsome, and Colubra sifting through the wreckage of the lodge. We joined them, embraces all around (except Colubra, who isn't the hugging type). "I'm so glad you two made it out," Toros said. He looked ten years older, face haggard, hair dirty and even messier than usual. "The cult caught us completely unprepared. Scores were killed, many

more grievously injured. So many of my cousins..." He bowed
his head. "I suppose we must have posed a real threat to the
cult, if they went to this much trouble to hurt us." His laugh
was a scattered, broken thing. "I don't know how they broke
through our defenses."

"The Pilgrim," I said. "He betrayed us."

Toros nodded, like that didn't surprise him; like nothing
could.

"Our Zax does have uneven taste in companions," Winsome
said.

"It's because he sees the best in everyone," I said.

"The Pilgrim did ask me an awful lot of questions about gods
I'd heard of, and about the cult," Toros said. "I assumed that,
as a religious person, he would consider the Cult of the Worm
heretics. I didn't realize he was thinking of joining them. He
knew everything about our defenses." Toros sat down in the
rubble and put his face in his hands. "I only wanted to save the
rest of the worlds from the fate of my own."

Sorlyn had told me Toros's history, and why he'd formed the
Sleepers – the devastation of his world by breaches in space-
time, and the ruination caused by the bombs used to seal those
breaches. Now, after listening in on the cult for so long and
interrogating our captives, I know the Prisoner caused those
cracks in the world, with all his endless pounding on the walls
universe. "It's not too late," I said. "We can rebuild–"

"I don't think so," Toros said. "In fact... I think now is the
time to strike back hardest, when the cult believes we're at our
weakest."

I frowned. "Strike back how?"

"Many of the outposts still stand," Toros said. "All those
missions I set in motion before I joined you in the search for Zax
and the Lector have begun to bear fruit. We've narrowed down
the homeworld of the cult – there are only a few possibilities,
now. I say we gather our survivors, arm them heavily, and
storm each choice in turn. Now that you've brought back the

shuttle, we can descend in numbers, with heavy armament. Once we definitively identify their homeworld… we set off our breach-bomb."

"The what bomb?" I asked. It was the first I'd heard of the weapon, and when Toros and Sorlyn explained what it could do – what much smaller versions had done, on Toros's homeworld – I was both intrigued and horrified. "Ignite the atmosphere? With all those people there?"

"Not people," Toros snapped. "*Cultists*. Murderers. They slaughtered our family, here, last night! We have to hit back, when they think we're still reeling. Sorlyn, load the shuttle with our best weapons. I'm going to gather the survivors. We'll head for the outposts soon. We will raise an army." He stomped off, Winsome and Colubra following at his heels.

I looked at Sorlyn. He looked at me. "Well," I said. "Are you going to do that? A last-ditch, desperate assault, where the best outcome makes us into mass murderers?"

"I am open to alternative suggestions," he said.

"I think I know what Zax would do," I said.

So we stole the shuttle. Without that, Toros couldn't deploy his bomb – it was too big for a traveler to carry. First we hit a known cult outpost on a world where trees grew upside-down from a cavern ceiling and the floor is covered in thick fog. We crept in, me in a shimmersuit and Sorlyn with his natural camouflage, and waited for a cultist to emerge from their crude wooden fort. We tranquilized him and stuck him in the back of the shuttle.

It took hours, but we got all five of the cultists there. The last one was pretty freaked out, wandering around, calling for her siblings; they were a family unit. A lot of the outposts were like that, it turns out. Once we had the cultists all bundled away, we traveled to a garden world twenty-four jumps away. Sorlyn had noted that world on an earlier survey. There were no other worm-trails there, and it had seemingly never been visited by the cult.

Their new home had lush trees with edible fruit; ample water; lots of fish; fat, slow-moving birds; and, in that region at least, an absurdly temperate climate. The only predators we identified were rat-sized egg thieves. The day-night cycle was comfortable, and the skies were beautiful and full of stars. "Sorlyn," I said, "why are we giving the cult this world? *I* want to live here."

We flew the cultists fifty kilometers from our entry point. We didn't want them carving spears and lying in ambush for our next visit. We stretched their sleeping forms out on the ground next to a pile of supplies we'd brought from their outpost, and headed back out again.

It took about a full Sleeper-standard day, round trip, to go from an outpost world to the paradise we'd started calling Wormwood and back again. It was slow work, since capturing them wasn't easy and, at some point, word got around that something was happening – they were more cautious, and on alert, and there were automated defenses at the better-appointed outposts. Sorlyn tweaked the chariot, something about adjusting the failsafes, so it could appear a kilometer or two away from the natural entry point, and that kept us from getting shredded by autocannons. At the time we were baffled about how they knew to be on the lookout for us. Who'd told them? Still, we were sneaky, the most experienced agents the Sleeperhold had, and good at what we did. The work slowed, but we didn't stop. Sorlyn was tireless and never lost his temper, no matter how cranky and tired I got.

Oh, Sorlyn. We were such a good team.

It took ages, but we cleared out a lot of cult outposts, and even managed to get some answers to our questions. The missionaries we'd encountered before were zealots who'd never talk willingly, but the ones left behind could be more pliable. They told us about other outposts, though none of them were experienced multiversal travelers, so we still couldn't definitively pinpoint the First World – being told it was "four sleeps" from one place or "six sleeps" from another helped, but none of it was definitive, since every world could lead to three or four others. We were narrowing it down, even without access to the intelligence Toros had gathered.

I lost Sorlyn on a cult outpost situated in the midst of a reeking swamp, all bugs and predatory reptiles. Their base was built on one of the only solid patches of ground in the area. The site was very hard to sneak up to, but we did our best.

For once, our best wasn't enough. The cult had better tech than usual, maybe thermal imaging, and they saw Sorlyn coming. A bunch of cultists boiled up out of the swampy water, wearing breathing apparatuses, and grabbed him, dragging him to their solid island. There were so many cultists, more than I could take out, even with my staff loaded with tranquilizer darts. They seemed intent on capture, not killing, so I decided to hang back and wait for my moment.

That was the second time I saw the Trypophile. She strolled out of the hut, carrying a gnarled wooden walking stick, wearing that horrible wasp's nest mask of hers, and prodded Sorlyn with her boot. "The Prisoner told me about you. That you'd been creeping from world to world, taking my people away. He told me *where* you took them, too. There's nowhere you can go that he can't watch, figment. I'm going to steal that shuttle of yours and bring them all home again. You've done nothing but waste your time. You should have killed them instead." She raised her voice. "Come out! I know there's another one of you out there, to pilot the shuttle! I'll kill this one if you don't–"

Sorlyn vanished. He'd taken Minna's neurological upgrade, and could travel at will. The Trypophile cursed and pointed to one of the cultists. "You! Go after him!"

"I'll get a sedative–"

"Now!" She struck him on the head with her walking stick.

He fell, but he didn't disappear – she'd hit him too hard, and instead of knocking him out, she'd killed him.

Even she seemed aghast, and there was a lot of commotion among the cultists, but finally she singled out another and said, "Take a sedative, go after the Sleeper, I'll be along to pick you up later!"

He ran inside the fort. "Should I go with him?" another cultist said. "This Sorlyn is formidable–"

"Then who would power the shuttle, fool? You and my driver are the only travelers left here! No, you and Skrayling go out, find the shuttle, kill the driver, and then pursue Sorlyn."

"If the shuttle is in stealth mode, Trypophile, how can we–"

She shook the staff at him. "There are only about a dozen places in this filthy swamp where you can even stand up without sinking! The shuttle is *huge*, it has to be parked somewhere! Hurry, before the pilot can move it!"

He scuttled off, grabbed a cultist I assume was Skrayling, and they ventured into the swamp... unfortunately heading in exactly the right direction.

I hurried back to the shuttle, considering my options. I didn't have a lot. I had to move cautiously, since even invisible I still left a wake in the water when I waded or swam. I barely kept ahead of the cultists, and only managed to do so at all because they blundered into one of those predatory reptiles, and had to spend some time screaming and shooting the animal.

I was ready by the time they reached the shuttle, though. I shot them both with tranquilizers. I left Skrayling there – out of the water, so he wouldn't *definitely* get eaten – and lugged the cultist traveler into the cockpit of the shuttle. I bound him, and wired him up, intravenous feeding tubes and all. Then I messed with the settings and overrides so I could keep him in a more-or-less constant state of sleep, reduced from a person to a propulsion device. It wasn't very nice, but what choice did I have? I went after Sorlyn, but he'd fled ahead of the cultists, flickering through worlds, and we were so close to the First World that every place I went was riddled with worm-trails, and I had no way to tell which one was his. I wasted a couple of days looking, and then resigned myself to the fact that he'd have to take care of himself. I would continue the work, on my own, and just hope we'd meet again.

The first thing I did was return to the swamp. I was angry and lonely, but I took all the cultists to paradise. I'm not sure I would have been so merciful if the Trypophile had been there, too.

I kept up my resettlement efforts, though it was slower going without Sorlyn. I would lie in wait on the now-deserted swamp world, sometimes, hoping the Trypophile would return to check on things, but she never did. Maybe the Prisoner warned her away. I knew if I wanted to catch her, I was going to have to hunt her.

That's about the time I started keeping this journal. So there you go: have yourself a full circle.

Of course, stuff has happened since I started writing this account. Occasionally I'd see a smooth trail, and know it must be Minna. I even tried to follow her a few times, but without knowing which direction to travel or how far away she was, I didn't have any luck. In the end, she found me, quite by accident. I was doing reconnaissance on the world with the radio telescopes and the beetles when she popped out of a hole in my attention and said, "Hello Ana, have you seen Sorlyn or Zax, I like you also but I am worried about them."

I told her and Vicki what had happened to Sorlyn, and they told me about their fruitless search for Zax – the reason they never returned to the Sleeperhold was because they were looking for him, and, unlike me, they didn't ever give up. Minna doesn't know the meaning of the word "quit". She also told me the Trypophile had tried to recruit her, offering to make her a queen of all creation, which tells me she didn't

understand Minna at *all*. If she did, she'd know the way to get
to Minna is to threaten her friends, not offer her rewards. (I
wish that wasn't so clear to me. My mind just notices these
things.) When the recruitment attempt failed, the cult tried
to kidnap her, but Minna escaped doing her fade-from-view
trick, learned from Sorlyn.

Minna told me she'd "had a good strange idea" to protect
herself from being captured again, but when I asked what it
was, she said, "Not where the big worm in the void can hear
us," and pointed to my sleeping cultist. OK then.

Minna and Vicki agreed to help me – my task wasn't
incompatible with looking for Zax – and things went faster
then. We cleared out every outpost but one – a Sleeper base
the cult had taken over – and also narrowed down the location
of the First World. Since we'd been attacking the outposts, we
reasoned the cult would probably focus their defenses on the
last one standing. Instead... why not sneak in behind their last
line of defense, and clear out their homeworld instead?

We tried to transition to the First World in our carriages, but
wow, there were a lot of guns. We talked about adjusting our
entry parameters so we'd pop into the air a kilometer above
the transition point, but worried they'd be on the lookout for
us, since we'd already tripped an alarm. We were in the only
adjacent world, debating the best approach, when the console
on my chariot beeped. Its breach-detection systems were still
active, and there was a *big* one here. We followed the signal,
and there it was: a hole in the world, invisible in the air, but
marked by a pair of standing stones.

We stealthed our ships, and then me and Minna and Vicki
just... walked in. The cultists had a guard on the other side
of the breach, but just one, and I crept up and took him out.
We hiked through that horrid red landscape for about an hour
before we found their central camp. What a squalid junk-heap
of a place. The things people will put up with in order to be
closer to god... Vicki messed with their automated defenses,

and put the shuttle and all other sleepercars on some sort of "whitelist" so the guns wouldn't shoot us when we appeared. Apparently making the change was easy, since there was already an exception in place to stop the guns from blowing away the chariot the Trypophile had stolen.

After that... well, it wasn't *easy*, but it was doable. We slipped in, all stealthy, and gradually cleared out the cult's home camp. Minna was unnoticeable, and I had the shimmersuit, and Vicki cakewalked through all their security measures. We crammed the shuttle full of cultists, though after a couple of loads the ones left became really paranoid. The last twenty of them huddled in a room together, with guns pointed in all directions. I wasn't sure how we were going to deal with *that*. But Minna spent a while staring at one of the unconscious cultists, and then these weird white flowers bloomed from her fingertips. The blossoms started to produce this pollen or dust or something, and Minna wafted them through an air vent into the room. The cultists all passed out, and Minna said, "They are having the nicest dreams, oh so sweet and fine."

We dragged the cultists out, bound them up, and took them to paradise. The Trypophile was off being a zealous dictator elsewhere with the Pilgrim, unfortunately, but every other denizen of the First World was gone.

Minna stayed there to watch for the Trypophile while I took the shuttle to the last outpost world, to clear that out. There were about a dozen of them there, but they were all together, and I had a glass bottle full of Minna's sleepy-time-pollen, so once that went smash in the middle of their gathering, it was all over but the carrying and transport. My back still hurts. They're all a big happy family on Wormwood now, though. OK, maybe not so happy, but they'll get used to it.

Now I'm back to the First World... and there's no sign of Minna and Vicki. I hope they're OK. I *did* see the Trypophile and the Pilgrim set off in their sleepercar, not across worlds, but just through the air, toward the volcano. They dragged someone with them, dressed in rags, tied up, with a hood over their head – I'm not sure who it is, but anyone those two assholes want to hold captive is someone I want to set free.

I've heard a lot about this Prisoner of theirs from the cultists who've opted to talk to me, and I gather that volcano is where you can hear the voice of their god, except the Trypophile doesn't like to let anyone *else* go up there. It's smart to control access to the divine, I guess, if you want to maintain power. She probably had to agree to let the Pilgrim talk to God to secure his assistance. At least, I hope he asked for that much proof. Who knows.

I'm going after them. I'm going to *catch* them, and take them away from this place. The Trypophile and the Pilgrim aren't going to Wormwood, though. I'll stick them on some other world – nothing unpleasant, just a world the Trypophile can't bully and boss and accidentally murder her followers anymore, and where the Pilgrim can reflect on the consequences of betrayal.

They'll have plenty of time to realize that, instead of worrying so much about God, they should have been worrying about *me*.

A Total Lack of Clever Plans • Parley •
A Sacrifice • Zaveta Meets the Pilgrim •
Final Dispensations • A Tricky Thing
• The First Breach • A Happy Ending

We transitioned to the First World, and flew across the lake, toward the volcano. I thought of its counterpart on the other side, spewing ice into the sky. That would have been less scary to approach. "Are we just supposed to… land on lava?" I asked.

"The chariots are not that durable," Vicki said. "According to the cultists who've spoken to us, there is a cave near the base of the volcano on the far side, away from the lava streams, where the Prisoner speaks to his chosen conduit, and offers them the sacrament."

"So, a squalid worm-hole. Got it." I looked at Minna. "Did the Prisoner say anything else?"

I'd never seen Minna look so miserable, even during our darkest times. I knew she'd spent a lot of time with Sorlyn, but I hadn't understood how close they'd gotten. In my defense, I was too wrapped up in being close to Ana to notice much of anything else. She said, "Just that we have to help them or Sorlyn dies, but I do not understand, why doesn't Sorlyn just close his eyes and leap away?"

"You can't sleep your way out of this place if you slept your way into it," I said. "There are no new adjacent worlds. It's the end of the line for people travelers."

"There must be a way to fix that," Minna muttered. "To make it so we can travel back as well as forward, even without these chariots."

The Lector had believed there was, but he hadn't been able to figure it out. I'd come to realize Minna was smarter than the Lector ever was, though, so if anyone could crack the problem, it was her.

"I wish we could come up with a clever plan," I said. "But the Prisoner is watching us, so even if we did, it would know."

"A shame," Vicki said. "I do love a clever plan."

We approached the volcano. It was a stark black cinder cone, with trails of sluggish lava oozing down the near side and into the lake, so the base was shrouded by steam. The mountain was not erupting so much as endlessly seeping. I wondered how big the lake had been before years of lava had turned its far edge to rippled stone.

The far side of the volcano, for whatever reason, was free of flowing magma. There was a visible path, presumably trod by generations of worm-priests, leading to a shadowed concavity in the mountainside. The mouth of the cavern glowed. There was lava in there.

"Look, the shuttle!" Vicki said. "Ana's here. I'm hailing, but... no response. She must not be on board."

I willed us to land faster, which didn't help, but soon we settled down next to the shuttle. I scrambled out of the chariot and looked into the shuttle's cockpit, but it was empty, except for a cultist snoring and drooling in the back seat, attached with more wires and tubes than Minna had been. I hadn't thought to ask how Ana kept traveling after she and Sorlyn were separated – but now I knew. Abducting a cultist was probably not a choice I would have made, but then, it wasn't a choice I'd been *forced* to make, and these were desperate times. Maybe Ana was in the back for some reason–

Someone crashed into me, and I gasped, but they were hugging me, not attacking me, and then Ana shimmered into view, dressed in her crinkly silver shimmersuit. She kissed me on the mouth for a long time (but not long enough) and then said, "Zax, Minna did it, she found you!"

"She did." Her face was smudged with ash, and I stroked it away. "What are you doing here? Did the Prisoner send you a message too?"

She frowned. "What?"

I told her about Minna's vision, and that we thought Sorlyn was inside, being held hostage. Ana swore. "What do we do?"

Zaveta stepped forward, smiling. "We get him out. You are the famous Ana? You are tiny, but comely enough."

Ana looked from Zaveta to me and back again and frowned. "Who are you?"

She bowed. "I am Zaveta of the Broken Wheel. I joined Zax of the Thousand Worlds to exact vengeance on those who stole my friends away."

""Zax of the Thousand Worlds?" Ana murmured. "I've been to a thousand worlds too, you know."

"Yes," I said. "But you have to admit… you did it in a flying chariot. I walked."

"The leader of the wormlings is in this cave?" Zaveta took the cudgel from her belt. "Then let us venture forth, and settle this matter."

"If we attack them, they'll kill Sorlyn," I said.

"If they do, they lose all leverage, but I take your point. I suggest going in alone, as an obvious threat, to draw attention. Minna and Ana can be more sneaky, and stab this Trypophile and the Pilgrim in their backs."

"What will I be doing during all this?" I asked.

"Averting your eyes from the violence, and preparing medical supplies in case we need them," Zaveta said.

"A good enough plan," Vicki said. "Except that, in theory, the Pilgrim and the Trypophile are in direct communication with the Prisoner, who is watching us even now, and certainly reporting on our activities."

"Hmm," Zaveta said. "Then... I suggest we parley, and see what terms they offer. We need not *accept* the terms, but perhaps there is a way to secure Sorlyn's safety."

"If we're trying talking," I said, "that's my area."

I went into the mountain, unarmed and alone. The cavern was surprisingly small, almost cozy, and not as horrifically hot as I'd expected, given that there was a literal pool of lava bubbling just a few meters away.

The Trypophile sat on a throne of natural rock, and the Pilgrim stood at her side, pointing his long rifle at Sorlyn's head, where he lay bound on his side on the stone. Even without the gun, the Pilgrim could have picked Sorlyn up and hurled him into the pool of lava from where he stood. The glow from the bubbling magma flickered redly across them; they looked like demons in a stage play. And so did I, probably.

The stone wall beside the throne was riddled with many small holes. It looked like a wasp's nest, or a lotus pod. Like the Trypophile's mask. That must be where the Prisoner whispered and birthed its worms. "So," I said. "This is the holiest of holies."

"Please do not blaspheme here, Zax," the Pilgrim said.

I could hardly stand to look at him. "You betrayed us, Pilgrim. I can't believe it."

The Pilgrim shook his head gravely. "I betrayed no one. I have always been in the service of God. I am indebted to you for helping me find my deity. I truly hope we can reach a peaceful resolution, with no further harm."

I wanted to tell him the Prisoner meant *everyone* harm, but the priest spoke before I could.

"Here are my terms," the Trypophile said. "Minna will surrender herself to our custody. She will make serum for us, and provide my people with all her other little powers, too.

We will take your shuttle, and the cultist Ana kidnapped. We will also need this breach-bomb, so we can dispose of it safely."

"Oh, is that all?" I said.

If she was annoyed, I couldn't tell through the mask. "In exchange, you can have Sorlyn back now. Once Minna has trained our people to make the serum, you can have *her* back, too. After that, I suggest you travel as far into the multiverse as you can. We will let you live your lives in peace. You could have many years of happiness before our great work intrudes." She leaned forward in the throne. "I would not have offered you such generous terms, but the Prisoner is merciful."

"You think we'll agree to help you infect millions of people and destroy all of reality, killing untold trillions?" I shook my head. "We want Sorlyn back, but no one could make that trade."

But Zax, a voice whispered from the rocks. This time, the Prisoner didn't sound like Ana. It sounded like a voice made of wriggling worms and cascading rocks. *You are clever. You are brave. And our plan, why, it has so many steps before it reaches completion. There are so many ways it could fall apart. If you save Sorlyn now, perhaps you can stop us later. You'll take that chance, won't you? To save him?*

The idea had occurred to me. Live to fight another day, and all that. "I–"

Minna shimmered into view beside me. I hadn't even realized she was there. "This is not Zax's decision," she said. "You want me, and the things I know how to do. I care about Sorlyn, really very much. If you let Zax take him away, you can keep me."

The Trypophile cocked her head. "Really? So easily?"

Minna shrugged. "I helped the Lector when I had no choice. I have no choice now. I am a practical creature."

"The Pilgrim can see through your little disappearing trick," the Tryphophile said.

The Pilgrim pointed to his eye. "Augmented vision."

"Don't think you can sleep your way out, either," the priest said. "We're going to take you to the second world in the shuttle, with the cultist Ana stole as the engine, and I'll watch you transition back here by sleeping. Then we'll follow you through, pick you up, and fly back here to the temple." She pointed at Minna with her stick. "There will be no escape."

Minna shrugged. "That is fine. I accept."

The Trypophile rose. "Pilgrim, stay here, and watch Sorlyn. If Minna's friends try anything, kill them all."

"It will be done," he rumbled.

"Minna, no–" I said.

Silence, the Prisoner said. *She has made her choice. Make the exchange.*

Minna took Vicki off her finger and handed it to me. Then she and the Tryphophile left the cave. I didn't. I put Vicki on my ring finger and then sat down, cross-legged, and looked at Sorlyn. "Is he all right? Did you bash him on the head?"

"He is sedated," the Pilgrim said. "Zax, please understand, I have spent my entire life seeking, and now, I am found."

Blessed are those who serve the cause of freedom, the Prisoner whispered.

I couldn't bear that voice anymore. I went outside, and found Ana standing by Minna's chariot. The shuttle was gone. "She's really sacrificing herself?" Ana said.

"I don't know," I said. "If she has a plan, she didn't tell me. Where's Zaveta?"

"Surveying the terrain, she said. I told her there was no point in trying a rescue, since the Prisoner can see everything we do, but..." she shrugged, "...it gives her something to do. She was... not happy about Minna's decision."

"I'm sure she wasn't. I'm not, either." We sat and waited. Vicki was uncharacteristically silent.

After a time, the shuttle came skimming across the landscape, settling down in the same spot where it had been parked before. Minna emerged, and the Trypophile came after her.

"Come along, my little acolyte." She poked Minna with her walking stick. "You too, Zaxony. We'll make the exchange."

Ana and I followed them into the cave.

"Go ahead," the Trypophile said. "I am a woman of my word." The Pilgrim hauled Sorlyn to his feet. He was groggy from the drugs, but came awake with the motion. He blinked at us. "Minna?" he said. "Darling, what–" The Pilgrim marched Sorlyn forward and thrust him toward Ana. She helped support his weight.

"Minna," I said. "We can find another way, you can't–"

She kissed my cheek. "We help people, Zax. Sorlyn needs help." Then she kissed Sorlyn, on the lips, and joined the Pilgrim and the Trypophile by the throne.

"Go ahead and take Sorlyn out," the Trypophile said. "So you know we're in earnest. Then you can come back and we'll work out the other details, about the bomb and so forth."

"If you need motivation to hold to the terms of our agreement," the Pilgrim said, "know that we can hurt Minna without reducing her usefulness–"

I held up a hand. "Stop, Pilgrim. Stop."

He looked away. "I am sorry. This is… it's important. God needs me."

"What's happening?" Sorlyn mumbled.

"Bad things," I said.

We returned to the shuttle, where Zaveta was waiting, cleaning her nails with a knife. "Minna has great healing abilities," Zaveta said. "Perhaps…" Then she glanced at the sky and scowled. "It is hard to plan under the enemy general's eye."

"Hmm," Vicki said. "That is true. But, ah… it is always wise to take cover, and it never hurts to prepare for the possibility of violence."

Did Vicki know something we didn't? Had they cooked up some scheme with Minna? If so, they couldn't tell us, not in the presence of the Prisoner. We followed their suggestion, though, and moved to put the shuttle between us and the cavern. The other cultist was still sedated into unconsciousness in the back. The Trypophile hadn't bothered to wake him up. We stood there silently for a while. Finally I said, "Is something going to happen, or–"

We heard the Tryphophile scream, a sound of rage rather than pain, and the Pilgrim roared.

"She's done it, then," Vicki said quietly.

Ana and I peeked around the edge of the shuttle, and saw the Pilgrim and the Trypophile emerge from the cave mouth. "Madness!" the Trypophile shouted as they stalked toward us. "Did you *know* she was going to do that?"

We exchanged quizzical glances. "Do what?" Ana called.

"The fool flung herself into the lava!" the Tryphophile bellowed.

Minna was dead? She'd sacrificed herself to save Sorlyn, and the multiverse? *That* was the secret plan? I staggered against the side of the shuttle, barely able to keep my knees from giving way beneath me.

"Please, Zax, do not lose heart," Vicki said. "We must keep our wits about us." I stared at the gem on my finger, suddenly hating them. Vicki was a cool crystal intellect, but didn't they care at all? It was *Minna*.

We did have more immediate problems, though.

"Kill them!" the Trypophile shrieked. "Slay them for their treachery!"

The Pilgrim raised his long gun, and Ana and I ducked out of sight.

"Did you know," Vicki said, conversationally, "that the Pilgrim's extraordinary deftness with that rifle is due to a neural implant? He is mentally connected to the gun's controls, synching its aim with his own eyes. He even fires the weapon by thought alone – and there's no manual trigger, to prevent others from using the weapon against him, I assume. But, of course, a system like that depends on wireless communication, and that can be... interfered with. There. The Pilgrim can't shoot us now. Of course, he still has a sword, and the reflexes of a predator..."

I stepped out of cover and held up my hands. "Pilgrim, this is over. Minna... she died to end this. No one else has to. We–"

My old friend pointed the rifle right at me. Nothing happened, and he looked down at the gun, shook it, and pointed at me again, still to no avail.

I stared at him. "You tried to shoot me?"

The Pilgrim growled. "We made a covenant, and it was broken."

"Technically, Minna just said she'd hand herself over, not that she'd remain alive in your custody," Vicki said. How could they talk about her death so calmly?

"Kill them!" the Tryphophile said. "Use your teeth if you must! The Prisoner demands it!"

"God asks difficult things of us, sometimes." The Pilgrim threw the rifle onto the ground and drew the curved sword from his belt. "This will do to end you all."

A hand fell onto my shoulder, and Zaveta stepped up beside me. "*All*?" she said. "Even me?"

The Pilgrim gazed at her. "Zax's new companion. Shall I begin with you, then?"

"I am Zaveta of the Broken Wheel," she said. "And I am pleased to match my skills against another warrior – even a traitor like you." She added, from the corner of her mouth: "Permission to engage, Zax?"

"Granted," I said, and she launched herself at the Pilgrim, cudgel swinging at his head. He blocked with his sword, but staggered back, clearly unprepared for the ferocity of her attack.

The Trypophile darted toward Zaveta's back, raising her staff, but then Ana shimmered into view behind her and snaked an arm around her throat. "Ah, ah, no cheating. Drop the stick or I'll crush your windpipe."

The Trypophile complied. Ana pulled the priest's hood down, yanked at the bindings on the back of her mask, and threw the grotesque thing into the dirt. Underneath it all, the Trypophile was younger than I'd expected, and looked like she could be Ephedra's mother. She hissed in outrage, and Ana squeezed her neck until her eyes rolled back and she sagged to the ground.

Then we turned to watch Zaveta and the Pilgrim dance.

"Should I try to shoot the Pilgrim with a tranquilizer, or something?" Ana said.

I shook my head. "This is Zaveta's specialty. We should let her do it."

The Pilgrim was larger than Zaveta, with a longer reach, and he was certainly formidable… but he came from a world of technology, and he was a better sniper than a melee combatant. This was basically the only kind of fight Zaveta of the Broken Wheel had ever had. She was in her element, laughing as she fought, finally able to operate at her full potential, metal-clad cudgel striking sparks against the Pilgrim's sword. She blurred, feinted at his face, and then dropped and struck at his knee. He staggered, and she clubbed his wrist savagely, making him drop the sword. She kneed him in the face, kicked his sword out of the way without even looking at the blade, and stood over him. "In deference to Zax, who hates to see unnecessary death, I will give you the opportunity to yield, on your word as a warrior and a man of God. Else, only death awaits you, and I do not think your God waits for you in *that* void."

The Pilgrim looked at her for a long moment, and then whispered, "I yield. On my honor as a pilgrim and a man."

"Good enough," Zaveta said. "But I'm going to smash one of your knees just to be safe."

We heard the Prisoner's thin and distant howl of frustration and rage from inside the cave, mingled with the Pilgrim's shout of pain.

* * *

"Come with us," I said. "We'll take you anywhere you want to go–"

"Leave me here, with my God," the Pilgrim said.

"You don't understand," I said. "The bomb, it's going to light the sky itself on fire, you'll–"

"I will burn," he said placidly. "But I will burn in the presence of my lord." He turned and limped back into the cavern, using the Trypophile's staff as a crutch.

I looked at Ana, who shrugged. "It's his choice."

"I have no interest in burning," the Trypophile said, rising to her knees. "Take me with you, please!" She clasped her hands. "Don't leave me here to die, I beg you–"

"You think we'd do that?" Ana said.

"It's what she would do to us," Sorlyn said. "She can't imagine anyone else is different from her." He was still moving slowly, but his mind was working again. I felt bad for him. I knew he admired Minna, and her loss would hurt him, no matter how stoic he seemed.

"You won't leave me here?" the Trypophile said. "You'll reunite me with my people on that garden world–"

"We didn't say that," I said.

Ana looked at me. "Zax. You mean you *aren't* going to do the nicest possible thing?"

With Minna gone, my desire to be nice was rapidly receding. A universe without her in it was a crueler, darker place by definition. "The cultists have a chance to make a new life, on a new world. If she's there, filling their minds with poison, manipulating them…" I shook my head. "I'm not being cruel to the priest here. I'm being kind to her people."

"Don't take me to the world with the beetles, please, or the terrariums, oh, god, no–"

"We aren't you," I said. We stuck the Trypophile in the back of the shuttle so we wouldn't have to knock her out or listen to her complaints. Sorlyn moved the other cultist into the back of the chariot. Vicki and Sorlyn set off together to deliver the captive cultist to Wormwood, while Ana and I took the priest and a load of supplies away to her final destination, with plans to reconvene back at the Sleeperhold when we were done.

I'd never been the propulsion system for a shuttle before, but it wasn't so strange. Ana put the diadem on my brow, kissed me sweetly, and then said, "Sleep for me."

After everything we'd lost in order to win, I welcomed the prospect of a brief oblivion.

I dreamed I was back on the First World, on the shores of the steaming lake. The Prisoner was there, looking like the Lector, sounding like Ana. "Must we do this?" I said.

"I just want you to know how pointless all this is." It paced back and forth on the shore. "You'll set off a bomb, seal me back into my tomb, collapse my worm-trails, close my peepholes – what does it matter? I'll just keep hammering away. I am tireless, and I am eternal, and I will break through again. You've only delayed the inevitable."

I nodded. "Right. But didn't it take you billions of years to make those breaches in the first place? The ones we're going to seal? Maybe you've gotten better at breaking things – maybe you'll take *half* as many billions of years this time." I shrugged. "That's OK. That gives a lot of people the chance to live full lives in worlds that aren't collapsing on themselves. I'm not eternal, like you, Prisoner. From my point of view, billions of years is as good as permanent."

"I can hold you here for what *feels* like billions of years," the Prisoner said. "I can make it an eternity of misery–"

I'd spent a lot of time with Zaveta. She'd taught me a few things, lessons that fit nicely with lots of other meditative practices I've developed over the years. My mind fortress isn't nearly as nice as Zaveta's – it's just a steel sphere, barely big enough to stand up in, so far – but it does have a window, and that window has a shutter. I called the fortress into existence, and pulled the shutter down, and the Prisoner's voice became the distant whisper of the wind. I suppose it could have made me wait there for a subjective eternity, but the Prisoner enjoys more active torment, I think. Soon enough, the darkness returned.

We took the Trypophile to a world the Sleepers had surveyed long ago, with an island sporting natural caves for shelter, mineral springs for water, ample fish and fruit, and even a beautiful lagoon. There were sea monsters, farther out – leviathans that rose and writhed and crested, and that maybe even had their own culture, who knows? – but they couldn't come anywhere near the shallow waters of the island. They would discourage attempts at sailing, though.

There were lots of tiny holes in the sand near the waterline, where tiny burrowing crabs lived. Seeing that was what made Ana think of this world as a final destination in the first place.

When we shoved the Trypophile out of the shuttle, she collapsed to her knees on the sand, and howled. "What am I supposed to *do* in this place?"

"Not commit multiversal genocide, for a start," I said. We dumped a bunch of supplies beside her and left without exchanging another word.

When we got to the Sleeperhold... Minna was waiting for us.

"Surprise!" she said. "I did a tricky thing and I am sorry you were sad or scared, but the Prisoner could see you all the time, so it had to be a secret thing–"

I gasped and flung myself at her, hugging her, then looked her over. She didn't have so much as a burn. "Did you figure out a way to make yourself *lava-proof*?"

"I did not," she said. "Vicki can explain it faster than me maybe."

Vicki loves explaining things. "I am so sorry I could not tell you her plan," they said. "I couldn't risk revealing anything where the Prisoner could hear. Do you remember when Minna was forced to grow a new version of Polly on the space station, working from a sample of the creature's flesh? And the way Polly encoded its consciousness into a sort of seed, so the Lector could transfer its mind and memories into the new body?"

"I do." I did not like where this was going.

"I kept a piece of the Polyp," Minna said. "Later, I grew it, but only into a body, without a mind – that was not so hard. It was just about making certain connections not connect." She interlaced her fingers and then pulled them apart. "You see, I was thinking and thinking about the way Polly's mind was passed around, and it didn't seem so different from the way I put my memories in a seed that time so *you* could see what happened to me when we were separated, Zax. I figured out a way to do what Polly did. I didn't think it was good for much except maybe a sort of emergency, um, what is it called, Vicki?"

"An emergency backup," Vicki said. "Or a restore point."

"A way to make a new me in case the first me got killed," Minna said, as if that were a perfectly ordinary idea. "So all that I am would not be lost. But when the ugly mask lady tried to recruit me, I knew they wouldn't stop trying to catch me, and if they did, I wanted to be able to escape to the one place they could never follow."

"Minna made a duplicate of herself from Polly's tissue," Vicki said. "Then she encoded her entire personality into a seed, and fed it to the copy. She did all this on worlds where the Prisoner had no eyes, to keep it secret. Then... there were two Minnas. One to go forth into danger, and one to stay back, safe. I had Sorlyn pick up this one on the way home from Wormwood."

"So the Minna who died on the first world... that was the copy?" I said.

Minna cocked her head. "What do you mean?"

I frowned. "You're the original, aren't you?"

Minna shrugged. "I am not sure. Polly's body is so versatile, and I made it even more so, until it *became* mine, every bit, down to the cells, and we have all the same memories of course, so who could tell one from one?"

"One of you would remember feeding the seed to the copy, though, right?" Ana said. "The memories can't perfectly match."

"Oh, we cut that memory out." Minna made a snip-snip motion with her fingers. "It didn't seem fair, for one of us to think they were more real somehow. We were *both* real. Both Minna. Both me. When the time came to decide who got to go on the mission and who would stay behind and be the backup, we just let chance decide."

"I generated a random number," Vicki said. "One was odds, and one was evens. And, no, I don't know which Minna was the original, either. I had to shut myself down to avoid the contamination of that knowledge, lest it alter our relationship. I have been persuaded to Minna's way of thinking, now – that it doesn't matter which one came first."

"You can clone a plant, and it is the same plant, until it grows into something new," Minna said. "I am sad the other me will not get to grow anymore, but one gone is better than all gone, we agreed. I would have died to save all the everything anyway, but this way, a part of me still goes on."

"It will… take me a while to get my head around this," I said.

"We have time," Minna said.

She led us through the remains of camp, to where Sorlyn and Toros and Winsome were bringing the bomb out of the vault on a levitating dolly. The breach-bomb was a cylindrical metal thing, almost as big as one of the chariots, wrapped with glowing blue pipes.

I approached Toros warily. "Are we good?" I said.

He looked at me coldly, then sighed. "You took an

unnecessary risk. Without Minna's quick thinking, all would have been lost. But... I am attempting to remain focused on outcomes. I like to think of myself as pragmatic above all else."

We loaded the bomb into the back of the shuttle. Sorlyn and Toros took it to the First World. Ana and I followed in a sleepercar. We flew to the breach we knew led to the second world – even if the bomb wasn't as effective as its creator predicted, we hoped it would seal *that* one, at least. There were other breaches in that world, it turned out, which made sense – the Prisoner had been bashing at the walls of his prison for a long time. Most of those breaches were underground, or on the icy night side, or led to uninhabitable worlds. This first breach was the one that let zealotry in and caused all the problems.

I looked to the volcano. "I could try to talk to the Pilgrim again..."

Toros shook his head. "He made his choice. We should respect it. We've meddled with other worlds and their inhabitants too much already."

I reluctantly agreed. We placed the bomb, set the timer, and retreated to a safe interdimensional distance, into the second world.

Then we sat, our chariot next to their shuttle, parked near the standing stones. "How will we know if it worked?" I asked.

Ana pointed to the console. "See that? It indicates the presence of a breach. So–"

"Now!" Toros said over the radio.

The indicator light on the console flickered and went out. "Breach sealed," she said. Toros and Sorlyn whooped over the radio, and Ana reached into the back seat to hug me. "We did it!"

"So let's go celebrate," I said, and kissed her.

Don't you love a happy ending?

Ana

I'm writing this in one of the notebooks I scrounged from the Sleeperhold, since I gave Zax his journal back. He's been reading my account, and I've been reading his. It's funny how often we had the same ideas or the same thoughts about things. Or maybe it's just natural. We do fit.

I didn't plan to write again like this. I thought I'd spend some time just *living life* instead, but with everything that happened with Toros... I'm having trouble processing it, and maybe writing again will help.

At first, everything went beautifully. We sealed the breaches in the First World, and trapped the Prisoner. Once we got back to the Sleeperhold, we found out we'd done even more than that. We noticed the phenomenon while we sat around a table set up near the ruins of the lodge, pretty much all of us except Toros and his cousins.

"Your worm-trail... it's disintegrating." Sorlyn pointed at Zax.

He peered at Sorlyn through his cute little spectacles and said, "Yours is, too!"

Sorlyn laughed, a rare sound from him. "Who knew reality could knit itself up like that? Why hasn't it been happening all along?"

"I think the Prisoner was reaching through the trails."

Minna wriggled her fingers. "Like bits of metal in a wound, preventing them from healing all the way."

"But we slammed a gate down across the First World," I said. "We cut off his tentacles or his eyestalks or pseudopods. He can still reach into the First World, but he can't reach any farther."

"I've got to tell Toros," Sorlyn said. "This is amazing news!" He took Minna's hand, and they ran off together.

"Truly a welcome outcome," Winsome agreed, and Colubra nodded. "I wonder though… what does this mean for the infected, here and scattered elsewhere? Will they continue to whirl through realities, or will this change remove their abilities?"

"Maybe the little worms will die *too*, and I'll get my cure at last," Durio said.

"I… guess we'll find out." Zax sounded a little stunned at the prospect. He was Zax of the Thousand Worlds – what would it mean to him, if something so fundamental about his nature changed? With Minna's ability, not dependent on the worm, we could still travel with her and even use a sleepercar… but we wouldn't *have* to.

I took Zax's hand. Wherever he went, I'd go with him. "What's everyone going to do, now that our war is over?" I asked.

"Toros's cousins are planning to stay here," Durio said. "I guess their world is a garbage pit now, and this one is nice enough. *I'm* going to return to my own world. Even if the parasites don't die, Minna's procedure means I can stay there as long as I like. Winsome here said he'd pilot the shuttle for me."

"Durio's world sounds like a delight," Winsome said. "Technology and luxury, without the ossification and stratification that so defined my own world of origin."

"They will return me to my hive along the way," Colubra said. "My honor debt to Toros is now discharged."

"I don't know what the other Sleepers are planning," Durio said. "Toros had some meeting with them in the wee hours of the morning, and I haven't seen any of them since. I was supposed to go, but I was *resting*, and I'd say I earned the break." He shrugged. "What about you lot?"

I leaned my head on Zax's shoulder. "We're going to see the worlds, and see if we can't do some good along the way."

Zax nodded, then pointed across the table at Zaveta, who was shoveling food into her mouth; she ate with the same intensity she did almost everything else. She wore Vicki on her finger. It turns out Vicki's addiction is fresh knowledge, and they'd been talking a lot about siege warfare lately. "Minna and Vicki and Sorlyn are coming with us," Zax said. "First we're going to help Zaveta find her friends – tracking them will be trickier than we expected, with the worm-trails disappearing, but we'll go back to her world, and fan out from there."

"My people may not have survived," Zaveta said. "They were shepherds and farmers, not warriors. But some might be saved, and at the very least I will bring their bodies home, and give them the appropriate rites."

"Noble," Durio said. "I'm just looking forward to getting drunk on *proper* liquor in a place that doesn't smell like dirt and leaves." He belched, then stood up. "'Scuse me, I have to do the necessary."

Colubra rose too. "I should pack my things." We waved as they departed.

We had no idea it was the last time we'd see them alive.

The rest of us were just chatting away when we heard a voice weakly say, "Zax."

I turned, and Minna was there, covered in blood. She collapsed, trying to crawl toward us, but clearly spent. "I couldn't – couldn't save them–"

Zax was at her side in an instant. "What happened? What's going on?"

"Toros and his cousins," she said. "They attacked us. Shot

us, then stabbed us. I pretended to be dead so they'd leave, and I think I saved Sorlyn, I filled his wounds with moss and he disappeared when he passed out. But Durio and Colubra, I found them, her head was broken, Zax, I couldn't fit the pieces together, and then one of the cousins found me, and I had to hurt him, so he wouldn't call the others, but he hurt me, too, and..." Her eyes rolled back, but she didn't transition, so she must have still been on the edge of consciousness. Unless she was...

I knelt beside her. I couldn't feel a pulse. I told myself, with Minna, that didn't mean much, but... "Why?" Zax stared at me. "Why would Toros do this?"

"Because it has to be done." Toros stepped out of the trees, four of his cousins flanking him. They all held terrifying weapons, from guns to bloody blades. "You travelers are abominations. We sealed the breach and we stopped the cult, but *you carry their sacrament*. Listen to you, making your plans, intending to spread your filth throughout the worlds. Colubra didn't have to die, but she tried to protect Durio. She doesn't understand. None of you do. Everywhere you go, you damage reality. If you die, you'll pass your worms on, and they will go on, eternally."

Zax stood up, putting himself between Minna and me. "Toros, the worm-trails are healing! That's what Sorlyn went to tell you before you attacked him! Without the Prisoner's interference, the damage to reality is temporary!"

I saw the flicker of uncertainty in Toros's eyes... and then saw him will it away. "Even if that's true, it doesn't matter. You carry the worm. Minna can make more like you any time she wants. You're *dangerous* – you were always dangerous, and just because the cult is gone, that hasn't changed. Everything needs to go back where it belongs. Every world on its own, complete and uncorrupted. Abominations must die. I'll give you a moment to say goodbye to your–" He frowned. "Where is Zaveta?"

A voice behind Toros said, calmly: "Drop."

Zax grabbed me and Winsome and pulled us both down to the ground, hard, so we fell next to Minna in the dirt. Toros and his cousins turned toward the voice – and then jerked wildly in place as a rapid series of bangs shattered the air.

The attackers fell to the ground, riddled with small holes. Zaveta stood behind them, holding a portable autocannon. She dropped the weapon on the ground, its barrels still smoking, and then stepped over Toros and the others to approach us. "Using a weapon like that hardly seems fair, but then, Toros and his cousins did not engage fairly, either." She held up her finger, jewel twinkling. "Vicki told me how to operate the gun." She looked at Zax, bowing her head, and her expression was – sheepish? "I am sorry I did not ask for permission to kill them, Zax. I did not believe there was time."

"You're forgiven," Zax croaked.

Recoveries • *Love Is Little Yellow Flowers* • *What Worlds May Come*

Ana showed me what she wrote last night, about Toros turning on us, and it's what I would have written, pretty much, although my version would have included more anguish and shock. She's stronger than I am.

She says she loves how I always look for the best in people, but it certainly does mean I get hurt a lot, doesn't it?

Oh well. So far, the trade-off still feels worth it.

Minna recovered. She went into some kind of temporary hibernation while her body fixed its wounds, and you'd never know she'd been shot and stabbed now. Physically, anyway. I assume some psychological damage was done, but it's hard to tell with her.

We found Sorlyn in an adjacent world, and he's stable, though he kept losing consciousness and flickering away. Minna fetched him back every time, and I guess he ran out of new worlds he can reach from the Sleeperhold, because he hasn't disappeared again. We don't have a good infirmary here anymore, but we're doing our best.

Ana says if Sorlyn doesn't improve soon, she knows a world with a really good hospital that's patched him up before. Minna says she'll take care of him, thank you very much. When she's done with him, she says, he'll be even *better*. I never thought

I'd see Minna fall in love. It's made her even more adorable. She's blossomed. Sometimes literally. Love looks like little yellow flowers in a crown around her head.

We buried Toros and his cousins. Colubra and Durio too. We found the other travelers and their companions, the ones Toros called in from the outposts, all murdered, their bodies tossed in the vault that used to hold the breach-bomb. Where we would have ended up, if Zaveta hadn't done what she did.

I still don't think killing is ever the best choice, but I must reluctantly concede that sometimes there aren't any *better* ones. I wish we could have subdued Toros and his cousins and stranded them somewhere they couldn't do any harm, but I can hardly blame Zaveta for saving us all.

Emptying the vault meant filling more graves. We just couldn't leave them like that, in a heap, you see. Winsome and Zaveta are tireless when it comes to digging holes, at least, but it's still exhausting. The aquatic people are also dead – poisoned, we think – and we left them in the water, not knowing what rites their people prefer.

We did notice that the worms aren't contagious anymore. Ana didn't get infected, despite getting the blood of dead travelers all over her during the cleanup. The parasites aren't really separate creatures, after all, but aspects of the Prisoner, extended into our worlds and our selves. Now that those extensions are severed from their "body", they're like sliced-off fingers, rotting away. My worm is probably dying, or already dead, and once the chemical it secreted leaves my blood, I won't travel anymore when I sleep. If that's true, Toros really did try to kill me for nothing. Even more nothing than we thought.

It's hard to wrap my head around the possibility of such a fundamental change in myself, and in all the other infected scattered throughout the multiverse – not just the cultists, but those unlucky carriers like me. They might all find themselves, finally, at rest, and I can only hope they end up in places where they can live in peace... though I don't know how likely that is.

I take comfort in the knowledge that no one else will be infected and suffer the loss that I did, torn away from everything they've known and cast into the unknown. The incalculable pain created by the Prisoner and the cult will no longer increase. I often wonder if my efforts to help people made any real, lasting difference – but in this case, I know they have. We've done good.

Minna says, if I want to keep the ability to travel, she can make that happen. She changed her body, after all; she can change mine. She's offered that ability to Ana, too. She says she's thinking about it. If the damage we do to reality heals itself now, there's no reason not to.

You'd think I'd want to be rid of this gift, this curse, this power... but I still have work to do, and people to help. We're all mourning right now. We're all staggering around in grief. But we're doing what we can, and what we must. In time, we'll be able to do more; to do our best.

For a long time, I hated what happened to me. My life was loss and loneliness and fear, sorrow and confusion and desperation. But being flung through the worlds this way... it's the reason I met Minna, and Vicki, and Winsome, and Sorlyn, and Zaveta. And Ana.

The Prisoner was evil – that's not a term I use often, or lightly – but it did bring us together. Even the worst events sometimes have threads of good running through them.

I don't believe the Prisoner is a god. Not exactly. But it worked at least one miracle. Do you know how rare it is, to find a person who's just right for you, even in the vastness of one single world? Let alone the impossible expanse of the multiverse? And yet, thanks to the Prisoner's curse, I managed it. I found Ana. Then I lost her, and found her, and lost her, and found her again.

No more loss. This time, I'm holding on, through whatever worlds may come.

Acknowledgments

Thanks to Eleanor Teasdale at Angry Robot for acquiring this book, and to Simon Spanton for editing it. They believed in me and my idea for a weird multiverse duology, and I'm grateful, because Zax and Ana are dear to my heart. Thanks as well to Gemma Creffield and all the other members of the Robot Army who make me look good. Rob Lowry's copyedit saved me from myself. (I can't be expected to get the names of my characters right *every* time.) As usual, I am indebted to my literary agent Ginger Clark, who always has my back.

My wife Heather Shaw and our kid River make my home life a delight, and always support my writing, even when I shut myself away at my desk for hours and wander around muttering a lot. Thanks to my closest confidantes, Ais, Amanda, Emily, Katrina, and Sarah. They're always there for me, even in the vicissitudes of a plague year (and more). My cohort of fellow writers always remind me that I'm part of a community. I'd like to particularly thank Molly Tanzer, to whom this book is dedicated, for countless conversations and moral support.

Finally, thanks to you readers, for taking this journey through the multiverse with me. I'll see you in the next book. Whole new worlds await.

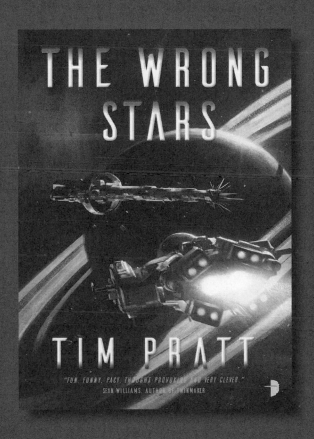

CHAPTER 1

Callie floated, feet hooked over a handrail in the observation deck, and looked through the viewport at the broken ship beyond. The wreck hung motionless, a dark irregular shape – a bit of human debris where no such debris should be. Was this a crisis, or an opportunity? Every unexpected event could be one or the other, and sometimes they were both.

The dead ship was long and bullet-shaped, pointlessly aerodynamic, apart from a bizarre eruption of flanges, fins, and spikes at one end that looked like the embellishments of a mad welder. The wrecked craft was far smaller than Callie's own ship, the *White Raven*, a fast cruiser just big enough for her crew of five people (or four, or maybe six, depending on how you defined "people") to live comfortably along with whatever freight or prisoners they had to transport. If the *White Raven* was a family home, the wreck was more like a studio apartment.

Ashok floated into the compartment, orienting himself with tiny puffs of air that burst from his fingertips and heels – showy and unnecessary, but he had a gift for turning simple things into engineering problems he could solve in complicated ways. He hovered with his head near hers, sharing her view – though it probably looked a lot different to him. "Oh captain, my captain."

She glanced at his complex profile and grunted. "You got new eyes?"

He shook his head. "These are wearables, not integrated. I'm giving them a test run before I implant them."

"That's almost cautious, by your standards."

He grinned, insofar as he was physically able. One of the lenses on the array attached to his face rotated and lengthened toward the viewport. "So do we get to crack the mystery ship open and see what's inside?"

She went *hmm*, pretending she hadn't already decided. "Last time I let you clamber into a wreck, you lost an arm."

Ashok held up his current prosthetic. The translucent diamond housing revealed glimpses of the mechanical motion within as he flexed his hand, which was really more like a nest of tiny, versatile manipulator arms. "That was just an opportunity for an upgrade, cap. I say we fly over with torches and cut a hole and poke our heads in and look around." No surprise there. Ashok believed in radical self-improvement, and every mystery was a potential upgrade in waiting.

"I like the enthusiasm, Ashok, but we're still factfinding. This doesn't look like any human ship I've ever seen, and it doesn't look like a Liar vessel, either, despite all that weird shit on the stern. Didn't the Jovian Imperative try to solve its toxic waste problem by launching tubes full of poison randomly into space? What if this is one of those?"

"Space is big, so throwing bad stuff into it wasn't such a terrible idea, as far as terrible ideas go. But that's not a waste container – our sensors sniffed it thoroughly. No toxins or bad radiation. Besides, your boy Shall just identified the vessel."

"He's not my boy," she said, but she was too interested in the wreck to put much growl into the ritual denial. "So what is it?"

"Once Shall filtered out all the weird stuff welded to the ship's ass, the profile matches a model in the historical database." Ashok lifted his chin, which, unlike the rest of his head, still looked like a baseline human's. "That, captain, is a goldilocks ship."

Callie frowned. He might as well have told her it was a Viking longboat or an *Apollo* module. "From the bad old days? Before we had bridge generators?"

"A genuine old timey antique. It's gotta be about five hundred years old." Ashok gave himself a little spin, changing his orientation so she was looking at his feet, because actually being still for any length of time was outside his considerable skillset.

"A goldilocks ship. Wow. Weren't they propelled by atomic bombs?"

"Pretty much, yeah, at least the first wave, and this was one of the earliest models launched. Looks like it's had some modification since then, though. The goldilocks ships were no-frills. They didn't go in for decorative S&M spikes."

"Maybe a pirate crew found it and tried to make it look more badass?"

"That ship is *old*, cap. No pirate would want it for anything other than scrap, or to sell to a collector."

"So what's it doing here? Goldilocks ships aren't supposed to come back. That's the whole point. They took one-way journeys, way out, trips of desperation and exploration. Now five hundred years later it's just floating in trans-Neptunian space? By cosmic terms it's practically back where it started."

Ashok nodded. "That's the big juicy mystery. No way that ship came back from anywhere, right? It's not like they had Tanzer drives back then. They weren't zipping around the galaxy. Unless they found a bunch of plutonium lying around on their colony planet and built more bombs to stick up the ship's butt, there was no coming back."

"No mystery at all, then, Ashok. This is just as far as they got. The crew took off on their brave voyage, reached the edge of our solar system, suffered some critical failure, and... that's it. Nobody ever expected to hear from the goldilocks ships again, so no one went looking."

"You think that ship spent the past five hundred years drifting among the iceballs out here and nobody noticed? With all the surveys and mining vessels tagging everything even halfway interesting?"

Callie shrugged. "You said it yourself. Space is big. The ship was just overlooked. What's the alternative?" The idea of this enigmatic ship breaking down centuries ago was comforting, in a way, because failure was common, plausible, and non-threatening, unlike most of the other possible explanations.

Ashok wasn't having it. "I don't know what the alternative is, but there's something else going on here. Who made all those modifications? Space vandals drifting by with buckets of epoxy and loads of sheet metal? Outsider artists among the asteroids?"

"Seems unlikely."

"And what about the energy readings? Parts of the ship are still warm."

"I know. They were made to run a long time, the goldilocks ships. Some of them are *still* completing their journeys. Could just be some old systems ticking along in the midst of critical failures."

"Nah, these readings are weird, cap. The whole thing is weird." Ashok sounded quite chipper about it, as he did about most things. "It's a mystery. Mysteries are great. Let's peel it open and see if it's wrapped around an enigma."

"I hate mysteries," Callie said, not entirely accurately. "You always think it's going to be a box full of gold, but usually it's a box full of spiders."

Ashok made a noise that might have been a snort in a baseline human. "And yet you always end up opening the lid, don't you?"

"What can I say?" Callie unhooked her feet and pushed off toward the doorway leading deeper into the ship. "I like gold more than I hate spiders."

"Launching magnetic tethers." The voice in Callie's headset had the clipped tones of someone who'd grown up under Europa's domes, which meant it was the navigator Janice, and not the pilot Drake – he was from one of the Greater Toronto arcologies, populated mostly by the children of Caribbean immigrants, and his accent was a lot more melodious to the captain's ear.

Watching from the window in the airlock, her angle was wrong to see the metal tethers bursting from the side of the *White Raven*, but seconds later Janice said, "Contact. Connection secure." Janice didn't have a particle of romance in her soul, which was a good quality in the person who was supposed to tell you where you were going and where you'd been.

As soon as the airlock unsealed and yawned open, Ashok launched himself out, snapping a carabiner on to one of the steel lines that now attached the *White Raven* to the dark wreck a scant thousand meters away. He would have spacewalked without any safety gear at all if Callie had allowed it: he liked spinning to and fro in the void with nothing but puffs of compressed air to get him back home, but Callie insisted on a modicum of safety in her crew, at least in micro terms. On the macro level, she sent them into danger all the time, with herself at the front of the line. Space had a billion ways to kill you, so you prevented the ones you could, and didn't waste time worrying about the ones you couldn't. If you got hung up on a little thing like the terror of the unknown, you might as well head down a cozy gravity well and become whatever people were down there. Wind farm technicians? Organ donors? Crime scene cleaners?

She attached her own line behind Ashok's, following at a suitable distance as he pulled himself along the tether toward the wreck.

They made the journey in near silence, the only sound her own breath in her helmet. They didn't need to talk. The *White Raven* did a lot of contract security work for the Trans-Neptunian Authority: skip-tracing, investigation, fugitive recovery, chasing down smugglers. They dabbled in freight and salvage work when other jobs were lacking. She couldn't count the number of times she and Ashok had crept silently up on a ship, not exactly sure what they'd encounter when they arrived. Neither one of them had died yet, though Ashok had come close a few times. If they ever perfected mind uploads, he'd be even more reckless with his physical wellbeing: he'd doubtless jump at the chance to stop half-assing it as a cyborg and go full robot.

They reached the wreck, the dark curve of its hull smooth and cold before them, the towering spikes all over the stern looming like a misshapen forest. Ashok's voice spoke in her ear, close as a lover. (What a terrible thought. She wasn't *that* hard up for companionship. She had access to useful machines that didn't come with Ashok's cheerful obliviousness attached.) He thumped the side of the wreck with his prosthetic fist. "The hull looks intact. I'd like to get a look at that mess they've got where their nuclear propulsion system should be. I guess you want to check out the interior first, though?"

Callie had an elemental aversion to slicing holes in hulls. That skin of metal was all that divided a bubble of life and air inside from the emptiness all around outside, and she'd spent her adult life living in places where a hull breach meant panic at best and death at worst. "Janice, are we *sure* there's nobody alive on this thing?" Janice wasn't just the navigator: she also ran their comms and squeezed every bit of useful information out of the ship's sensor array.

"You can't prove a negative, captain," she said. "But if there's anyone on board, they aren't transmitting or receiving any communications, and we did everything short of knocking on the door and yelling 'Hello, anybody home?' You two could try that next. There *is* a strange set of energy signatures, so some systems might be functional. Could be life support. No way to tell from here."

Callie's executive officer Stephen, who was also the ship's doctor, joined the conversation, his voice a sedate rumble. "I've been doing some research. If the ship really has been out here since the first wave of goldilocks ships took off in the twenty-second century, the crew could still be alive, in cryosleep."

"Oh, damn. They still used cryosleep back then?" People didn't do a lot of centuries-long voyages anymore – the bridges had made such projects seem pointless, for the most part – but there were better options for human hibernation nowadays, with stasis fields and induced zero-metabolism comas. Cryosleep was a lot less reliable, from what she'd learned in history class, and could have short- and long-term neurological impacts on those who went through the process... if they could be successfully thawed out at all.

"Somebody made modifications to the ship and left it here, though," Ashok said. "The original crew, or someone else. The joyriders could still be on board. Maybe it's Liars. You know they like to tinker with things."

"Do they now? You don't say." Drake's accent was melodic, but there was a spiky edge to his tone that made Callie wince. Ashok was tactless because he was clueless, not malicious, but it took a special failure of compassion to talk about Liars that way when Janice and Drake were on the line. They'd experienced the Liar predilection for technological improvisation firsthand.

"Settle down, children," she said. "Mommy's working now."

Stephen chuckled over the comm. When it came to running the crew, Callie was the stern disciplinarian, and he was the deep well of patience. She pressed her gloved hand against the side of the ship, imagining she could feel the cold through the thick layers of fabric and insulation. "If there's someone awake on this boat, they had ample chance to announce themselves. See if you can get inside the nice way first, Ashok, but if not, slice away."

Ashok floated close to the hull, sliding both his gloved hand and his unprotected prosthetic one around the airlock until he found a panel he could pry open. Filaments sprouted from his mechanical hand, and he hummed to himself over the open comms channel as he tried to convince the ship's ancient and rudimentary control systems that he was authorized to open the door. "Ugh. This is like trying to punch soup."

Callie considered. "Punching soup would be pretty easy. Assuming it wasn't too hot. I've punched lots of things worse than soup."

"Yes, fine, but punching soup wouldn't *accomplish* much, is what I'm saying... ah. There it is. Have I told you lately that I'm a genius?"

"I'm not sure. I don't usually listen when you talk."

"I'm really sad the door opened for me. I've got a new integrated laser-torch I wanted to try out in the field. Maybe next time."

The hatch unsealed, and Ashok grabbed a recessed handle and hauled it open. Callie turned on her helmet light and looked into the airlock beyond. Ashok gasped – it was *almost* a shriek – and then coughed to cover it.

"I thought they were bodies for a second, too." Callie watched a couple of old-fashioned, bulky gray spacesuits float in the airlock, but they were empty, their helmets hovering nearby. Callie unhooked from the cable, clambered into the ship, and deftly stowed the suits out of the way in the sprung-open locker they'd probably escaped from. Ashok came in after her, and then sealed the door.

"We're inside," she told the comms.

"Your heart rate's up a bit," Stephen said. "Is the ship full of space monsters?"

"I assume so. How are Ashok's vitals? I thought he was going to faint when we saw a vacuum suit float by."

"Ha ha." Ashok peered around the dark with his multi-spectrum lenses.

"His vitals seem fine, but since he installed those hormone pumps to regulate his physiological responses, it's impossible for me to tell what's going on with him based on his suit data. He doesn't need a doctor, he needs a small engine repair shop."

Ashok was normally happy to trade banter, but he could focus when the need arose, and he was working on the control panel for the interior airlock door now. "There's pressure on the other side, cap. I'll sample the air, see if it's breathable."

"Ugh. I might leave my helmet on anyway. These little ships always smell like recycled farts."

"People on ice probably don't fart too much, but suit yourself." The airlock hissed as the pressure equalized, and after a few minutes a light above the door turned green and there was a *whoosh* of seals unfastening. After the inner door swung open Ashok entered a dim corridor, his helmet light shining on blank gray walls, and he held up a finger like someone planetside trying to feel which way the wind was blowing; there were sensors embedded in his prosthetic digits. "Hmm. A little oxygen-rich for my taste, but if we don't play with any open flames, we should be OK." He unhooked the latches on his helmet, removed it, and took a tentative breath. "Smells fine. Not as good as the spinwise gardens on Meditreme Station, but it'll do."

Callie took off her own helmet and sniffed. The air was stale, but fine. It didn't smell like death or burning, which she found reassuring. "I guess it won't kill us."

Ashok glanced at her. "Your nose is a feat of structural engineering, cap. I bet you can smell all the way out to the asteroid belt."

"That's big talk coming from a one-armed man with a computer stuck to his face." She tapped the side of her admittedly considerable nose. "This is the Machedo family pride. Signature of a noble lineage. Some say it's my best feature."

"Everything is somebody's fetish."

"Do you think making fun of your captain's nose is a good idea?"

"No, but it's no worse than my other ideas. Like poking around in ancient spaceships full of zombie space suits."

The banter and insults were a form of whistling in the dark. For Callie, every disabled, drifting, battered, or broken ship was a reminder of the fate that could await her own crew if she made the wrong decision, or ran into a situation where bad decisions were the only ones available.

Ashok took the lead, his light sweeping back and forth across the corridor to illuminate every step. He was doubtless peering around with other, more advanced senses, too, so they might get some warning if there were nasty surprises lurking. "Shall managed to find some old interior schematics for ships like this. There's only one set of living quarters, since the crew was mostly expected to be frozen, with the ship waking one of them up for a day every year or so to do a manual check of the systems. Most of the space is given over to supplies – seeds and embryos and communications equipment, tools, crude old-school fabricators. Maybe we can find a collector interested in obsolete pre-Liar technology." He stopped by a closed metal door. "The cryochamber is through here."

Callie hit the button by the door, but nothing happened, not even the whine of a mechanical failure. The ship was pulling power from somewhere, for something, but apparently not for opening doors. Ashok shrugged, then worked the fingers of his prosthetic hand into the minuscule crack where the door met the wall. He could exert a startling amount of pressure with those fingers, and the metal squealed and shrieked as it slid forcibly along its groove and disappeared into the wall. The room beyond wasn't entirely dark: a faint blue glow shone off to the left. Most of the cryopods were dark, but the instrument panel on the last one in the row was illuminated.

"Do you think they made the pods look like coffins on purpose?" Ashok took a step inside. "As a way of getting the people inside used to the idea that they were probably going to die on the trip?"

There were six pods, each roughly rectangular and big enough to hold a human, but they didn't make her think of coffins. They reminded her more of big chest freezers – which, in a way, they were. Five of the pods were open and empty, which gave her a chill right up her spine and into her backbrain. She couldn't help but imagine dead crew members, blue-skinned, frost rimed on their faces, lurching through the black corridors of the ship, eager to steal the heat of the living.

"There's someone on ice over here." Ashok stood by the last container, its glowing blue control panel casting weird shadows on his already weird face. "Most of the power on the ship has been diverted to maintaining life support and keeping this pod functional, I think."

Callie joined him and looked into the pod. There was a window over the inhabitant's face, and the glass wasn't even foggy or covered in ice, the way cryopod windows inevitably appeared in historical immersives. Artistic license. The figure inside was a petite woman with straight black hair, dressed in white coveralls. She looked like a sleeping princess (peasant garb aside), and something in Callie sparkled at the sight of her. *Uh oh*, she thought.

"Can we wake her up?" she said. Not with a kiss, of course. This wasn't a fairy tale, despite the glass casket.

Ashok shrugged. "Sure. We can try, anyway. The mechanisms all seem to be intact, and Shall says the diagnostics on the cryonic suspension system came back clean. Want me to pop the seal?"

"Let's get Stephen over here first in case she needs medical attention." Callie activated her radio. "XO, get suited up and come over. We've got a live one on ice."

Stephen groaned. He didn't like EVA. He preferred sitting in a contoured acceleration couch and listening to old music, and only showed real enthusiasm for physical activity during his religious devotions. "Isn't it bad policy for the captain *and* the executive officer to leave the ship at the same time?"

"He's right." Drake's voice was amused. "With both of you off the ship, leaving me and Janice unsupervised? We could get up to anything. The only thing keeping me from crashing us into the nearest icy planitesimal is your strong leadership. Janice, hold me back."

Callie clucked her tongue. "It's only a thousand meters, Stephen. I think we'll be OK. Ashok and I will finish checking out the ship while you come over."

Their survey didn't take long. The cargo area was a mess – the seed banks seemed fine, but the refrigeration for the more fragile biological specimens had failed. They both put their helmets back on, because the stench was bad in there. There was no sign of the missing crew members.

"What the hell happened here?" Callie floated in the dim cargo hold, scanning the walls. It looked like an ugly, irregular hole had been cut in the ceiling and subsequently patched.

"The crew went somewhere, woke up, welded a bunch of crap all over their stern, one of them got back on board, set a course for Trans-Neptunian space, and went back into hibernation." Ashok fiddled with the buttons on an ancient fabricator, meant to build machine parts on a colony world the ship had never reached. "The 'what' is pretty clear. The how and why are totally mysterious, but if we can wake up the ancient ice mummy back there, maybe she'll have some answers."

"She's more like Sleeping Beauty," Callie said. "Mummies are gross."

"Beauty, huh? You see something you like back there, cap?"

"Shut up. She's a thousand years old."

"Five hundred, tops, and she doesn't even look it."

"Shut up double." She waved him away. "See if you can get any sense out of the ship's computer, especially the navigation system, and try to find a crew manifest. It would be nice to know where this ship's been… and who our sleeping beauty is." "I'd rather see what's going on with the propulsion system. Engines are way more fun than cartography and human resources."

"You can tinker after you gather intel. Shoo. Do as you're told." She returned to the cryochamber, where Stephen had arrived and was now stooped, examining the control panel on the one active pod. "What do you think?" she said. "Is she going to survive?"

Her XO shrugged. Stephen was a big man, and his default expression was doleful, so he tended to resemble a depressed mountain. "She's frozen. We'll see what happens when we thaw her out." He activated something on the panel, and they both stood back as the cryopod rumbled, the lid sliding down and icy vapor pouring out in a condensing plume of fog.

"The system should be warming her up now." Stephen seldom sounded excited, and he was hardly vibrating with enthusiasm now, but he *did* sound interested: for him, that was the equivalent of jumping up and down with glee. "These cryogenic procedures are barbaric – they're on par with bloodletting and trepanation, medically speaking – but from what I've read, after she's returned to a reasonable temperature, her heart will be jumpstarted with electricity or adrenaline or both. Apparently the initial reaction can be quite dramatic–"

The sleeper screamed and jolted upright, clouds of vapor eddying around her. Some collection of straps and restraints around her waist and legs kept her from floating up out of the pod, but her upper body was free. She stared around, eyes wide, then reached out, grasping Callie's gloved hands in her bare ones, and pulled the captain close.

"First contact!" she shouted, loud enough to make Callie turn her head away. "We made *first contact!* I had to come back, to tell everyone, to warn you, humanity is *not alone*–" She stopped talking, her mouth snapping shut, and then her eyes rolled up and her body sagged.

Callie squeezed the woman's unresponsive hands. "Is she dead?"

Stephen floated closer, removed his gloves, and touched the woman's throat. "No, there's a pulse. The jolt that started her heart shocked her into consciousness, but it wasn't enough to keep her awake. There are a lot of drugs in her system. Some were keeping her healthy while she was in hibernation, and some are trying to bring her metabolism and other systems back up to baseline. She's going to be sluggish for a while. I'll examine her more thoroughly back on the *White Raven*, but I don't see any immediate cause for concern." He paused. "For someone born in the twenty-second century, she's doing quite well."

Callie let go of the woman's hands and pushed herself away from the pod to float near the center of the room, considering.

"So." Stephen peeled back the sleeper's lids and shone a light into her eyes. "After she wakes up, do *you* want to tell her we've known about the aliens for three hundred years, and her first contact bombshell is old news?"

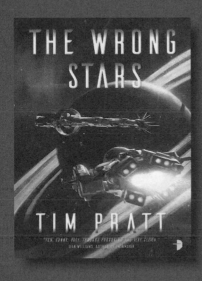
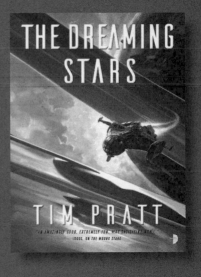
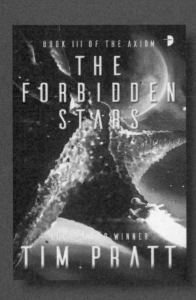

ANGRY ROBOT

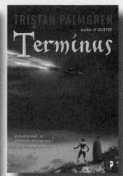

We are Angry Robot

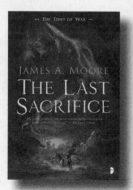

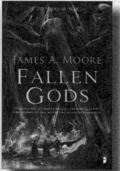

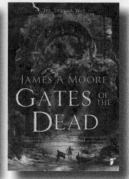

angryrobotbooks.com

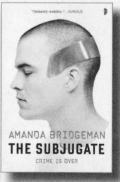

Science Fiction, Fantasy and WTF?!

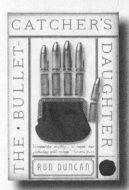

@angryrobotbooks

We are Angry Robot

angryrobotbooks.com